DEAD INSIDE

A DEAD INSIDE NOVEL

DEAD INSIDE

Cover design by: Miblart

Marginal Impact Publishing LLC

ISBN-13: 979-8-9898848-2-7

Ebook ISBN-13: 979-8-9898848-3-4

Second Edition: May 2024

Printed in the United States of America

Dead Inside

PIPER ANDERSON

MARGINAL IMPACT PUBLISHING

For my little people. Those who love me for all that I am and all that I am not. Without these people, I would truly be... Dead Inside.

Content Warning

Be forewarned, this series deals with vampires and other supernatural beings. Their moral compass is vastly different than mortal morals. Dead Inside vampires closely follow the traditional lore surrounding vampires and their dietary needs. They're vampires doing vampire things. Be sure to understand that and your sensitivities before going forward. If none of that bothers you, then please read on. Enjoy the ride.

Glossary of Terms

the Awakening *n.*: three-hour process in which a being is buried alive while The Fates supernaturally change said being's physical make-up or bestow them with new abilities. Only occurs when new royalty is sealed. Afterward, the vampire must feed on fresh human blood immediately though bouts of bloodlust persist for a decade after or until control can be learned.

bind *v.* 1: to join in binding 2: to take an eternalmate

binding *n.* 1: a binding ceremony usually with accompanying festivities: nuptials 2: the state of being united to another supernatural in a formal ceremony where each makes an exchange of eternal vows.

Book of Being *n.*: a sacred magical tome entrusted to the High Priestess or Priest of the White-witch Advisors. Contains magical rituals, spells, chants, incantations, and supernatural bylaws. 2: a magical conduit for The Fates to pass down prophecy. Cannot be touched or read by evil beings.

bound *v.* 1: to take, give, enter into, or join in binding: Bind 2: to unite firmly in a blood exchange whereby a male vampire takes blood from the femoral artery of a female. The female takes blood from the male's carotid artery.

Centripetal Impulse *n.*: an electrical shock or jolt felt when a male of any supernatural species feels a soul-deep emotional attachment to his predestined mate. A physical unavoidable pull toward one's true mate.

GLOSSARY

cleansing *n.*: a ritual by which the High Priestess of the White-witch Advisors invokes the spirits of their ancestors who have passed on to Raj. All White-witch Advisors are placed in a coma-like state, and their minds are read for the presence of evil or malign influence. Traitors are stripped of their powers, exterminated, and their souls sent to Pakao-Brava.

Commoner *n.* 1: any breed of supernatural having no rank of nobility but swearing fealty to the Vampire Royals and abiding by the laws set forth by them.

courtier *n.*: any supernatural who attends court of the Vampire Royals and who is ordained by The Fates or the king or queen as noble. Usually, descendants of the Sanctioned and the most powerful of each race of supernatural are included in this class. They set rules for and hold control over the compound in the absence of a king or queen.

created *v.*: the act or fact of being born or bringing forth young 2: caused to exist 3: vampire equivalent of being born. The gestational period for a vampire child is three months. The gestational period for a hybrid of any kind is six months.

crypt *n.*: vampire residence wholly underground.

The Dark Majesty *n.*: fallen brother angel of The Fates. Fell from grace in much the same manner as archangel Lucifer. Cast out of Raj and into Hell by the Most High. Lucifer made him a king, ruler of his own Hell domain for supernatural, Pakao-Brava. Commands two hundred legions of demons including three races of supernatural created before his fall.

GLOSSARY

Daywalker *n.*: 1: any supernatural who has sworn allegiance to the ex-King Balkan 2: a vampire in Balkan's army who has been gifted with a blue sapphire amulet—worn in a wristband, ring, choker, or brooch—cursed by the late Dark-witch High Priestess Lilith Luca 3: can be Rogue but doesn't have to be; also called a Walker.

defective *n.*: derogatory term describing a supernatural that defies their station, such as refusal to mate within ones breed or a rogue Royal Guardsman or courtier 2: a mentally ill supernatural.

eternalmate *n.*: 1: supernatural equivalent of a husband or wife 2: the only supernatural a vampire can take blood from without being poisoned. Predestined mate. Long periods of separation cause acute withdrawal symptoms, pain, and eventual death.

expulsion *n.*: banishment or termination ruling passed by a unanimous vote of the courtiers in the absence of a king or queen. Banishment: a White-witch magically induces amnesia, wiping all memory of the compound and its inhabitants. Termination: carried out by a Royal Guardsman of the supernaturals breed.

The Fates *n.*: The supreme reality for the supernatural; *esp.*: angel creators and supreme rulers of the supernatural. Three angels possessing god-like powers gifted to them by the Most High.

flatline *n.* 1: a death-like sleep state during which time a vampire's injuries heal and energy is restored.

GLOSSARY

Immortal Age of Maturity *n.*: painful twenty-four-hour process ten years after a natural-born vampire's creation when a vampire young passes from fledgling to full power immortal. Heart and respiratory systems cease functionality. Digestive systems no longer process mortal food. May grow in mass or height at this time; aging and physical changes stop. Demon conscience becomes internally audible. No longer requires a White-witch governess.

Pakao-Brava *n.*: 1: nontemporal realm of the Dark Majesty in northwest corner of Hell where damned supernatural spirits reside 2: a place of torment or destruction

Raj *n.*: 1: Paradise 2: Heaven 3: abode of The Fates and the blessed supernatural 4: an ideal place or state 5: where White-witch spirits dwell until called upon for guidance.

rejuvenation *n.*: when a White-witch Advisor reaches the end of their lifecycle they are given the option of rejuvenation. Through an Awakening, their youth is restored, and they rise as vampire sans magic.

retinue *n.*: The body of attendants of the Vampire Royals *i.e.* White-witch Advisors, chief guardsman and his men, vassal, the VRs entourage

rogue *n.*: 1: a corrupt vampire who follows no law and has allowed their demon dominance by taking death into themselves by killing its prey 2: any corrupt, dishonest, evil supernatural that follows no law and kills indiscriminately. Wholly evil and can't be near any sanctified people, places, or objects *i.e.* crosses, holy water, churches, pastors, priests, and nuns.

GLOSSARY

royal guard *n.*: the strongest supernatural male of any breed; responsible for guarding and protecting Vampire Royals, supernatural, and mortals from supernatural.

the Sanctioned *n.*: three humans with psychic abilities and formidably strong souls that no matter how hard the demon tried it couldn't cage the soul and take possession of the body. The Nephilim, angel-human hybrid, Grigori Dimir, was deemed the strongest of the Sanctioned due to his natural psychic ability from his angel blood.

sanguinary demon *n.*: created by the Dark Majesty before his insurrection, they possess grace and magnetic beauty of angels. Humanoid in appearance, but possess an animal's predatory nature and some features *i.e.* retractable fangs and claws, spectacular sight and night vision, agility, and preternatural speed. They are charming, apathetic, beguiling, and seductive. Their psychic abilities include: compulsion, or mind control, and telekinesis. Can sublimate into fog or mist, and have limited conjuring abilities. Possess powers of regeneration and accelerated healing. When exposed to sunlight their skin burns.

seal *n.*: a distinctive mark, brand, of nobility gifted to the Vampire Royals and the Vampire Royal Guardsmen by The Fates 2: a tilde (~) seared into the heart and inside of the left wrist of Vampire Royals 3: an infinity symbol (∞) seared into the heart and middle of the right forearm of Vampire Royal Guardsmen

siren *n.*: Beautiful humanoid seductresses with the ability to enchant and enslave others with their music, voices, and beauty. Possess an unusually high level of pheromones, which draws others to them. No being, mortal or immortal, can resist the call of a siren.

GLOSSARY

transition *n.*: Certain physical and biological changes taking place over a six-month time frame and are completed during the Awakening. Amelia is the only being to ever transition.

witch *n.*: a male or female who possesses varying degrees of magical power and or psychic ability; *esp.*: sorceress or sorcerer; they come into their power at the age of fifteen. Play a large part in vampire procreation. Abides by the Wiccan Rede: "And it harm none, do what ye will."

- **Dark-witch** *n.*: a witch, who abandoned the Wiccan Rede, swears allegiance to the Dark Majesty, and practices black magic. They're evil and use their magic for personal gain.
- **White-witch** *n.*: a witch that uses his/her abilities for good and lives by the Wiccan Rede. They use their magic for benevolent purposes.
- **White-witch Advisor** *n.*: males and females chosen from the most powerful White-witches to be right hand to the Vampire Royals. Bound by blood oath to the Vampire Royal king or queen. Dispatched as midwives and governesses to vampire young.
- **High Priest/High Priestess** *n.*: a teacher and ruler of any coven of witches. The High Priest/Priestess is the most powerful and skilled of the coven. Leads the coven and initiates others. They perform bindings and preside over funerals.

vampire *n.*: 1: created by the Dark Majesty, named by The Fates. Part Sanguinary Demon and part mortal. Hearts and respiratory systems do not function. Inherited their demon half's traits. Nearly immortal, they're vulnerable to sun exposure and silver. Can be destroyed by piercing the heart or decapitation. Certain breeds can convert humans through blood exchange.

GLOSSARY

- **Convert** *n.*: a mortal turned vampire. Stops aging at the time of change. Stronger and faster than a mortal but weakest of their supernatural breed.
- **Dhampire** *n.*: offspring of a mortal and a vampire. Will never become a vampire, and most will not have any notable vampire traits. If a Dhampire and a mortal mate, the offspring have a 50/50 chance of being either a mortal carrier of the dormant recessive vampire gene or being pure mortal. If two offspring carrying the dormant recessive gene mate, the offspring have a 25% chance of being mortal, a 50% chance of being a carrier of the dormant recessive vampire gene, and a 25% chance of manifesting vampirism at the Immortal Age of Maturity (twenty-one in mortal years).
- **Hybrid (Dark-witch & Vampire)** *n.*: soulless, wholly evil offspring of a vampire and a Dark-witch. Have all the weaknesses of vampires, but are significantly more powerful due to their ability to wield magic. However, they don't possess all vampire strengths, *i.e.* cannot compel or sublimate. Feed by draining the blood of their prey completely and consuming the carcass.
- **Hybrid (Dark-witch-Vampire & Mortal)** *n.*: extremely rare offspring of a Dark-witch & vampire Hybrid and a mortal. Not born evil, they turn evil by killing their mortal parent. This causes them to lose their mortal soul. Have slower-than-average heartbeats and digestive systems, giving them the ability to consume small portions of mortal food. They wield magic and possess their Hybrid parent's weaknesses. Sensitive to sunlight, but can walk in daylight. Until they lose their humanity, they feed on only blood.

GLOSSARY

- **Natural-born** *n.*: 1: any supernatural born of two supernatural parents can be Commoners, Vampire Royals, offspring of Converts, or Royal Guardsmen
- **Vampire Royal** *n.*: are descendants of Grigori Dimir the Nephilim Sanctioned. All are born with tilde seals. The Fates bestowed them with more heightened senses than other vampires, more strength, speed, agility, and intelligence. Possess control enough to convert humans. Have extra psychic ability. Can track all supernatural telepathically and can communicate mind-to-mind with their retinue. When their seal is activated they take on the last name Dimir. *Also known as,* VR.
- **Vampire Royal Guardsman** *n.*: males marked by an infinity symbol seal. Are the offspring of rejuvenated White-witch Advisors and descendants of the second strongest Sanctioned. Formidable warriors, protectors of the VRs and mortals, and endowed with more physical strength, speed, agility, and cunning than other supernaturals—including the VR—making them harder to destroy. Exceptional control enables them to convert mortals. Males they sire become members of the Royal Guard. Also called: VR

vassal *n.*: 1: a mortal under permanent compulsion. Immortal servants to the being who compels them. Under the protection of their sire, they die when, and if, their sire is destroyed 2: a trusted mortal under the protection of a supernatural whom he/she owes homage.

DEAD INSIDE

A DEAD INSIDE NOVEL

The Inauguration of Chaos

Delphi, Greece, 1,020 years ago

The supernatural would cease to exist. Danae Rossi couldn't breathe. Her lungs burned. Erratic thumps of her heart sounded loud to her ears. Each footfall against the cold, stone floor of the grandiose Radulescu crypt rivaled the fiercest thunderstorm.

Crypt—hmph? Danae would have laughed at the ease with which she thought the word if anything could be humorous in this moment.

Decades ago, such musings would've wrought light-headedness and palpitations. Supernatural: beings capable of shifting shape. Beings that possessed magical abilities and outlived mortals. Beings, like her. She'd been young, ignorant then. Neither description suited her any longer. These people were her friends, family. This place, her home. Her heart palpitated for a different reason now. For this news, she bore.

...to everything, there is a season, a time for every purpose. So it is written, now is the time, a time to fall. The time for more hate than love, more sow than reap, time of chaos for all ye supernatural. A time of great sorrow, time of much woe. Now is time for Vampire Royals, to Raj they must go...

The prophecy filled the limited space unoccupied by terror in her mind. This mystical passage catapulted her from her quarters, sent her running through the massive underground dwelling.

She passed *Chief Vampire Royal Guardsman*, Sebastian Cantemir, his second-in-command, Gawain, and the newest addition to the guard, Sebastian's son, Emilio. Her heart ached for the oblivious males.

Would they survive? Would any of them?

These morbid ponderings hastened her steps. She needed to reach the queen.

"Your Majesty," Danae blurted seconds later from the entry-way of the nursery. She paused, swallowing hard. "It has been written. Your cousin and his army shall attack. The Vampire Royals will not survive."

Soft, ethereal laughter came from the petite, gold-cloaked, hooded figure standing beside an intricately carved wooden cradle. "Ah… dear, White-witch. I could destroy the barriers guarding your thoughts with much ease."

Danae wiped a sweaty palm down the front of her red ser-vants' cloak. She knew the queen would sense her shields. How-ever, she'd hoped to ease into the discussion her abrupt delivery belied.

"My queen, this is prophecy from the *Book of Being*, not a vision. We must take it seriously."

A pale white hand extended from the gold cloak. Glided back and forth across the top rail of the cradle.

With her back facing her, Danae could not gage the queen's reaction. Her own heart constricted. The hair on her nape and arms stood on end. Intuition bellowed time was of the essence. The queen needed to understand the magnitude of the situa-tion.

"What can Balkan do, which has not been done?" Queen Ana-Marie drawled in a bored tone. "His Daywalkers have failed time and again. And they walk in sunlight. If that advantage has not aided him thus far, what could?"

Danae sighed. If only that reasoning staved off the inevitable. If she were a mere servant this knowledge might be easier to bear. On second thought, it would not. Queen Ana-Marie brought order, peace, to the supernatural. Things her cousin, the ex-King Balkan, never did in his six-century reign. Not one sound-minded supernatural could relay such news and not recognize it for the catastrophe it was.

In the decades since the queen's ascension to the throne, she and Queen Ana-Marie had forged a friendship. Dare she be so bold as to say they had become sisters? That knowledge doubled her burden. How did one inform their sister of her and her family's imminent demise?

"Fifty years have passed, madame," Danae pointed out, voice cracking. "His army has grown in strength and number, along with his hybrid young. We do not possess similar advantages."

"How does he continue to find reasons to be unhappy?" the queen mused. She turned, pinned Danae with narrowed, beguiling eyes. "The Fates should have destroyed him. Simple deposing for creating those hybrid abominations was too good for him."

Danae pushed back the hood of her cloak, ran a hand through her chin-length, ebony hair. Legs aching from her sprint through the crypt, the weight of Queen Ana-Marie's gaze nearly felled her.

The queen's flawless white skin glowed with eternal youth. High cheekbones and a small, pert nose were perfect complements. But her eyes were the *pièce de résistance.*

Hypnotic and almond-shaped, one iris was deep green with a jagged pool of golden-brown citrine reaching out from the pupil. The other iris was yellow with the same pool of golden-brown citrine reaching from its pupil. When Queen Ana-Marie set eyes upon someone, she could be denied nothing.

With untraceable speed unique to her breed, Queen Ana-Marie crossed the room. She sat in a large, floral-engraved, throne-style chair and lowered the hood of her cloak. Lustrous, deep red waves cascaded to her waist. "Come. Sit with me, dear Danae. I worry for your health. You look unwell."

"Your Majesty, please," Danae pled, voice cracking. She cleared her throat. "I would never come to you with such distressing words with any uncertainty. Ana-Marie, I implore you, prepare the guard."

She never addressed the queen informally, even when requested. The queen's knitted brows confirmed Danae's words had the intended effect. A wave of the queen's hand pulled out a smaller chair, scooted it near hers. She patted the seat.

On shaky legs, Danae entered the nursery and sat.

Queen Ana-Marie was silent, eyes fixed on nothing in particular across the room. "I see," she whispered moments later. "When is the battle to take place?"

Danae's heart became lead in her chest. Her stomach dropped. This was what she wanted, the queen to grasp the seriousness. Now that she had, her friend's forlorn look was unbearable. A hot tear rolled down her cheek. She shook her head. "The time is undisclosed. However, intuition says the time is near. Less than one rising."

She once envied the immortal inhabitants of the royal crypt. Although long-lived, witches grew old and passed on to *Raj*. Secretly, Danae wanted to be as the half-human, half-demon vampires were, forever young and beautiful. Here, watching the queen's expressionless face, empty eyes, and stiff posture, she didn't wish to be witch or vampire. All would meet their end... soon.

Reaching over the cloth-covered arm of her chair, Danae placed her warm hand on one of the queen's much cooler ones.

For long moments they were still, absorbing the quiet comfort the other offered.

The queen's gaze shifted.

Danae followed her line of vision to the cradle. No, not the cradle. Through it, to what was held within. Princess Valora. A crimson tear slithered down the queen's cheek. She roughly brushed it away.

It occurred to Danae then, she would never know the obvious pain the queen experienced. The loss of young. The joy of bringing life into the world. Prophecy stated they would all perish, servants and Vampire Royals alike—her. Her heartache soared. Shifting fabric called her attention to the present. Danae focused on the queen.

Her upper lip curled away from lengthening fangs. Unique eyes glowed. Queen Ana-Marie yanked her hand from underneath Danae's.

Danae started.

"What of my young?" the queen snarled, facing her.

"The book did not say. It stated a time of chaos would befall the supernatural. Races will fight each other to near extinction. The warring will lead to exposure to mortals, which will incite the Most High's wrath. Eventually, he'll destroy The Fates and all supernatural."

"What. Of. My young, Danae?" she demanded.

Danae gulped. "Prince Isaac and Prince Nico have long since reached the Immortal Age. They must battle with the king consort, the guardsmen, all of us to protect you."

"And what of my Valora?" Queen Ana-Marie turned slightly, as if to glance toward the cradle. She jerked to face Danae. "I refuse to stand idly by, helpless, cradling my young while we are destroyed. You and the Royal Guardsmen are sworn to protect me. *I* am bound by a force beyond even The Fates comprehension to protect my young. Must I choose between my—" Her voice broke.

Half-crazed, desperate eyes bored into Danae's.

"If there be nothing I can do for my sons... please" — she swallowed; seconds passed before she finished — "help me spare my daughter our fate."

Tears welled in Danae's eyes. She fought them, for once started, they'd never cease. The panic and despair she observed in the queen's frantic gaze was a punch to her abdomen. What could she do? The Fates' will would be done. Perhaps—an idea came to mind. Danae chanced a brief glance toward the cradle then back to the queen. "There may be a way, Your Majesty."

Queen Ana-Marie's fangs retracted. Red eyebrows furrowed. "A way?"

"To save Princess Valora."

Hope sprang to life in the queen's eyes. "Why such suspense, dear friend?" She took both Danae's hands in hers. "Our time is short. Speak now."

Her mouth went dry. She hadn't meant to give the queen false hope. There was no guarantee she could still perform such magic. If The Fates became aware... the consequence would be death. "I have not attempted this in years. And I have never performed such magic on a person—vampire or mortal. But, I may be able to cloak the princess. If successful, she will be incapable of being sensed by supernatural or The Fates."

Before the last word fell from her lips, Danae was alone. One second, she sat hand-in-hand with the queen. The next, her hands were folded in her lap, and the queen's chair vacated. Not even wind denoted the speed at which the queen traveled.

"Do it," Queen Ana-Marie commanded from beside the cradle, hood covering her bowed head once more. In another, faster-than-discernible movement, the queen had the infant vampiress swaddled in a gold velvet blanket and in her arms.

They needed to hurry, but the abruptness with which the queen made the decision concerned Danae. If Ana-Marie did not understand the ramifications of such a request, all could be lost.

"Your Majesty," Danae hurried to elaborate, "if The Fates trace my magic they will destroy the babe with me. If successful and the royal family is destroyed, Valora can never rule. Her seal will be dormant. It will be as if she no longer exists."

"Is this your lone objection?"

Nodding, Danae stood.

In the span of a heartbeat, Queen Ana-Marie approached. Wide, crimson tear-filled eyes leveled on Danae. She placed a feather-light kiss on her forehead and one cheek. Then she handed Danae the baby.

Danae cradled the infant in wooden arms.

"Go now," the queen ordered. "Cloak her. I care not for the throne. Raise her among the mortals. Protect her with your life—as if she were your own. If I, Victor, or either of the princes survive the impending battle, we will call to your mind. Remain open to us." She gazed lovingly at her daughter, brushed back a blood red curl from her daughter's forehead. Crimson tears streaked Queen Ana-Marie's pale face. Somber eyes fixed on Danae. "Promise you will love her, care for her as your own."

Unable to speak past the lump in her throat, Danae nodded. *How could this be the end?*

Queen Ana-Marie pulled Danae into cool, strong arms. Squeezed. She pressed a kiss to the baby's forehead. "Leave this place. Now!"

The command came not from a queen, but wrenched from the soul of a grieving mother.

Danae spun around. Ran as if *The Dark Majesty* was on her heels. Wind tousled her hair, ruffled the ends of her cloak. She sprinted toward the secret tunnel that led out of the crypt.

Dense fog and mist whooshed past her. Seconds later, the thud of several pairs of booted feet on stone sounded behind her as fog and mist morphed into males. Guardsmen. The queen must have summoned them through her telepathic link to all royal servants.

A short time later, Danae emerged from the underground passageway. Gazing around the lush, green mountainside and up the stone benches of the Delphi theatre, she wrapped Princess Valora tighter to protect her skin from the deadly sun's rays. A muttered incantation cast a transportation spell.

The first battle cry sounded as they teleported through space and distance.

Light, reassuring touches of each member of the royal family fluttered against her mind. She and the baby rematerialized in an unknown village where night had fallen.

Danae quickly located a vacant domicile, entered, and cast a protection spell over it. Her heart pounded. For hours, she cowered in a corner awaiting news of the battle. She clutched the resting young to her bosom. Then...

One by one, the Vampire Royals' presence vanished from her mind. Prince Isaac. Victor. Prince Nico. And last, with a strained, whispered *"Thank you,"* Queen Ana-Marie. The vampire royals were destroyed.

Tuesday, June 27th, 1000 years later, St. Joseph's Hospital Phoenix, Arizona

Hanging above closed double doors, a standard circular clock's long, black minute hand struck twelve, midnight. Cries of a newborn baby pierced the doors of the delivery room.

Elsewhere in the world, and for the first time in a millennium, a new entry appeared in the *Book of Being*. It read:

> For unto the supernatural an heir of
> pure noble blood is born, a daughter
> is given: The government shall be
> upon her shoulder: and her name
> shall be called Zenith Royal, Portent
> of Peace, Most Powerful, Princess of
> Compassion, The Everlasting Queen.

Chapter One

Present day Rome, Italy

Talon Cantemir's gaze traveled the length of his muscled forearm. His large hand rested atop a black marble counter. Long, pallid fingers obscured an object fisted in a vise-like grip.

Squeezing tighter, a lion-sized roar tore through his lips, piercing the silence. Reverberated through the room followed by a loud...

Pop!

Dense red nectar of life seeped between his closed fingers, ran over his knuckles, pooled on the marble.

"Dammit!" a thunderous male voice shouted from beside him. "That was the last one! You know what this means. And not only did you get it all over yourself, but your mother's new counters. Does this make you proud?"

Oh, yes, very. The one vampire warrior in existence disgusted by blood. No, not blood. Bagged, donated blood. Yeah, he was real proud. Was it his fault he had taste buds?

"Four rogue vampires attacked me, night before last," his father rehashed in a low, gruff tone. "I'd just left one of the courtier's palazzo. How do you suppose they knew of my whereabouts? Or breached the compound's shield?"

Talon bowed his head. Strands of golden-blond hair slipped over his forehead, tickled his eyelashes. He studied the bloody mess he'd made of his hand, glanced at his white silk shirt. Lots of blood stains there, too; it'd be a bitch to scrub off.

He kept his head down, but not out of shame. Nor did he fear his father. Talon feared what *he* might say. Anyway, it wasn't as if Sebastian Cantemir expected an answer. His father adored talking at him. Not to him. Fates forbid his son might say something intelligent.

"Your mamma narrowly escaped decapitation leaving the Liakos palazzo last night. Luckily, she sublimated to fog before the silver-plated machete pierced her flesh."

"I get it, *Comandante*," Talon bit out between clenched teeth. This wasn't new news, just one of many training tactics his father employed. Guilt. The *compound* was magically shielded, invisible to mortals, rogues, and non-privileged supernatural. The walled-in city housed the largest concentration of supernatural. *Vampire Royal Guardsmen* and their counterparts of other breeds protected it. Somehow, the *courtiers* had become the unofficial law. If rogues were getting in...? "I will not allow the courtiers to continue their plotting. I'll make you and Mamma safe."

"How? By bending over? Handing them the blade to sever your head from your shoulders? This will help you blend with the mortals. Yet this simple task is too hard for you."

Thanks for the sunlight to that wound.

"That's what I'm trying to do now," Talon continued, ignoring his father's gibe. "This solution—finding the Vampire Royals mortal descendant," he said in an ominous tone, "seems facile and farfetched."

"It is not for us to question The Fates' will," Sebastian snapped, hitting the countertop. The sound of cracking marble rent the air. "We've been over a millennium without their guidance, punished for things not of our doing. No sealed queen or king. We're not converting mortals. White-witches haven't spelled our females' bodies, giving us no vampire young. If the incessant warring doesn't bring about our race's extinction, the lack of young will. The supernatural won't survive another thousand years. The prophecy must be fulfilled."

Talon couldn't concentrate. The sulfuric and burnt rubber stench of old blood made him sick. He felt it drying on his face and hand. No matter, he knew how this song and dance went. His father's blind faith in the mystical trio of angels who'd created the supernatural astounded him. Sebastian refused to see reason.

"Your inability to do this jeopardizes us all, *Talon*." Contempt turned his name into a curse.

He was the prophesied savior of the supernatural and his family. Why couldn't he do this?

Hand-to-hand combat?

Check.

Weapons?

Master of all, there wasn't one he didn't know how to use, dismantle, and rebuild.

Feeding from a donor bag...?

Couldn't do it to save his existence.

Talon turned. His eyes traveled up, up, up the mountain that was his father looming beside him. Their resemblance was striking. Both were broad-shouldered and lean. Sebastian appeared larger from Talon's sitting-on-a-barstool vantage point. In truth, they were the same height, six-six. They shared dark blue eyes. However, the similarities ended there.

His haircut was shorter, modern. Sebastian's golden-blond locks were shoulder-length. Their most important difference could only be seen when one examined the non-beating heart of the individual male. He didn't possess his father's blind faith. Talon preferred solid, indisputable proof. Perhaps there were other differences, too. He knew he had dried blood on his face, but his father...

Jaw tight, his pale face harsh, livid. Arms crossed over his chest. Blood spatter peppered his cheek and forehead.

Non bene.

"Father."

Sebastian growled.

Damn! He never slipped and called him that. Sebby didn't allow it. But the need to appeal to whatever got his father dubbed chief by the *Vampire Royals*, whatever once made him an esteemed leader, made Talon forget himself.

He began again. "*Comandante*, there is no proof Princess Valora existed, or that she ever bore young to produce this descendant. This journey to America to find the alleged descendant could be a hoax. A trick to leave you and Mamma unprotected."

"I am far from weak!" Sebastian smacked the countertop again, almost breaking it in half. "You forget, I trained you and your brother."

Talon stared at his father, deadpan. "If this is a false prophecy and you and mamma are destroyed, how could I restore our name? How would the supernatural be saved? They would be in the same chaos they'd lived in for over a millennium. The only difference—no royal guard to protect them."

"I can't speak for the other breeds of guardsmen, but if I were to perish, my second would succeed me. If we both should perish, you would lead the Vampire Royal Guard."

He wouldn't touch the remark about his father's second-in-command. Talon considered Gawain family. The male was loyal to Sebastian, even trustworthy, but dedicated to the supernatural? Not in a way that mattered. However, he would set his father straight on one thing.

"No. I will not." Implacable resolve steeled his tone. "If this turns out to be a fool's errand, and you and my mamma are destroyed, I will not lead the VRG." No matter how misguided, these were his parents.

"Will you be joining your brother then?" Sebastian asked evenly.

Talon wasn't fooled. This was no innocent question. It was the calm before the storm. And the storm would be off the charts. Beyond a tsunami if he didn't defuse it. The topic of his brother, older by over a thousand years, inspired many long rants.

"Disgrace your family further," his father barreled on, preventing Talon from interjecting. "Force your *cara* mamma into hiding, shame her for delivering two *defective* young." His eyes lit up, glowing orbs of blue fire. "You would sentence her to destruction by my hands or that of the rays of the sun? All because you believe you know better than The Fates?"

Sebastian stepped close enough that Talon's elbow bumped his torso. His top lip pulled back from his teeth; incisors and canines lengthened.

Talon peeled back one finger at a time from the palm of his fisted hand. The small, deflated plastic pouch slid from his blood-soaked hand onto the counter. Eyes locked on his father's, he stood with slow deliberation. In response to the aggression, his own fangs lengthened in his mouth. Pricked his tongue.

Sebastian stepped nose to nose. "You'd do that to your family?" he snarled. "Turn your back on your responsibilities?"

"I'll do what is right," Talon growled, keeping his lip over his fangs.

Yes, his stance was hostile. He couldn't help his response to the rage his father vibrated. Such antagonism called to the male, warrior, and demon within him. Especially the demon; it thirsted for bloodshed. He didn't want to go a round with Sebastian. As his father, he respected him. As a warrior, they were too evenly matched.

"One son has disgraced my name," Sebastian yelled, his face a contorted mask of fury. "Turned me and mine into hunted beings by those who once revered me. Now you want to increase my burden, force my hand?"

He struck.

A large hand engulfed Talon's neck. Dagger-like nails bit into his throat, threatened to liberate his Adam's apple. Sebastian hoisted him off the ground. Wasn't necessarily uncomfortable. He didn't need air, but it was painful as fuck!

Usually, he could endure. But in an effort to make him thirsty enough to drink bagged blood, Sebastian hadn't allowed him to feed in weeks. Meaning, he wasn't at full strength.

His face tingled. Tightened. As if cotton were stuffed in his ears, noises became warped, muffled. White spots danced before his eyes, which felt as if they'd burst out of their sockets. Vampires didn't handle sensory deprivation well, and he'd started at a disadvantage. Talon's perfect vision blurred. Oh, shit! He was gonna pass—

A gasp came from somewhere in the distance. In seconds, Talon went from being held midair to a massive, crumpled heap on the gray, granite, kitchen floor. His senses came back online quickly. When he looked up, his jaw dropped open.

Slender, five foot five, Lea Cantemir's back faced him. She wore a knee-length, red, pencil skirt and black lace tank top. Long, dark brown hair hung to her waist. In her left hand, she held her *eternalmate* by the jugular. Sebastian's feet dangled above the ground. With blinding speed, she slammed Sebastian against the wall across from where Talon lay on the floor. The wall cracked. Tiny fissures spiderwebbed behind his father's head.

"Retract. Your. Fangs," Lea demanded in a clipped tone. She turned. Glowing green eyes locked on Talon. "You, too," she snarled, lips curled away from elongated fangs.

He and his father's fangs receded at once.

"What is the meaning of this?" his mother asked, facing his father.

Talon was shook. Both his parents were acting out of character. Sebastian prided himself on his control. He rarely allowed his demon to sway him. If Sebastian were the sultan of control, then his mother was the reason the word was invented. This mission had them all on edge.

"He makes a mockery of our family and the supernatural," Sebastian said tightly.

"Nonsense," Lea asserted, "he's an investigative thinker." She lobbed a prideful glance over her shoulder at Talon. Her fangs retracted.

"He doesn't need to think. The old witch foresaw his role in bringing about peace for the supernatural."

If Talon heard about that damn witch and her vision one more time, he'd lose his shit. One hundred and twenty years ago, an old White-witch told his parents she'd seen the future. Said she'd dreamt that she was supposed to spell Lea's body so she could conceive. The young would play a major part in restoring peace to the supernatural by aiding a new, more powerful line of royalty. That's it.

That was all it took to convince his devout, Fates loving parents to go against the law that stated only The Fates or the *Vampire Royals* could grant permission for vampire conception.

When Talon heard the cockamamie story he thought, *bullshit!* He'd never have bought that shit. But, his misguided parents, when they heard the story all those years ago, thought: *Great, let's do it—lady we don't know. We trust you completely.*

They conceived him that night.

He was born three months later.

"Go ahead, Talon. Explain your position to your father," Lea said sweetly. Glancing askance at Sebastian, she tightened her grip. "You'll listen," she growled.

Odd. He'd never been offered this luxury before, had even gotten used to holding his tongue, so much so, it'd become a personality trait. He thought things through, then put those thoughts into action. No talk.

"I don't believe a mortal female is the key to the supernaturals' salvation. The entire story seems...convenient," Talon explained.

"If we took that approach, you wouldn't exist," Sebastian grumbled. The sound cut off abruptly. His mother must've tightened her grip. Lea's permissive smile encouraged Talon to continue.

"The idea Queen Ana-Marie had young no one knew of conveniently spirited away by her White-witch Advisor before battle? Right. A vampire child couldn't pass as mortal. Wouldn't the rapid aging, blood diet, and bursting into flames in sunlight call attention to her?"

"She had her White-witch to raise and protect her. Danae was Chief White-witch," Lea pointed out. "Very powerful. If Princess Valora hadn't been introduced to the supernatural, it makes sense no one knew of her."

All good points, but he wasn't convinced. "What vampire, of any breed, would willingly take a mortal mate? Not only take a mate, but crossbreed with one?"

Lea glanced at Sebastian, who she retained a firm grip on. Her glower softened. Sebastian returned her gaze. His glare lost some intensity.

Talon wanted to lose what little bagged blood he'd managed to ingest.

His mother turned to him, head shaking. "Oh, *figlio mio*. What has hardened your heart so? Love is a powerful emotion. It makes fools of even the strongest of us."

Good thing he didn't intend to let that particular emotion overtake him. Enough outside forces were fucking with his existence.

He shook his head. "Even if that is true, the prophecy stated it would be a descendant of *pure* noble blood. A Dhampire isn't pure. And after so many centuries of gene pool dilution, wouldn't any of Valora's children's young be totally mortal?"

His parents were silent.

Uh-huh! Neither of them considered that, had they?

Sebastian broke the silence. "I saw Danae running through the crypt that day, felt terror vibrating from her. The guard had just been summoned by the queen. I couldn't stop to investigate what she carried. Though, she and the queen were close. If Queen Ana-Marie asked, she would've done it."

Talon appreciated his father's heartfelt explanation. Really, he did. However, for him, there were too many plot holes.

"We'll never know, Talon," Lea said, sounding put out. "Princess Valora chose to end her existence to be with her mortal when he died. What we do know is that there is a mortal descendant, an heir to the Vampire Royals. She is transitioning and probably scared."

He struggled to hold back his eye roll. Far be it for him to point out the stupidity in that plan. Supernatural went to *Raj* if they were good or *Pakao-Brava* to be tortured by *The Dark Majesty* if evil. Humans went to Heaven or Hell, according to his research. Valora and her mortal would be separated in the afterlife—if such a thing existed.

"Now" — glancing at her *eternalmate* — "we understand our son. He will do what is right." The penetrating look she gave Talon said, *"You'll do what we think is right."*

Sebastian looked on the verge of passing out. Good.

"And you, Sebastian Cantemir," Lea drawled. "I love you more than my own existence. You are an extension of me—my right arm—if you will." Snarling. "But, I would cut off my right arm, should it do something as offensive as to harm my young. *Capisce?*"

There it was... the reason his family was no longer respected and instead hunted. The explanation for why his treacherous older brother, Emilio, still walked the Earth's surface.

Talon gazed at the stars, ran his fingers through damp strands of his hair. Cleaning blood off all the counters had taken an hour. After his mother, The Queen of Clean, thoroughly inspected his work, he was permitted to shower. Now, he stood bare-chested in the backyard, wearing black and gray BDU pants and steel-toed SWAT boots for two hours of playtime.

Joy!

Sebastian Cantemir was a tyrant, a grueling taskmaster. He allowed Talon only two hours of freedom a night. During this time, he was authorized to train in a backyard the size of a box—a large box—but a box nonetheless—or work out.

With options as plentiful as they were, Talon chose to work out.

He stomped across the grass to the back wall. His father kept a steel fireproof storage cabinet stocked with all things necessary to vanquish rogues of any kind. Silver bullets, daggers, athames, silver-coated throwing stars, swords, and flame throwers—yippee!

The toys were meant to hone Talon's skills, as if he hadn't trained every night since he reached the *Immortal Age*, one hundred and ten years ago. Training and working out were his father's ideas of fun.

Old Sebby, the original party animal.

Talon chose a jump rope. Why they kept such mortal equipment, made no sense to him. Ten years after birth, a vampire reached the *Immortal Age*. Meaning they ceased to breathe, change, or grow. He was as fit as he was ever going to be.

If not for his guides, his father's second-in-command, and Anton, he wouldn't have known other interpretations of fun existed. They helped him stay abreast of popular vernacular and trends, so he'd fit in with mortals on his mission.

Thanks to Anton's White-witch governess, Anton spent a lot of time with mortals. When it came to befriending the mortal descendant, he'd be better suited for the task than Talon. Unluckily for Talon, Anton wasn't a VRG, nor was he the prophesied savior.

Actually, no one knew Anton's background. Not even Anton. His father, Victor, had appeared at the *compound* with an infant Anton almost ten years ago. The *courtiers* were suspicious as hell since the red-haired, American vampire somehow found the compound's location and breached the shield. Victor was interrogated for hours under a White-witch truth spell. Finding no malicious intent, Victor was granted sanctuary.

Baby-loving Lea instantly attached to the hapless Victor and his motherless young. She arranged for them to have a White-witch governess and mansion near the Cantemir palazzo. Not that securing a palazzo on the outskirts of the compound was hard. Nobody trusted Victor's intentions, and the outskirts were reserved for the ostracized.

The putrid stench of rotten flesh hit Talon with the subtlety of a battering ram. His nostrils flared.

Speak of the Devil...

The backdoor slid open.

"Dude, I gotta get me one of those seals. Females go liquid for a vamp with tats. Bet you got 'em in puddles, son."

Jumping rope, Talon turned a glare on the lanky, auburn-haired, golden-eyed fledgling. Anton Liakos dressed like some rapper turned fashion designer regurgitated on him.

And, Fates! He reeked. Drinking donor blood to practice control and eating mortal food made fledglings smell old. Stale.

He rubbed his *seal*, an upraised infinity symbol branded into the middle of his right forearm, and growled. "It's not a tattoo, *idiota*."

Anton stepped back, hands raised in surrender. "I'm just saying" — he jerked his chin toward the *seal* — "had I been born with something that cool... Well, I'd work with what The Fates gave me, know what I'm sayin'?"

No. He didn't. Because of the *seal*, his entire existence consisted of honor, duty, integrity, training, and courtly manners. Those were the ways of the VRG. Talon had been deprived of everything, including carnal knowledge about females of any species. So, unlike Anton, he wasn't abreast of all things coitus.

As well as filling him out and bringing him to full power, Talon hoped the *Immortal Age*, which Anton would reach in about three months, changed his personality. The fledgling annoyed the hell out of him. Pondering Anton's impending milestone had him wondering about the descendant's transition—if he believed it, which he didn't, but if he did...

Vampires were born or converted. None ever started as one species and transitioned into another. She'd be the first. Would she understand the changes? She'd need to be Awakened, buried alive by the exact time of mortal birth on her twenty-first birthday. Talon was curious to know what—if any—inborn ability she possessed and which resulted from the transition. Guess he'd find out, if this prophecy proved true. If it didn't, he'd kill a mortal.

Thinking of dead things...

"Where is your White-witch?" he demanded.

Anton and his father were as despised as the Cantemirs on the *compound*. Being a fledgling, Anton was easy pickings for anyone looking to eliminate a perceived threat. He wasn't supposed to be out without his governess, Lea, or Talon.

"Man, you gotta calm down. I don't need a fuckin' babysitter," Anton snapped. "And anyway, your mom asked me to bring more donor packs for your trip."

"Doesn't matter. You shouldn't be wandering around alone. You should have waited for Vanessa."

"Whatever. Lea asked me to come. I'm here. If somebody wasn't being a bitch—" he broke off, gagging.

Talon moved quickly. One minute, the fledgling stood next to the open sliding glass door watching him jump rope. The next, the glass door was closed, and Talon had him by the throat against the stucco wall beside it.

His eyes heated. Their glow reflected off Anton's pale skin. Fangs lengthened, promising a painful death. Nostrils flaring, he growled, "I'm nobody's bitch, youngblood. Got that?" Something about being called *bitch* filled him with murderous rage.

Anton's eyes bulged. He struggled to breathe. Purple splotches formed bruises under his eyes. Capillaries ruptured. Blood vessels burst in his eyes. Tiny red fissures streaked his sclera. Unlike Talon, Anton hadn't reached maturity. This wouldn't kill him, but he needed to breathe. He nodded around the monster mitt turning his neck into a twig.

"Glad we understand each other." Talon smiled humorlessly, dropped him, and sauntered across the moonlit yard. "You stink."

Anton fell to the ground with a *thud*. He gasped and coughed for a moment before standing on unsteady feet. "Damn" — cough — "been eatin' your spinach, huh, Popeye? Be grateful I don't offend easily. Cuz if I did...I wouldn't give you that shit you need for your trip. You'd have to go out there and bake, *patna.*"

That got his attention. He turned. "What do you got?"

Anton took his time answering. Straightened his shirt, brushing off his jeans. Give the little leech some power, and it went right to his head.

"Just a little bromantic somethin', somethin'." Anton smirked. "Man, your parents are a trip. Lea was laying into old Sebastian, good, about something when I rolled up." He laughed. "If that's what having an eternalmate's all about...take me off the list. I don't want some female on my ass telling me what to do."

He stared blankly at Anton. "Don't worry. I don't think The Fates want you to have an eternalmate either," he teased. He picked up his discarded jump rope. "An eternalmate holds no appeal for me. I work enough."

Of course, there were other reasons for him not to want a mate, none of which were Anton's business. With the exception of being forbidden to mate outside their breed, *commoners* got the freedom to choose their mates. Guardsmen didn't, for the most part. They were permitted to choose from a small pool of *rejuvenated* White-witches. Not a lot of choice. Plus, his choices had been taken from him since birth. Taking a mate would be just as limiting. He wanted to be free. After this mission, he would be.

Putting the jump rope away, he spied butcher knives. Might as well train. Talon grabbed six ten-inch knives and then closed the cabinet. He turned to Anton.

Eyes wide, Anton backed away. He stopped when he hit the wall.

Talon chuckled. "Now who needs to calm down?" Moving fast, he approached Anton. Handed him the knives. Auburn brows drew taut.

Off Anton's confused look, he explained, "I need to test my reflexes. Throw those at me." He was across the yard in a nanosecond.

Mouth agape, Anton gazed at the knives in his hand, then at Talon. "You're kidding, right?" He glanced down and up again. "You want me to throw knives at you? For real?"

Talon lifted an eyebrow. "Did I stutter?"

"Why does a vampire at full power need to test his reflexes? You're a guardsman. Shouldn't you be faster than everybody?" Anton's voice squeaked, bewildered.

"Throw the damn knives, youngblood."

Anton shook his head, palming a knife. He lifted it to eye level, inspecting the blade.

"You ever gonna stop stalling, give me whatever you got? Share any info? Did Vanessa get any names? I can't go to Arizona yelling, 'Descendant! Anyone see a descendant?'" He shifted his weight foot to foot, waiting for Anton to throw the knife.

Flipping it once, Anton caught then chucked it with expert skill.

The moron wasn't bad, but Talon was faster. He stepped to the side a fraction of a second before the knife would've pierced his throat. It landed on the ground beside him.

Readying another knife, Anton shook his head. "I'm offended. I really am. I walk all the way over here, courageously put my life at risk to bring you more blood, and you think my White-witch governess is the only one with skills. *I* got you names." He threw the knife.

Talon spun. The move put him in his starting position and the knife on the ground.

"Fine. Did *you* get any names?" He'd be shocked if he had. Anton was a goofball. A help thyself screw thy neighbor vampire.

"Vanessa finagled you and the descendant pretty little keepsakes to keep you from living like bacon. *I* did you one better. Got you her name, and the name of some friend of hers. Mortals don't get a lot right, but they make up for it with Google." Laughing, Anton prepared another knife.

Talon rolled his eyes. "I don't care about the friends. What's her name?"

Anton answered at the same time he threw the knife. "Amelia Marie Keeler."

Talon was shocked immobile. Who would've thought the little shit had brains? Anton no doubt saved him a whole lot of—

Oh, shit!

Warm liquid ran down Talon's torso. He glanced down. The black handle of a knife protruded from his abdomen. Pierced his belly button. Blood oozed. Dripped onto the toe of his boot, painted the grass red.

Relief spread through him.

Thank The Fates he wasn't in the kitchen.

Chapter Two

Tuesday, April 20th

   Hey Mom and Dad,

Happy Anniversary! It's that time again. Tis' the season to be bitchy. Don't worry, I'm not gonna do anything crazy—again. I know what you're thinking: "Amelia's always up to something." Well, not this year. No, really, this year I'm F.I.N.E. Freaked out, Insecure, Neurotic, and Emotional. Yep, totally fine.

Evan's okay, I guess. NAU seems to agree with him. If not for Kasey, I wouldn't know anything about him. Speaking of Kasey—they're back together. For whatever reason, she's his one. Tessa's doing well too. Still... Tessa. And she still has Dan firmly under thumb. Wall continues his bid for sainthood. Seriously, why he puts up with me, I'll never know. He deserves so much better.

Oh! Last but not least, drum roll please... my birthday. Exactly one week and two months from today. Yep, I've started the old proverbial trudge up the hill. Kill me now. No, really, kill me now. Twenty-one. Feels... anti-climactic.

You go all your teens anxious to turn eighteen, so you can do whatever you want. Then turn eighteen, wait with bated breath for twenty-one, so you can drink. Twenty-one comes, and you're all... meh. Of course, I've been... meh since seventeen so, whatever.

Well, gotta go. Time to put on a happy face. I love you so, so much, Evan does, too. See you later.
Forever,
Dead Inside

"Fourteen, eight, fifteen, twelve, exhale," Amelia Keeler whispered the words, her lifeline, over and over upon exiting her bathroom. Maintaining a firm grip on her black leather-bound journal, she wrapped her bath towel tighter. Entered her bedroom. Some people did light reading in the bathroom; she did her best writing in there. "Fourteen, eight, fifteen, twelve. Inhale. Fourteen, eight, fifteen, twelve. Exhale."

Fourteen steps to the bureau across the room. She opened the top drawer. A luxurious sea of overpriced, multi-hued bras and panties greeted her. The hand holding her journal dove into the tangle of undergarments, hid the book underneath them.

Victoria's Secret, eat your heart out.

Her mother would be proud of her ever-expanding collection. Mom believed retail therapy cured everything from profound sorrow, stab wounds, the flu, to a stubbed toe.

Mom, you couldn't have been more wrong.
No, focus!

Runaway thoughts were counterproductive. She had to get through today. Slowly, and a little distracted, she closed the drawer. Eight steps to the—

Amelia spun toward the dresser, nearly losing her towel in the process. Why she bothered with the towel, she didn't know. In Hell, things dry instantaneously, and she did live in Hell, literally and figuratively. Arizona. Peoria, Arizona, to be exact. Hell's waiting room, or Heaven's, depending on how one chose to look at it. She chose the former. Standing on the sun would probably be cooler than living in Arizona. But, it was home. All she knew.

Yanking open the drawer, she anxiously dug through the ocean of underclothes. *Pay attention,* she instructed herself. For the first time she saw, or didn't see, what she should have seen before.

Get pissed.

"Tessa!" she hollered, head thrown back, ensuring she'd be heard through her bedroom door. She slammed the drawer shut. "Tessa Renee Wilde! I told you to stop taking my damn socks!"

Eight steps to her four-poster queen-sized bed. Tightening her hold on her towel, she flung back ruby and gold sheets, felt around underneath them. Dammit! Nothing.

She gritted her teeth.

Damn Tessa and her compulsive need to control everything. If she didn't adore her best friend and roommate, she would've kicked her out long ago.

Kneeling to one knee then the other, she bent over and checked under the bed. She groaned.

"Eww... gross. Please tell me you're not assuming the position for Walker. I just ate."

At the flat, sarcastic voice, Amelia jolted upright from her previous, butt straight up in the air, pose.

One good thing about being five-three—no risk of giving Tessa more of a show than her rent paid for. The oversized towel fell almost to her ankles, concealing the goods.

She looked over her shoulder at Tessa standing in the doorway.

Dressed in a clingy black T-shirt and tiny white shorts, something she'd wear while teaching one of her dance classes. Tessa pulled an Oh! Henry candy bar from seemingly nowhere. She leaned against the door jamb, leisurely unwrapped it, and took a bite. "Hey, I thought I told you that you look better in heels?" she asked, mouth full. "You don't need socks for those."

Amelia curled her lip at her friend's snack. "You make me sick, you know that? How do you eat like that and stay so skinny?"

Tessa shrugged, unconcerned.

Gripping the side of her bed for support, Amelia heaved herself off the ground. Fifteen steps to the walk-in closet. She sifted through her clothes. How did Tessa do it?

Bobbed dark brown hair, snow white skin, rail thin, five foot five, and a crap diet.

She changed into her work uniform. Sharp pain twisted, and knotted her insides. Could have been the craving she refused to indulge or a jealousy pang. It was the latter, hopefully. The other could not be sated. Not that she wasn't happy with her physique. But it took work to maintain, a lot of work. Tessa could sit around eating bonbons and sticks of butter and not gain a pound.

"What do you have planned today?" Tessa called.

Rolling her eyes, Amelia emerged from the closet. And discovered Tessa had invited herself in and gotten comfy on her disheveled bed. She pinned Tessa with a droll, *duh* stare, and waved a hand over her attire. "Well, after I reinvent the wheel... I figure I'll take a stab at calculating the actual price of beans in China."

"Jeez, thought I'd make some conversation, grouch. I—" Interrupting herself, Tessa scowled, green eyes scrutinized Amelia's outfit: black slacks, short-sleeved white dress shirt, black vest, and black silk tie. Black Jimmy Choo pumps dangled from her left index and middle finger. "You look like a boy," she mused. "Why don't you suggest a better outfit for that theater? I mean, it's the least you can do, if you're gonna make a career outta that craphole."

Even devoid of emotion, she knew a dig when she heard one. Although, grief and anger were emotions. She felt those, no problem. The last three years fostered the sole cultivation of both, leaving no room for her to feel anything else. Three years had taken both sets of grandparents, her other best friend...

Shaking her head scattered those thoughts. They'd lead nowhere good, fast. She had to stay in the present. And at present, she was getting shit about her job. Again.

"Thanks for the news flash, Ms. Couric," she said dryly. Pushing a couple throw pillows aside, she sat on the end of her bed and put on her shoes. "I don't have any pull over what we wear."

Tugging at her vest to illustrate her point. "So, boy-looking or not... this is it."

"Whatever, I guess." Tessa sighed. "Maybe you should sleep with Tigger or Gordon? That'd get you some clout." She wagged her eyebrows. "Ooh... I know! Sleep with Heidi, and let Tigger and Gordon watch. That'd really get you some say over uniforms and anything else you wanted."

"Tessa, sweetie, baby, please try to remember what I told you. Some things are better in than out."

"Hey, freedom of speech is as much my right as it is yours. So, how you doin'?" Tessa asked jovially. The forced casual tone did a piss poor job of masking genuine concern.

Horrible, suicidal, bewildered...

"Fine."

Penetrating, narrow, green eyes studied her.

"The regular fine, promise," she fibbed, rising to escape the probing stare. Eight steps took her to her dresser.

Lying was necessary. No one would understand the cravings. The voices. Not voices, one specific voice. Hers. Not the normal daily instructions she gave herself. This one was sinister, deeper, but hers. Its horrid suggestions caused severe mood swings, made her reactions and responses extreme. If anyone found out about either issue, she'd come home to nuthouse orderlies ready to cart her off. She wasn't crazy.

"Mm-hm..." Tessa nodded, lifting a discerning well-plucked brow.

Evanescence's "Bring Me to Life" drew Amelia's attention to her purse on top of her dresser. She plucked her cell phone out of it.

Certain songs evoked specific emotions, memories. She'd chosen that particular song as her text ringtone for that reason. Unfortunately, it never brought her back to life. For three years, she'd lived in a quasi out-of-body experience. Watching herself go through the motions of daily life. Breathe in, breathe out. One foot in front of the other. But she wasn't present. She'd become numb. Hollow. Dead inside. The nothing the lead singer sang about? That was her.

Amelia caressed the screen with the pad of her thumb. She felt like an elephant planted itself on her chest. Why couldn't she feel more? Walker deserved so much better than her. How she treated him. To think her only ambition in life used to be to help people. She'd wanted to care for the sick, lonely, and mentally ill. Now, one person she should be able to help, should want to help, she couldn't. All she did was strive not to hurt him—more.

> *Ditto! Have a good day!*

Tessa's throat clearing brought Amelia's eyes to her friend's curious gaze.

"Captain Codependent?" Tessa smirked.

She didn't answer. Wisely, Tessa didn't push the issue. Good girl.

"Stoked about tonight?"

"What?"

"Are you stoked about tonight? It'll be fun." Tessa grinned, swinging her feet back and forth with childlike exuberance.

Tonight? Fun? Maybe a lack of nutrients killed brain cells. Tessa could be such a bobblehead.

After picking up her brush and hair tie from the top of her dresser, Amelia brushed her wavy, damp hair, and worked it into a ponytail.

Tessa nodded towards her hair. "I see your dye job lasted this time."

Rolling her eyes, Amelia shook her head. "Yeah, right. A whole twelve hours."

"Give or take." Tessa snickered. "Took longer to dye than it did to come out."

Don't get her wrong, she loved her blood-red hair; it was healthy, manageable, fast-growing. Contrasted nicely with her deep caramel skin—if she may say so herself. That aside, last night she'd spent hours dying it black to match her soul. It came out beautifully. Then she showered this morning, and it washed out. No matter what color she dyed her hair it wouldn't hold artificial color. Like a tantruming toddler, it refused change. Even when she cut it, it grew back to its original length, and then some, within days.

A cold chill rocked Amelia. She shivered. She'd been experiencing regular cold and hot flashes for months. More in the last couple of days. Just another of many weird symptoms she suffered as of late. Like extreme empathy. Off and on, she literally felt other people's emotions. Similar to static cling, feelings vibrated off people and clung to her. Brought a whole new meaning to the Beach Boys song "Good Vibrations."

"Tessie, I think I'm getting sick or something. I'm all achy and blah."

"Nice try. You're not getting out of dinner. Evan can't make it—he has some test—but he made me swear we'd still do it. The boys will be here though, and they're expecting perfection. It'll be a good time. Take your mind off things. You need this."

Yeah, like a severe case of the clap.

Setting her brush on the dresser, she traded it for her Louis Vuitton purse. "If they were lookin' for perfection... they should've gotten different girlfriends."

"Hey!" Tessa jumped to her feet in mock outrage. "Speak for yourself. They don't come more perfect than me."

Amelia hoped it was a joke. With Tessa, it could go either way.

Pushing past her roommate, she took the steps she had down pat. The steps she counted each day just to get from minute to minute, to stay alive. Ten steps to her bedroom door. Nine down the short hall. Turn right. Twenty steps through the front room to the front door. When would the pain go away? The need to count.

All part of the daily song and dance she performed for her puppet masters, the spies. Her wardens. Eyes were everywhere. Looking for any fissures in the glass, watching for any signs she'd break.

So, the show was necessary if she didn't want to end up in a padded room with drawn-on windows, rocking in a corner and knocking her head against the wall.

"Hey!" Tessa shouted, stopping her. Amelia hadn't realized she followed.

The expectation to keep up appearances and conversation today was unbearable. The façade was slipping. She needed out of this house, pronto.

"What?" she snapped without turning. "I'm gonna be late for work."

"Oh, however, will they get by without your expert ticket-taking skills?" Tessa drawled in a faux southern accent.

Having reached her destination, and nearest escape route, Amelia paused hand on the knob. "Did all you want is to insult me, or did you actually have something to say?"

"That purse, those heels, and that outfit... you look like a transvestite."

Shocked, Amelia turned, cocked her head, and *smiled*—sarcastically, but smiled, nevertheless. She put her hand to her heart. "Aww... I love you too, schnookums. See ya tonight. I'll get tater tots and cheese on my way home."

Well, look at that. Apparently, this old show pony had one last trick in her. Amelia left without another look back. Fifteen steps down the cracked stone walkway through what used to be a lush, flourishing lawn, but was now dead grass, weeds, and rocks. She didn't want to think about the symmetry there.

"Hey!"

The serious edge in Tessa's voice froze Amelia. She turned. Taking her sunglasses out of her purse, she put them on, so she didn't have to squint to see her friend in the doorway. "Yeah?"

"Have a good day, okay?" Tessa smiled weakly. "Smile though your heart is aching."

Mom...

Felicia Keeler sang those words to her whenever she was sad. Then took her to purchase body armor, mood lifters, aka all the trendiest designer clothes.

Amelia nodded, a curt, jerky motion. Pressing unlock on her key fob, she hotfooted it to her royal blue Mustang, got inside, and slammed the door.

"I'm not going to cry, I'm not going to cry," she chanted. "Start the car."

Crying showed weakness; she hated crying and never did it in front of people. Tears wouldn't change anything. Doing as instructed, she pushed the button to start her car. An oldie, Limp Bizkit's "Break Stuff" blared from the speakers.

How appropriate.

A traitorous tear slid down her cheek. Swiping a finger under her sunglasses, she flicked it away. Checked out the passenger window, making sure Tessa hadn't seen. She hadn't. The door was closed.

Good.

She needed peace, if only for a minute. Peace was the great unobtainable, something she hadn't had in three years. Nothing would fill the hollow spots in her heart, especially nothing today. The anniversary of her parents' death.

Chapter Three

"Calin," a female voice pleaded in agony.

Calin Luca stared blankly into pain-filled eyes the color of fog. The only way to decipher the actual iris from the white of the eyes was the black pupil and silver ring around them. Even if the anguish was genuine, he'd rather gouge out his eyes with a serrated blade than do anything that benefited his mother.

"Son, this is another chance," his mother, Eliza Luca, croaked. "Imagine both of us free of the ties binding us. You, your humanity. Me, my curse."

He smacked the desk he sat at in his quarters. Everything traced back to her curse, didn't it? The vampiress didn't do anything not ninety percent selfish.

Curse or no curse, Eliza Luca was a Dimir to her bone marrow. A power-hungry sociopath through and through. Really. Her father, his grandfather's, forbidden indiscretion not only led to him being deposed by The Fates, but also, a rare breed of vampire. Part vampire, part Dark-witch. His offspring with his Dark-witch concubine were wholly evil, amoral to the core.

Eliza didn't care about his soul. If 200 years hadn't convinced him of his mother's self-centered nature, nothing would. This ten minutes? The longest amount of time she'd spent with him in the five years since suckering him into coming here.

"Mother, this is ridiculous. You, yourself, told me the only way to get rid of my revolting—that is the word you used, right?" Calin rolled his eyes at the memory of her exact words 180 years ago. The night she abandoned him and his father. He stroked the underside of his goatee with his index finger in mock thought. "Revolting? You said my revolting partial soul could only be destroyed if I killed my mortal parent. News flash, Father died well over a century ago—of natural causes."

"I misspoke. How was I to know?" Crimson tears filled Eliza's eyes.

Damn curse!

Calin fought the urge to put his boot to her face. Thanks to her curse, his mother couldn't lie for shit. He didn't believe for a second that this wasn't her plan from the beginning. Stupid him, he'd allowed himself to be wheedled from his home in Paris, France, for this bullshit.

"Papa wouldn't approve of such a mission if he didn't trust this information," his mother finished, voice rough from unshed tears.

"Sure he wouldn't," Calin muttered. Then louder, he said, "You do realize he's already sacrificed three of his children for his cause, don't you? You're cursed, expendable."

His grandfather may have accepted his mother back into the family, but that was due in large part to the fact that she'd finally produced an evil little holy terror, i.e. his five-year-old half-sister. For centuries, no one had realized Eliza survived the battle her father waged with his army of *Daywalkers*.

Eliza had been discovered in Paris while fleeing the battle, at her mother, Lilith Luca's, behest. She killed her captor, the then reigning White-witch High Priestesses sister. Sadly, not before being cursed to not only feel mortal emotions, but also experience severe pain with them. Acting on the feelings dulled the pain but didn't alleviate it. For his mother's breed of vampire, her curse was a fate worse than destruction. Ashamed, she went M.I.A. on her family.

During that time, she met his father and, because of her curse, created a new even rarer breed of vampire than herself. Him. A vampire, Dark-witch, mortal Hybrid. Not wholly evil because of his partial soul, he had a barely traceable heartbeat and could eat small portions of mortal food. Not even her curse kept her from being a horrible bitch for long. She'd left him with his bastard father when he was twenty and capable of keeping his existence secret.

Calin wasn't entirely sure how his father hadn't realized his mother wasn't mortal, or that his son went from infant to adult in ten years. Whatever. Mortals were stupid at best and ridiculous Neanderthals at worst. How they didn't fall down more amazed him.

He'd gone a blessed one hundred and eighty years without seeing her. Then, five years ago, she'd blinked into existence, materialized right before his eyes, holding a baby. A tiny, beautiful, blond-haired, blue-eyed, rosy-cheeked murderer. At two weeks old, the baby had devoured her mortal parent. Sucked him dry. Ate him bones, teeth, hair, and all. Although the same breed as him, his half-sister lacked what he needed to get rid of. The thing that made him the stain of his family. His humanity, aka his soul.

To his grandfather, the only thing worse than his mother's curse...? Him. Of course, the ex-king would sacrifice them. They were the weakest link.

"Calin." His mother's strained voice broke into his ruminations.

"What the hell do you want from me?" Calin pushed his swivel chair back from his desk and stood. He'd been in the middle of whittling wax, one of two favorite pastimes. His father had been a famous Parisian sculptor—maybe he inherited the talent. It calmed him, he'd been carving a heart for his sister, not the cute shape but an actual four-chamber human heart—at her request. Now, heart be damned. Eliza pissed him off. Raking a hand through his brown hair, he paced in front of his king-sized bed where his mother sat.

He glared askance at her. She sat with perfect regal posture, legs crossed, wearing a long, figure-hugging, red silk gown. Her hip-length blond hair hung loose. An air of entitlement clung to her. Spoke of the princess she would have been, had his grandfather not defied The Fates.

"Son, are you listening to me?"

"Yes, Mother," he ground out. "You didn't just find this out, did you? It's why you brought me here. Why you decided family was so important. Why you regret abandoning your only son."

Eliza's expression morphed into a mixture of disgust and sorrow.

Looked painful. He pitied her.

Damn soul!

Calin scrubbed his face with his hand. Retaking his chair, he pushed it under the desk. Had he gotten rid of his soul when he should have, he wouldn't have been lured here with false promises of family and belonging. She also wouldn't have anything to appeal to now.

He despised the cocktail of love and hate she stirred in him. And the longer she sat here... the more scales tipped against love.

"It isn't," she lied. He knew it. The low whimper she emitted confirmed it. "Siring young means making hard decisions. I hope one day you know such a burden. This will help us all. Imagine, you without your foul soul. Me, without my curse. Papa, king again."

Grandfather had made that very same declaration in an uncharacteristic discussion with him weeks ago. Not about Calin being free of his soul, but about him being king again and his mother without her curse. When Balkan made the vow, Calin assumed he spoke of the distant future. Not months from now.

"This prophecy could be a ruse. A trap laid by the VRG." Censure hardened Calin's tone. "Are you willing to stake our existence on this? A flimsy prophecy from the same Fates that took the families seal to begin with? I'm not. Not my existence, or yours."

As much as he detested the witch, she was his mother. He might want to throttle her, but he couldn't let her be destroyed on some fruitless mission to America.

Waves of palpable anguish and terror vibrated from Eliza, which meant she was about to do something emotion driven.

Getting to her feet with preternatural speed, she crossed the room and approached Calin. A trembling hand rose to his head and began harshly stroking his hair. Calin's whole body stiffened.

Damn curse!

Just what everybody wanted, forced affection.

Kill. Me. Now.

"Your grandfather assures me his source is credible. There's no risk." Eliza tried to convince him, but her pained, tight voice contradicted her statement. Her hand shook so much it felt like an earthquake rolling through his hair, trying to crack open his skull.

This was torture. He'd tell her to stop, but she couldn't. The curse didn't work that way. She had to ride out the emotion.

How lovely for him.

"White-witches are the only supernatural who can touch the book. Since when do they aid us?" He flinched. "Again, you can't take the risk. I won't let you," Calin said, resolute, attempting to ignore the assault on his scalp.

The vampiress didn't have a clue how to give a tender caress.

"Papa has someone on the inside of the royal White-witch coven. I believe I heard it referred to as an..." She paused as if searching for the right word. "'Informant' on the television. But..." Eliza paused again.

"But what?" Calin growled when it didn't seem as though she'd continue.

Eliza retook her seat at the edge of his bed.

Thank, The Fates.

His head hurt.

She folded her long legs beneath her on the bed, fidgeted with the tear-drop-shaped sapphire gemstone hanging from the black velvet choker around her neck. The choker was a necessary accessory. It allowed her to walk in daylight. Before being killed in battle, his grandmother spelled amulets for her hybrid children and the *Daywalkers*.

His mother seemed oblivious to the nervous habit.

Not Calin. "Mother! But what?"

She looked around the room, everywhere. But at him.

"Mother!"

"Your grandfather isn't requesting that *I* risk being destroyed," Eliza hedged meekly after several moments. She lifted wide, foggy eyes on him.

This bitch!

Regarding her through narrow eyes, Calin clenched his jaw. Everything clicked into place.

"You have to understand," his mother hurried to explain. "This is the only available way to exterminate your humanity. You'll be one of us... and I'll be free."

He sucked his teeth. "He doesn't want *us* to go; he wants *me* to go. It's my mission, then? And here I was looking out for you." Calin speared her with an icy glare. "I won't make that mistake again."

Bloody tears crested her waterline. "You're young, relatable. The Awakening is a simple process. You bury the descendant alive by midnight June twenty-seventh. It will dig its way out of the grave. Destroy it." Her voice broke. "And the activated seal magically activates your dormant deactivated seal."

"Why, after sentencing me to the farthest corner of the mansion, where no one so much as trips past my rooms, am I being entrusted with this oh-so-sensitive mission? Why not delegate the task to an idiot Daywalker? Or, here's a better idea, do it yourself."

"Our feeding methods aren't..." She paused, searching for the word. "Inconspicuous. And our amulets are... easily detectable."

Finally, some truth. Eliza and her siblings' breed of vampire fed by total consumption of their prey. They also fed more. Hundreds of missing people would be quite noticeable. He'd require the same special diet without a soul. With his soul, he fed the way all rogue vampire did. He drained his prey. Also, his mortal blood allowed him limited exposure to sunlight without the assistance of an amulet. This need for anonymity implied more risk than her original assurance.

"It must be a being of noble blood, but not of the original line," Eliza croaked. A fat red tear rolled down her cheek.

Damn, curse!

"Bianca is too young." More tears escaped as she continued. "Neither I, your aunts, uncles, nor grandfather can do it. That leaves you. Papa will find a way to strip the active seal from you and restore it to himself when you return." Tears flowed freely now.

Please, no more spontaneous, brutal acts of affection.

She might feel the pain of an emotion, but she possessed the mind of a sociopath. The knowledge and understanding behind emotions eluded her. Stupidly, part of him craved sincere affection. A hug, a pat on the shoulder. His father never embraced him. Men didn't behave in such a manner in the 1800s. Moron that he was, Calin wanted to experience genuine... anything. Damn, he couldn't wait to be rid of his soul.

Heavy footsteps shook the floor. Eliza jumped. Calin's eyes shot to his closed door. Sounds equivalent to nails dragged down a chalkboard rent the air. Dread settled in the pit of his stomach. The raucous noise grew louder, closer.

After a wide-eyed double-take at the door, then him, Eliza kicked into action. Using the back of her hand, she wiped away all traces of tears. She lifted. Rubbed her hands on his navy blue comforter, erasing the red tear stains. She sat on the spot to hide it. Grandfather hated her curse. It reminded him of what he'd lost in battle.

Not the loss of three sons, his *eternalmate*, or his concubine. No, what pissed Grandfather off was the knowledge that after destroying the *Vampire Royals*, his cousin, he didn't reclaim his seal. His power.

The Balkan Dimir bloodline was about power. Grandfather sacrificed his title to create his hybrid offspring for it. Eliza was all for sacrificing him, her offspring, in her power quest. At least television's depiction of vampires got something right. They were obsessive.

Chasing power was a lost, damning cause. Hell, his grandfather was the poster child for it in supernatural history. Try as he might, Calin craved it, too. There was power in belonging, being accepted by his family, in having them and the *Daywalkers* behind him. Power begot respect.

Boom!

The bedroom door exploded. Wood bits flew everywhere.

Eliza yelped. Slapped a hand over her mouth. Suffocated a scream. Calin didn't do either, but he saw why one might. If the Bogeyman was real, then the hulking figure standing in the doorway would be him.

The bastard was freaking enormous. Balkan couldn't fit through the doorway without ducking and turning sideways. Only *The Dark Majesty* vibrated more concentrated amounts of evil than Balkan. Although dethroned more than a millennia ago, Balkan still wore his gold royal cloak over mafia-style pin-striped suits at all times. The hood of his cloak completely obscured his face.

Calin doubted anyone, save his offspring, had ever seen Balkan's face. The only part of his grandfather he'd ever seen was his monstrous hands and random strands of dark blond hair. Balkan Dimir was true to his reputation, a sick SOB. Malevolence, depravity, and wickedness personified—with an odd scraping and clicking coming from behind him.

Initial shock worn off, Calin and Eliza jumped to their feet as if tased. His mother curtsied. Calin bowed his head respectfully. In unison, they said, "Sire."

"Sit," Balkan snarled the command.

They complied.

"Papa, I—"

Balkan's hooded head whipped around toward Eliza.

Her mouth snapped shut.

"Speak when you're spoken to, *daughter*."

The way his grandfather said the word, he'd think it also meant trash. Calin glanced at his mother in time to see her bottom lip quiver.

Oh, shit!

So not the time for her curse to make an appearance.

In one swift, dizzying move, Balkan angled toward Calin. "You will go to America. Track the so-called descendant." He sneered. "Make nice with it. Gain its trust. Explain how great being a vampire is. Mortals love the idea of becoming immortal. It'll let you perform the Awakening," Balkan said, sounding almost happy, if such a thing were possible. "I have it on good authority that this act will not only end your insufferable mother's curse but also do away with that reeking soul of yours. More importantly, it will restore the seal to its rightful owner."

Calin didn't know this "good authority," but the harsh way Balkan said the words shouted he didn't want to be them if they were wrong.

"If I may, Grandfather? How are we to trust such a prophecy? The informant might be playing both—"

"Do you question me?" Balkan's roar reverberated through the mansion.

Oh. Shit. He woke the beast.

Rather than fuckup an already fucked situation, Calin stayed quiet. Shook his head.

"If anything were to go awry, no one would suspect you. Your breed is unknown. With your repugnant mortal blood, if Sebastian, White-witch, or any member of the royal guard happened upon you, they wouldn't detect what you are. If my authority is wrong, you've killed a mortal—who cares?" In a deadly tone, he added, "And I've killed a no one."

Crisp, honey-scented fear permeated the air, splitting Calin's focus.

Where did that come from? It smelled delicious.

No way was Grandfather Balkan secreting such a magnificent aroma. Trying to keep her lip from quivering, Eliza played with her choker. Distress vibrated from her, not fear. The fragrance was clouding his mind.

"The two of you leave tonight. Dark-witch, Athan, will supply further instructions before you depart," Balkan informed him.

Two of you?

Calin knew he'd regret this. "Mother doesn't need to—"

A bolt of electricity ran from the wall outlet towards Calin's desk lamp. Traveled through his desk and up his arm. Calin gripped the desk; the wood cracked. Electricity lit him like a traffic light. Involuntarily, his fangs elongated. He barred his teeth against the torture.

Eliza cried out, the sound a cross between misery and concern.

Balkan laughed a hearty satisfied sound.

Smoke seeped from Calin's body. Multiple scents, burning flesh, singed hair, filled the air. Fought for supremacy.

"I am not sending your" — Balkan's hooded head turned briefly toward his daughter then back to Calin — "unstable mother on such an important errand. I'm sending the only being I trust to be my eyes and ears and to keep you in line. Now, what say you to this task?"

The question was rhetorical. Calin was as sure of that as he was of the fact that his balls were fried. It'd take a good fourteen hours for his skin to regenerate.

Nobody refused Balkan and continued to exist. No, this was masturbation for his ego. He loved to stroke it by ordering others around. Hearing them acquiesce to his will made him jizz power. Normally, Calin would leave him with a monster case of blue balls, but he wanted to go on this adventure. Once it was done, he would have power over Balkan.

He accepted the challenge with a nod.

"That's what I like to hear," Balkan drawled. "Now, I've brought something for you." He pulled a struggling, portly, brunette woman from behind his back by the collar of her shirt.

Oh... The good smell.

Muffled pleas came from behind her duct-taped mouth. Black pumps scraped the hardwood floor as she tried to wriggle free. Seeing Calin's charred skin, brown eyes widened in fright.

She looked...

Scrumptious.

Balkan shoved her into the room, then left. With lightning speed, Calin and Eliza descended on their prey.

Chapter Four

Blazing Arizona sun shone brightly on the movie theater, an ominous spotlight on the red brick and chrome building. Amelia alternated between glancing out her driver's side window at the place she'd worked for six years—her first and only job—and staring unseeing out the windshield. Her grip on the steering wheel tightened. She breathed deeply. In through her nose, out through her mouth, trying to pull in courage from the universe. Today, work would be her stage and the world her audience. She'd be turning in an Oscar-worthy performance.

Amelia Marie Keeler, starring as: Normal Person.

She'd laugh on cue, frown if necessary, roll her eyes, or bat her lashes. Whatever proved to the world, and the so-called friends her brother didn't think she knew he had watching her, checking on her mental health, that she was *okay*.

Never mind the fact that she was cursed. Death personified.

Far from ignorant, she knew her thinking was unhealthy. Flawed. But until someone provided irrefutable proof to the contrary... Her thinking worked. None of the counselors Evan forced her to see when she initially shut down gave irrefutable suggestions. Neither did they provide adequate proof that she wasn't the catalyst behind her loved ones' deaths. The facts as she knew them were clear: anyone she showed soul-deep love for died.

No one understood how powerless she felt. Her parents died in a freak accident where a drunk driver going the wrong way on the 101 northbound plowed head-on into their car. She'd dreamed it. Thought it a nightmare until she was startled awake by a phone call confirming it.

Three months later, her father's parents, her grandparents, were rushing to her because she'd had a bad feeling. Had they not stopped at their house to get the special soup she requested, they wouldn't have encountered the burglar who murdered them. The suspect? Never found.

Six months later, her mother's parents decided to come for an extended vacation after Evan told them she'd been increasingly more depressed. Their RV, their residence at the time, burned to a crisp the same night. With them in it.

Her male best friend, Jon, wanted to take her away for her nineteenth birthday. That night, he'd been on his way back to Arizona from Utah. He overcorrected on a winding mountain pass, flipped his truck, and ejected through the front windshield. Died on impact.

If someone else she loved died...

She couldn't take it.

Amelia considered herself made of tough stuff, but no one should expect her to be that tough. Her parents' death started the shutdown process. Jon's completed it. But she didn't call undue attention to herself. She faked emotion. Displayed enough to skate by.

Evan seemed to forever have people lurking in the shadows, waiting for her mask to slip. It wouldn't. She regained power by eradicating outward emotion. Who would've guessed her psyche would take it a step further and extirpate every internal emotion, too—save pain and grief? And she'd endure it. Because she couldn't escape the truth that no one she loved had died in the three years since she'd died inside. So, she would be cold and distant. To protect them.

Thank, God, for mood swings. They fooled the universe into thinking she had no loved ones left. The pain she dealt with on the daily, marrow-deep. Yet everyone expected her to get on with it. Let bygones be bygones. *Que sera, sera. Carpe diem.* Yeah, right!

She wasn't seizing anything, not letting anything be, and she for damn sure wouldn't let anything go.

Oh... she wished she had a penis, then she'd have something for the world to blow. The phrases "suck it" or "blow it" were less impressive when one didn't possess the proper hardware to back them up.

She'd get through today like she did every day. Fake it. Three years had taught her well how to pretend to give a damn. To think, she used to despise fake people. Now she was a big ole hypocrite, faker than the explosion of BBLs in Hollywood.

To top it all off, she was in pain today. The gums over her incisors and eye teeth were on fire. Add that to her weird stomach cramps, mood swings, hot and cold flashes, and all of a sudden, her life felt sponsored by menopause. Something she hadn't expected to happen for a long time.

After a ragged breath, she mumbled into the silence of the car, "I can do this. I. Can. Do. This. It's just one day." She adjusted her tie.

My public awaits.

"Hey, Amelia Badelia, what's shaken?" Gordon, her boss, asked from where he stood on top of the concession counter. The sun bounced off his shiny, burnt sienna, bald head as the door eased shut behind Amelia. He flashed a white, gap-toothed grin.

Breathe, smile, and be polite, she reminded herself.

A spark of something close to contentment rose inside Amelia, then flickered out. It happened whenever she entered her beloved job. Dark inside, it fit her to a T. Daylight made her sad, not happy like it did most people. It never had. Since everyone started dropping like lead balloons, it made her feel worse. Each new day reminded her of all she'd lost. Inside the theater, it was always night. But nowadays, even her joy of the night never lasted long.

Decorated like a disco, Super Saver was one of the nicest theaters in Arizona, which said a lot, considering the three-dollar admission. Strategically placed chandeliers resembling neon, abstract, twisted balloon art provided scant light. Glass brick walls flashed multiple colors that changed to the beat of the Muzak playing through the lobby speakers. As usual, the smell of fresh popcorn filled the air.

Standing on the large, blue, circular countertop, Gordon toyed with a drink special sign.

"Am I the first one here?" Amelia practically shouted, unsure if he would hear over the popper.

The answer walked in before Gordon spoke. Tall, gangly, good-looking—if the just rolled out of bed fully dressed look appealed—Christopher appeared at the rear of the theater. He hopped the blue velvet rope separating the theater hall and lobby. Raking his long fingers through shaggy blond hair, powder blue eyes locked on her.

"'Bout time you got here." Christopher's wide smile creased the corners of his eyes. "I thought we were going to have to open, and you wouldn't get your surprise."

He means well, be polite.

Amelia pursed her lips, her brows scrunched. What in fresh hell was going on? Rounding the counter, she went into the concession area and locked Louis in her drawer under the first register. "Are you speaking gibberish again?"

"Give it a second." Christopher chuckled. "You'll see." He tilted his head, ear lifted heavenward as if waiting on instruction from God. Music started a second later. Dread consumed her. Christopher extended his hand over the concession counter. "May I have this dance?"

No. No, you can't, dillhole.

Damn, the voice again.

Be nice. Be. Nice.

"Umm...are you kidding?" She stared at his hand as if it were covered in feces, then looked to Gordon for help.

He shook his head. "Don't look at me. This is all him. I told him he was stupid, but" — a lazy shrug — "it wasn't new news. You got ten minutes until we open."

Peaches and Herb's "Shake Your Groove Thing" filled the lobby. Like a baby stuck in a highchair refusing peas, Amelia shook her head no.

Christopher wriggled his fingers at her, his lower lip jutted out in a pout. Or he could've been doing a puppy dog face. Didn't matter; both looked ridiculous.

Why did everyone expect her to be old Amelia? If in three years she hadn't magically reverted back to fun, Disco-adoring, people-loving, sweet Amelia, it wouldn't happen. Surrender the fantasy. Yet every year on the anniversary of her parents' death, they went overboard trying to do the impossible. Change her back.

Wouldn't work. But she had to play the part. The theater had eyes. Or, at least, her brother did. His spies were everywhere. *"For her own good."*

So, play the part she would. She walked around. Met Christopher in the lobby where he moved side to side, swayed, and mouthed the words to the song. She wanted to applaud his rhythmically challenged effort to cheer her up but couldn't. What she could do was pretend. Like every other year, she broke out halfhearted disco moves to one of her old favorites.

Gordon got in on the action, too, busting out his best John Travolta *Saturday Night Fever* impersonation. His dance partner was the sign he'd been fixing.

Petite Cicely sauntered into the theater. Coffee-brown skin shimmered in the sunlight a second before the doors closed behind her. "I work with crazy people." She laughed. Cat-like brown eyes lit in amusement. She strode around the concession stand and locked her purse under register two. With all her seventeen-year-old enthusiasm, she skipped to Amelia and Christopher. Long, black micro-braids bounced behind her. "You guys aren't doing it right. You're supposed to do the hustle."

Christopher laughed. "What do you know about the hustle? What're you, four? Maybe five years old?"

"Hey, I'm a Blaxican. Rhythm and all dance moves are encoded in my DNA," Cicely retorted, exchanging a booty bump with Amelia.

A couple hustles later, the sun illuminated the dark theater once more. Short, chubby Matt entered. Cutting bourbon-colored eyes at each of them, he shook his crew-cut head of hair.

"What the—? You guys are losers. Headed over to Studio 54 after work?" He smirked.

Amelia stopped dead in her tracks. Went back into the concession area. The weasel was disgusting. Vile. She half expected raw sewage to spew from his mouth each time he opened it. He was wet sand in her underwear, and right. How could she allow herself to even pretend to go along with them, today of all days?

Ice-cold waves of guilt poured over her. Her parents were probably turning in their graves at her callousness. This was a time to mourn, not jump around like an idiot.

As soon as the song finished, Christopher jumped the velvet rope and ran down the hall to change the sound system to Muzak.

"Smooth move, Ex-lax," Cicely grumbled, fixing Matt with a frigid glare. "We can always count on you to be insensitive—dumbass."

Wonderful, now babies were feeling sorry for her. Anger was a brush fire, fast-burning and all-consuming inside her. People were always treating her like cracked glass—one wrong move, and she'd shatter. Honestly, she felt that way sometimes, but she didn't need their pity.

"Can't minors get fired for cussing?" Matt taunted, following Cicely behind the concession stand. "Isn't there some type of labor law about that?"

Fists balled, Cicely lunged at Matt.

He covered his manhood. "Gordon! Cicely's sexually harassing me again," Matt tattled, flinching away.

Cicely rolled her eyes. Snorted. "Yeah, right. You wish I'd sexually harass you, douchebag. That's the only way your fat ass would get any."

The corners of Amelia's mouth threatened to turn up. Cicely was hilarious. A deep breath kept the unwelcome smile at bay as she finished checking her candy drawers.

Gordon hopped down off the counter. "Enough, guys. We need to open." He headed toward the back door, which led to the kitchen, storage area, and upstairs to the manager's office. "Fill the cups, stock the candy. Somebody fill the butter. Umm...

Amelia?" he hesitated. "If you wanna do box office today, you can."

Eyes narrowed, Amelia glanced over her shoulder at Gordon. Hand hovering over the doorknob, he gave her a pitiful I'm-doing-this-because-I-care frown. She hated special treatment. These people knew way too much about her personal life. She gazed at her co-workers, who were all giving some form of the same pathetic face.

Wonderful!

She slammed her candy drawer. "Give me an effing break! I'm scheduled for the concession stand. I'll work the damn concession stand."

Should she cuss at her boss? No. But pity seemed to be synonymous with job security. She could call out his momma and not get fired.

"You get off earlier in the box office," Gordon reminded her as if it mattered.

Amelia glanced at her co-workers again. They were trying to be sensitive to her needs, and yes, their intentions were good, but—what did her mother always say? "The path to Hell is paved with good intentions."

She grabbed her purse out of the drawer. "Un-fucking-believable," she muttered under her breath, storming through the lobby to the box office, keys in hand. "I need a new fucking job. One where everybody minds their own damn business."

Amelia unlocked and opened the box office door. A small, dark cave. If not for two ticket windows, there would be no light at all. Normally, this was her refuge, but today, she was exiled here. She hated being told what to do. Turning to the concession stand, she shouted, louder than necessary, "Christopher, bring me a cup of ice before you open the doors?" Her damn teeth hurt like crazy.

Christopher nodded.

"Call upstairs if things get too—"

If he didn't stop talking, she would rip out his larynx. "I'm fine, Gordon. I wouldn't have come in if I wasn't," she snapped, cutting him off.

Gordon disappeared behind the back door.

Before slamming the box office door, she yelled, "Remember my ice!"

Hours later, Amelia pulled to the curb and cut the Mustang's engine. She glanced at the dashboard clock, then frowned out the window. Her house. The saddest reminder of her parents that she couldn't get away from and couldn't bear to sell.

"Aww... memories," she sighed.

She scowled at the cars in the driveway. Tessa's purple Dodge Charger parked next to Dan's silver Jeep Wrangler. Walker's black Dodge Ram parked in the gravel on the side of the red brick house. How nice of them to not save her a spot. Leaving room for her to pull into the two-car garage must have been too much.

Assholes!

Amelia groaned. The gang was all here, and in the mood for it or not, they were going to have a nice group dinner, according to Tessa. She got out of the car.

Before she put her key in the front door, it opened. Dan. Poor Dan had gained weight. Not a lot, but being only five-seven, he appeared thick. Beefy. Didn't help that his shaved head and scruffy goatee made him look like a bum. He was a cross between a pudgy, dull, green-eyed Leonardo DiCaprio and a real-life teddy bear dressed in jeans and a snug white T-shirt.

"What it be, A? Tater tots and cheese in the car?"

"Oh, shit! I forgot."

Aha! Maybe this would cancel the stupid dinner. Her stomach growled in loud disagreement. Okay, maybe not. She was starved. More than starved, ravenous. It hit fast, like seeing Dan made her hungry.

"It's cool. I'll get it. I'm headed to the store anyway. Apparently, I didn't follow proper protocol and bring flowers for the hostess," Dan commented snidely, then chanced a quick glance behind him. Probably making sure Tessa wasn't within earshot.

His girlfriend scared him shitless. Tessa absolutely wore the pants in that relationship. She'd turned a testosterone-filled ex-jock into a neutered house cat.

"Where's Wall?"

"He walked to the park with a basketball about... hmm... an hour ago." He squeezed by her. "Do you care what type of cheese it is?"

"Uh... get the already shredded kind; it's easier. Two pounds of tater tots, too, okay?"

Nodding, Dan got into his Jeep.

Amelia went inside. The phone rang as she closed the door.

"Hello?" Tessa answered from somewhere down the hall.

Entering the makeshift dining area, she threw her Louis Vuitton on the island and sat on a barstool. She needed a shot. Not alcohol, but an actual shot. To the head. Today had been one of those days. One she didn't see ending any better than it started.

The front door opened and closed.

Sniffing, Amelia cringed. The ripe musk of sweat and Axe Body Spray reached her before Walker did. Gah!

Long, sweat-dampened, tattooed arms wrapped around her waist. Walker molded his hard, lean body to her back. "Hey, butternut," Walker whispered in her ear then kissed her neck.

Twisting out of his arms, she turned to face him. Walker's normally mohawked brown hair was slicked into one strip down the middle of his head, whether with sweat or gel, she couldn't be sure. Wearing black basketball shorts and a white wife-beater, his completely tattooed arms and neck were visible. Wide armholes displayed his tattooed ribcage. Soulful cognac eyes screamed come-hither. No surprise there—his eyes always looked that way, and usually, that's what they were saying.

People judged him harshly based on his outward appearance; even Amelia made unfair judgments before she knew him. Inside, he was beautiful, and the tattoos and piercings made him masculine, sexy.

"Hey, you. How was your game?" She wanted to be disgusted. He smelled rank, but his flushed face made him oddly gorgeous in a manly sort of way. She hadn't experienced this type of attraction for him in a long time.

Leaning in, Walker planted a kiss on Amelia that sent her body into overdrive. Her heart raced. Her stomach knotted with desire. Weird. He'd kissed her before, but this one packed a punch. She threw her arms around his neck, desperate to get closer.

Walker's lips contorted under hers. He pried her arms off him. "Damn, babe! You been lifting weights or something?"

"No, why?" Amelia frowned. Was he making fun of her? She could barely lift a gallon of water.

"Milk must really be doing you good. You've never grabbed me and hurt me before." Wall grinned mischievously. "You wanna... grab me in your room?"

"Shut up." Amelia shoved him. He stumbled backward. Whoa.

"Who's Queen Bitch talking to?" Walker asked, jerking his head toward the hall where Tessa's voice came from.

Amelia hated his nickname for her best friend. She couldn't challenge it though. Tessa didn't do nice, especially when it came to Walker. Like beer, Tessa was an acquired taste; either you liked her, or you didn't. And she and Walker had a love-hate relationship. They hated when they weren't able to do what they loved: piss each other off.

They strained to hear Tessa's phone conversation.

"No, she's not," Tessa said, answering a question from the anonymous caller. "Yeah, I'm sure...Probably as soon as you hang up." Dressed in another easy-movement dancer out-fit—sleek, slim-fit black yoga pants and a white, stretchy tank top—Tessa walked past them and into the kitchen. She hung up the phone, set it on the island.

They stared at her in expectation.

Tessa shifted foot to foot. "What? Do I have a bat in the cave?"

"Who was on the phone, dork?" Amelia asked.

"Oh, nobody, just the Visa people," Tessa replied flippantly while getting food out of the refrigerator.

Amelia and Walker exchanged glances.

"And...?" Amelia prompted.

"And what? They asked if I was here. I said no. They asked when I thought I'd be in, and I said probably as soon as they hung up. Then I hung up—the end. Now, Smelly McAsshole" — she leveled a glare at Walker — "needs to go shower. He smells like ripe ass."

Kissing her cheek, Walker growled in her ear. Her stomach churned with the same extreme desire she'd undergone seconds before. He flipped Tessa the bird.

"I'll be back. Feel free to join me. I'll leave the door open for you," Walker offered.

"Gross! Please close it," Tessa complained, making gagging sounds as Walker walked away. She turned to Amelia. "I hope you've been tested. Make sure he double-bags it. You don't want cooties or worse... the nine-month flu."

"Thanks for the advice, Dr. Drew, but double-bagging is less effective than one. Anyway, I'm not the one you should be worried about. What's Dan in, his second trimester?" Amelia smirked.

"Fuck you! He's retaining water," Tessa defended. She grabbed a knife from a drawer and the bag of soy ground beef from the freezer. Holding the bag of soy ground beef at eye level, she stabbed it with the butcher knife.

Amelia gasped. "What are you doing, stupid!"

"What?" Tessa asked oblivious to the issue.

"You're gonna cut your finger off or stab out your eye!" Reaching over the island countertop, she held out her hand for the knife and soy beef.

Still trying to open the bag, Tessa backed away. "I know what I'm doing. I'm a pr— Shit!" she cried out, dropping the bag and knife.

Amelia jumped to her feet, intent on helping. She froze midstride. Everything seemed to move in slow motion. Sounds amplified. She heard blood travel through Tessa's veins. Rush to freedom. It oozed from the cut in her left index finger. Slid down its length. Dripped onto the floor. Each drop sizzled like frying bacon and smelled tasty. Amelia's gums throbbed. Ached.

Blood flowed freely from her friend's wound. No more fighting her craving.

Amelia was entranced.

Chapter Five

R un, bitch, run!

Pure, unadulterated, cold, hard fear sliced through Tessa Wilde. The frantic pound of her heart could give a drummer wood. Her mouth dried. Actual sweat beaded on her forehead. Yuck. Her knees knocked.

Cut finger, be damned!

"A?" she said, shocked at her steady voice. Her nervous system was the extreme opposite. Amelia looked at her like a cartoon wolf eying a lamb, picturing it all buttery and rotating over an open fire. Kinda weird since Amelia was a staunch vegetarian. "A, what are you doing? Bring me a towel."

If Amelia heard her, she gave no indication.

Tessa took a wobbly step back.

Her best friend gave a barely perceptible shake of head, a silent command. And kept coming. She prowled around the island, eyes dropping to lock onto Tessa's finger.

For some reason, she was scared. It made no sense. She'd never been scared of Amelia. Not when she lost her favorite royal blue Coach purse, washed and dried her royal blue leather pants, and threw away her laminated Eminem poster all in one day. Everybody knew not only was royal blue one of Amelia's favorite colors, but messin' with her stuff—and she considered Eminem her stuff—was signing their own death certificate. That disastrous day should've been her last. Yet, she hadn't been scared—much. But right now...

An underwear change was in her future. Near future.

Stalking toward her, Amelia's every step was slow, measured. A bit forced. As if she fought someone invisible.

Whoever it was, Tessa hoped they won. She didn't know what was happening. Another step back. Freeze. The handle of the fridge met her spine.

Dressed in her work uniform, black vest over white button-down, black silk necktie, and black slacks, Amelia resembled a limo driver. A serial killing limo driver. Her top lip curled away from her teeth. Speaking of teeth, something funky was up with them.

The gums over Amelia's incisors and her canines were noticeably swollen. Inflamed. Looked like they were breathing. Movie-special-effect-style, pulsating.

Ohmigod! Tessa's eyes widened. *Maybe somebody slipped me some crack at the dance studio.*

Click... click... click.

Her eyes darted around in search of the sound's origin. The floor.

Amelia's heels collided with the linoleum, adding an eerie Jaws-closing-in soundtrack to the already surreal moment.

Her gaze flicked to her friend. Tessa started. *Holy shit!* Her eyes grew impossibly wider. Moisture coated once dry orbs. Amelia had used her momentary distraction to get *way* closer. But that wasn't what made her jump. Two specific changes did.

One, the teeth under Amelia's swollen gums shifted. As in, grew. Not a lot, but definitely grew longer. Sharper. Incisors shorter than the canines, they stair-stepped each other. Tessa half expected a twinkly ping to dance on top of the razor-sharp tips.

Two, Amelia's freaky eyes—she meant that lovingly—got freakier. Normally, Amelia's peepers—as Evan would say—were cool, OMFG-style. Unlike anything she, or anyone else, judging by the stares Amelia received on the daily, had ever seen before. The right iris was an emerald-green pool, but it looked like someone jumped off a high dive into the black pupil. A champagne brown shot out, frozen mid-splash. The left was yellow, like, actual gold, like follow the yellow brick road, with an identical champagne splash reaching out of the pupil. Neither splash obscured the color of the iris but crawled out just enough to be totally noticeable. Although they, *so,* weren't, for lack of a more fitting description, hazel. At that moment, Tessa called them glowing.

Fucking! Glowing!

Like her favorite childhood toy, the Lite-Brite. Ooh... that thing was dope. So awesome!

The effect in real life, however? Not so awe-inducing when coming from a frickin' person. Shit was scary. The predatory gleam convinced her that even if she could move, Amelia would catch her. Even in the dark. Hunt her down and eat her.

Luminescent eyes glazed. The corners of Amelia's mouth turned up. A feral smile. Her nostrils flared as if she smelled something yummy.

Please don't be me. Dumb thought. It was her.

Without a shadow of a doubt, she knew that although this—creature?—was Amelia in body, Amelia wasn't there. Amelia had left the building. Amelia, *no en casa!* Her replacement, a predator. A graceful, methodical predator. Moving closer and closer. Ice-cold fear skittered up and down Tessa's spine. She shivered.

She'd been wrong. Amelia didn't look like a limo driver. She was a tigress in a limo driver's outfit.

In the blink of an eye—a gesture Tessa wouldn't contemplate doing right now—Amelia closed the distance between them. She flinched. Couldn't help it, what should've taken several more lazy, slinky steps took Amelia— hmm... She didn't know how many steps. In truth, although she hadn't looked away, she couldn't say with certainty that she'd seen Amelia move.

Amelia grabbed her upper arms, a bruising grip.

Damn! Bench press much! Through her T-shirt, she felt—claws? Glancing down out of the corner of her eye, Tessa saw that, like her teeth, Amelia's nails had grown sharper. Claws bit through the fabric of Tessa's shirt and skin, drawing blood.

Amelia shook her. Hard.

Apparently, she needed to witness her best friend in the whole wide world lick her lips and gaze hungrily at her—finger?

One hand released her upper arm. The abrupt return of circulation to that part of her arm burned. Hurt like a bitch. She would've grabbed it, soothed the ache, but suddenly, her injured hand was otherwise engaged. Amelia took possession of the wounded digit, inching it toward her mouth. All the while, studying it like it was speaking Japanese to her.

What the hell is going on here?

She didn't have a clue. What she knew? She couldn't stand here looking all tasty and delicious. Since her legs obviously decided to forgo safety, she figured she'd try using her mouth. Although she didn't know why. It never did anything for her before, except get her in trouble. Whatever. Words? Or her finger inside Amelia's mouth?

Before she uttered a word, the sound of crinkling plastic reached her ears.

"Oh, God! What happened?" Dan shouted from somewhere nearby.

Tessa wouldn't risk a glance at him, no matter how close he sounded.

More bags rustling, then a *thump*. He dropped the bags.

She assumed. No way would she take her eyes off the Amelia monster. Not when she still had her finger in a chokehold, causing more blood to bubble out of the now purple digit.

Dan's heavy footfalls clomped against the kitchen floor.

Amelia blinked. Her teeth receded, going back to their prior perfection. Her eyes dimmed and returned to the awe-inducing kaleidoscope of colors. Just like that...

Back to normal.

Eyes flying wide open, she dropped Tessa's hand like it burned her. She released her hold on Tessa's upper arm at the same time and backed away.

Dan hurried to her, rushing past Amelia as if she weren't there. Gently taking hold of her injured hand, he led her to the sink. She followed on stiff legs, yet her eyes never detoured from a bewildered Amelia. Her heart continued to race. The *whoosh* of the running faucet broke her inquisitive stare. Tessa sagged against Dan's side in relief. Unfortunately, her mind wasn't as relieved. No longer numb from fear, chaotic thoughts ping-ponged around. The most prominent:

What. The. Fuck?

Had she imagined it? The ordeal, which seemed like an eternity, in actuality had only lasted a couple minutes.

She glanced over her shoulder at Amelia. "What the hell is wrong with you?"

"I'm—I'm—" Amelia stammered.

"A saber-tooth tiger!" Tessa provided, unable to help herself.

"I'm sorry. I'm sorry." Amelia stepped back. The sharp corner of the island countertop impeded escape. It must've cut into her back. If it did, she made no face to hint at being hurt. Without glancing backward, she stepped around it. "Uh... I don't know. I'm—I'm having a shitty—sorry." Inarticulate apology finished, she turned. Booked it through the dining room and down the hall.

Tessa studied Amelia's retreating form. Dan continued washing out her cut.

Something was seriously wrong. She understood Amelia's depression. Not that she would handle it the way Amelia did, but she got it. The thinking if she kept everything exactly the same she wouldn't lose anyone else. Kinda made sense. She'd lost Jon, too. However, she hadn't lost her parents, then both sets of grandparents before that. Shit, she didn't know what she'd do if she lost her parents and all Amelia had. That's why they'd planned the dinner to make her day a little easier. Damn, test or no test, Evan should have been here. Clearly, Amelia needed her brother.

No. Scratch that. Tessa was exactly who Amelia needed. Depression didn't cause cannibalistic behavior. But something else might.

Once dinner ended—Taco Bell since tater tot casserole was now and forever off the menu—Amelia sat in the front room on the white wicker daybed, waiting for Tessa.

She'd begged Tessa to talk. Coerced her into meeting in neutral territory with fancy words like: "I promise I'm full." "No, dumbass, I won't eat you."

She didn't know what to say, how to smooth this over. To be honest, she didn't remember what happened. All she knew for sure was that she'd done something to terrify her friend. She never wanted anyone afraid of her, especially Tessa. She had to fix this, but she had no memory of what *this* was. It was like a drunken blackout without the shit side-effects. At this point, she'd almost prefer those to this maddening feeling of missed time. This black void where memory should be.

Green eyes regarded her with wary suspicion as Tessa entered the room. She gave the side of the daybed Amelia occupied a wide berth and sat on the extreme opposite end. Amelia frowned at the way Tessa settled herself on the edge of the tacky, pastel-covered seat. She appeared a second away from making a break for it.

She plucked at loose threads of the covering. Her mom used to wait up for her and Evan here back in the day. Felicia Keeler—rest her soul—the queen of tacky. Amelia once hated the peach, kiwi, and orange pastel covering. Now, she'd kill anyone who tried to get rid of it.

Her palms sweat. Woo! She was nervous. Something she'd never been with Tessa. Confession time. "I don't know what's wrong with me."

"Is it okay to sit this close?" Tessa scooted an infinitesimal degree closer. "You're not still hungry, are you?" She held her hands up in surrender, said in a mocking tone, "Don't eat me."

"Tessa!" she chided between clenched teeth. "I'm being serious. Something's wrong with me. I'm having... weird cravings."

Expression blanked, Tessa arched a fine-trimmed brow. An unspoken *duh* hung between them.

Amelia went on deciding not to reopen a wound she had no memory of inflicting. She needed to garner sympathy, so Tessa knew she wasn't some zombie lunatic. "I told you I've been sick lately. Hot flashes, cold flashes. I know you know I've been moody—even for me. PMS to the twentieth power. My gums are sore, bleeding. I'm going through ice like a monkey with an unlimited amount of crap to throw."

"Wow. Could've gone my whole life without that last piece of imagery," Tessa muttered. She reached a hand as if to touch Amelia's in comfort. Stopped. Pulled her hand back. Reached again. Stopped. Two failed attempts later, she made contact and rubbed the back of Amelia's hand soothingly.

Amelia tried not to be offended. She understood the hesitance. But that didn't mean she liked it. *I'm not crazy.*

"Chill, Hannibal. I know you didn't mean to almost eat me. Calm down, okay? Breathe in through your nose. Exhale out through your mouth."

She did as instructed. Didn't help.

"After my..." Tessa paused for dramatic effect. "Brush with death. I broke some shit down. I think I know what's wrong with you." Another pause.

Hmph! Somehow Amelia thought there'd be more to that statement. But Tessa just sat there giving her a weird wide-eyed look and nodding as if that said it all. It didn't. Not unless Tessa expected her to absorb her theory through osmosis. She was wound tight right now. In no condition to deal with Tessa's cryptic bullshit.

"Tessie!" she snapped when two silent minutes passed. "I will punch through your forehead if you do not finish your sentence." Amelia's eyes widened at her uncharacteristic aggression.

Tessa, just as shocked, flinched. "Jeez, since when do you go all WWE SmackDown?"

Afraid to say anything else, she glared at her friend.

Her expression must have done the trick.

Tessa went on, voice grave. "Okay, sorry. I get it. You know the whole single or double bag debate we had earlier?" She bit her lip. "Let's just say you don't need to worry about that anymore."

Amelia froze.

"The low down. Now!"

"Hello to you, too, Evan. I'm fine. And you?" Amelia stretched. Yawned. Her brother's harsh tone didn't faze her in the least. One hand held her cell phone to her ear. The other shoved the gold comforter off her overheated body.

Damn it! Another hot flash day.

She rolled to her side. Empty space. Alone. Shame and relief dueled inside her. Most girls would be heartbroken or pissed to discover their boyfriend had snuck out at some point during the night. Not her. Relief won. Thank, God, Walker hadn't taken her lapse in judgment as a sleepover invite. Quick on the heels of that revelation—shame. Walker treated her like she hung the stars and moon. And here she was happy he was gone.

I'm such a bitch.

Okay, so, maybe relief hadn't won. It was a tie.

Her head felt stuffed, full. Weighted down with the amount of crap she had to think about. Nothing like a shitty night's sleep and a rude awakening to her phone playing The Bloodhound Gang's "Why's Everybody Always Pickin' On Me" to start the day. And everyone said breakfast was important.

Liars.

Another yawn slipped past her lips.

"I don't have time for this, Nugget. Tessa already made a little dil-ya-ble to me. Said something's wrong with you."

Her heart constricted. Rolling to her stomach, she kept the phone to her ear. Slammed her face into her pillow a couple times. Hard. Or as hard as one could slam their face into a pillow. Walker's nasty Axe scent filled her nostrils. *Ugh!* One more reason to hate herself. Those were piling up lately.

The ache in her heart increased tenfold.

Had Tessa told Evan everything? Everything, everything? They'd gotten over the... Event That Shall Not Be Mentioned.

But, the talk afterward? She didn't want Evan to know. To be disappointed in her. Amelia hated his nickname for her: Nugget, short for Butt-nugget. He'd called her that for as long as she could remember. Yes, it annoyed the shit out of her, especially when used in mixed company. But now, she considered it a term of endearment.

Would he still call her that if he knew of her stupidity? She could've gone her whole life without the knowledge. The proof. *It* was a truth she wasn't ready to face.

"Give me the skinny," Evan ordered in his weirdo talk. He saw one old gangster film when he was, like, seven, and ever since, he'd thought he was one. Even dressed like it. Diptard! "The truth, dig? And quick. I got class."

"Wh-wh-wh—" Damn, childhood speech impediment rears its ugly head. Nope, didn't give her away at all, did it? Deep breath in, she started over, "What did Tessie tell you?"

If she told our secret, friend or not, the bitch's head will roll.

Shit! That voice again.

"Stutter much, Nugget?" he asked, smug. He knew her too well. "Don't worry, she didn't spill whatever your big secret is. She just said to call."

Amelia wanted to release the breath she absolutely knew she held. But, she didn't want Evan to know. Talk about giving herself away. Mashing the phone screen—and by design, the microphone—into the bunched comforter at her side, she exhaled. Loud.

Tessa better thank her lucky stars. She just got saved by the hand of God. Her friend might have provided her with the answer, but that didn't mean she could spread business not hers to spread. Amelia never wanted this news to get out. Although, sooner or later it would.

Her mind drifted to their conversation last night.

Pregnant.

She didn't feel pregnant. Didn't pregnant chicks feel... heavy or something? Or excited? She felt neither. How could she be so stupid?

The Lifetime channel was all she watched. Every other show had something to do with the consequences of unprotected sex.

She watched the channel as if the programming choices were made specifically for her. Shook her head at girls who ended up in this situation. Judged them openly. Tsked when they said dumb shit like, "How could this happen?"

"It's called birth control, ya silly slut. Use it!" she'd yell at the TV.

Now, look. Her. A fucking statistic.

The role of mom didn't appeal to her. Maybe she'd wanted it once upon a time. But not now. Not anymore. With her nonexistent emotions, she wouldn't respond to the baby's cries. She could drop it or something. Did Vera Wang make maternity clothes? What about baby clothes?

Amelia's gaze slid down her torso, stopping on her flat stomach. If a baby was in there wouldn't she just... know? She didn't. And didn't want to. She didn't want to get fat. Would Walker hate her for ruining his life? They couldn't live happily ever after. Mommy's supposed to love Daddy. Not be with him because she didn't want to lose anyone else. What if she lost the baby? People died around her. She couldn't handle it. This.

Time.

Still time. There were options. This thing wasn't that advanced.

Her breath grew shallow. Where'd all the air in the room go?

A garbled, muffled noise—yelling?—reached her ears. Brought her back to her senses. Shit!

Evan.

She lifted her phone to her ear.

"Amelia! Amelia! What the fuck are you—?"

"I'm here. Sorry. I dropped the phone. Sorry." Oops!

"I asked if Walker was givin' you shit?" Evan obviously repeated. Frustration colored his words.

He'd given her something all right.

This situation would absolutely be blamed on mood swings and the voice. Until six weeks ago, sex wasn't on her radar. It required emotions she didn't possess. She and Walker had been in a sexless relationship for years.

Then one night she'd—for lack of a better word—mauled him. Sexually assaulted him. Last night after... The Incident...

she'd done it again. She'd gone from scared shitless of herself to sexual predator in a nanosecond. Walker hadn't minded. Amelia did.

"You need me to check him? Realign his nose for him?" Evan offered, breaking into her thoughts.

Right! God, she was tired of this. Their beef. Neither one of them could fight. Both were cowards behind the swagger. The most Evan and Walker could do was have a staring contest.

"Uh... No. It's all good." No way in hell would she slip and tell him anything. First, he'd find a way to kill Walker. Second, talking to her brother about sex in any form—nasty. But, she really wanted a guy's opinion. Hmm... "Can I ask you something?"

"Shake a leg, doll."

Ugh! "Can you act normal? Please."

"That your question?"

"Evan," she pleaded.

"Fine. Ask your question, Miss Keeler. I'm happy to oblige."

Ass! Whatever. She'd take what she could get. "What would you do if Kasey told you she was pregnant? Hypothetically." Quiet stretched between them for so long she checked to see if her phone dropped the call. It hadn't. "Evan?"

When he finally responded his tone was empty, flat. "What's your story, morning glory?"

Oh, no! Why didn't she consider that he'd take it seriously? Oh, damn. "Evan, no. It was just a question. No, Evan. Listen."

"You're pals, see? You wouldn't tell me if she did. Broads before Joes, right? I knew she was acting weird. Surprise visits aren't her shtick. She stalks. Oh, my God..."

Rambling. Soon, she wouldn't be able to understand him at all. When they were kids Evan rambled when he felt cornered. Trapped. His equivalent to pacing. He always panicked, rambled, and told on himself instead of staying calm.

"She's not pregnant, Evan. I promise." Amelia tried to assure him.

"Yes she is. She told you first. Wanted you to break it to me, huh? That's why Tessa was skittish earlier. I'm too young to be a dad," he babbled.

Great. She imagined him raking his fingers through his black hair, pulling tuffs of it. Normally, she would talk him down, but running on empty herself, she couldn't. She didn't want to, but she'd have to leave this for Kasey to fix. She'd leave her a voicemail and explain. Right now, all she wanted to do was go to work and pick up her paycheck. Mom had always said, *"There's no problem shopping can't fix."* That theory would get the shit tested out of it today.

"Evan, talk to Kasey. She'll make it better."

"No!" he shouted. "It's a trick. You're trying to set me—"

"Love you, Evy. Bye-bye." She pressed End.

Chapter Six

For the umpteenth time, sunlight poured into the dark theater lobby as another waste of skin entered the building. Two full movies later, the "descendant" still hadn't shown. Roughly four hours of eternity Calin would never get back. Not that he cared. What was four hours in the grand scheme of things?

He preferred solitude. Not traipsing about pretending to be one of these pigs in a blanket. Calin didn't possess any social graces and didn't care to acquire any. The sooner this charade was over, the better. Should be easy. Throw a couple compliments the stupid mortal's way. Tell it "Being a vampire is, like, the bee's knees." Perform the *Awakening*, kill it, and walkway holding the metaphorical keys to the castle. Then...

All hail King Calin.

Correction, all hail King Calin Dimir. Bestowal of the surname occurred at the time of the *seal's* activation, or in his case, once he murdered the descendant and stole it. And if his grandfather expected him to go back and hand over the activated *seal* like a good lapdog, his ancient ass had another thing coming.

Did Balkan really think Calin was *defective*? Think he believed for one minute there was some mystical way to spare him and recover the *seal?*

Riiight!

He knew exactly how Balkan planned to "magically" strip the seal from him. There wouldn't be anything magical about it. Not unless decapitation meant magical experience. Balkan didn't care about him. Like he'd told his mother, they were expendable. Soon Calin planned to disprove that notion.

However, before his plans could take flight, he needed to find the damn descendant. When he'd asked the scrawny, blond-haired mortal behind the counter, the guy said he couldn't give out information about fellow employees. Ridiculous!

Hybrids—no matter the breed—couldn't compel mortals to do whatever they said, to think however they wanted. One of many abilities they didn't possess that "normal" vampires did. Calin had never wished to be normal; he wielded power, magic, of his own. All hybrids mixed with Dark-witch did. Each harnessed one or two magical abilities unique to the individual. But he couldn't deny compulsion would come in handy at times. Like now. That'd be nice.

"They should serve buckets of mortal parts."

Teeth gritted, Calin glared at the tiny abomination seated on the bench beside him. They'd taken up residence here in the darkest corner of the lobby ten minutes ago after their movie ended. It provided a covert location to observe the entire lobby without risking sun exposure. While tolerable, bake time was best kept to a minimum.

"You know, arms, legs, maybe some eyes," the small, tinkling voice continued. "It could be a combo deal with a forty-four-ounce cup of blood included." Excitement saturated the suggestion. "Yep, I like it. Let's make them do that, Brother."

This was who Grandfather Balkan trusted to be his eyes and ears. Bianca, his baby sister, a five-year-old fledgling who thought a mortal movie theater should carry buckets of human limbs. Good choice. How was he supposed to focus on gaining the descendant's trust and plotting murder while babysitting?

"Bianca," he said, dryly.

She upturned her cherub's face. Big, beautiful, deceptively innocent, crystal blue eyes framed by thick, mile-long, black lashes gazed at him.

For a second, he was almost suckered in. No wonder her prey never saw death coming. Mortals would never suspect the little darling had committed murder at two weeks old. Or that she was strong enough to take down a sumo wrestler. "Mortals don't eat each other. That's called cannibalism," he informed her.

Bianca would've had a comeback. He would've taught her another lesson, but before either occurred, their attention was diverted. His nostrils flared. Invisible rope constructed of peculiar fragrant wisps of mango-almond, cherry blossoms, and the barest hint of sweet, coppery, mortal blood drifted to them. Swirled around them. Lassoed him.

"Eww," Bianca hissed, pinching her nostrils between two fingers. "What's that smell?"

Ignoring his sister, Calin's eyes locked on the mortal slinking up to the concession stand. This wasn't the gruesome Hell demon he'd expected to find in a state nicknamed: The Valley of the Sun. Upon discovering Arizona would be his destination he'd researched the place online. When he saw the weather forecast, he assumed the state would be plagued with charred-skinned freaks.

And it was, for the most part. Okay, not charred-skinned, but mortals were ugly.

"Brother—"

"Shut up," he snapped, unwilling to be distracted. "I'm trying to listen to what they're saying."

This was it—her. The descendant. Due to their angelic origins, the *Vampire Royals* were renowned for their incredible beauty. His aunts, mother, and even uncles proved it. If he'd ever seen his grandfather's face, he would've probably seen it there, too. Of course, the packaging startled him a bit. Supernatural were highly evolved. Unlike mortals, skin color didn't matter. The flawless, medium mocha skin of the petite descendant perplexed him only because he knew the VR were white, or Caucasian, in PC mortal terms. No matter. Beauty was beauty, and this creature surpassed beautiful.

Assorted-colored, almond-shaped eyes hid under heavily tinted sunglasses. With his preternatural vision, he clearly saw the yellow, lemon drop candy-colored, emerald, and brown gemstone orbs. Long, blood-red hair hung to the middle of her back, framing an oval face affixed with a small regal nose and high cheekbones. Pouty, gloss-coated lips begged for thorough kisses.

What. The. Fuck!

This was his mark. Letting his mind wander down this road would lead to nothing good. Nor did he want it to.

"Wait! Don't be so hasty. The body doesn't have to be warm if you want to take things down that road," coaxed his demon conscience inside his mind.

"Shut. Up!" Calin growled low, teeth clenched. "This is a job. Pussy's a dime a dozen."

"Yucky, Brother!" Bianca blanched. Turned appalled eyes on him. "What did I say?"

He shook his head to clear it. Damn, he was 200 years old. Calin never made those types of mistakes. Talking out loud to himself? What the fuck?

Embarrassment didn't look good on him; he kept his eyes forward. "Just shut up. I'm listening."

"Ow! Sexy thang," Christopher catcalled.

Amelia rolled her eyes. Fat lot of good it did. Big-ass glamorous sunglasses hid her agitation. She removed them and hung them off the side of her purse. Visible outrage was needed here. Ogling was not. She plopped her purse down on the concession counter.

"Dayam," Matt shouted from the usher stand across the lobby. "Amelia, come sit on my lap. I got a... point... to make."

Nasty!

She wouldn't have worn the black tube top, jean miniskirt, and wedge flip-flops if today wasn't another hot flash day. Well, body temperature had nothing to do with the wedges. Heels were her thing; she always wore them. They made her tall—ish. Every inch counted when you were five-three. No, the shoes definitely didn't matter; the heat did. She was hotter than R.

Kelly at Chuck E. Cheese. The jaunt across the parking lot didn't help things either.

"Oh, yeah?!" she called to Matt. "Yesterday, I was a loser. Now, I'm all... *damn?*"

Shit! Yesterday.

The word sent her thoughts careening down a road better left untraveled. Of course, the more she tried not to think about it, the more it banged at the back door of her mind. Avoidance, more than likely, was the wrong way to handle the situation, but a better solution hadn't presented itself. Plus, knowing something and knowing what to do about something were two very different things. Her head hurt from the number of times the P-word flew to the forefront of her brain since her rude awakening this morning. Coping mechanism for the day—for the next two days: Shopping.

Maybe distance would help her decide how to proceed. Interestingly, the longer she stayed awake, the more removed she felt from the first part of last night, aka The Event. It had taken on a foggy, dream-like quality. Fine by her. She would relish no memory of the day.

"Hey!" Matt shouted.

She felt his hot gaze rove over her body from here. Shudder. Gross!

"Loser and fine do mix sometimes," he continued, voice lowering as he sidled up to the concession stand opposite where she stood. He leaned against the counter. "You keep comin' up here like that" — another too appreciative gaze up and down her body — "and I might have to holla."

Her lip curled of its own accord. *Dis-gusting!*

If he holla'd, she'd scream.

Why were people—mainly Matt at the moment—drawn to her? She had to be giving off leave-me-alone vibes. Closed body language dissuaded approach. She was doing it now. Her arms were crossed over her purse atop the counter. Even her legs were crossed. Yet people kept on coming. Crackheads drawn to the unwilling pipe.

"I'll wear sweats next time I come in," she muttered. Then turned her attention to Christopher. He was safer. Safe, from her, that was. One more repulsive look from Matt, and he would lose a testicle today or find one uncomfortably lodged inside his body. "Are the checks here yet?"

"I don't know. I haven't seen the courier, but one might've come. I was taking tickets earlier. We've been slammed. Wanna suit up and join ranks?"

"After how awesome yesterday was?" she asked sarcastically. "Uh... no thanks, I'm good. But I noticed how packed the parking lot was. I had to park next to Hooters."

Ow! Stunning pain lanced her gums. As if it would help, she cupped a hand over her mouth. Damn teeth. Of all the days not to be working. Demanding ice from Christopher wouldn't work—again. He expected it yesterday, but today? No, go. This was one of those times where normal emotions were necessary. How would a regular girl get her way?

Flirt.

She flinched. The voice, again. Least it helped this time.

"Kissy-fur," she crooned, leaning forward, calling the girls to the plate. As she'd assumed, he snuck a peek. Men! Sheesh! "Will you get me a cup of ice?"

Groaning, Christopher yanked out a drawer, retrieved a Styrofoam cup. He shoveled ice into it. "You know," he grumbled, handing her the now full cup, "you better stop writing checks with those eyes that your ass can't cash. Walker's a good dude and all, but... I'ma steal his chick if he's not careful."

Rolling her eyes, she plucked a cube of ice from the cup. "I can't be stolen."

God, she was hot, burning from the inside out. Tilting her head back, she closed her eyes, ran the ice cube across her exposed collarbone, up the column of her neck and down.

Sooo... good.

Upon contact with her overheated flesh, the ice melted. Each time a cube melted, she blindly retrieved another and repeated the process.

So, so, good.

Seconds, minutes, passed in—silence?

What was with the lag in conversation? Even the Muzak seemed to pause. Amelia cracked open an eye. The other eye.

Christopher and Matt stood mouths agape, eyes wide. They stared at her as if she'd suddenly sprouted wings.

She straightened. "What?"

Christopher shook his head.

"Uh... I gotta go... get the townspeople underhand," Matt said hoarsely. Not waiting for a reply, he hurried to the bathroom, shoved open the door.

No. Way. Amelia gave Christopher a curious look. "Is he?" She let the question hang. She'd vomit if she had to explain.

He nodded. "It's the only action he's gonna get. If it makes you feel better, you'll never go iceless again as long as he's around?"

Yuck!

Christopher laughed. Sudden unease slithered down Amelia's spine. Turning her head to and fro, she scanned the lobby. Didn't see anyone. But someone watched her.

"What're you doing?" Christopher asked, copying her movements.

"Have you ever felt like you were being watched?" No sooner than the words passed her lips, goosebumps broke out on her arms. Her arm hair stood on end. Superstitions, black cats, and voodoo weren't Amelia's bag, so it wasn't like she would know, but an evil presence felt near. Something dark, intrusive, like icy IV fluids running through her veins.

Christopher's snort halted her musings. "Uh... Anybody with a pulse watched your little ice tease."

"Shut up. I mean for real."

Laughing, he peered over his shoulder. His laughter died. Christopher pivoted toward her, expression blank, guarded. Cautious.

Her internal alarm blared. "What?"

He shifted his eyes left and right, as if assuring himself no one could hear.

Weird. The movies were all started, and other than a few stragglers going to and from the bathrooms, they were relatively alone.

"Over in the corner." He gave an almost imperceptible jerk of his head.

She gazed in the direction he indicated, pretending she saw whatever he had. Nodded.

"You see them? Scary guy? Freakish, *Village of the Damned*-looking little girl. They were waiting outside when I got here this morning, an *hour* before we opened. Been here ever since." Leaning in, he lowered his voice. "Somethin' ain't right with them. I felt like I should run to church after talking to him. The guy asked about you—sort of. He asked if a strange girl worked here. Do you know them?"

Thanks for the compliment, assmaster!

She shook her head. "I don't think so. I've given some kids freebies, but no kid was freakier than any other." Squinting, she tried again to see what Christopher saw in the corner. She couldn't. Someone exited the theater, bathing the lobby in blinding light.

"How are you, Duchess?"

Ho-ly, shit!

Her heart battered her sternum. Hand to Bible, she hadn't seen anyone move. Not in her peripheral or anything. The jaw-dropping, eye-bulging horror on Christopher's now sheet-white face echoed her sentiments. One minute, it'd been the two of them, her searching the corner, him talking. The next, a rich, slightly—Spanish?—French?—a combo of both?—accented, husky male voice came from behind her.

"You okay?" the sinful voice asked, amused undertones belying genuine concern. "Did I scare you?"

"No. I always wet my pants and raise my heart rate at this time. Keeps me young," she responded, spinning around to face her adversary. Breath rushed out of her in a huff.

Great balls of fire!

Amelia felt like she'd been bitch slapped by a lit torch. Another hot flash? Impossible. She was already in the throes of one. It was as if a nuclear bomb dropped on her. No, that wasn't right. She was the bomb. Heat exploded within her body, turning blood into molten lava, making her hot in a way she'd never been before. There was something about this man, something... familiar. Her body, her essence, everything about her recognized him. Although, they'd never met before. She'd remember meeting him.

How did this guy find clothes that fit? He wasn't fat. Far from it. Black wash jeans clung to legs and hips built for thrusting.

Oh, for a look at that butt.

If he wore the ginormous gunmetal skull and crossbones belt buckle to call attention to his midsection? Mission accomplished. She craved to know what kind of heat he packed in those jeans. A brown, death and glory Ed Hardy T-shirt stretched over the widest chest and broadest shoulders she'd ever seen.

Take. It. Off.

Wait!

What?

She must be a special blend of scandalous whore. What was she—damn voice! Had to be the voice. These thoughts couldn't be hers. She had Walker.

Who does as much for you as wet socks. We like 'em tall. This guy's over a foot taller. Definitely tall enough to ride this ride.

What? No!

Must... distract... self... from muscles so ripped that grooves were evident through his shirt. She forced her gaze away. Epic mistake.

Just then, he crossed his arms over his massive chest. Guns didn't do the bulging, pale biceps peeking from under his sleeves justice. Missiles? Much better.

She bit her lip to keep her teeth and tongue busy. Licking or nibbling strangers sent the wrong message. Didn't it? *No.*

Yes!

But, oh, that strong jaw.

Five o'clock shadow surrounded the faint dusting of a well-groomed goatee. Giving him that, *"Oh, this? I grew it overnight,"* look even though he clearly kept it that way on purpose.

Scruffy guys had never struck her fancy. He was an absolute exception to the rule, all rules. Roman nose, dark brown hair in a stylish bedhead cut. His outrageous good looks defied physics.

And his eyes? Outlandish. Piercing, clear, teal eyes reminded her of pictures she'd seen of the ocean where the water was so transparent you could see to the bottom. Thick, long, black lashes made his eyes pop.

What's wrong with me?

This wasn't her. Other than Eminem—whose lyrical genius and delicious eye-treat status couldn't be denied, lest ye be shot—she didn't lust after guys. Worse, this wasn't mere lust. It was more, scary, don't-want-to-think-about-it, put-in-the-file-marked-things-to-think-about-later: more.

Need. To. Look. Elsewhere. She forced her gaze—

Wow!

Beside Mr. McHotdamn sat the most precious child. No more than ten or eleven, the little girl was a walking talking Precious Moments figurine. At least, Amelia assumed she talked and walked. She'd witnessed neither. Both people seemed to... appear. Shiny black barrettes parted strands of dirty blond locks. Held them in place on either side of her head, like waist-length, Shirley Temple-curled curtains. Rosy cheeks, scarlet heart-shaped lips, and large doe eyes the color of light blue diamonds adorned a pale angelic face.

The frilly, deep blue, knee-length taffeta dress, white tights, and black patent leather shoes completed the doll look. Adorable beyond compare, it hurt to look at her—for more reasons than one. Amelia got the sneaking suspicion that the girl would hurt anyone. Period.

Button cute, her eyes seemed flat, empty. Matter of fact, a sense of menace and foreboding stuck to *him* stronger than gum on the bottom of a shoe. Even the carpet under his combat-booted feet seemed straighter, as if it feared tripping him.

"You sure you're alright, Duchess? You don't look so good."

His voice catapulted her thoughts down an alley dirty enough to make porn stars uncomfortable.

He embodied the phrase "work it, be it, own it, love it." Every move he made appeared calculated, premeditated, like the crooked grin delicately lifting the left corner of luscious lips. A brow quirked—expectantly?

Did he say something?

Chapter Seven

*D*id I say something?

Calin couldn't remember. Standing this close to the descendant clouded his mind. Hardened his cock. Good thing he wore baggy pants today. Of course, if she kept looking at him with those awestruck, beguiling eyes of hers, it wouldn't matter how loose his pants were. He'd be giving her a real salute.

What the fuck had she done to him? No mortal had ever garnered this type of reaction from him. Not that he hadn't bagged a mortal, or five hundred. Shit! Treasuring solitude didn't mean he wasn't male. He had needs. Itches to scratch. And control.

Had control, he corrected mentally, as more blood rushed to The Terminator—his cock's formal name, it was that good. The feelings of desire and need she stirred inside him were something else. Something primal, uncontrollable.

Pissed him off.

He'd have to bone her. It'd aid them both. Get her out of his system. Uncontrolled equaled dangerous for him.

Calin didn't do feelings. Unlike his mother, he didn't have the excuse of a curse to explain away his... extreme behavior. Emotions put him on edge. Made him act out. As it was, it took every ounce of self-restraint he possessed not to rip through the throats of every blood sausage in this theater. Starting with the one staring at him, evoking these unwanted longings.

Her mango-almond scent was potent, addictive. It stung his nose, dulled his common sense. Small, dainty, a foot shorter than him, she had the petite version of a Coke bottle figure.

Damn! He needed to kill her. Soon.

Must. Calm. Down. Focus. Before he put someone's eye out.

"What's your name?" Conversation good. Good distraction.

Bianca tensed beside him. Shit! Another good distraction. If mass murder could be deemed a distraction. Tearing his eyes away from the descendant, he shot a warning glare at Bianca. She was too young to be around this big of a concentration of mortals. At best, her control was iffy, at worst, nonexistent. If he noticed the warm blood traversing under the skin of the fragile mortal man behind the counter, she did, too.

Gazing at him, she smiled sweetly. Batted heavy lashes. Yeah, she didn't fool him. Her hunger vibrated off her and beat at him.

The dumbest animals sensed danger. Shit! Opossums fell to the ground, foamed at the mouth, and feigned death at the first sign of it. Did feeble-minded mortals? Nope. They basked in their false sense of security. They'd become prey in a matter of seconds and were none the wiser. Sadly, he wasn't the threat. He preferred his quarry intelligent. It filled him with a sense of accomplishment when he took them down. Bianca was nowhere near as picky. She eased closer to the concession stand, to the unsuspecting man leaning on the counter.

Calin shadowed her actions. The inadvertent position placed him closer to the descendant and forged a barrier between the man and Bianca. He glared his disapproval at her. Bianca's snack's—Christopher, per his nametag—worried voice tugged Calin's attention back to the group.

The descendant's breathing had grown labored. Her chest rose and fell in rapid succession. Desire to place a hand over her heaving chest, between her full breasts, almost dropped him to his knees.

"Umm... Amelia?" Christopher said alarmed. "Amelia! Do you need a paper bag or something?"

"I'm available for mouth-to-mouth," a stocky, blood beast offered, coming from the restroom to join them. He stood outside the concession stand opposite Amelia. His name tag read *Matt*.

That seemed to clear whatever respiratory issue she, Amelia, had been having. A-mel-ia. He liked her name too much. Yep, killing her was imperative.

"I'm fine," she flatly assured. "No mouth-to-mouth required."

Her soft, raspy voice hit him like a shot of adrenaline-laced blood. Went straight to his groin, hardening him to the point of pain. Calin was torn between wanting to suck the shit out of that plump bottom lip and tearing her head off with his bare hands.

He extended his hand. "Nice to meet you, Amelia? Pretty name. You don't meet many Amelia's these days."

"These days?" A glint of humor, or possibly agitation, sparked in her eyes. "Like, Wednesdays? Or does my old lady name amuse you?"

Ooh... feisty. The words had bite. He loved females who bit.

Despite her obvious annoyance, she placed her elegant, velvet-soft hand in his. A smile capable of putting the sun out of business spread across her face. On each cheek, a deep dimple. Both sparked something inside him that Calin wouldn't dare explore.

He didn't know how long he stayed, her hand in his, hypnotized by everything Amelia. An absurd amount of time must have passed—she didn't move either, or stop smiling—because someone cleared his throat loudly. Unable to hold it, a growl built low in Calin's chest, tumbled out.

Amelia jerked her hand away.

He wanted to howl, protest, the loss of contact.

Christopher thrust his hand into Calin's line of vision.

How dare the mortal presume to touch him? Calin didn't do touching unless forced by his mother, fucking, or feeding. And he didn't fuck males. Nor did he do examining the whole touching contradiction since he'd obviously touched the descendant for none of the above reasons.

He glared at the man's hand. Then at the man. If he took that hand, he would keep that hand. Literally. Message received,

Christopher's hand slowly retreated. He backed away from the counter as well.

Good mortal.

Calin glanced at Amelia. Game on. "I'm Calin Luca." He nodded at his sister. "This is my sister, Bianca. That's... uh... you've got a crazy grip for such a *petite dame*," he remarked, remembering the tighter-than-the-average-mortal-woman handshake.

"Is that supposed to be a compliment?" she asked haughtily.

"Not if you're Walker," Christopher muttered under his breath, too low for mortal ears.

Calin heard it. He snickered at the lewd innuendo. He didn't know this Walker, but he got the joke.

Amelia scowled. "Do I know you?"

Such a feisty thing. Nothing excited him more than a chase. His fangs itched for freedom, for a taste of her. Of course, her hardly mortal blood wouldn't provide the same sustenance pure mortal blood did. Might poison him. No vampire of any breed fed from supernatural.

Not entirely true. Vampires fed from their *eternalmates*, but that was a bonding experience. Not sustenance. Supernatural blood poisoned vampires. Put a vampire in an indefinite coma, leaving them vulnerable to all manner of possibilities. For some ridiculous reason, he couldn't care less about the consequences.

He wanted her blood.

"No. We're from out of state—out of country actually. Bianca saw you a couple days ago and wanted me to see how pretty you are," he lied smoothly, answering her question.

She offered both him and Bianca a bashful smile.

Got her.

Mortals loved cheesy flattery. However, in her case, it wasn't mere flattery but understated truth. "Sorry, didn't mean to put you on the spot. I don't have much... game?" Mortals loved humility, too.

"Nor should you ever say *game*," Bianca interjected in a low aside.

Unfortunately, not low enough. Everyone snickered.

Calin's temper flared.

The phone behind the counter rang, breaking into everyone's mirth at his expense. Matt jogged around the counter to answer it.

"Who's playing manager today?" Amelia asked Christopher.

He opened his cash register, inspecting its contents. "Let's see it's—what time is it?"

Amelia glanced up; her gaze briefly landed on him but quickly went over his head.

Did she find him lacking?

A clock hung above a door at the front of the theater.

Turning to her co-worker she said, "Ten to four."

"We're about to have another rush. I have one quarter even though I called up for more before we opened." Christopher slammed his register closed. "You tell me whose manager?"

Understanding shone in Amelia's eyes. She nodded, calling out to Matt, "Hey, ask Tigger if the checks came!"

"Tigger?" Calin asked. What respectable parents named their young something so absurd?

"His name's Phillip," Amelia answered, turning the full force of those radiant eyes and dimpled smile on him. "But since he's always hoppin' around in a methy haze, we call him Tigger."

He nodded. "Ah... I see."

"Amelia!" Matt shouted, hanging up the phone. "Tigger says your check's on the desk upstairs."

"And why can't he bring it down?" she asked, propping a hand on her hip.

Matt rejoined the group. "Apparently, he's going out to the alley."

Amelia frowned. "Wh—"

"Don't ask," Matt interrupted, which seemed to tell her and Christopher all they needed to know about their boss.

"Whatever. I have my keys. I'll get it," Amelia said, sliding her purse strap onto her shoulder.

"What's a meth haze?" Bianca asked, causing Amelia to stop.

Usually, Bianca specialized in being a living nightmare, but at that moment, Calin could've kissed her—something he'd never done. Again, for reasons better left unexplored, Calin wasn't ready for their interaction to end.

Christopher and Amelia traded uncomfortable glances. Christopher rested both his elbows on the countertop, bent as much as possible down to Bianca's level. "Umm... maybe you should ask your mommy or daddy that question, sweetie."

Just like that, Calin regretted his previous appreciation, because true to form...

Bianca leaped for the mortal's throat.

Chapter Eight

"**O**w! Brother!" Bianca whined, struggling against the bruising grip on her upper arm. "Ow! Stop. Let go. Calin, you're hurting me."

Good.

Calin dragged Bianca "The Horrific,"—a new nickname he'd be throwing into the rotation—into their hotel room at the Red Roof Inn. She should be thanking God, The Fates, the *Dark Majesty*, or whoever she worshipped, that he didn't do more to her.

Attacking a mortal in broad daylight with several witnesses? C'mon!

If he hadn't moved faster than mortal perception, inserting himself between Bianca and the witless mortal who thought her an innocent child, he'd be with the mortal police, trying to explain the inexplicable. Or they'd both be in some secret research facility being probed. His powers were impressive, extensive, but he couldn't work magic on an entire theater that no doubt—and rightfully so—would be dismayed by witnessing a bloody massacre.

The room door slammed shut behind them. Relinquishing his hold on Bianca, he, none too gently, shoved her away from him. She tripped, fell, bounced atop one of the double beds.

Calin cast a longing glance at his guitar case propped against the wall on the other side of the room. Why couldn't he be alone? Playing guitar helped clear his head. And boy, could he use a spring cleaning right now. He had a laundry list of things to consider. Unlike wax whittling, guitar playing was an activity he did alone. No one would ever hear him play. Didn't bode well for his hard-edged, I-run-shit persona to have people see him singing and playing guitar like some backwoods moron.

"I'm hungry, Calin," Bianca groused, righting herself on the bed. "You saw what nearly happened. I need to feed."

Calin threw a sideways glower at Bianca. Shook his head. Another issue for him to think on—Bianca's containment. Balkan might trust her, but Calin? Not so much. Yes, he loved her, had a ridiculous sense of loyalty to her, wanted her happy, blah, blah, blah. All brothers felt the aforementioned for their sisters. Didn't mean it made him stupid. Nor did it cloud his judgment. Bianca was a menace to society and his goals.

"It's been two days, Bianca. You haven't even reached the immortal age yet. Feeding this often isn't necessary," Calin replied, taking a seat at the rinky-dink desk. The chair creaked under his weight.

Mentioning the *Immortal Age* brought a bigger obstacle to the forefront. Or rather, aging did. Even if Bianca's insatiable appetite wasn't a problem, she was. Two months was a long time to spend among mortals. In that time, Bianca would change significantly. The observant eye would notice the subtle nuances: hair a few inches longer, height off, maturing facial features. Things a person wouldn't pick up on if they saw her every once in a while, but if they saw her every day? Even the most obtuse mortal would question the differences.

Sending Bianca with him? Did Balkan want him to fail? Grandfather might be using this impossible mission to justify destroying him. Calin knew his mother's curse wouldn't allow her to agree to his destruction. Grandfather Balkan knew it, too. That could be why he sent him. Botched mission, punishable by death. Wouldn't be the first time Balkan went to such extremes. After all, the mission—if real—wouldn't have been necessary if Balkan hadn't slaughtered his cousin Queen Ana-Marie and her family because of his actions, which led to The Fates deposing him.

"You're doing it again, Brother," Bianca said, pulling him from his thoughts.

"Doing what?"

"Ignoring me. I specifically recall telling you I need to feed."

"And I told you, you don't need to feed so often at your age. You can also eat mortal food. Helps you grow. We have to play it cool. All things in moderation. You fed a couple days ago. You can feed again in a few more."

"I'd hardly call that feeding, Brother. Besides, you know what they say about the Chinese. An hour after you've had one, you're hungry again." Bianca burst into tinkling, villainous laughter.

Calin rolled his eyes at his sister's off-color joke. The little vamp was volatile, a grenade without a pin. He couldn't risk taking her around such a large concentration of mortals again. What if she attacked Amelia? His worry had nothing to do with the descendant and everything to do with Bianca. Really, it didn't. Bianca could be poisoned if she tried to feed from Amelia.

Amelia was a means to an end. A mouthwatering, cock-hardening, means to an end. His attraction to her was chemical. More than likely a product of him spending so much time alone.

Then why didn't you want her to leave? You stopped her. Called out to her when she would leave you. Why would you do that?

Fuckin' demon conscience. Piped in at all the wrong times. He didn't know the answer to those questions. Two things he did know? One, he needed to get Amelia off his mind and get his head in the game. Thinking with The Terminator caused trouble. Two, when he called out to her, she remembered Bianca "The Terrible's" name without prompting. He'd had to remind her of his to be bid a proper farewell. For whatever reason, he wanted her to remember him. Wanted to scratch his name into her arm with a rusty nail so she'd never forget it. Infection made an impression on mortals. He'd taken that ego blow as his cue to leave before his emotions got the better of them.

I'm powerful, damn it!

Not easily dismissed like some besotted, insignificant mortal. No matter what she would be, Amelia was mortal. Inferior. Attractive, she might be, but that wouldn't save her head.

The opportunity to lose his humanity meant too much. Moreover, the *seal* would provide unfathomable power. Even if his uncles, aunts, and all the top *Daywalker* soldiers perished, he wouldn't obtain the type of power the *seal* supplied. But with one death, Amelia's, he could rule absolutely. Rule all supernatural, his grandfather, the Daywalkers, all breeds of *Royal Guard*, the *courtiers*, Dark-witches, White-witch Advisors and return his mother to royalty.

Booyah!

On the off chance this mission was the real deal, he'd follow protocol to the letter. Minus returning to Romania with the *seal*, of course. That he wouldn't do. Calin scrubbed a hand up and down his face. Raking his fingers through his hair, he caught sight of his watch.

Shit! Time to check-in.

He dug his phone out of his pocket, pressed "2" on the speed dial. Before anyone answered, he glanced askance at Bianca. A finger to his lips demanded her silence.

Lips pursed, eyes cut, she leaned over, snatching a previously discarded magazine. Photographs of mortal teens littered the cover. Leaning back against the wall, she kicked her feet up on the bed and crossed her legs at the ankle. She flashed a tight-lipped, humorless smile, and then proceeded to flip the pages. Loudly.

Brat! He would—a deep familiar voice answered the phone. "Mordred, it's Calin. Is one of my uncles around?"

"Nope, they're feeding with Rielle. What do you want?"

His anger, a lit match dropped on a trail of gasoline, ignited. Calin's fangs descended. News his uncles would feed with his aunt didn't upset him. What did? The blatant disregard for his authority the Dark-witch displayed. Family treating him as if he were trash was one thing. Dark-witches and *Daywalkers* doing it? Unacceptable. King Balkan Dimir's blood ran through his veins. He'd be damned if some two-bit servant spoke to him with anything other than the utmost respect.

Much to Grandfather's consternation, he'd taken out several Dark-witches and *Daywalkers* to prove his superiority. Blinking, moving from place to place with nothing more than a thought, drained his strength reserves the farther the destination. He'd risk it to make a point.

"Have you lost your mind, witch?" he growled, wishing the bastard were in front of him. "Do you need to be reminded to whom it is you speak?"

"Ooh..." Bianca chuckled. "Is the passive-aggressive, Big Bad Vamp angry? I love it when you get mad. You ferocious koala bear."

Beams of teal light illuminated Bianca's pallid face with the acerbic glare and accompanying snarl Calin threw her way. He could've killed her. Undermining him twice in one day? His patience with her grew thinner by the minute.

Lucky for her, he loved her deeply for logic-defying reasons. Calin's mind rebelled against the notion of her death, period. Until she reached the *Immortal Age of Maturity*, killing her could be achieved with great ease, even with her supernatural strength and budding magic. She wasn't at full power. One of several reasons why he didn't want her here. Never mind the fact that she didn't know when enough was enough. But then, if she knew that, she wouldn't be Bianca.

Flipping long curls over her shoulder, she ignored him.

Mordred, on the other hand, did a complete about-face. "I apologize, sir. Would you like to speak with your grandfather?"

Hell, no. That would be counterproductive. Amelia already had him off balance. He needed to regroup, to plan. Grandfather Balkan's brand of motivation, i.e. insults, wouldn't help.

"Yes, put my grandfather on. Now." What could he do? Showing any weakness would further serve to undermine his authority now and in the future.

"As you wish, sir. Just a moment."

The phone line went completely silent, meaning Mordred muted it. Probably so Calin wouldn't hear him talking shit before fetching Grandfather.

"What's wrong, Brother?" Bianca drawled in mock concern. "Cranky? Your fangs are descended. Somebody need a nap?"

Keep pressing me.

Oh, yeah, she'd need containment—for her safety. He could only take so much. Unlike his unique blinking ability, inherited from his mother, all vampires slept. It sped healing and built strength. Fledglings required more sleep than mature vampires. Calin could go days without it… Oh, yes, he would find a way to contain Bianca.

Grinning, he retracted his fangs. "Keep talking, *Ma petite*. Remember which one of us sleeps more."

Crystal blue eyes widened in outrage. Nostrils flared. Bianca tossed the magazine—he knew she hadn't really been reading—down beside her. She undid the buckle of one patent leather shoe.

With a slight shake of his head, Calin narrowed his eyes. Tightened his jaw. She wouldn't.

Bianca chucked the shoe across the room. She would!

Calin dodged to the right. The shoe hit the wall, narrowly missing his eye. And kept going. Through their room wall. Across the room next door to theirs. Through that room's far wall. He gazed wide-eyed at the holes, through the holes. Then at Bianca.

"Why the hell would you do that? Someone could have been in those rooms. Do you not recall the instruction given to us? 'Main-tain. A. Low. Profile.'"

With a minuscule tilt of her head, her dainty shoulder lifted lazily. The corners of her mouth curled into a smug smile.

"You pissed me off. Don't provoke me when I'm hungry. Looks like you have a mess to fix. Got any spackle?" She grabbed her magazine and flipped through it.

Maybe he could kill her. How could—

No. Bump that. He knew how the little psycho could do that; she was spoiled rotten. He'd already fixed a hole she made in the door last night after they arrived because he forbade her from feeding on the rude hotel manager.

Noise on the other end of the phone line prevented Calin from responding to her. He braced himself for the worst.

"Calin?"

Mordred. Thank goodness.

"Your grandfather's in a meeting. He can't be interrupted. However, he would like a progress report. Has contact been made?"

"Yes."

"And you've gained her trust?" the *Dark-witch* asked, tone hopeful.

"Uh... No. I've met her once." *Moron*, he added mentally.

"Your grandfather expects results. Failure is not an option. You need to gain her complete trust quickly."

Everyone wanted to test him today. He might have to blink back to Romania after all. Calin tightened his grip on the phone. Hearing a crack, he loosened up.

"We have two months!" he shouted. "Let my grandfather know the situation is under control."

"Bet you wish you napped now," Bianca said in a sing-song voice.

That's it!

Calin stretched his right arm toward Bianca. Sizzling energy raced through the veins of the extended appendage and danced on his outward-facing palm. Slowly lifting his arm, she levitated. The magazine fell to the ground. Back pinned, Bianca slid up the wall. He halted her propulsion before her head hit the ceiling. Her arms and legs flailed. Before she complained, cried out, or otherwise alerted Mordred or passersby, Calin balled his fist. Her eyes bulged as the air was choked out of her.

Satisfied, Calin finished his conversation. "Watch. Your. Tongue," he gritted out, punching each word for emphasis.

"My apologies," Mordred said grudgingly. "I relayed the message verbatim, as instructed."

He didn't have time for this. Past introductions, he'd made no progress with Amelia. At this rate, he'd be lucky if she remembered him the next time they met. "I'll call back in a couple days. Make sure my uncles are available," he commanded then pressed *End* not waiting for a response.

Unballing his fist, he let his arm fall to his side. Bianca dropped onto the bed, bouncing once. She gasped for breath. Crimson tears brimmed in wide eyes. She stood, smoothed down her dress.

"I'm telling!" In a burst of preternatural speed, she left. Wind stirred from her departure, and slammed the door shut.

Damn, he shouldn't have done that. The carnage left in the wake of this tantrum would be significant, mass casualties. Fuck! It'd take days to do damage control, but...

Calin smiled to himself.

"Totally worth it."

The last customer, a big man with eye-watering breath, lumbered toward the usher stand large, buttered popcorn, large Coke, and thanks to Amelia's expert upselling abilities, Junior Mints, in hand. It'd been a hell of a feat, but she'd talked him into buying the candy. She hoped he ate the whole box. Anything to neutralize that breath.

Amelia retrieved a bottle of cleaner and a towel from the cabinet below her candy drawers. Squirting down the counter next to her register, she sighed. Usually, Saturdays were busy, but with the temperature at ninety-five degrees, people flocked to the theater in droves for free A/C. The closer to summer it got, the busier the theater got.

For the first time since opening, the lobby was as empty as possible with every theater filled near capacity. It'd only get worse when school let out and temperatures hit triple digits. Would she still be able to work by then? Would she be show—

Nope. No, no, no, no-no. Don't go there.

Thinking about it would lead nowhere good, and she was avoiding the issue at the moment. Every time the condition came to mind, she went into panic mode. According to Google, she shouldn't be experiencing symptoms yet, being on the accelerated track doubled the issue—literally. She refused to consider the prospect. Irresponsible or not, she had to let it burn until confronting it didn't make her want to pass out.

Amelia glanced down. Oh, damn! Caught up in thought, she'd scrubbed the counter so clean the white rag actually had blue paint on it. See? Proof she couldn't cope. If that wasn't enough, her severe mood swings almost made her kick the ass of the kid who'd spilled the dried, sticky Pepsi she'd just cleaned off the counter.

Poor kid looked like he wet himself when she threw an F-bomb and a few other choice words at him. Good thing he was alone, otherwise she'd have angry parents to handle. Still might if Heidi caught wind of the situation. Heidi didn't give her the same leeway Gordon did and paid way more attention to detail than Tigger's drugged brain ever could.

Speaking of Heidi's attentive management style... Amelia grabbed a new rag, her squirt bottle, and went around to the front of the concession stand. The counter wasn't the only casualty in the Great Pepsi Debacle. Syrupy Pepsi remnants streaked the candy display case in front of her register. Nice.

She stooped down and got to cleanin'.

"Long-sleeves today... Duchess?"

Breath puffed out of Amelia's mouth, fogging the glass in front of her. Her heart palpitated in part fear, part excitement. Warmth enveloped her, surged through her. Pooled between her thighs.

Better. Than. A heater!

Today was a cold flash day, which was why she wore a long-sleeved dress shirt under her black vest. She'd secretly wanted to see the owner of the rich, accented voice again.

Thursday, her day off, and before retail therapy, she'd come to the theater. Why, she didn't know. He'd been here once, twice, if she were to believe his assertion that his sister had seen her before. Either way, two visits did not a routine make. They were tourists. Arizona had more, not a lot, but more than Super Saver Cinema to offer. Anyway, three hours passed without one tall, dark, sexy sighting. Cicely, The Hot Guy Spotter, said she'd call if she saw an indefinably gorgeous man. She hadn't. So, Amelia assumed he'd never be back. Yesterday, she'd worked from open to close—no Mr. McHotdamn. This morning, Walker brought her a blueberry muffin—her favorite—before going to help his mom prepare a room for some long-lost cousin. After Walker left, she'd darted out of the house like it was on fire. Getting to work early, inexplicable shards of hope Hottie would return, stuck to her.

And he did.

Okay, so, maybe her desire hadn't been as covert as she thought.

Why she felt complete in his presence? Better left unexamined. Too many logs were on the pyre of her mind. He made her feel. An arduous venture, according to her brother or friends. Evan went to NAU to get away from the mean-spirited, lifeless shell she'd become. Yet this stranger evoked emotion. Maybe the high of meeting someone new, a person with no expectations, no preconceived notions about how she should act or who she should be was addictive?

Her hair was in a high ponytail, the thick red veil provided the perfect shield for exploration. Peeking through the strands, her gaze crawled across black rainbow-speckled carpet. Scant inches from where she knelt, wheat Lugz boots—size thirteen, maybe larger. How did he sneak up on her? Her gaze wandered up faded blue, jean-clad legs. Damn, what'd he do? Collect unacceptably large belt buckles? This one: a silver flamed skull. A huge pallid hand thrust into her eyeline.

Her breaths came rapid now. She stared at the proffered hand. For some reason, the simple gesture felt packed with all the tension and anxiety of being a contestant on *Deal or No Deal*. His hand: $0 or $1,000,000. Standing unassisted: $750,000. Amelia snatched her rag and squirt bottle in one hand. Her other hand... she placed firmly in the unknown.

A light tug brought her to her feet. She meant to finish her thorough inspection, but her eyes stayed riveted on a wide, hard-looking, black T-shirt-covered chest.

Mmm. Mmm. Good!

"Your name's Amelia, right?"

Was it?

Shit, she couldn't remember.

He remembers your name, the creepy voice purred.

That frightening nuisance succeeded in stopping a dreamy sigh from escaping her lips. Biting her lip, she nodded. Her heart hammered her ribcage. She didn't dare raise her head. Look at him, take that step, while standing this close, when he hadn't let go of her hand, but instead, stroked the back with his thumb? No way. She hadn't even let herself think his name, fearing it'd make this—whatever it was—real.

"You shouldn't be working here, Amelia." His voice dropped to a seductive level. "This is beneath you."

Aww... He cares.

Shake it easy, hornball, you've got a boyfriend.

"Well, until I find the end of that rainbow? This'll have to do," she joked, attempting to relieve some of the tension between them. It didn't.

His laugh was mesmerizing. "I can give you rainbows, duchess. And all the gold you could ever imagine." Breath, a tropical breeze, blew past her ear.

Amelia shivered. Swallowed hard. She hadn't seen or felt him move. One second, he stood, the next, he leaned. Spoke near her ear but not into it. The scent of dark spice wafted off him. Seeped into her nostrils, her skin. Just as he'd bent with no noticeable motion, he straightened, keeping hold of her hand.

"What are you, a pirate?" she chuckled, or tried to, but it sounded wrong.

"If you want me to be."

"Somebody's been working on their game." Her knees weakened. If she didn't get away from him soon, she'd dry hump him like some big, overexcited dog. "I gotta get back to work."

"Say my name first."

The request startled her. She looked into his magical, transparent blue-green eyes. Dammit! A sigh slipped out. He was more beautiful than she remembered. Mussed brown hair, perfect five o'clock shadow.

Mmm...

"You don't remember my name, do you?" he asked, gruff. His liquid eyes froze. Lips mashed into a firm line.

Amelia yanked her hand away. A terrible sense of loss bombarded her. Distance. She needed distance. Going around into the concession area, she put away the cleaner and dirty rag. A counter, register, and... going over to the back of the concession stand she grabbed the broom from between the crack of the never-used popper and small sink. Taking a minute, she stood there, concentrating on breathing in and out.

Yep, a counter, register, and a whole popper was a reasonable, safe distance to answer. "I remember your name," she called. "Kinda."

"What is it?"

If she strained, Amelia would swear she heard his teeth grinding.

Ha. Ha. *Got him!*

"It's a girl's name, right? Something like... Caitlyn?" She peeked around the corner, making sure she had him.

Anger marred his rugged features. His mouth gaped.

"Of course, I remember you."—Borrowing a page from Tessa's book, she paused for dramatic effect, smiling when she caught his eye. —"Calin."

Calin's expression cycled through wide-eyed astonishment, tight-lipped suspicion, and lastly, his mouth lifted into a crooked grin.

"You were teasing me?" He sounded surprised.

"It's been two days. I'd like to think my memory's still able to extend that far. Where's your sister?" She started sweeping moving fully into his line of vision.

"You're funny," Calin said dryly.

"I try." Amelia shrugged. "So, where's that sweet little sister of yours?"

His smile intensified. "I don't know. I'm not my sister's keeper."

Silence stretched between them. Muzak bumped some Katy Perry song, compensating for the lag in conversation. Sweeping a full circle around the inside of the concession stand, Amelia replayed their conversation in her head. She swept the trash into the dustpan and threw it out. Calin leaned on the counter to the left of her register. A well-groomed brown brow rose.

What was he—

She got it.

Lifting her eyes heavenward, she smiled humorlessly. "You're a dork." He had to be the only guy to see the movie *My Sister's Keeper*. She laughed. A real, genuine laugh. "How long were you waiting to use that one?"

"It was off the top of my head. I swear." He chuckled.

God, he had the sexiest laugh.

Amelia rolled her eyes. "Seriously. Where's your sister? —No stupid movie humor," she warned, wagging her finger at him.

"Off terrorizing a small village or something." Calin shrugged.

Fine. Whatever. She could take a hint. Wasn't any of her business.

"You're by yourself? You guys are busy," he said, looking around.

"Yeah, tell me something I don't know," Amelia agreed. "Christopher and a guy you didn't meet, Ruben, are cleaning theaters. I let Matt and Kim—I don't think you met her either—go to lunch while we're slow."

He nodded. "Oh. Right-handed people live longer."

"Excuse me?" Her brows scrunched together, punctuating her question and emphasizing her confusion.

"Right-handed people live longer." He repeated matter-of-factly, which didn't help since she had no idea where he'd pulled that tidbit from or why he chose now to share it.

"What does that have to do with anything?"

"Nothing. You said tell you something you didn't know." He winked and gave a cocky grin. "Did you know that?"

Heat rose up her neck, warming her cheeks. Awareness slammed into her, stopping her heart momentarily. What a smile. "Shut. Up." She laughed, going to stand at her register across from him. "You're frickin' funny, dude."

Weird. Emotions came easily when he was around. One part of her wanted to understand how a complete stranger succeeded where her friends failed. A smaller part didn't consider him a stranger. A greater part, which overrode the other parts, said ignore those two. And she obeyed.

"I try." He smiled, stealing her line.

Their eyes fastened on one another. Her smile melted. His did, too. Time stood still. Something ineffable passed between them. Could he feel it, too?

"Amelia!" The squeal from the front of the lobby severed their connection.

Gazing around Calin, she caught sight of Cicely. The box office door banged closed behind the young girl as she ran out. She made a beeline for the concession stand. Dashing inside, she sidled up to Amelia. Undeterred by a pesky term called personal space, she poked Amelia in the ribs with the tips of her bony fingers.

Amelia flinched. "Cicely," she snapped. "How many times do we have to have this discussion? This is my bubble." She pushed Cicely back a couple paces. "Keep your little ass out."

"Sorry," Cicely apologized without losing an ounce of pep. She clapped excitedly. "Introduce me to Walker's friend."

Walker's friend?

Before she asked what Cicely meant...

"Who's Walker?" Calin asked.

Shit! For the first time, she wanted to do something she'd never done, never considered: deny Walker. Because of whatever power this stranger had over her, she wanted to say, "No one."

I'm such a scandalous bitch.

Cicely must not have truly seen Calin before rudely interrupting. The comical, bug-eyed stare she trained on him suggested she did now. "Holy, shit!" she shrieked, then whispered in Amelia's ear, "I need to hang out with you more. Damn!"

She would've found her coworker's proclamation funny if Calin didn't seem to be staring at the chocolate-skinned teen, too. The look was heated. Amelia couldn't tell if it was sexual heat or aggravation. Either way, she didn't like it. Her gums throbbed in direct correlation with her displeasure. She was pissed.

Mine!

Wow! Where did that come from? Had to be the voice. Jealousy and Amelia didn't mix, and she for damn sure didn't have a claim to a total stranger. If he wanted Cicely, that was none of her business. He appeared to be in his early twenties, not much older than the seventeen-year-old. What'd she care?

Mine! Definitely, the voice. She wouldn't think that word regarding a person. Walker worshipped and adored her. Calin was nothing to her. No-thing.

Empowered by the thought, she answered. "Walker's my boyfriend."

Dragging his gaze from Cicely, Calin turned hard eyes on her. Which didn't make a bit of sense since Cicely held his full attention mere seconds ago.

Amelia focused on someone she understood, sort of. Sometimes.

"What are you talking about, Cicely?"

That brought Cicely's attention to the matter at hand. "Gurl...*puh-lease!* Dumb is not a good look on you. Are you growing hot guys or something?" she teased. "If you're starting some kind of cult? Sign. Me. Up!"

"What are you...?" Amelia's question trailed off. The answer was sauntering through the lobby door behind Walker.

Whoa.

Chapter Nine

"Hey, good-lookin'," Walker greeted, but the steel-edged tone was directed elsewhere. Winking, he stepped almost directly in front of Calin as if he weren't there.

Ugh! Male posturing, how annoying.

"What're you doing here?" Amelia asked, sighing. Her annoyance doubled as Cicely, in a particularly girly move—and disregarding all previous bubble talk—hooked her arm through Amelia's, giddy over possible drama.

Tattoos covering every square inch of visible skin—minus his face—gauged ears, spiked mohawk, Walker intimidated most people on sight. If his physical appearance didn't work, then his standard attire of white wife-beater, khaki Dickies shorts, and Chuck Taylors did the trick.

Neither affected Calin. The glacial size-up he gave Walker shouted, "I eat guys like you for breakfast!" Not to mention, the six-inch height advantage he had on five-foot-ten Walker and muscles. Yeah. Calin won that contest hands down, even against the giant, super-pale, Adonis posted behind Walker like a bodyguard or assassin waiting for orders.

He can guard my body any day.

God, I'm a faithless whore. I should be stoned.

Some kind of hot guy convention must be in town. Had to be, 'cuz Arizona don't grow 'em like this. First Calin, now this golden blond-haired man who, as cliché as it might sound, looked like a fallen angel warrior? Sheesh!

Drool, actual drool, almost dribbled from her mouth.

Someone needed to send this guy's parents a fruit basket or something to thank them for creating such a perfect specimen. He could be a police officer. Maybe military? No on both counts. Although the same law enforcement power-authority vibe oozed from him, it was too much. Dangerous. Concealed weapon carrying, dangerous. His hair stopped just off his nape, and the front hung over his eyes. Too long for military. He moved through the theater with sure-footed confidence, all lithe panther stealth. His shrewd, midnight-blue gaze tracked continually as if assessing possible danger and locating all exits.

Seriously, black boots, leather pants, silk shirt, fingerless gloves? Did he not get the black absorbs heat memo?

The gorgeous man dwarfed Walker and Calin—well, barely Calin. Everything about him was severe, overtly so, arrow straight posture, prominent Adam's apple, and chiseled features that appeared carved from stone. His shirt draped over a broad-shouldered swimmer's build. Fabric didn't hide but accentuated a torso that looked like one of those Roman breastplates with defined abs.

"What?" Walker asked.

The falsely innocent question snapped Amelia out of thoughts dirty enough to make Larry Flynt blush.

A hint of a devious smile tilted his lips. "I can't visit my woman at work?"

Not when you're being an ass, no.

"Yeah, I just didn't know you were coming... or bringing a friend." She threw in the last bit on the sly. Couldn't let her curiosity show. Walker would flip.

His jealous streak stretched a mile long. Almost six years they'd been together. She'd never cheated or done anything to warrant distrust, yet he remained insecure. The unprovoked stink-eye he trained on Calin further validated her claim. What didn't make sense? Mr. Tall Pale and Deadly and Calin eyed each other like rival gang members in a turf war. It all seemed very old western, high noon standoffish.

Cicely gripped her arm tighter. Grinding her teeth, Amelia leered at the horny teen. Okay, so, the overabundance of testosterone clouded her mind, too, but she handled it, kinda. Alternating between Mr. Sex on a Stick and Calin gave her eyes whiplash.

Shouldn't you be looking at your wonderful boyfriend?

That's beside the point. She grew more accustomed to the voice each time she heard it, but this Devil's advocate bullshit got old fast. As did Cicely's randy ass. Presently, the hornball was making goo-goo eyes at the "angel among men" and sensually tracing her full top lip with the tip of her tongue. Her hold on Amelia's arm squeezed blood pressure cuff tight.

Enough!

Amelia peeled her coworker's fingers off her and pushed her away. Harder than intended. Cicely's feet tangled. She tripped. Amelia caught the teenager by the arm before she cracked her head on the corner of the popper. She steadied her and settled her a few inches away, outside the bubble.

Touching, any physical contact, inferred a relationship. Platonic or not, it set the recipient on a collision course with tragic death. It took all she had not to flinch when Walker touched her. But keeping things the same—her being the only change—was paramount. It kept those she loved safe from her curse and retained the memory of her lost loved ones.

Dark burgundy blush stained Cicely's cheeks. Humiliation and anger warred in her eyes. "Damn Hercules! What the hell?"

"My bad," Amelia apologized.

Of course, Cicely recovered quickly. "Hi, Walker," she said, sounding breathless.

"'Sup? What're you two doing?"

"Talking. Calm down," Amelia replied. She would not aid Walker's fishing for information expedition. He couldn't act innocent with her. Right now, he was probably taking mental stock of his bank account, calculating the cost of hiring a hitman to take out Calin. Or maybe he'd use Mr. Hot and Rigid.

"And who are *we* talking to?" Walker smirked.

So, he wanted to be an ass, huh? Two could play that game.

"As far as I know, *you* weren't talking to anyone—unless yourself counts. *I* was talking to Calin before Cicely ran out here like one of the last of the Mohicans."

Did Calin just smother a smile? She couldn't be sure; she caught it in her peripheral. The greater part of her mind would swear The Jolly Stone Giant did the same. Weird!

Walker, still being a total ass, half-angled his body toward Calin. Implying he wasn't worth looking at head-on.

Yeah, that'd prove something—jackass!

Expression impassive, Walker extended his fist. "Hey, I'm Amelia's boyfriend, Wall or Walker—Walker Palmer."

Sparing Walker and his friend only the barest murderous glare, and ignoring the proffered fist, Calin turned gentler oceanic eyes on Amelia. "Do you work tomorrow?"

Ho-ly, crap! Gauntlet thrown!

Cicely's audible draw of breath mimicked Amelia's low gasp. Even the lobby seemed to hold its breath. How the hell could she respond when Calin had just issued the male equivalent of a bitch slap to none other than her boyfriend?

Nervous, she glanced at Walker. Walker wouldn't brush off the slight like Christopher had. He thrived on his don't-fuck-with-me rep. Didn't appreciate it challenged. How would he respond? Hopefully not by fighting. She wasn't in the mood to watch her boyfriend get his ass kicked.

Walker let his fist plop to his side.

Thank goodness.

Speak for yourself. I would've liked to see the prick get his ass handed to him.

"Umm... Yeah," she answered Calin to drown out the voice chanting "fight" in her mind.

Calin rapped the counter with a knuckle. Close to where her hand rested. Almost touching it. "See you tomorrow, Duchess." He winked, stealing her breath. "Bianca wanted to see another movie."

God, something about his *whatever* attitude made her sinfully hot... and worried. Did he treat everyone he deemed unworthy that way? Would he do it to her? She forgot her concerns, and her name, as the left side of his mouth rose into a slow, lopsided grin as if meant for only her.

"Oh, o-okay. See you tomorrow," she stammered. This couldn't be more awkward, she thought until she became aware of—three?—pairs of eyes on her, gauging her reaction. Two pairs were pissed.

Once again, neither fazed Calin. He spun on a dime, striding away in that menacing way of his, but not before mock saluting Walker's friend. Turning at the exit he bared his teeth and—growled?

Days ago, when he introduced himself, she'd thought she heard something similar. She wrote it off as insanity since she'd been strung out on lust. Now, she knew she heard right.

"So, Walker, you gonna introduce us to your...*friend*?" Cicely asked, wanton invitation lowering her voice.

Amelia rolled her eyes.

Walker turned hard chestnut eyes on her. "You will not see, or talk to him again. Do you hear me?"

Excuse me?

He must be brand new. That or he suffered a TBI on the ride here.

"He's a customer. I have to talk to him. But," she added in a chipper tone, "if it makes you feel better, I'll keep my eyes closed while I do it." She smiled, tight-lipped, in case the sarcasm wasn't apparent.

"You will not see him again."

Amelia's brow quirked. Her mouth dropped open. Hearing a double—*POP!*—other mouths falling slack, affirming she wasn't the only one shocked by Walker's previously silent partner's gruff words. Her gaze shot up, up, up over Walker's shoulder, and locked onto deep, penetrating blue eyes.

His words alone weren't completely responsible for her reaction. One, the guy's voice was deep and resonant, making James Earl Jones's sound soprano. Two, if the voice didn't get panties tumbling down, the odd visions it elicited did: Hot chocolate on a cold winter's day, warm apple pie, chicken noodle soup. Even its harshness soothed like a long soak in a hot bath. The contradiction unnerved her.

She stepped away from the counter to better peg both domineering men with glacial eyes. "Who. The. Heelll," she dragged out the word, "do the two of you think you are?"

"That's my cousin, and he's right," Walker said, as if the question weren't rhetorical, jerking his head toward his friend. "Other people can help that guy. He's a douche."

Unbelievable. Walker still thought he could tell her what to do. Amelia scrubbed her forehead with the back of her hand. Everyone stared in confusion. Great! She had a point to make.

"What're you doing?" Walker asked, brows almost touching.

"What?" She lowered her hand, shrugging. "You mean the name Bella Swan or Elena Gilbert isn't written up there?" Amelia swiped a hand over her forehead. "Whew! Good to know. For a second there, I thought one might be. I mean, if you thought I'd listen to you like some fictitious subservient bitch, I figured one must be written up there." Then hardening her voice, "You're not my boss." She turned toward Walker's cousin. "And I don't even know you, so, I for damn sure won't be listening to you."

"Walker," his cousin barked, mouth set in grim determination.

Walker turned and locked eyes with the man.

"Move."

To Amelia's complete amazement, instead of responding with his usual aggression, Walker stepped aside. His cousin took his place at the counter. Leveling sapphire eyes on her, he crooked a thick finger. Her breath hitched.

When she didn't move, he curled his finger again. An expectant blond brow arched.

Her mouth went Sahara dry. She tried to swallow. Couldn't. Intense blue eyes bored into hers. Demanded obedience. And forgetting where she was and everyone around, she moved as close as possible to him. If the counter hadn't impeded, she would've been head to chest with him. Or head to pectorals, considering his foot-and-a-half height advantage.

Who was this nameless man? If she remembered right, Walker said he was from Nebraska. But as far as she knew, Nebraskans didn't have smooth Italian accents. And since when did corn possess growth hormones? He and Walker shared no resemblance. The two might as well be different species. Refinement and raw masculinity had him in a chokehold. She wouldn't be surprised if he could kill a man with the small fork of a formal place setting—the one she never knew what to do with—and not get dirty.

He offered his hand. Curious as to his intent, she hesitantly placed her smaller palm down in his larger callused one. In an old-world gesture, she'd only seen in movies, he wrapped a tender hand around her fingers. Head bowed over her hand. His severe gaze never relinquished hers as he brought her hand to his lips and pressed a gentle kiss to her knuckles.

"I am Talon, milady." A simple introduction made with firm lips still against her hand.

Uh... She couldn't breathe. His mouth and peculiar, cool breath chilled her skin. The world stopped. Condensed. Narrowed. Until they were the only two left. Was it possible to burn and freeze at the same time? His touch? Cool. Her insides? On friggin' fire. It took everything she had not to jump over the counter and throw herself into his muscular arms. And he'd catch her. His arms were made to carry a woman. Or hold one up against walls.

Someone gasped. Amelia jerked her hand free.

What am I doing?

Talon allowed her to reclaim possession of her hand.

What the fuck am I doing?

Taking her hand? Idiot!

To think, today started off well. His flight to this Fates' forsaken state no vampire in their right mind should ever live arrived on time. Why mortals here didn't forgo the state and reside on the sun was beyond him. A vehicle treated with special tint and bulletproof glass waited, parked in Sky Harbor International Airport's parking lot, as had been confirmed. Compelling the Palmer family had been far too easy.

The Palmers took to the implanted suggestions as if they'd waited all their drab lives for someone to feed them utter bullshit. Most mortals required a firm mental push to bend their will. Their minds tended to hold fast to memories. Didn't take to them being manipulated or altered. If not handled with the utmost care, the mind rebounded. Real memories ricocheted off false suggestions, causing insanity. One misstep could result in permanent brain damage. He needn't have worry about either scenario with the Palmers.

Other than his stab wound, which would've healed overnight, but waylaid him twenty-four hours due to his lacking the nourishment live blood provided, things went well. Until he entered the theater.

The bitter, sickening sweet scent of evil assailed him. He wanted to pinch his nose and cover his mouth. Imagine his surprise at finding a rogue in the exact same state, city... theater as him. No coincidence there.

It meant one thing. Somehow, Balkan knew of the prophecy. Evil couldn't touch the *Book of Being* or read it. The pages went blank in evil's presence. Only *White-witch Advisors* could touch or read the book, further meaning: the *compound* had a spy.

Didn't that pull this mission out of the complicated pile and into the extremely screwed *Pakao-Brava* pits?

Being in the company of so many mortals without succumbing to bloodlust signaled the rogue had better than average control. Not surprising! Balkan and his *Hybrid* offspring trained *Daywalkers*. What disconcerted him? The obviously established relationship between it and the descendant. And, yes, Talon was pragmatic enough to admit the tale of a descendant was true, after seeing proof. Didn't mean the rest of the story held water.

Although her small stature and brown skin threw him for a loop, the prominent bone structure, high cheekbones, garnet-red hair, and outrageous eyes matched paintings of the *Vampire Royals*. Specifically, Queen Ana-Marie. Her pert nose, gloss-coated, bee-stung lips...

Her tantalizing mango-almond and cherry blossom scent did unexpected things to him. Tightened his leather pants. Lucky for him, his shirt covered his body's response. No one saw his skin tingle or his mind fog. Felt the electrical current surge through his entire body raising arm and leg hair.

This brought back his original question. *What the fuck... am I doing?*

Twenty-first-century mortal women didn't get their hands taken. He knew that! Over his one hundred and twenty years, he'd spent countless hours under Sebastian's second's tutelage. Trained in each decade's customs, vernacular, popular slang, and mannerisms. Century, decade, or country of the descendant's birth unknown, he'd been instructed in all he'd need to know to acclimate to the descendant's time.

Suffice it to say, no one prepared him for what the descendant would look like or for his inappropriate physiological reaction to her. Taking her hand? Kissing it! What the hell?

Although he'd been taught to treat females with the utmost respect, this was a new day and age. Mortal women weren't the same as *compound* females. Unaccustomed to being treated as ladies. They devalued themselves. Sought equality with their males. Never embraced their femininity and spoke out of turn. Their use of foul language and disagreeable natures, as demonstrated by Amelia, repulsed him—should repulse him.

Talon looked at Amelia, really looked. As if he hadn't been doing that all along. He needed to discover what about her called forth this unacceptable reaction in him and extinguish it. Besides the obvious issues apparent in being attracted to someone he'd been dispatched to murder, for lack of a better word, The Fates forbade it.

Servants and *commoners*, supernatural with no rank of nobility, were forbidden to mate *Vampire Royals*. Neither could achieve *Centripetal Impulse,* the magnetic pull and accompanying shock supernatural males experienced when a soul-deep attachment formed between him and his predestined mate. The decree was explicit, written in the *Book of Being* near the interdiction against vampires mating outside their breed.

Royals mated with *courtiers.* No exceptions. Anyone hoping to circumvent the edict would be destroyed. Both points were moot. He didn't want an *eternalmate*, royal or otherwise.

"You have a man. Let me have this one."

The low aside delivered by the bubbly dark-skinned girl Amelia called Cicely grabbed his attention. No mortal heard her words. Not even Amelia appeared to, and they were spoken into her ear. Amelia stood stock-still. Eyes stared into the distance. She seemed stunned. Didn't move when Cicely nudged her aside.

Cicely stood in front of Amelia, extending her hand. "Hey, Talon—is it? Cicely."

General rule of thumb, Talon didn't touch mortals unless feeding. But his dumbass stepped in it when he took Amelia's hand. If he wanted to escape suspicion, he needed to do the same with her coworker. So, he did.

"Nice to meet you," he said, lifting his head and releasing her hand.

That's when he found Amelia's gaze refocused. On him. He heard her heart bang a staccato beat. Saw her jaw tense. The audio-visual cues signaled anger, yet the emotion made no sense.

Released from compulsion, Walker approached the counter, denying Talon further examination of Amelia's strange response. Jerking his head, Walker beckoned Amelia. She approached the counter. He caressed her cheek with his thumb. Talon considered homicide.

"Babe, you know I don't mean to sound jealous," Walker crooned. A well-plucked eyebrow rose, Amelia didn't look convinced. He smiled wryly. "You're cute. Guys always push up on you. The asshole wouldn't even fist-bump me. Please, don't talk to him."

"Wall, you have too much testosterone for your own good. Someday somebody's gonna kick your ass." Amelia chuckled, then added seriously, "Just because you like me doesn't mean everyone does. Plus, I'm not some mindless bimbo who falls for a guy just because he looks at her."

"I'm sorry." Walker's smile was slow in coming. "We good?"

Amelia nodded. The fact she didn't return Walker's smile didn't escape Talon's notice.

Lips puckered, Walker braced his hands on the counter. Pushing off with his feet, he lifted himself so his body angled toward her. His arms supported all his weight. Amelia hopped up and met him halfway. Their lips met.

Talon saw red.

How dare the unworthy mortal kiss her? He clenched and unclenched his fists. Ground his teeth. His fangs begged for release. Talon wanted nothing more than to pull Walker's weak legs out from under him. Take pleasure in the thwack of skull meeting counter. Render Walker unconscious. Bust his lip open and hopefully rip out that ridiculous labret piercing. Talon's mouth watered. He liked the image his thoughts conjured too much. Could almost smell the sweet copper scent of blood spilling from Walker like an overturned bucket of water.

Mortals were killed easily. Snapped neck here. A well-placed stab to the gut there. Hell, a strategic blow to the head terminated one. A simple slit of the wrists had them leaking like sieves. Mmm... appealing.

"So, how long are you in town, Talon?" Amelia asked, her euphonic voice erasing his delicious ruminations.

Engrossed in said thoughts as he was, he hadn't seen her and Walker separate. Good. Now he wouldn't have to shank the mortal.

Enraptured by the way her full lips moved as his name rolled off her tongue, Talon forgot she'd asked a question until anticipation twinkled in her eyes.

What was wrong with him?

"For a while," he answered, noncommittally.

"That sucks." She frowned. "Walker's apartment smells like butt."

Walker shot Amelia a droll stare and flipped her off. "He's not staying with me—loser. He's staying with my parents."

"Oh, that's right. I forgot." She grinned at Talon. "Lucky you."

Dimples.

Shit! Hello, erection. It sprang to life as if eager to accept some unspoken offer the twin indentations posed. He might not have a pulse, but his dick did. Made him want to jump the counter and release one hundred and ten years of sexual frustration on her.

"Do you have a girlfriend, Talon?" Cicely blurted, twirling a long, braided strand of hair around her finger.

Walker turned a wide-eyed warning look on him and shook his head. "Don't answer, bro. It's a trap. That right there is R. Kelly bait. She'll get you five to ten."

"Nuh-uh!" Cicely protested, stomping her foot. "I turn eighteen in ten months."

Walker laughed. A second booming male laugh from across the lobby joined in. Apparently, Walker said something funny. The stocky man taking tickets at the usher stand doubled over in laughter.

"Fuck you, Matt!" Cicely shouted.

"Hey, don't proposition me either," he fired back. "I'm not going to jail for you."

Cicely's mouth tensed. Her nose wrinkled, and her nostrils flared. Shoulders squared, she stomped out of the concession booth and over to a closed door at the front of the theater. Talon assumed it led to the box office, given that's where he'd first spotted her from the parking lot.

Opening the door, she yelled, "You guys are stupid. Next time you need a shift covered don't call me." She entered the room and slammed the door behind her.

Shaking her head, Amelia *tsked*. "That could've been your wife," said in faux pity, then sighed. Her slender shoulders lifted infinitesimally. "Now we'll never know."

Talon rolled his eyes. He got the joke. But just the thought of taking an *eternalmate*, even in jest, made him shudder. Never did he want to experience the physical pain of needing to be near his mate. The pull to protect her above all others. The need to share himself mind, body, and blood. However, watching a mischievous grin slither across Amelia's mystifyingly beautiful face, he felt shackled.

Fuck!

Chapter Ten

"M an, you're lucky you're staying here," Walker said, tossing up and catching some collectible football he'd gotten off the desk of the office-turned-guest room Talon would be staying in. "Mom worshipped Uncle Harold. No offense, bro, but I kinda thought he was gay the one time I met him. Guess there's someone for everyone. Anyway, you'll get treated like a king here. Fuck," he groaned, stretching. "I could use breakfast in bed."

"I don't require breakfast," Talon grumbled.

"A giant-size boy like you? I don't believe it."

Talon couldn't respond. He ran a weary hand over his face, through his hair. For two hours, he and his simpleton "cousin" had stood around the theater warning males away from Amelia. While more fun than it should've been, scaring off mortal men who dared breathe in her direction, Walker's jealousy knew no bounds. It'd gotten so bad that although they were busy, there were only women in Amelia's line. At which point, a plump blonde woman, Heidi, suggested they leave and not return. Needless to say, he'd had his fill of one-on-one time with this mortal. And he was thirsty.

Back at Walker's parents' house, Talon stupidly assumed Walker would be just as eager to end their family bonding. Hunger caused him to emit danger vibrations. Mortals sensed them and gave him a wide berth. The males at the theater had. Did Walker?

Nope.

The waste of skin set up shop in the ugly forest green recliner of the sports-themed guestroom. If he couldn't stand a few hours with the mortal, how the hell would he survive the next two months until the *Awakening*?

Fuck me...

Weren't mortals supposed to be considerate? Talon had feigned jet lag, yet Walker stayed. Shit! If Walker had any sense of self-preservation, there'd be a Walker-sized hole in the door. The mohawked jackass looked tasty.

Get him out of here. Keep up pretenses.

Could he resist the sweet allure of Walker's blood? Yes. But he already possessed an aversion to the prick for reasons he wasn't quite sure of, and the idea of draining him... *Get him out. Now!*

"Walker—"

"Wall," he interrupted. "Friends and family call me Wall."

"We're not friends," Talon corrected, steel infusing his tone.

"That's the beauty, bro," Walker continued, smiling and tossing the football to himself. "We're family—instant friends."

Drain him.

Shit. He couldn't. Draining prey to death allowed the demon conscience dominance. That turned vampires rogue. It caged the human soul, relegating it to an easily avoidable conscience. The process was irreversible. His demon half craved it. All vampires' demons wanted out, which is why they talked so much.

Fine. Don't drain him. Take a pint or two then break his neck.

Yep, time to get Walker out before he succumbed to his inner demon. The succulent blue vein in Walker's neck and the ebb and flow of life's warm elixir rushing through it had Talon dizzy with need.

"Oh, hey! I'm playing ball at the park later. You gotta come. These guys will fuckin' flip when friggin' albino Shaq walks up." Walker chuckled.

Talon turned away from his suitcase, staring deadpan at the dumbass mortal. Kneeling in front of Walker, he captured his gaze. Walker's pupils dilated. His eyes glazed. The football he'd been tossing fell.

"Do you enjoy living?" Talon asked, pitching his voice low. Even.

Walker nodded. A stiff movement of his head.

Talon arched a brow. "Thought so. You're going to leave. Alright? Immediately."

Walker nodded again.

"I knew you weren't as stupid as you look. Now, after your basketball game, you're going to call Amelia. Tell her I'll be picking her up tomorrow to run errands. Say whatever you have to. Just convince her to go with me. She will be with me a lot over the next few weeks. You will not interrupt our outings. Not with annoying phone calls, text messages, or petty jealousy. If you do, I will kill you. Understood?" he asked, no inflection betraying the depths of his emotion.

"Understood." Walker's response was wooden.

Talon began to stand, but sudden inspiration struck. "Also," he added. "You will not refer to me as albino again. Nor will you ever invite me to play sports. Are we clear?"

Another stiff nod.

"Now leave," Talon ordered. He straightened and returned to his suitcase on the bed and the shirt he'd been folding as if nothing happened. Clearing his throat released Walker from compulsion. "Yeah, that'd be cool, Wall."

Walker blinked several times. His brows furrowed. Eyes darted side to side.

"What?" he asked, shaking his head as if to dislodge an unpleasant thought. "Never mind, bro. I gotta jet. Get at me tomorrow when you wanna hang."

Still confused, Walker stood without another word. His foot encountered the football. He stared at it, perplexed for a moment, before picking it up and placing it on the desk. He left.

Talon's relief was palpable. He needed to feed before the Palmer clan got home. Dumping the clothes out of his suitcase and onto the bed, he located the false back panel. Unzipped it and found the freezer compartment containing six dozen donor packs of blood.

Yum... Not!

A tormented groan slipped past his lips. He removed two pouches. On the off chance one of the Palmers returned early, he replaced the panel and repacked his clothes. Talon glared at the fetid blood. He didn't want to do this.

Maybe microwaving it might trick his taste buds into believing they were getting the good stuff. Pulling his phone from his pocket, he eyed the blood again. Yeah, right. If he thought the microwave would help, he might as well play in sunlight without his ring. Embrace insanity.

Without Walker tempting his senses, feeding could wait. There were other matters to address at the moment. Pressing speed dial number "2" on his cell, he placed the device to his ear.

"Anton's Boom Boom Room. You shake 'em we squeeze 'em."

Lifting his eyes skyward, Talon rubbed the back of his neck. Twisted his head left and right to relieve some of the day's tension.

"Do you even understand what it's like being your bitch?" Anton asked.

He didn't possess the patience required to deal with the fledgling today. What he expected to be a fool's mission morphed into much more. He needed to reassess the situation. Reevaluate Amelia's protection. With a *Daywalker* in their midst, he needed to stick close to her. Where there was one *Daywalker*, there were more.

Balkan despised the *Vampire Royals*. In his mind, they were responsible for his deposition by The Fates. With a new queen sealed and able to reorganize the supernatural, Balkan would feel threatened. He'd pad his bet. Send as many *Daywalkers* as possible to kill Amelia.

"I need to speak with Vanessa."

"Well, hello to you, too. You know, you catch more flies with pee than you do honey," Anton quipped.

"What?" He was out of his depths today. Jokes were flying over his head. Amelia caused his body to act independently from his brain. Anton's idiom made no sense. Not that Anton's slang ever did, but Talon usually deciphered the meaning.

"I don't know the exact saying. But be nice to me. Vanessa's not here, and anyway, she gave me lead on this. So, consider me Giles, Buffy. Or Genie, Aladdin. Poof! What do you need?" Anton asked, then chuckled.

Yes, references he understood. Decades ago, they'd believed the descendant would be a child. Talon had suffered through several Disney cartoons. He also endured several horrible teen dramas about vampires. A petite mortal girl slaying vampires? Talon laughed from a healthy place over that. His fascination with mortals and their vampire myths started then. He collected books and graphic novels on the subject.

"How are you supposed to help with this mission? You're not at full strength," he reminded the fledgling.

"I don't have to be. But thanks for rubbing sunlight in that wound," Anton retorted. "You gotta let me do this, dude. Give me a chance."

The uncharacteristic seriousness in Anton's request gave Talon pause. "What's going on?"

"Why's anything gotta be going on? I've helped you, man. Got you names, those addresses, the descendant's name. Let me do this."

"And what a name it was. Walker Palmer is Amelia's boyfriend. Not the friend you claimed he was," Talon informed him.

Although, he worked with the development, playing the long-lost cousin angle. Walker presented an unwelcome challenge.

"My bad," Anton apologized, less than repentant. "Ain't like people get relationship licenses. You can't hold that against me. I got you the ring, which, by the way, you need to take off eleven hours a day. Our voodoo don't doo-doo like Dark-witch voodoo. The ring'll weaken you. It can't be worn all the time like Daywalkers' amulets. I suggest flatlining while it's off."

Great. This mission kept getting more complicated. To build strength or heal, vampires *flatlined*, or as mortals call it, slept. But they didn't dream. Didn't breathe. Nor was it a nightly requirement. It could be days before a vampire *flatlined*. The hours he took off the ring would undoubtedly coincide with daylight. Leaving Amelia unprotected.

"You can't help, Anton. This is bigger than you. When I arrived at the theater where Amelia's employed, a Daywalker was there. Somehow, Balkan knows about the prophecy."

"The courtiers have issued an expulsion order for me and my dad," Anton said, voice grave. "I'm not like you, Talon. There's no predetermined path for me. If I don't prove myself useful by the time I reach *Immortal Age* in July... we're out. Please, let me do this."

Shit. Talon pushed his suitcase aside and sat on the bed. Scrubbed his face with his hand. *Expulsion*. The courtiers had become more ruthless with their assumed power, but *expulsion* for no reason? Incredible. Those expelled had all memory of their time in the *compound*, its inhabitants, and location erased. Now he understood Anton's newfound envy of the *Royal Guard*.

The fledgling annoyed him but in a younger sibling way. He didn't wish him thrown out of the only home he'd ever known. Some supernatural memories were harder to erase than others. When that occurred, the expelled were destroyed.

Talon acceded with a groan. "The Daywalker's name is Calin. I need all the information you can find on him. Something was... off about him. And he didn't have a wristband."

"You like me. You really, really like me," Anton said, reverting to his light-hearted jocular tone.

"Don't press your luck, fledgling. Screw with my mission, and I'll relegate you to a memory."

"No, you won't." The confidence in Anton's assertion pissed Talon off.

When did he lose his power in the scenario? He preferred the youngblood afraid of him.

"I get why you have to say that," he continued. "You don't want me to think you're soft. I dig it. Look, I'll hack some shit. Tap some contacts—literally. And keep my ear to the streets. I'll get answers. In the meantime, you're on the descendant like a fat guy on a fritter."

"Amelia!" Talon snapped harsher than intended.

"What?"

"Her name is Amelia. Call her Amelia. Calling her 'the descendant' makes her sound like a thing. Some tool we're using." That quick, Talon understood his response to Amelia.

He mistook sympathy for attraction. Made perfect sense. Being created only to serve some ulterior function, he understood her plight. The plight she didn't seem to be aware of, given her occupation and behavior. What a relief!

"Sorry," Anton said, sounding anything but. "Didn't realize you two were all buddy-buddy."

"Nobody wants to be treated like an inanimate object. Existing only to do others' bidding without choice in the matter."

"Alright," conceded in a wary tone. "Now can I tell you about the present I procured for you and the descend—Amelia? It's pretty dope, brotha. I got mad skills."

"Make it fast." Talon glared at the donor packs, trying not to gag. "I have things to do. This better not be like your last *gift*."

Anton burst into laughter.

Humor was lost on Talon. He saw nothing funny about a mortal prostitute tied to a chair in his resting quarters. Anton had called himself killing two birds with one stone. Helping Talon lose his virginity and sating his thirst. Neither would've been bad if his mother hadn't beaten him home. Lea flipped the fuck out.

He cleared his throat. "Done?"

Anton sobered. "Umm... yeah. Anyway, I got you a bona fide castle. Well, not you the—Amelia is the owner."

A castle in Arizona? "I thought you said you could handle this."

"Hear me out."

Talon remained silent.

Anton went on. "I figured living with mortals wasn't your shtick. So, I searched online and found that the Arizona government owned a castle but wasn't using it. Since I read Arizona's hurting for money, I electronically transferred funds from the courtiers' fund into the government's account. Presto change-o, the castle's ours."

"What good will that do? Amelia won't be safe there," Talon pointed out.

"Already taken care of. Amelia's the owner, and for now mortal. I contacted a local coven of White-witches—who you now owe a favor, FYI. You go in first then have her enter. It'll activate the threshold shield mortal residences have but allow those within to come and go as they please. It'll stay active even after she's awakened. Downside, she's the only one who can permit new entrants."

Once again, Talon was impressed. Seems the fledgling was quite resourceful with proper motivation. If that were possible, maybe Talon could feed from the donor bags without regurgitating.

"Text the details."

Chapter Eleven

Pushing open ornate, mahogany doors, Anton Liakos slipped inside the foyer of his palazzo. Careful not to make a sound, he eased the doors closed behind him.

Please don't let me get caught—again. His gaze darted from one side of the luxurious entryway to the other. Something wasn't right. His Spidey senses were tingling. Taking mental inventory, he scanned his surroundings.

The gargantuan 24-karat gold chandelier twirled an infinitesimal degree. Its soft light made shapes on the cathedral ceiling and walls. The dumb decorative table Lea swore served a purpose rested in the middle of the room. A big ass plant of some sort sat atop it. Black and white marble, curved, double staircase. Of course, they wouldn't move. Things seemed fine, quiet.

Anton tiptoed across the black and white marble tiled, stadium-sized vestibule. Dodged a bullet this time. If someone saw him before he reached his rooms, he'd be screwed. Besides, what the fuck would he do if something were amiss? As everyone liked to remind him, he was a fledgling. Not at full power. Unable to go out alone.

Whateva.

They could kiss his entire white ass. He made it back unscathed this, and every other time, he snuck out. Intuition and awareness kept him safe. Maybe some shit like residual epi-nephrine from the high of possible discovery contributed to his unease. Everything appeared in order, unless he'd gotten the wrong house.

Again.

Last time that happened, he was four. Somehow a rogue werewolf infiltrated the *compound*. Piss-pants scared; he'd run into the wrong house. One clean slice of Sebastian's silver Japanese Katana sword decapitated the werewolf, right beside Anton. The severed head rolled over the toe of his boot.

After eight puke-filled hours, he decided he didn't have the stomach for guardsman life. Or to ever enter the Cantemir palazzo uninvited again. Had it not been for the fact Lea dec-orated both homes, Anton never would've gotten disoriented. Only now he realized how dissimilar the homes were.

Quiet moments were nonexistent in the Cantemir house. Something gruesome was always going on there. Talon being a Vampire Royal Guardsman might be dope, but it'd suck to be him. Living with constant threats to his and his parents' existence. The *courtiers* didn't trust or care for him and his father, which explained their need for constant security. But they didn't pretend to be their friends, and then secretly send once loyal beings to destroy them either.

Lea and Sebastian lived on high alert. He often wondered if Emilio cared what his defection did to his family. Jealousy of Talon's prophesied destiny drove him to Balkan, the *Daywalk-ers*. He claimed. It also earmarked his family for destruction. Only no one had the balls to confront Sebastian head-on. Emilio was a cold piece of work for that mess.

Talon never talked about it, but Anton suspected it got to him. Up until seven years ago, he'd had a brother who fought be-side him. Now, he fought against him. And Emilio was a worthy adversary. For centuries, he'd studied his father's fighting style and thought processes, he knew his family—his enemy—well. The insane part of it all, Anton could relate to the douchebag.

The jealous portion anyway.

If he'd reach the *Immortal Age* already, he could do some-thing dope like sublimate into fog or mist to sneak to his quarters. But nooo... he had two months and sixteen days—yeah, he was countin'—until then. So, for now, he had to 007 it so his father or *White-witch governess* didn't catch him.

They didn't seem to understand his need for alone time. He might be young, but a playa had needs that were unfulfillable in mixed company. Well, the cute little nymph he messed with was a freak, she might be with it, but him—not so much.

Prepared to head to his rooms, angry male voices coming from his father's study stopped him. He detoured down the middle of the foyer to the black doors positioned between the grand staircases. On to his second favorite thing—the first being females—eavesdropping.

Nobody ever visited them. The Cantemirs were his and his father's only real friends. With Talon gone, Sebastian wouldn't leave Lea alone for a second. The courtiers shunned them. Thank The Fates, his father wasn't as strict as Sebastian. Victor allowed him to watch television, play video games, listen to music, and do anything he wanted, pretty much. His one rule: don't leave the palazzo without Talon, Lea, Gawain, or Vanessa. Those were also the only beings they knew. So, who was Victor talking to?

Too many vamps and other supernatural on the compound didn't trust them. His father's vehement refusal to disclose their origins hadn't won them any friends. So, it wasn't a new friend, or friends, by the sounds of it.

Anton sympathized with the *courtiers*. He probably knew less than they did about his background. All Victor ever told him was that his mother and her White-witch were assassinated by a rogue vampire the night after his birth. Whenever he asked about extended family, his father told him, "Sharing blood with another is overrated." Then bought him a new gaming system, computer, or device, or gave him cash.

Last week, he'd asked about his father's parents, and...BLAM! He had a Sony Playstation 6 and a new DSLR camera. His quarters consisted of six rooms. If he asked enough questions, he'd need another three to hold all his loot. And after what he just heard... Hello, in-home movie theater.

"We're brothers, think of all we could do," an unfamiliar male voice said.

Anton had to pick his jaw up off the floor. And not because of the nut crunch the word "brothers" delivered. The voice didn't have the Italian, Greek, or Romanian accent most *compound* dwellers possessed. He'd only ever heard this accent on television or from his dad. It was American.

The whisper of fabric signaled someone standing. "How did you discover this?" His father's demanding voice. Old Victor must be doing his signature pace. A constant source of aggravation, Anton knew that pace well.

"We did the math. And... a little birdie helped put the missing pieces together." Another man who, if not for enhanced hearing permitting him to distinguish the subtle differences, Anton would have sworn was the first speaker, answered.

"Math? What pieces?" Victor's incredulous questions. "Ophelia can't touch the book. Speaking of witch, how is Mommy Dearest?"

Anton couldn't have been more stunned if his father's study doors flew open and smacked him square in the face.

Mommy Dearest?

Shut the front door! Vic wasn't hatched, he had a mother and, from the sounds of it, two brothers. Why would his father deprive him of a family? Let him believe they were alone? Anton's head reeled over the implications of what he'd just heard.

The front doors opened.

"I'm unsure." Vanessa's authoritative, yet genteel, voice came from under the regulation raised hood of her ankle-length red velvet cloak. Members of the Vampire Royal *retinue* were required to wear the garment when out, or in the presence of a VR. If not annoying as fuck, and like a second mother to him—Lea being like a first—Vanessa would've been smokin'. Statuesque, long brunette hair with red highlights—most of which the unflattering cloak hid—he got the appeal. She must've been using earbuds on her phone.

Hmm... a welcome change from her normal spot on his ass. Good thing she hadn't seen him yet, or she'd be right back there.

Anton ducked behind a floor-to-ceiling stone column to the right of the study doors.

"I was told there was a serpent in the garden. I presume he or she's cavorting with Dark-witches, and or, Balkan. He's always had a predilection for concubines."

A serpent in the garden?

Damn her and her old-school gibberish. Couldn't she step into the twenty-first century with the rest of them? Shit! Trying to eavesdrop on two conversations was hard enough without having to crack her archaic code.

"Come tomorrow, the reptile shall be flushed from our midst," she went on, preparing to ascend the staircase, oblivious to Anton. "Yes," she answered an unheard question.

"Meet me here at dawn, and we'll go to Fay's for the cleansing together."

Cleansing? Oh, shit! Now he got it. "Serpent" was code for spy. The same spy Talon believed fed information to Balkan. Unequivocal proof more *Daywalkers* would descend upon Arizona, and Talon. Damn! Talon needed reinforcements, and knowing him, he wouldn't appreciate Sebastian showing up. Crap! He'd told Talon he could handle this. Who—

"Anton Isaac Liakos!"

Busted.

Straightening to his full six-two height, he stepped from behind the pillar. Vanessa lowered her hood. Anton met her perturbed bronze glare.

She folded her arms over her ample chest. "May I ask what you are doing, young one?"

Getting caught by a real force to be reckoned with, if you don't shut up.

He put a finger to his pursed lips. Wrapping the fingers of his other hand around her upper arm, Anton guided her away from his father's study.

At the foot of the stairs, Vanessa shook off his hand. She speared him with a reproachful glower. He knew that look well. The witch had formidable abilities. Given the fact that he was barely stronger than a mortal until the *Immortal Age*, he made no further move against her. Her voice might be breeze gentle, but she had the potential to turn into a tornado.

"Do you believe no punishment is warranted for your blatant disregard for others' privacy?" Vanessa scolded. "Have I taught you nothing of decency and respect?"

He didn't have time for this. He had phone calls to make, flipping out to do.

"It seems you're in need of a history review. You need to understand how prudent it is that you keep a strong hold on your vices. Your demon will gain dominance with ease if you be so weak-willed as to not control your..."

Blah... blah... blah. Anton felt his eyes glaze as she nagged him.

"...urges," she continued. "Is it so difficult to be decent? Have you absorbed nothing I've taught you? Yes, you absolutely need a refresher history lesson. No charge of mine will go rogue. How would you feel if someone eavesdropped on you?"

These weren't questions so much as statements meant to rebuke, and by the way she droned on and on, she clearly wasn't looking for answers but...

"Maybe I was absent the day you covered all that." He shrugged, smirking innocently. "Seems like a lot of material."

Anger sparked in the depths of Vanessa's copper eyes; she smacked the back of his head. Hard. Her touch transported him to his room.

Fine by me.

Yanking his phone out of his back pocket, Anton stomped into his sitting room. He had calls to make.

Chapter Twelve

D id all guys read from the same book: *1000 Ways to Manipulate a Woman?* Must be written by the same guy who wrote, *Just the Tip.*

"He's my cousin. It's important you two get along. If you loved me, you'd do this," Walker cajoled the previous night.

Ugh! Amelia twisted the hot water knob to off. Shoving the black shower curtain aside, she stepped out of the shower. She could kill Wall. Lobotomy ranked higher on her list than running errands with his giant, pasty cousin.

The audacity of Walker! Asking for favors after the stunt he and his sidekick pulled yesterday. Them mad dogging every Tom, Dick, and José pissed her off. She dried herself with her plush beige towel. Wrapping it around her, she padded out of the bathroom and into her bedroom. Goosebumps erupted over every inch of her skin.

What was the air conditioner set on? Alaska?

Her teeth chattered. She half expected to see her breath when she breathed. Lotioning up never went so fast; Amelia got it done in less than a minute. Standing at the end of her bed, towel snug around her body, Amelia studied the outfit laid on it. She'd chosen the strapless, gold, regal brocade corset and black velvet shorts before her shower and subsequent cold flash.

Accessorize or freeze me bum off.

Her foot tapped a staccato beat against the carpeted floor, for warmth, and in anger.

Heidi didn't treat her with kid gloves the way Gordon did. She'd threatened to fire her if the big bad Palmers turned up at the theater again. The loss would kill Amelia. Might not be a loss of a person, but it was a gateway to further losses. She wouldn't allow Walker and his cousin to cause problems.

Showing off for his cousin, stupid Walker strutted like a peacock. He'd gone as far as to chest bump some random man. Made a complete spectacle of himself, and by extension, her. His cousin intimidated with no more than a look. Everyone had lines stretched out the doors in front of their registers. Hers was much shorter with only women and children. What they hoped to accomplish with their machismo, Amelia hadn't a clue. What they achieved was her disdain for, and suspicion of, Talon.

The guy reeked of danger. Whereas before she thought it some magisterial vibe, she now recognized it as a crime boss vibe. One of her old favorite soap operas had a mob kingpin. Ladies loved the sexy, brooding, dimpled, mystery bad boy with gel-slicked hair and tailored suits. Until they found out what he did. Or fell victim to it.

His intense blue gaze tracking her every move. The way he watched—no, not watched—concentrated on her was unnerving. He saw too much. She could admit he was beyond gorgeous. Blind women saw that. But with distance, and her libido in check, came clarity. Talon had secrets. Bodies buried under houses, bombs strapped under cars, big secrets. She didn't trust him. No one that imposing was harmless. The idea of going anywhere with him scared her. There was too much... Talon.

Cousin or not, she didn't understand Walker's insistence on them hanging out. Wall suspected the mailman of unsavory intentions if he lingered at the mailbox. She doubted Talon's honey-blond, inexcusable, fall-from-heaven handsomeness escaped his notice. Calin's didn't. And Calin didn't fall from heaven.

Judging by what little she knew of him, she'd say Calin jumped.

Why would Wall want her alone with Talon? Unless there was something she didn't know. Talon was a man. A virile—two loud gongs made Amelia jump. Her heart palpitated.

Good, Lord! She clutched her chest.

I forgot my alarm?

In three years, she'd never forgotten about her alarms. She lived by them and counting to get through each day. This alarm gave her a thirty-minute heads-up before Talon arrived. See? Another reason for suspicion. He threw her off kilter. Although, if she were being honest, she'd admit she'd stopped counting her steps after meeting Calin. Thank goodness for self-delusion.

She got dressed. Long-sleeved, black, shrug bolero sweater and four-inch heeled, thigh-high, Stella McCartney boots completed her corset and shorts outfit. A black lace choker with a ruby teardrop dangling from the center brought the look together. Might be a bit much for spring, but Arizona spring was summer in most places. Amelia didn't care. Her teeth were knocking hard enough to shatter.

Fifteen minutes provided the time to do her makeup and flat iron her hair. In the hall, she stopped at the A/C control panel mounted on the wall.

Eighty degrees!

No frickin' way! Either the air conditioner was broken, or she was.

"Tessie!" She called as she rounded the corner into the makeshift dining area between the stools set at the island and small living room. "Is it cold in here to you? I'm freezing."

Tessa lay on the navy blue couch with tiny white sailboats embroidered all over it. Her laptop sat open on her lap. Some reality dating show played on TV.

Once again, Tessa managed to sneak more of her decorative touches into the living room. Amelia noted Tessa had added pictures of herself—of course—to the mantle above the red brick fireplace built into the far wall. A new brown wicker basket sat on the ledge in front of the fireplace. Each violated their agreement to leave the room and house exactly as her parents left it, tacky matching loveseat and couch and all.

"Uh-uh. I'm hot. I was actually gonna turn the A/C down," Tessa answered, eyes glued to her computer screen. "You okay?"

"Yeah," Amelia lied, resting her hands on the headrest of one oak chair positioned around the circular oak dining table.

"Is Gabby Reece dead?"

Ooookay. Let's talk about that.

"The former volleyball, model chick?"

"No, the ice cream man, Gabby Reece," Tessa quipped, unwrapping a Milky Way candy bar, which seemed to materialize from nowhere. She took a big bite.

Amelia rolled her eyes. "Hey! You can't expect me to immediately hop on the track of every errant thought you have. Provide a map or something," she scolded. "Why do you care if she's dead or not?"

"Cuz she has a bucket list online."

"Well, exhale. I think she's safe," Amelia assured. Sudden pain lanced her gums. Chills skittered down her spine. Both sensations turned her casual lean against the chair into a perilous struggle to stay upright. "A bucket list means she's alive," she explained, making certain discomfort didn't leak into her words.

"No way." Tessa shook her head, finishing her candy bar in one huge bite. "Bucket lists are for," she said with a mouth full, turning she saw Amelia for the first time. Green eyes bulged. "Hey, Diamond, what time do you get off the pole," Tessa chided, interrupting herself. "Where exactly do you think we live? You're gonna die of heatstroke."

Amelia would've balked at the stripper reference if her gums didn't feel twice their normal size. Or if she thought she could talk without biting through her tongue. The only option available to her, scrunching her face into a disgruntled frown. However, she feared it presented as a cross between constipation and messing her pants now.

Tessa wrinkled her nose and pursed her lips. Squinting, she continued scrutinizing her.

Amelia squirmed, uncomfortable with such a thorough examination. "I told you I was cold," she defended through gritted teeth.

Ding! Dong!

They both jumped. Startled by the chime of the doorbell. Amelia groaned inside.

Oh, joy! Her unwelcome captor. Here to whisk her off on some mystery errand. What kind of errands did someone visiting have to run anyway? Nebraska, her ass. If Talon was a native Nebraskan, she was a Martian.

"Yeah, but you do realize outside it's, like, one hundred degrees, right?" Tessa announced, paying no mind to the doorbell. "You're gonna spontaneously combust."

"Okay, Ann Landers." Amelia sighed exasperated. "How about you answer the door and spare me the advice," she suggested. Although closer to the door, the pain wouldn't allow her to relinquish the chair.

With a huff and eye roll, Tessa hefted her laptop from her lap. Standing, she sat it on her vacated seat and went to answer the door. She looked Amelia up and down as she passed.

Hand on the doorknob; she turned to Amelia. "You look pale. Are you okay?"

A blank stare and raised brow got her roommate back on track.

Tessa opened the door. Gasped.

There is a way to shut Tessa up.

The open floor plan provided Amelia with an unobstructed view of the front room, and by proximity, the front door. Illuminated by the harsh Arizona sun, dressed in black Dockers, a white T-shirt, and a black overshirt, Talon. Why did he have to be so... delicious?

He lifted the sunglasses covering his profound blue eyes. Rested them on top of his blond head. Damn black fingerless gloves. Talon seemed married to them. Anyone else would look stupid in them. On him, they added to his sex appeal.

Mine!

Damn voice. When did her brain start associating that word with people, aka, random men? If related to her boyfriend wasn't enough, his bossy, arrogant nature repelled ideas of ownership.

Hand braced on the doorknob, Tessa pulled the door with her as she took a small step back. Staring at Talon, she hunched over. Her other hand was on her knee like a runner catching their breath after a race. She breathed several loud, exaggerated breaths. From her place behind Tessa, Amelia couldn't see her face. Whatever expression she donned must've been something else because the corners of Talon's mouth twitched.

"You're... related... to Walker?" Tessa asked between breaths.

Talon nodded. Yet he made no move to enter.

Could the mean giant be scared of the itty-bitty woman? Wouldn't be the first guy Tessa scared. It was a wonder Dan didn't piss himself every time he was around her.

"How are you and the walking Magna Doodle from the same family tree?" Tessa straightened. Shaking her head, she raked a hand through dark brown tresses. "I knew having a sense of humor wasn't a sin. Apparently, God has a big one. You and Walker in the same family? And everybody gets on me..." Having said her piece, she let go of the door and ambled toward the living room.

With Tessa gone, Talon's eagle eye zeroed in on Amelia.

"Invite me in," Talon demanded. "I'll carry you."

Blinking, she recoiled at his offer. "Umm... No, thanks. I'm good."

Her knees weakened. Now she held onto the chair for an entirely new reason.

Jaw set in a firm line, his pale skin was so smooth and hard in appearance she doubted it'd ever been marred by a smile. He stood feet shoulders width apart. Hands behind his back, body braced, and chin high. An unnatural amount of confidence exuded from him.

Made her want to ruffle his feathers on purpose. Get some emotion out of him.

"Is this how you normally greet company?" he asked in his deep, accented bass. "Leave them standing outside and insult their family?"

She scoffed. "As far as greetings go? Yes. That's how Tessa does it." Amelia smirked. "As for the leaving outside part? *I* leave you outside." Nothing good would come from him coming inside. Or something good and nasty could, which was why he would stay outside. "You don't need to come in. I'll be out in a second. Gotta grab my purse. Wait here," she ordered then hauled ass to her room.

He made her hot and angry. If they were spending alone time together, she needed a minute to regroup. She also had to figure out how not to be rude to him. It just kept slipping out. Amelia sat on her bed.

Tessa entered the doorway, eating a Popsicle not even a second later.

So much for a minute alone.

"Why's he outside?" Tessa asked, amusement tilting the corner of her mouth. She wagged her eyebrows. "Afraid he might be a cookie crook?"

Amelia shot her a droll stare. "Are you slow?"

Inviting herself in, Tessa plopped down on the bed next to her. "Think about it, A?" A wicked grin slithered across her face. "You can't get re-impregnated. This is the perfect chance for a freebie without getting caught. Then you come back here, tell me, and I can live vicariously through you. Could work." She sucked her Popsicle suggestively.

Amelia glared askance at Tessa, the little devil on her shoulder. Which would've been fine if there'd been an angel on her other shoulder. There wasn't. Another little possessive devil told her to take what belonged to her, which made no sense. Talon wasn't hers. She didn't want him. Besides, both devils were overlooking a bigger issue.

"You do realize Talon is Walker's cousin, right? Walker would find out if we did the hibbidi-dibbidi."

Puh-lease!" Tessa snorted unladylike. "Tens don't talk to twos. How close could they be?"

Moments like these made her question their friendship. "So, you think it'd be a good idea if I slept with my baby's daddy's cousin?" Amelia snorted in derision. "I can almost hear the crowd now... Jerry! Jerry! Jerry!" Cutting off mid-chant she glowered at Tessa. "I love Walker. I don't want to do the old boop-scudo with his cousin. No matter how hot he is." *Liar!* But Tessa didn't need to know that since she wasn't confronting it.

Sitting quietly, Tessa considered Amelia's words. A wide Kool-Aid smile spread across her face.

"Gross. No!" Amelia knew that smile. She hopped off the bed and grabbed her purse from the top of the dresser. "I'm leaving."

How could Tessa consider doing that to Dan? Without a backward glance, Amelia stormed out of the room.

"Hey!" Tessa whisper-shouted close behind her. "Ain't no fun if the homies can't have none." Lowering her tone further she added, "He may not even know Dan. Plus, he looks like the strong silent type."

Entering the front room, Amelia rounded on her friend. Lips pressed tight, eyes bulging, she put a finger to her mouth. She turned toward the open door. Talon hadn't moved an inch. She smiled, tight-lipped. "Let's go."

She pushed past Talon. Stifled a groan when her elbow made contact with his rock-hard abdomen. Nice.

What the hell am I thinking?

Tessa's thoughts must be seeping into her brain. After slamming the door in Tessa's grinning face, she stomped across the broken stone path through her dead grass lawn toward her Mustang.

"Where are you going?"

Amelia jumped. Too close. Talon managed to get too close without her noticing. Peculiar, cool breath tickled her neck. His bass-filled voice in her ear made her shudder.

Damn...

Although her heels added four inches to her height, making her five-seven, she barely reached pec level on him. Talon's stone torso was damn near pressed against her back.

My, my, my... Impressive. Please let that be because he's happy to see me.

Tramp! What are you thinking?

She resisted the inexplicable urge to lean into him.

"My car's over there," he purred.

Strong, heavy hands came down on her shoulders. The stiffness of his hold told Amelia those hands were capable of inflicting great pain, yet his touch was gentle. She might not be opposed to some rough handling at his hands. Dammit! When did she become such a hornball? He shifted her toward a dark gray Chrysler 300 parked behind her car.

Prepared to scold him for disrespecting her personal space—and get him off her before she did something impulsive like lick his hand—she swiveled her head to the right.

His pasty skin quelled her argument. Having deep brown skin, she didn't tan. She hadn't a clue about tanning conversation etiquette. How did one tell someone they were in desperate need of a tan? His skin practically glowed in the sunlight.

She turned all the way around. Talon released her long enough for her to face him. Then put his hands right back on her shoulders. Grinding her teeth, Amelia glanced left at his stark white hand and then right at the other. Again, what she saw sidetracked her. Stunned her quiet. Okay, another topic she'd need to broach with him: the gaudy, ruby, class ring-looking monstrosity on his right ring finger. Who'd he think he was? A pimp? Maybe the Godfather?

Ripping her gaze from his skin and colossal pimp ring, a thought made her glance at his car.

Gaping, she turned wide eyes to him. "You can't have your windows tinted that dark. It's illegal. I can't even see your steering wheel. I'm not driving with you." She wiggled and shrugged her shoulders to extricate herself from his hold. He didn't move a muscle. Not a smile. Frown. Nothing. His grip never wavered. "Get. Your hands. Off me."

To her amazement, he did. Briefly.

Amelia turned her back on him. Glared at the death machine he expected her to ride in. She tossed a bratty moue over her shoulder. Blue eyes trapped her gaze. Hers stayed on his. Watched as he walked a slow, menacing circle around her. The rest of her body remained stock still. He loomed over her. Neck straining, she endeavored to maintain eye contact. Her stomach knotted. Breath caught in her throat at his smoldering, potent look.

Unable to handle it, but incapable of breaking the connection, Amelia nibbled her bottom lip. She'd been frozen to the bone since she stepped out of the shower earlier. Under his severe stare, his nearness, her body thawed. Their fronts touched enough to confirm there wasn't a banana in his pocket. He might look mad, but part of him was happy to see her.

She hadn't felt alive since her parents' death. Part of her died when they did. Each subsequent death of a loved one took its pound of flesh. With so many pieces gouged out, she figured she'd never truly live again.

Until now.

Staring into the abyss of Talon's midnight blue eyes was like being shaken awake from a nightmare. Amelia experienced a sudden acute awareness of the sun beating down, warm against her skin. The scent of freshly laid asphalt pricked her nose. Subtle nuances in the chirps of area birds she'd never noticed before became decipherable. Her heartbeat. Her every breath. Were absurd in their volume. Something about Talon brought her to life. And although undeniably attracted to him, she despised him for it. If she lived, the deaths of her family, and her friend, became real.

Her gaze fell to the ground. A long, thick finger under her chin forced her focus to return to him. Did no one respect boundaries anymore?

"First, you won't be driving with me," Talon's emphatic statement. "I'll drive, and you'll sit in the passenger seat. Second, I know being difficult is your specialty—milady—but you will allow this."

Amelia wanted to be offended, but she couldn't. Not with his cooler-than-ice breath distracting her. The minty-sweet aroma made listening nearly impossible. It wasn't like breath, as weird as that might sound. It reminded her of air rushing out of a stuffy room when someone opened a window. Or better yet, like if a person found themselves stuck in one of those As Seen on TV Space Bags when the vacuum hose sucks out the air. He seemed to draw on the air around him to speak rather than use his own breath. Crazy.

Figuring she looked like an idiot standing there reveling in his delicious breath, she forced herself to concentrate.

"Why does it matter who drives?" she asked, recalling his command. "If it makes you feel better you can drive my car."

Talon cocked a golden brow. "Are you hearing yourself? If I can drive your car, why can't I drive mine? Pretend we're in your car."

"Impossible," her dogged retort. "I can see out my windshield."

Fates! The mortal could try the patience of a Balance Deity. Neither supernatural nor mortal, Talon had encountered the beings responsible for maintaining balance in the universe a time or two.

Amelia's stubbornness could drive one of those beings to act outside themselves.

His first responsibility was her safety. Part of his protection detail included driving his vehicle. The windows might appear dark to her, but from inside they were clear. Special tint prevented the sun's rays from penetrating the glass, which would help on the off chance he found himself sans ring. Also, he didn't know how far into the transition sun sensitivity started. Amelia would need the tint as much as himself. In addition, the car's body was bulletproof.

Being a Royal Guardsman, he needed to plan ahead and assess possible danger. Guard against the unexpected. Quick on the heels of that thought came the real reason for his irritation. Amelia had left him standing outside. These mortals weren't big on manners. Their failure to invite him into the residence meant if anything supernatural or mortal threatened Amelia inside the home, he couldn't protect her. Compounding his agitation was his complete inability to control his responses to her.

Why couldn't he quit touching her? He thought he'd discovered the source of his unacceptable physical reaction to her. Through his discussion with Anton yesterday, he'd learned he sympathized with her plight. No one deserved to be objectified. He knew firsthand how deprivation of choice destroyed on a profound level.

The insight should have relieved the ache in his balls. Put the kibosh on his hardening by the second dick. It didn't. In fact, the peek-a-boo glimpses of plump brown ass cheek each time she took a step had him drill-bit hard. The strip of soft flesh visible between her short shorts and leather boots... Too. Much. He wanted to run his fingers through her hair. Caress her cheek.

Crush his lips to hers. Sit her on his car, spread those brown thighs, plow into—

Time to go. To deter further argument, he resorted to forbidden tactics. He wouldn't normally break protocol, but this fell under the guidelines of "protection at any cost." Given her advanced state of transition, it might not work. Her mind could be more supernatural than mortal.

Talon stooped to her eye level. Captured her gaze. Magnificent eyes glazed. She stared. Her pupils dilated. Pitching his voice low. Even. He changed her mind.

Chapter Thirteen

T alon put the car in gear and followed memorized directions to the castle. In the passenger seat, Amelia sat secure and tranquil. Hands followed in her lap. Still under compulsion. He couldn't believe what he'd done. Compelling the soon-to-be queen? Not okay. But the female's pertinacious attitude infuriated him.

Although the ring protected him, an existence worth of fear of sun exposure died hard. Being in daylight was uncomfortable. New. Combustion a too real a possibility. He hadn't wanted to stand outside arguing about driving. His vehicle was safer, plain and simple.

He adjusted his sunglasses. The quantity of time this wasteland spent drenched in sunlight astounded him. No vampire could thrive here. Talon couldn't wait to get the *Awakening* over with and leave. This place was unsuitable for—he glanced sideways at his hostage—a queen.

How was this fragile mortal destined to be the queen of such a vicious race of beings? Talon had a hard time justifying ending her life to save the supernatural. He chanced another brief glance at the delectable mortal in question. The rise and fall of her even breaths forced her breasts firm against her corset. One exaggerated inhale, and her swollen brown globes would pop out. Fuck!

He had to quit thinking this way about her. Until she completed the transition to immortal, she was his charge. Reservations about his role in her fate or not, death would come for her in one form or another. If she didn't transition, she would die a permanent death. Her ruined life would haunt him. Talon wouldn't permit her a true death. Amelia's health, safety, and continued existence were his personal onus. He would see to her every need, even those she had no knowledge of. First, he needed to squash his forbidden attraction. Her unreasonable attitude would repel the horniest male.

A loud clearing of his throat released her from compulsion.

Amelia scanned her surroundings. She ran a hand through her hair, tossing it over her shoulder. Brows furrowed, she patted the seatbelt secured across her chest. "How did—What—I-17 south—Did you put me in here?"

Talon would've laughed at her confusion if her heart hadn't accelerated. Her fear worried him. She could have a heart attack. Mortals often died from those. He hurried to allay her fear. "You entered of your own volition. Relax."

She didn't.

"What do you mean relax? You relax! Why did you beg to drive if you're not comfortable with it?"

Her astute observation surprised him. Yes, he knew how to drive, but it wasn't his preferred mode of transportation, nor had he practiced often. "What makes you think I'm uncomfortable?" From the corner of his eyes, he caught her gimlet stare.

"The way you're gripping the steering wheel." She inclined her head toward the object in question. "You look like a drowning man desperate to stay afloat on a cheerio."

Talon attempted to loosen his grip. Failed. An elderly woman driving a silver Buick chose that moment to slow down as he merged onto the I-10. He hated driving. Sublimating would be simpler. Of course, the point was moot. Mortals couldn't sublimate.

Dense waves of tension rushed through the vehicle's interior, interrupting Talon's ruminations. He became conscious of Amelia's shortened breaths. Her plummeting heart rate. Salty anxiety tickled his palate. Tempted his fangs to descend. She clung to the "Oh, shit!" bar. Unbidden, her thoughts penetrated his mind.

Oh, my God! He's crazy. He almost killed that poor old lady. Why did I let him drive? Must. Distract. Myself. Talk, or tuck 'n roll out this bitch.

A smile threatened to curve his lips. He held it at bay. While he despised driving, her safety wasn't ever in jeopardy. In normal circumstances, he preferred not to read people's minds. One assumed their psyches were private. Invading that privacy seemed wrong to him. But to protect Amelia, he'd do it. If anticipating motorists' actions through their thoughts didn't work, he had other tricks up his sleeves. Talon didn't want to expend energy using telekinesis to keep her inside the car. Thankfully, she decided to talk.

"So, why did you need me here?" she asked. "You seem to know where you're going."

Talon gazed at her. The way she clutched the handle, sitting ramrod straight and eyes glued to the road, was comical.

"Whoa! Eyes on the road, buddy," she shrieked. "That car's breaking! Keep those hands where I can see 'em. Ten and two. Ten and two."

Oh, my God. He's gonna kill me. I actually almost wet my pants.

Snickering at her absurd thoughts, he turned his attention to the road. "I need to get a gift for a friend," he said, creating the excuse on the fly. He couldn't tell her he needed her to enter a castle, which was hers, to set the magical veil. "I assumed you could help. You seem to know your way around shops."

Out of the corner of his eye, his gaze ran over her body from head to toe. Without conscience thought, he made a second sweep, lingering too long on the swell of her breasts. They were exceptional for her petite frame. On his third go-round, he saw her frown out the window as they merged onto Loop 202.

"What mall are we going to? Fashion Square or Arizona Mills?" she inquired. "You know we could've shopped online, right? That's where I get most of my stuff."

"Ah... yes, speaking of your 'stuff.' Do you always dress like a runway model prepared for winter in one-hundred-degree weather?"

Amelia snorted. "Look who's talking? Don't you know black attracts heat? I happen to have been taught to never step outside my door looking less than my best. And I'd rather be a supermodel dressed for winter than a pimp ring-wearing giant. All you're missing is a cane, goblet, and fur coat." She gave him a covert once over.

At least she thought it was covert. He saw it, and her little pink tongue snake out to lick her glossy lips. His erection stiffened so much that his stomach knotted in pain.

"And, FYI, what I wear, or don't wear, is none of your business," she finished her rant.

Mmm... Fiery.

Talon hadn't meant to offend her with his question, but now that he had... He wanted to press more of her buttons. This was the first time his inexperience with females benefitted him. The fear, confusion, and sweet arousal she vibrated might as well be an aphrodisiac. Smelled better than adrenaline-spiked blood. No good could come from these inappropriate desires.

Vampires suffered from overt, excessive sex drives. All their emotions were more intense, extreme. Talon possessed impenetrable control specific to royal guards. His libido hadn't ever ruled him. Until now.

This mortal is your future queen, not a viable choice for any sort of torrid encounter.

His brain understood that. His demon and dick didn't share the same sense of duty and honor. Even if she were an option, she wasn't. An eternalmate held no appeal to him. If it did, his choices were *rejuvenated* White-witches. No one else.

If you're so sure then why do you keep looking at her like she hung the stars and moon?

Shut the hell up!

Damn, he needed to refocus. He rarely paid attention to his demon's mutterings. In truth, he'd ignored it to such an extent its attempts at influence were sparse.

He glanced at Amelia. Why did she—something in her lap caught his eye.

"Hey! The speed limit's sixty-five, pervert! Watch the road."

Pervert? Talon shifted his gaze back to the freeway.

"God, didn't your mom teach you any manners?" Amelia groused.

What was she—

He glanced at the object in her lap again. The reason for her reaction occurred to him at once. He burst out laughing. "You're the pervert, naughty female," managed through spurts of laughter.

Her brows furrowed, and her nose crinkled in cute confusion.

He sobered enough to say—pointing to her lap, "I was looking at your keychain."

Deep rouge flooded her cheeks.

In a miniature rectangular plastic frame, a picture of a black-haired male with long sideburns and sky blue eyes. The man wore a black, three-piece zoot suit with a red and black striped tie and red fedora.

"Are you cheating on my cousin?" he asked amused.

"Uh...ew! No! That's my big brother, Evan, you freak."

"Pardon me, *signorina*, I did not notice all the family resemblance."

"Umm... it's called adoption," Amelia snapped. "Read a book or something."

Adopted? Shit! Just when he thought this mission couldn't get more complicated. Of course, she was comfortable in her mortal life. How had this tidbit escaped their research? Damn The Fates and their cryptic prophecy! The Fates, who his parents had infinite faith in, hadn't taken the slightest measure of care for their precious descendant. They expected him to tell her everything? This couldn't be happening.

"How long have you been adopted?" he asked, holding onto hope she'd at least known her biological parents.

"What?" her wry question. "All my life."

"Do you know anything about your birth parents?"

She scoffed. "What's it matter to you?"

"I'm curious." He floundered to think of a plausible excuse for his nosy request. "I've always wanted to meet someone adopted. Answer the question."

"How's it feel to want? I don't usually go around telling strangers my life story. And, FYI, adopted people don't like to pick at that wound too often."

"I'm a friend, not a stranger," he persisted.

The sooner she accepted that reality and stopped treating him like an enemy, the better. Like it or not, they'd be spending a significant portion of her life together for the next few weeks. Embracing that idea might make his eventual reveal a lot easier to handle.

"My birth mom was fifteen and had my skin color," she answered to his astonishment. "Some older pervert took advantage of her. She never held me but insisted my name be Amelia Marie—some crap about family tradition. The end. That quench your thirst, Mr. Phillips?"

"Mr. Phillips?"

"Stone Phillips," she explained, "former reporter... Dateline NBC?"

Whatever. He kept silent.

Amelia reached forward, turning on the radio. Electric guitar and a number of other instruments blared through the speakers. Some male sang of a living dead female. Yeah, way too close to home there. Forgetting to control his movements, Talon switched off the radio. He hoped she didn't notice the speed.

"Jeez!" She jumped and her heartbeat accelerated. "What's your problem? Got something against Rob Zombie or living dead girls in general?"

He wouldn't touch that with a ten-foot pole. "I don't like music."

"At all?"

"No. And that song is far too...spot on for this situation."

"What situation? Driving?" Her voice rose in disbelief.

Before he manufactured a good lie, the air between them filled with apprehension once more. Unable to pinpoint the reason or spot danger, Talon peeked in on Amelia's thoughts.

Where the fuck is he taking me? This isn't the mall and definitely doesn't look legal. I knew he was a criminal.

Talon could've laughed. How did she get criminal when she saw him? Taking a side street, he drove down a short gravel road. He parked outside a tall, whitewashed, stone boundary wall integrated with a wrought iron gate. His eyes landed on an industrial steel chain wrapped several times around the gate, locking it shut. Fuckin' Anton!

Why did he trust the fledgling? How were they supposed to get through? There was no key. Using his abilities was out. He looked at Amelia.

She'd seemed relaxed during the last leg of their journey. Now she sat board stiff. Hands gripping the edge of her seat. Gaze darted here, there, and everywhere. Sweat glistened along her hairline.

"Where are we?" she asked inflectionless.

A better male would relieve her anxiety. Maybe if she hadn't challenged him at every turn, he would've taken mercy on her. Since she hadn't...

"Don't worry. The less you know the better," he responded affecting a grim frown. He opened the door. "I'll be right back."

Amelia grabbed his arm before he got out. Her face paled. "I don't think you should do this. Take me home."

You can't be attracted to this girl, no matter how adorably gullible she is.

Careful of his strength, he removed her dainty hand from his arm and took it in his. He rubbed the back of her hand with his thumb, brought it to his mouth, and kissed her knuckles. Oh, how he wanted to nibble those long, slender fingers.

"I was being facetious," he admitted, loathe to relinquish her hand. He did. "You really think I'd bring you, or anyone, along while I committed a crime?"

Her features hardened. "I don't know you. For all I know, you could be a weekend serial killer."

"You think Walker would trust me with you if I were a killer?" Talon asked, getting out of the car. He leaned into the open door.

Amelia appeared to consider that. "I don't know. I love him, but he's not always the brightest star in the sky."

He didn't know which pissed him off more, the fact that she loved Walker or that Walker "The Dolt" would put her life in danger and she knew it. "Get out of the car, milady," he grumbled, shutting the door.

"You could say *please* you know," she said, getting out and slamming her door.

"Why? You show no overt familiarity with the term," he fired back.

As her servant, such insubordination was punishable by destruction, but she wasn't queen yet. Plus, he couldn't put a clamp on his anger, which he directed at her—for no good reason—and Anton. He glared at the locked gate.

Fucking brilliant, Anton, really, very helpful.

Now Amelia would surely believe this was some illegal operation.

She regarded him through narrow eyes. "What? No key, Mr. Serial Killer?"

"I forgot it. I'm going to scale the gate."

"And what am I supposed to do?" she asked. "Fry in the sun? Squeeze through the bars? I'm not that skinny."

"Is the sun bothering you?" he asked, alarm making his tone brusque. "You should have informed me immediately."

"Whoa! Settle down, hoss." Reaching into her handbag, she retrieved large black sunglasses and put them on. "These work wonders. And even if the sun bothered me, I wouldn't tell you. What're you, my dermatologist? How are we getting over this gate?"

Good question. Talon looked her up and down. Something told him she wouldn't be a fan of this next idea. "I'll carry you on my back." He knelt in front of her, gazed over his shoulder. "Hop on."

Amelia stared deadpan at him. "Oh, yeah? Just hop right up on your back?" She gibed. "While you, what? Scurry up the gate like an ant? Then toss me like a javelin off your back once we reach the top?" She pantomimed the action. "Now who's not hearing themselves talk?"

Why must everything be a fight with her?

"How do you propose you get over?"

Bending with measured grace, Amelia grasped the mid-thigh zipper of one boot. Slid it down the contours of her leg. Leather peeled away, exposing smooth brown skin. When finished, she started on the second.

Talon almost swallowed his tongue.

Chapter Fourteen

"What are you doing?" he asked, voice hoarse.

"Well, Spiderman, it would appear I have a gate to climb," she said, sitting on the ground. "And since these" — a hard tug freed the right boot — "are an almost two hundred dollar pair of Stella McCartney's" — another tug removed the left boot — "I'm doing this barefoot." She pulled off her stocking socks.

Talon arched a brow, surveying her actions. He appreciated a female unafraid to get her hands dirty. Quick on the heels of that thought came an even dirtier image: him buried to the hilt inside her. Beneath him, her dark red hair splayed across black silk sheets.

Stop it! He chastised himself.

Searching for a distraction, Talon found the perfect one on the outside of her right ankle.

"What's that?" He pointed to the artwork.

A white-eyed vampire fairy with a black rose crown of thorns dressed in a lacy Victorian gown. Blood welled from a crescent slash over its right breast. Several drops also trickled from her mouth. Underneath the fairy, black Old English read: Dead Inside.

Amelia twisted her leg, giving him a better look. "Wall suggested I get one. I got this after my parents died. Fits me perfectly."

Did it ever! "Kind of morbid, don't you think?"

Shaking her head, Amelia stood and dusted off her bottom. "Since you're the genius who forgot the key, you get to hold these." She shoved her boots into his chest. "You break... you buy. Let's get it movin'. I work tonight."

Thirty minutes later, Talon stood on the opposite side of the gate. Stubborn, difficult Amelia struggled up the gate on the other side.

He rolled his eyes. "Amelia, milady, let me help you."

Stepping onto where padlock met rusty, thick chain, she shook her head. "No. I almost got it." Her foot slipped, and she dropped to the ground. "See what you did?" she accused, getting up and wiping dirt off her hands. "Your talking made me slip. Shh!"

Of course, it did. She'd used a similar excuse when he looked at her, when he shifted from one foot to the other, and when he brushed dirt off his pants. Made sense that talking would do it, too.

"Let me give you a boost," Talon offered.

"No. You didn't need a boost."

"True, but I'm a foot and a half taller than you. Almost as tall as the gate."

"Shut up," she barked, placing her foot on the chain for leverage and pulling herself up. "You know, I used to have this best friend—Jon. He was so accident-prone. If there was a way to get hurt, he found it. He actually cut his hand off a few years ago." She hoisted herself to a bar at the top of the gate.

"Was it capable of being reattached?"

Damn, her determination was sexy.

"Yeah. Anyway, in eighth grade we went to Castles-n-Coasters." Noticing his confusion, she explained, "It's a place with rides and stuff. Kind of like a fair."

The explanation didn't help. What was a fair?

Oblivious to that she went on, "So, we're leaving, right? And we're allowed one last ride. Me and my friend Melody are in line for a roller coaster. He wants to shorty cut so he can go on with us. But there's this red spiked fence between us and him. So, he climbs the fence, goes to jump over, and... BAM! One of the spikes goes right through his shoe. Ripped his heel totally open to the bone. Blood. Everywhere."

Finally, she hopped down, on his side of the gate. "Gross, huh?"

The victorious smile she bestowed upon him would've brought weaker males to their knees.

He wanted to kiss that smile from her face. Instead, he handed her her boots. Waited while she put them on.

"Does he still get hurt all the time?"

Amelia's smile faltered. "No. He's dead," she said with indifference that didn't fool him.

He saw the light in her eyes fade as she uttered the words. This person had clearly meant a lot to her.

"I'm sorry."

"Whatever. It's not your fault."

On impulse, Talon reached to comfort her as they walked along the rocky trail. She sidestepped his gesture. His arm fell to his side.

Smooth...

They trekked along in silence. Whitewashed stones, like the ones the wall was made of, lined their way. Prickly pear, Ocotillo, Saguaro, and cacti of all variations surrounded them.

"So, how come you weren't at the Palmer family reunion last year?" Amelia asked, breaking the silence.

Shit! He hadn't thought that far ahead. Compelling the Palmers had gone so well he hadn't considered creating more backstory. On-the-spot story fabrication went beyond his capabilities. He compelled. Because of her advanced state of transition, compelling her once had been hard enough. Twice, impossible. *Fuuuck!*

"So... is this as hot as it gets here?" he asked, evasive on purpose.

In all honesty he couldn't feel the heat. Vampires were a homeothermic race—maintained a constant body temperature no matter what the ambient temperature.

"What do you care?" Amelia glanced at him. "It's not like you've broken a sweat. You're not even breathing hard. Now, answer the question."

Damn, relentless.

"I was in the middle of finals," he lied.

"What college has finals in July?" She turned to him again. Lowering her sunglasses, she threw him a skeptical glare. Replacing them, she kept moving. "And what are you doing? Getting a PhD in everything?"

"What's that supposed to mean?"

Amelia paused, giving him a once over, then continued. "What are you—twenty-six? Twenty-seven?"

Ouch!

Why did she love to rile him? *Natural-born* vampires retained their youthful appearance for eternity. He was supposed to be, if nothing else, appealing to mortals. His innate charm worked on Cicely yesterday, but Amelia seemed immune to him. Shouldn't bother him, but it did. He wanted to set her straight. Couldn't. Shouting he looked good for a one hundred and twenty-year-old would do more harm than good.

Using the immortal age as a marker, he answered, unamused, "I'm twenty-one. Thanks."

"Really?" she asked amazed.

Good thing he didn't offend easily, or this conversation would've bruised his ego.

Talon watched Amelia's awed expression as she took in the scenery. An impressive cactus garden filled with tall Saguaro cacti surrounded them. Those would come in handy for protection after the *Awakening*. Not that they would spend much time here. His instructions were to get her to Italy as soon as supernaturally possible once she rose as queen.

Watching her careful steps around rocks and small Notocacti, hair blowing in the breeze, guilt assailed him. Would she hate him for deceiving her? For his part in taking her life? He couldn't bear it. And he saw her preparing to ask more deception-breeding questions. He needed to shift the focus pronto.

"I hear you sing," he said, recalling a bit of information Walker mentioned yesterday.

Amelia's answering glare, lethal. "Umm... No. You hear wrong."

Note to self: never mention singing again.

"Oh. Well, you draw, right? Wall showed me a picture you drew him a few years back. A rose or something?"

Another murderous look. "What? Are you writing a book about me or something?"

"Why don't *you* tell me something about yourself then?"

Amelia was quiet so long he didn't think she would answer.

"Tell *me* about you," she retorted.

He thought wrong.

"Since when do Nebraskans have accents? And how are you related to Wall? Are you close to your parents? What about siblings? How many you got?"

Oookay... Operation getting-to-know-you aborted.

"That's a lot of questions."

"Annoying, huh?" she asked, flashing him a snotty smile.

What a firecracker.

Again, he'd inadvertently set her off, which he didn't mind one iota. Amelia angry equaled Amelia sexy.

"My mother is Greek, and we lived in Italy for a time while I was growing up; the accent's a combination of both," he lied, sort of. She seemed to buy it.

The trick to lying seemed to be sprinkling it with elements of truth. His mother was Greek. They lived in Italy. All he left out was his brother and Romanian father.

"I lived in Nebraska only after I met my father," he explained, using the lie fashioned for the Palmers. "As for my relation to Wall...? My father Harold is the estranged second cousin of Wall's mother, although she calls him her uncle."

That pacified her for a while. Until...

"What about siblings?" she asked.

That question resurrected feelings better left dead. Did he have a brother? Yes. Did he dare mention the traitor? No. Logically, he understood Emilio was now the enemy, but the fledgling in him wanted to be close to his brother. He also wished Emilio had the predestined future to save them all.

"No siblings. I'm an only child."

Amelia stopped dead in her tracks. He allowed her to pull him to a stop. Mouth agape, she lifted her sunglasses and pointed straight ahead.

"Tovrea Castle at Carraro Heights," she said, breathless.

He followed her gaze, zeroed in on the three tiered, cream-colored castle with cupola on top ringed by more cacti. Arched windows dotted each tier—those would need blackout curtains ASAP.

"You know this place?"

"Uh... yeah! I can't believe I didn't realize this was where we were. I've only ever seen it from the freeway. Wow!" She stared impressed momentarily then, turned on Talon. Her features pinched. "How do *you* know this place? Why are we here?"

Because I'm a special breed of vampire sentinel who serves the vampire royalty who rule all supernatural, which—surprise—happens to be you in a little over a month and a half. I was created specifically to protect and guide you through the transition from mortal to immortal. Sadly, I couldn't stay with your boyfriend or his family because I've been starved of mortal blood. I was ready to gorge myself on them like a wino trapped in a liquor store. So, I have to stay here. Yeah, somehow, he didn't see that explanation going over well, so instead...

"A friend of mine's family bought it. I'm going to be staying here." He was getting good at lying.

The blank stare she pegged him with said she thought otherwise. "You're staying here?" Amelia asked in flat incredulity. "In a friggin' castle?"

"What? You don't believe me?"

She shook her head.

Good, you shouldn't.

"C'mon." He grabbed her hand. "Let me show you my crib."

Anton used that word all the time; Talon figured it applied here.

Upon approaching the front door, Talon paused, expanding his senses. Something wasn't right.

"You're really breaking in here, aren't you?" Amelia accused as he pushed her behind him. Her tone screamed she knew she'd been lied to.

She didn't know the half of it. If she did, she'd shit a brick. More than that, she never would've come here with him in the first place.

He took his keys from his pocket. Inserted a key in the lock. Careful not to let Amelia—who watched him like a junior detective—see, he unlocked the door with his mind.

Since vampires were able to enter vacant residences without invitation, Talon crossed the threshold with no problem. His unease tripled.

"Stay. Here." He emphasized each word. Wouldn't surprise him if she ignored his edict in favor of being difficult. Through clenched teeth, he reiterated, "Do not leave this spot until I instruct you. No matter what you hear. Understand?"

She nodded. Talon stalked into the castle.

Boots clomped on dark maple hardwood floors. Let whatever intruder hear him. Know death stalked them. Once out of Amelia's sight, he conjured his dagger and silver knuckles. Amelia considered his fingerless gloves a fashion faux pas, but he wore them for moments such as this. Silver burned, scarred vampire skin where nothing else could. Killed some supernatural. His gloves protected his skin. The trespassers wouldn't be as lucky.

Back pressed against the parlor wall, he sidestepped toward a hallway. Amelia vibrated fear so strong the acidic taste stung his tongue from here. She'd referred to him as the Big Bad Wolf in her mind when he'd commanded her to stay. The last thing he wanted was to scare her and lose ground. He'd worry about that later. Something was in the house.

Talon moved with predatory stealth through the front room. The interior was bare except for heavy red velvet drapes hung over the windows outlining the room's walls. A large, familiar crate sat in a far corner. Two fireplaces were spread several feet apart, one on each side of the room.

On closer inspection, he realized the curtains were made of the royal servants' fabric: Red on the side facing him, black on the other. Royal servants wore cloaks of this material. The gold royal seal, a tilde, was embroidered on the red side. VR wore similar cloaks of gold and black. The material was impenetrable. Seems Anton wasn't completely useless. Maybe some—

Another male's thoughts interrupted Talon's musings. He whirled around, dagger at the ready.

"Hey, now."

The voice surprised him. "Gawain?"

Gawain Simeonescu Sebastian's second-in-command, stepped from behind a pillar leading down a long dark hall. Six-five with unkempt black hair, the muscle bound vampire fancied himself a playboy. Being out of commission so long, he'd found television and women. All women.

Unlike Sebastian who clung to the days of old, Gawain acclimated to modern times well. It was why he'd been chosen as Talon's mentor. Gawain's presence wasn't a good thing. Either his father didn't trust his ability, or more than Calin lied in wait for the *Awakening*.

"Man, they might as well live on the sun here. What vamp in their right mind would live in Arizona? What is there—seven minutes of night here? For those of us without a nifty ring, shit gets boring," Gawain rambled, lowering the hood of his red cloak yet remaining in the shadows.

"What are you doing here?" Talon demanded. His dagger dematerialized. "I could have destroyed you."

"Hey." Gawain raised his hands in surrender. "Cool out. Heard you weren't staying with the mortals anymore; thought you might like a house guest."

Yeah, right.

"What'd my father promise you?" He really didn't have time for this shit. Amelia was probably having a panic attack outside.

"Nothing. I wanted to come. Maybe we could have a housewarming party?" Gawain suggested. "You know, invite some snacks and libations over." He winked an aquamarine eye and clucked his tongue. "Get it."

Talon glared.

"C'mon, I got all this vamp love to give. These sun monsters need this vamp game."

"You don't have game."

"I've got sixteen hundred years of game. I'm game personi-fied. When other Beings spit game, they're spittin' little pieces of me."

Talon folded his arms over his chest. "You can't be here; Amelia's outside."

Donning his hood, Gawain peeked around the corner, stole a glimpse of Amelia. He straightened and stared at Talon, face dead serious. "That's the heiress?"

He nodded.

"Times... they are a-changin." Gawain smirked wickedly. "If she wasn't royalty me and her would be making a vamp swirl cone. I envy whoever the book prophesies to be her eternal-mate. Damn... She's small. What I call a flipper. The positions I'd—"

Talon struck, pinning Gawain against the wall. His sil-ver-knuckled left hand, fisted, dangerously close to Gawain's cheek. His fangs elongated.

"Speak of her that way again, and I'll chop you in such small pieces it'll take a century for you to reassemble yourself. And I'll start with your dick."

"Talon!" Amelia called. "FYI, chocolate melts in the sun."

He released Gawain, silver knuckles disappeared.

"Better let her in. I'd hate to see her melt." He grinned. "At least, not outside anyway," Gawain said, heedless of Talon's threat.

Talon ground his teeth but otherwise ignored Gawain's lewd comment. "You need to leave."

"Nah... I'll go hide in a closet or something. Once she steps inside, the veil's activated, and no supernatural can enter with-out her invitation."

Exactly why he wanted him to leave.

Gawain clapped him on the shoulder. "It'll be fun. We can stay up all day and tell human stories," he said in a spooky voice.

Talon wanted to throw the Hugh Hefner of vampires out and let the sun have at him. But that would only incur the wrath of The Fates and his father. He glowered at him.

"C'mon, Tal, this is your game. I'm just warming the bench. You need me? I'll suit up. Otherwise, I'm on vacay."

Yeah, he fully intended to keep Gawain on the bench, too. He didn't need help. With a slight bow of his head, Gawain sublimated into aquamarine droplets of mist and drifted down the hall.

"Amelia!" Talon yelled. "Come in."

F inally! Sheesh. Amelia lifted her sunglasses, resting them on top of her head. She approached the double doors of the... castle. Her mind stumbled on the word. Couldn't help it. Who lived in a frickin' castle?

The oddest sensation, like walking through Jell-O or foam, overwhelmed her as she crossed the threshold. Hmm... Maybe she was suffering from heatstroke. Climbing that fence took forever. At least she proved to Conan the Quiz Master she could do it. His me-big-strong-man-you-fragile-lady act convinced her of his relation to—

Whoa! She tripped.

Strong, corded muscular arms encircled her waist before she and the hardwood floor made out.

"You alright?"

No. The vibration of his sinful voice did funny things to her lady parts. The spark of desire that hit her threatened to set her on fire. Oh, and his smell. She considered herself an expert on man smells and cologne. That's why Wall's penchant for bathing in Axe Body Spray infuriated her. Talon didn't wear cologne. Camping and being skinned alive were equal forms of torture in her book, but Talon smelled like the woods after it rained. Natural. Earthy.

"Did you hurt something?" Talon asked.

Damn, his voice! It so didn't help keep her from wanting to rub against him like a human scratching post. She righted herself quickly. None of that!

"Thanks," she muttered. "You really plan on staying here?" Gazing around, she searched for a distraction.

She crossed the room to inspect some fantastic burgundy drapes hung from golden, wrought-iron, medieval hook curtain rods. The click of her heels on the floor echoed through the room. She ran her hands down the luxurious, soft material. An almost 3-D gold tilde was embroidered in the center of each curtain. Had every window been covered and the doors closed, it would've been pitch black in here.

"Who did this?"

"I told you, my friend's allowing me to stay here. His family owns it. Must be theirs."

Wow, some friend. Made her friends look pretty shabby.

She faced him. "It's empty in here? Does that crate" — she pointed to the corner — "have magical pop-up furniture in it?"

With burning eyes and a confident lope, Talon neared her. The curtain end she'd been admiring slipped through her fingers as their gazes met. Her insides melted like butter at the needful look in his midnight blue eyes. He had a strange effect on her. It'd be so easy to forget everything and get lost in him.

You are such a bitch. He is your boyfriend's cousin.

That snapped her out of her fantasy.

"What are you looking at?"

He shook his head. "I have a proposition for you."

Why did that sound naughty? His gruff bass did that to even the most innocent words. Something about the way he continued to stare unblinking made it sound dirtier.

"What," she croaked. Clearing her throat, she tried again, "What would that be?"

His grin made her heart flutter. He should do that more.

"Walker tells me you're a champion shopper?" He cocked an eyebrow. "Is that true, or another thing I got wrong?"

Not trusting her voice, she rolled her eyes and nodded.

"Good. What would you say if I asked you to decorate for me?"

"I'd say it'd cost a lot of money. This place is frickin' huge. I don't even want to guess how many rooms there are. And that's not including bathrooms and the kitchen. I don't even know what to call this room," she said, waving a hand encompassing the space.

"What if there was a liquid budget? Could you do something with that?"

Liquid budget! If her mother were alive she would've had a stroke. Liquid budget? Who'd he think he was? Donald Trump?

"Shut up! I think the sun's getting to you," she joked. "It would cost thousands to decorate this place. And when I shop, I do it big. No Target. No Wal-Mart."

Talon pulled his wallet out of his back pocket. The four items he retrieved were faint-worthy.

Black American Express card.

Black Visa *and* Mastercard.

And...

A fat wad of hundred dollar bills.

Amelia was far from a gold digger. She might have designer things, but that came from her spoiling herself. She didn't expect, or think, others should spend money on her. To her, the heart of a person mattered more than the outside. Loving a poor man was as easy as loving a rich man. That being said...

This is gonna be fun.

Chapter Fifteen

Amelia glanced at the enormous black and white clock hanging above the box office door. Almost one thirty in the morning. She wiped sweat from her brow with her forearm, careful not to get any oil from her hand on her face. The popper needed *a little* elbow grease, her ass!

"Damn it!" she muttered.

She scrubbed the inside of the kettle. Bad idea, letting everybody leave early. She'd underestimated how disgusting the popper could be. A can and a half of Easy-Off, two cups of scalding hot water, and a massive amount of elbow grease later, and the popper finally looked capable of popping edible popcorn again.

Amelia released a loud breath, stood on her tiptoes, and inspected the inside of the popper. Well... it was as clean as it was going to get, and way better than anybody else would do. Time to bounce.

First, to put the cleaning supplies away. She opened the storeroom door. Froze. The back door to the alley stood wide open. Sheesh! Tigger sure didn't waste any time leaving.

Breaking out of her momentary shock, she placed the supplies on the rack to the right of the entrance. She crossed the room to close the door. Halfway there, chills skated down her spine. Amelia literally froze. Like left foot stuck in mid-step, froze. Her heart hammered her sternum. There'd been no noise. No telltale signs. But something was out there. She felt it.

Great!

Her second B-movie moment in less than twenty-four hours. Earlier with Talon she'd been scared shitless standing outside while he went all German Shepard sniffing out crime inside the castle. Now she was the stupid girl who stood in front of an open door, knowing danger lurked. She so wouldn't be that girl. Breaking her fear-induced paralysis, Amelia hauled ass to the door, slammed and locked it.

If Jack the Ripper wanted to kill her, he'd have to do it through a locked door.

Get through that, *Jason*.

As she turned to head into the lobby a frightening thought occurred to her. She gazed left, up the flight of stairs leading to the managers' office. The four steps to the landing were shrouded in complete darkness.

What if someone's up there?

Her breath caught in her throat. Oh, hell no! This shit was way too *Nightmare on Elm Street* for her tastes. Amelia darted through the door. Went behind the deserted concession stand, grabbed her Louis Vuitton—right, like she'd let Chucky get her Louis...*puh-lease*. She got a cup of ice for her teeth, set the alarm, and exited the main doors all in the span of a heartbeat.

Once in the safety of—well, shit, outside wasn't much safer, but at least she had her car to hide in if push came to shove.

Damn. Sweat trickled behind her ear. Either it was still hot, or she was hot flashing. Whatever. Beggars can't be choosers. At least she wasn't inside with a murderer.

She double-checked the theater doors. Locked. With no moon and all the other businesses in the strip mall closed, it would've been pitch black if not for sparse streetlights. Making matters worse, her Mustang was parked as far as possible from the theater. Nice.

Of all the nights to park in BFE...

What'd they say in self-defense class? Oh, yeah. Getting her keys out of her purse, she found her car key. Wedged it sharp point out between two fingers, prepared to use it as a weapon.

She crossed the parking lot. Every few steps, she checked behind herself.

Nearing her car, she squinted. Tilted her head side to side. Had it always been that low to the ground? She figured out the problem as she closed in. Oh, perrrfect! Yeah, this was straight up scary movie shit. How the hell did all four tires go—

Psst!

Amelia spun around. No one was there. Ho-ly crap monkeys! This night got scarier and scarier by the minute. She hadn't heard any footsteps, but somebody was behind her. Turning back around, she quickened her pace. No way on Earth would she turn around again.

It might be a bitch move, but what'd she care? Those stupid people on the news who said you should face your attacker weren't her.

Psst...

Never in a million years did she think someone potty trained could be scared enough to piss their pants. She was wrong. That seemed a very real possibility at the moment. The person was closer now. She sensed it. Fine hairs on the nape of her neck and arms rose.

Staring into her driver-side window—keys still in hand, any thoughts of them being a useful weapon abandoned—she saw only her own reflection. God, how stupid was she, whoever thought of keys as a weapon? There were no stories of someone being murdered by a key.

Psst...

She jumped.

Whoever it was was right behind her. Before she could stop herself, she turned.

Great, now she'd see death coming. Exactly what she didn't want—terrific. Her heart stuttered, then took off like wings of a bird.

"Hey, why are you ignoring me?" the night stalker asked in a slight whisper.

About twenty blinks and seventy hard swallows later, she recovered enough to speak. "Wh-what the hell are you doing here?"

"Nice to see you too, Duchess." Calin ran his fingers through his hair.

He looked amazing. His bluish-green eyes were bright in the darkness. The night seemed made for him. It embraced him. Amelia bit her bottom lip. If this wasn't so awkward and scary, he'd be sexy as hell in his khaki shorts and black muscle shirt. Against his pale skin, the shirt accentuated his rippled biceps and delectable, muscled pectorals.

"Why are you here this late?" she asked, eyes narrowed on him.

He grinned his infamous crooked grin. "My sister and I are staying at the Red Roof Inn behind the theater."

Sounded reasonable. They were at the theater a lot. Still didn't explain him being here now!

"Why are you out here? The theater's closed."

Calin gave her a flat stare. "I know. I couldn't sleep, so I decided to take a walk. When I saw you, I came over to say hi." He tilted his head toward her Mustang. "You know... I heard these ride better on inflated tires."

Amelia glared. "Ha, ha, ha. Aren't you a damn comedian. You should be a clown."

He shrugged, a casual ripple of muscles. "I know. How're you getting home?"

She scanned the deserted lot. This situation couldn't be any more inappropriate. Walker would have a conniption if he knew she was with Calin—alone. The one guy he specifically asked her not to see. Although, technically, she hadn't promised... She'd avoided making that vow because some part of her, on some level, suspected she couldn't keep it. Compounding her guilt, she wrestled with impure thoughts about the clear, impressive bulge in his khakis.

Stop! Focus, girl. You have a boyfriend.

"I guess I'll call my boyfriend," she answered. I guess? Could she be more suggestive? Hopefully, he didn't catch it. She took her phone out of her purse.

"You guess?" He smirked.

Dammit, he caught it.

"Why don't you come back to the hotel with me? I have a car. I'll get my keys and take you home," Calin offered.

Fate must be playing a cruel joke. Why did this guy have such an effect on her? It should be easy to stay away from him. But she did need a ride…

"I can't," she declined, knowing it was for the best. "We'd have to walk there, and the killer could be on the loose."

Calin started to object. She shushed him with a raised finger.

"Going with you would be like volunteering to be the new abduction story of the week. And I don't want to be abducted in my work clothes."

Calin laughed. "You are so adorable—you know that?"

Amelia's mind blanked. Every objection she had went right out the window, along with Walker's request.

After a pause, she said, "Okay, let's go. Hands where I can see 'em at all times—got that?"

Calin nodded stiffly.

She continued her rant, "And if there is a killer… I'll push you into him to save myself. We clear?"

"Crystal. You don't have to worry about serial killers with me," he assured, turning towards the road. "Come on."

I'm so gonna regret this.

Amelia clutched her purse like a life vest. She was the stupid girl who fell for a line and then ended up a statistic on the news. Great.

From the corner of her eye, she gazed at Calin. God, he was tall. Not Talon tall, but still tall.

"So, what makes you tougher than a murderer?" she asked, recalling his previous statement. "Are you serial killer kryptonite?"

Calin glanced at her. Their gazes met. Her heartbeat skyrocketed.

He nudged her playfully with his elbow. "I make you nervous." He smiled.

An eighteen-wheeler passed on her side of the sidewalk. Her ponytail blew into her face. In the time it took her to brush her hair out of her eyes, Calin wrapped a strong arm around her waist. Lifting her off her feet, he traded places with her. He now walked on the outside closest to the road and she on the inside.

She flinched away. He couldn't touch her. When he touched her, her body reacted in unacceptable ways.

"You agitate me," Amelia retorted. "I have a boyfriend; he makes me nervous."

Calin snorted, nodding. Unconvinced.

"And don't avoid my question. What do you got—a bullet-proof ass?"

"Nah, trust me, I'm the scariest thing out here tonight."

Amelia laughed. "Oh, really? And why is that?"

"I'm a vampire," he stated matter-of-factly.

Amelia waited for him to laugh.

He didn't.

Fantastic! A walk with a lunatic—she knew he had to have a flaw. She hoped he just had a weird sense of humor.

"*Right...* and I'm the artist formally known as Prince." She chuckled.

Calin stopped walking. Out of curiosity, Amelia did, too. He placed his hands on her shoulders, turned her toward him. She gazed into his turquoise eyes, and was lost.

She should look away, she wanted to, but couldn't. *Please don't kiss me. Please don't kiss me.* He leaned in. Amelia forgot how to breathe. With his forefinger and middle finger, he tilted her chin up.

Please kiss me. Please kiss me.

His lips slid into a sexy grin. "Hmm... I don't know. Prince is short but not your type of short" — turning her face side to side — "and you don't wear enough makeup."

He dropped his fingers and started walking again. Amelia stood immobilized and breathless for a couple seconds before following him.

Calin looked over at her. "Speaking of Prince, what type of music do you like? You sing, play any instruments?"

"No," Amelia answered fast, too fast.

She might believe they had some cosmic connection, but she didn't talk about her reasons for not singing. Not with anyone.

Calin cocked an eyebrow.

She rolled her eyes. "I used to sing, but not anymore. Don't ask why."

A flash of her parents' funeral tore through Amelia's mind, twisted her heart. The last time she'd sang. After that, she vowed never to sing again. Tears burned behind her eyes. A lump clogged her throat. She had no interest in opening that can of worms. Thankfully, Calin didn't ask her anymore about it.

They were near the hotel parking lot the next time she spoke. "So, why are you guys staying in a hotel?"

"Like I said the other day, we're not from here. I'd planned to go to Vegas, but then Bianca wanted to come, so I picked Arizona instead. We live in Romania so..."

"You chose Hell as a vacation spot? You know California has Disneyland, right?" Amelia laughed. "Wow, Romania. What do you do there?"

"Nothing. I don't work I'm... independently wealthy."

"Gee, must be nice," she mumbled. Of all the people she could meet, she'd managed to stumble into two of the richest. What were the odds? She should buy a lottery ticket. "You had to study or something. Your English is excellent."

"I have a master's in philosophy. But I learned English from traveling," Calin answered, leading her through the front lobby and onto an elevator. He pressed number four.

They rode in silence until nerves got the best of her. "Don't you want to know about me?"

He studied her with open interest. She felt it as if he'd actually touched her. "I'm sure you'll tell me what you want me to know."

Amelia regarded him with suspicion. People weren't this cool. They poked and prodded, butted their noses in where they didn't belong. Proof apparent by the grilling she received from Talon. However, when she stared into Calin's eyes she saw sincerity.

The elevator stopped on the fourth floor. She followed Calin down a dimly lit corridor to room 422.

Butterfly wings fluttered inside her stomach as Calin opened the door and went in. She stayed in the doorway.

Calin flipped on the lights.

Normal hotel room setup. Dressers, huge, outdated TV, king-size bed with ugly pastel comforter. A desk and chair were set in a corner. Yep, a regular hotel room, all except for the gargantuan man turning it into a shoe box. The guy might as well have been playing house in a cardboard box. Calin had a definite presence. He overwhelmed any room he entered.

Bending down, Calin pulled a black duffel bag from under the bed.

Oh, crap.

What if he was a mobster and that was where he kept his weapons? Why had she come here? She didn't want to be rubbed out, or sleep with the fishes, or whatever it was called. Why was she so stupid for him? For God's sake, he thought he was a vampire. She could be standing at the door of a deranged killer with a vampire fetish.

Calin turned the full force of those turquoise eyes on her.

Gee Willikers! He was potent. Big, strong, solid, and the way he looked at her—pure possession. He touched without permission. Flirted without shame. Calin consumed a person—her. Yet, he had an untamed, lethal, quality about him. Something dark seethed just below the surface. When he said he was the scariest thing outside, part of her believed him.

He smiled. "I won't bite."

Yeah, but she wanted him to. Hard.

Shut up! You have a boyfriend, you dirty whore.

Damn her! No, damn him and all his hotness. She wouldn't take one step into that room.

His smile widened, exposing a set of blindingly white teeth. "Amelia," he pleaded, "come sit down, please. I've got to find my keys. I promise my hands will always be in view," he said, holding his hands up to stress his point.

Smooth talking SOB. He probably used that line to lure all the girls into his web. If he thought she'd buy into it he was...

Right.

Amelia stepped into the room with false confidence. How could she be confident when the air between them was rife with better left unnamed tension? She felt like Little Red Riding Hood locked in a cabin with a wolf in grandmother's clothing.

He might have gotten her in the room, but she wouldn't sit anywhere. She meandered around while Calin continued searching for his keys.

On the desk sat the most intricate, detailed, wax figure she'd ever seen. She'd know the orange and pink fur, those googly eyes, and bushy black brows anywhere. Picking it up, she turned to Calin. "This is Animal, right? From the Muppets?"

Rifling through his bag, he answered without looking at her, "Umm... yeah. Why?"

Umm... yeah? Calin didn't make such unsure statements. She hadn't known him long, but she knew that. She'd bet her life on it.

"Animal's my favorite Muppet. Where'd you get it?"

That got his attention. He turned, scratching his whiskered chin. "I made it."

God, what couldn't this guy do?

"You should make me one," she joked.

"Maybe," he answered, returning to his search.

Since he didn't seem comfortable, she decided to drop the topic. She returned the figurine to the desk.

He must have sensed her discomfort because he said, "Do you really think I'm some murderer?"

Yes.

"I don't know. If you are, it serves me right." She shrugged. "I've already put myself in quite the fucked up position."

Calin zipped his duffel bag and shoved it back under the bed. "You're not afraid of dying?"

Whoa! Out of left field much? What a great way to put a guest at ease when they already thought you were a murderer. He needed serious lessons in being a good host. Her heart kicked up a notch.

Play it cool.

If he was a killer, he probably got off on fear. She wouldn't give him that.

She responded with nonchalance. "Life and death are..." She searched for a good word. "Unappealing to me." Not the best word, but whatever. Better than saying what she really felt: Both life and death frightened her. "Everything that lives dies," she went on, "we all expire. What about you?"

She didn't know why she asked. Even if he said yes, he needn't worry about her killing him. He outweighed her by well over a hundred pounds of solid muscle. Looking around, she wandered to the vanity area. When Calin didn't answer she glanced over her shoulder.

He shook his head in answer to her question.

Turning, a black guitar case under the long white counter caught her eye.

"Trust me, Amelia, there are things more worrisome than life or death," Calin said as if he knew something she didn't. "And as far as I know, there's no expiration date stamped on your butt." He snickered.

Amelia bent toward the case, stopped before touching it. Was this a regular guitar case or some secret weapons holder made to fool people? Hmm...

"Well, I'm very afraid of death," she admitted absently, absorbed in her speculations. "How about I bend over and you tell me when I expire." She looked at him, mortified. Wishing she could recall the words.

Calin's uproarious laughter filled the room.

She had to sidetrack him, quick. She didn't want some strange guy, who may or may not be a murderer, thinking about her booty. Inspiration struck; this would kill two birds with one stone.

Pointing to the guitar case, she asked, "Do you play?"

Calin shrugged. "Kind of. I'm self-taught. Gives me something to do when I'm alone—which was all the time until recently."

How sad. How in the world could Calin be alone? Women at the theater stayed tongue-tied near him. Even she had problems keeping it together. Hard to believe he wasn't given that same treatment everywhere. She wouldn't have believed him if not for the look in his eyes. Amelia recognized it. He was lonely. Maybe that was what drew her to him. Not sexual interest, but a kindred spirit vibe.

With the grace of a hunting panther, Calin advanced on her. Got so close she felt his strange tropical breath on her face. The way he sized her up, she thought he might kiss her. His gaze burned, warmed her insides.

After a minute, he bent down, undid the clasps on his guitar case, and lifted out an acoustic guitar with flames engraved on it. He moved the desk chair, set it facing the end of the bed. He studied her as if searching for something. Long seconds passed.

"Sit," he said finally, pointing to the end of the bed.

Another twinge of fear shot from the base of her neck to the end of her tailbone. This fear wasn't what she'd felt outside the theater. This fear made her take the six or seven nervous steps to the bed and sit. This type of apprehension was what a person felt when someone confided in them, and they worried they weren't worthy of such trust.

She wanted, more than anything, to be what he needed right now.

Locking eyes with her, he cleared his throat. "I've never played for anyone before. If it sucks... just... plug your ears or something. I'll get the hint."

She didn't know what to say. It's not like she'd really plug her ears. Yeah, she could be mean sometimes, but not ruthless.

Amelia nodded. Under normal circumstances, she would've made some sort of sarcastic joke, but Calin seemed nervous. Cool and confident, arrogant even, since they'd met, this vulnerability shook her. She braced herself for what was to come.

He strummed the first chords. They sounded vaguely familiar. Calin played beautifully. He even added a few embellishments. He gazed at her, smiled a bashful smile, then...

Sang a perfect rendition of Gavin Degraw's "Follow Through," and stole her heart.

Chapter Sixteen

Calin parked his black Phantom in the Red Roof Inn parking lot a little after four a.m. What to do with Amelia's car? She didn't work in a rough neighborhood, but still. He didn't want her to come for it and—

Stop!

What the fuck was he thinking? He'd flattened those damn tires for a reason. Now, he worried about what happened to the car? Or rather, how she'd respond to possible vandalism. Oh, he was fuckin' slippin'.

He got out of the car. Cleaning up after Bianca's temper tantrum cost him major ground. Even without bodies to dispose of, because Bianca fed like all soulless hybrids—drained and consumed her victims' remains—he'd been forced to lay a false trail for law enforcement. He didn't mind killing a few mortals to implant suspicion of a mortal serial killer. What Calin minded? The advantage he'd forfeited due to his distraction. He smelled it, *him*.

The Vampire Guardsman.

No amount of popcorn or cleaner masked the caustic icy forest in winter scent. She reeked of the asshole guardsman. Calin didn't like that. He glanced in the general direction of the theater.

Let her car sit there.

He glanced right, left. No one watched him. Murmuring an enchantment, he cast a disguise spell. To would-be vandals, larcenists, and other criminals, his Rolls Royce would appear to be a POS. That spell worked better than any mortal alarm system and mirrored the concealment spell he used to contain Bianca. He plodded toward his room.

He'd staged the entire night to get close to Amelia. Blinking into the kitchen/storeroom had been child's play. He had only to visualize the place he wanted to go, and he was there. His senses ensured he never blinked into an occupied room. Calin had watched Amelia for several minutes from the storeroom. When she made to enter he'd opened the door and blinked himself outside. She'd been afraid. Fear motivated. Caused even the most cautious to make irrational decisions. Amelia acted no different.

By the time he approached her outside, she'd been scared enough to agree to anything. Inability to cast a reflection, a trait inherited from his mother, added a nice surprise element. Their walk provided the perfect opportunity to drop the vampire bomb on her. And he'd dropped the ball. He'd alluded to it, started, then crapped out, and couldn't begin to explain why. His intentions and his mouth wouldn't synchronize.

Maybe on a subconscious level, he didn't think it was the right time. This had been their first time completely alone. Considering the unpredictable nature of mortals, news of that magnitude might have caused her to jump out into traffic. He could've caught her, but still. Plus, she looked radiant under the night sky. Had she not been wearing the hideous uniform; she would've been mind-frazzling. If his behavior in his hotel room qualified as an indicator, then she did frazzle his mind.

He never played guitar in front of others. And singing? No question about it. As a young man, his father would've bludgeoned him to death for such a display. French men might be known for their passion, but whoever said that hadn't met Maxime Depardieu. His father believed men were providers, protectors. Men weren't coddled, didn't require reassurance, or affection of any kind. A man definitely didn't express or acknowledge soft emotions.

All things considered, Calin didn't know why it hadn't been easier for him to murder the bastard.

Damn, soul! Got in the way every time.

Just as it had when he gazed into Amelia's unique brand of hazel eyes. He'd seen nothing but genuine curiosity. She wasn't playing some angle or trying to get anything from him. He had scared her when he'd said he was a vampire, coaxed her into his room despite her nervousness, yet she wanted to know him.

For that reason alone, he'd lapsed in judgment. Played for her as if he were in concert. Self-doubt, something he never experienced, seeped past his defenses as he began. Never having played or sang for anyone before, he hadn't known if he was any good. In general, he didn't do anything he wasn't positive he did well. But Amelia seemed to enjoy it. He smelled the salt of tears. So, either she liked it, or she was a great actress. Several songs and a promise to sculpt her a wax figurine later, he drove her home.

That's it.

That's fuckin' it!

Didn't try to fuck her or nothin'. Talk about slippin'. Behavior of this nature wouldn't get his goals met. He had to stop thinking of her as a candidate for a relationship he didn't even want. Everything hinged on the success of this mission. If he didn't get the *seal* from her, he'd be destroyed. Whether or not he retrieved it for his grandfather, or walked.

If he walked, nowhere in the world would be safe for him. He would be hunted. The bounty his grandfather would place on his head—astronomical. Rogues, *Daywalkers*, and, hell, maybe even *commoners* would be after him. If he got the *seal* and returned to Romania, Grandfather Balkan would destroy him to take it. That left secret, and his favorite, option C—for Calin. And he was so team Calin.

He'd destroy Amelia after the *Awakening*, take the *seal*, which without his soul, would turn it and the *Book of Being* evil. All the power and extra abilities bestowed upon the VR would be his without the limitations of good, and The Fates couldn't touch him. No one could.

Yep, he needed to regroup. Amelia had him twisted. She skewed his sense of self, his perception of right and necessary. Right and wrong were subjective. What was right to one person could be wrong to another. People never did what they perceived as wrong for no reason. In the proper circumstances, wrong could be right. Calin did the necessary, always.

This philosophy led him to cast a spell that masked the adjoining door to his and Bianca's new room. The incantation also locked and soundproofed Bianca's room. He should release her; it'd been hours. The room probably resembled a demolition site. But...

A maid's cart filled with towels, extra toiletries, and cleaning solutions sat outside room 217. Two floors below his. Calin expanded his senses.

Damn, soul!

He actually felt bad for leaving Bianca alone. Shock of shocks, he heard the flutter of her rapid fledgling heartbeat. She rested. Good, because he caught a whiff of something irresistible. Erotic musk crept from behind the closed door in front of him. Danced on his tongue, whetting his appetite. Aha! What he needed to center him, reenergize him from the drain of using his powers.

Calin smiled. Someone was lying down on the job. Two someones, to be exact.

Moans of pleasure wreaked havoc on his body. His fangs elongated, piercing his tongue with their sharp tips. The Terminator went from six to midnight in his pants. When lengthened, vampires' fangs became erogenous zones capable of giving and receiving pleasure. For a vampire, carnal desire and feeding were closely related. Some males ejaculated and some females orgasmed while they fed.

This probably accounted for the reason mortals romanticized vampires in their books and films. Idiot, blood beasts! They had no idea only *eternalmates* fed during sex. Taking blood from a mortal during intercourse, more times than not, ended in necrophilia. Although morbid, vampires—at least this vampire—didn't get down like that. Mortals got a lot wrong about vampires. One thing they managed to get correct: vampires' animal magnetism. Vampires were masters of seduction.

He unlocked the room door with his mind. It swung open.

Well, well, well... Look what we have here? Score!

The women's expressions were trapped between embarrassment, terror, and half-mast eyed lust. Strawberry blonde on bottom was naked from the waist down. Her maid's uniform hiked to her navel. Naked, olive-skinned woman on top, straddling the blonde's face, was a brunette who'd tried to dye her hair blonde. The resulting color was a burnt orange hue. Evident by the sheen around both their mouths, their faces had been planted between each other's legs. His powers of seduction weren't necessary here; his prey had arousal covered.

The heady sweet aroma of sex hung thick in the air. Hunger detonated inside Calin. Two women in the throes of passion... too much! He flew headlong into predator mode. Both women stared at him through wide brown eyes.

Calin leaned against the door frame. "Don't stop on my account, ladies," he drawled in amusement. "Please... as you were."

Bet neither of them thought their release would be this explosive. Pushing off the frame, he entered. Shutting the door behind him telekinetically, he sauntered over to the bed. Calin ran a finger the length of the olive-skinned woman's sweat-dampened cheek. She shivered in fear under his touch. He didn't have to have the ability to read minds like normal vampires to know the women were afraid. Fear seeped from their pores, holding their screams at bay.

If they were vampires and not useless mortals, things might've gotten interesting. As mortals, they were nothing more than sustenance, which brought his conflicted emotions for another mortal to the fore. His demon didn't do emotion. It rose to the surface, suffocating his humanity.

Saliva inundated his mouth. Wrapping the orange-haired woman's hair around his hand, he yanked, granting him full access to her throat. Light from his glowing eyes illuminated soft pliant skin, her carotid artery pulsed. In one bite, he tore through the tender flesh. Blood poured into his mouth. Groaning in contentment, he gulped her life's essence.

Mmm...
He felt better already.

"How do you not have a key to your parents' house?"

Walker turned and glared at his best friend. His parents were home, he knew it. For some reason, they were taking their sweet ass time answering the door. It was hot as balls out here.

"I have a key to my parents' house. What do they think you're going to do—steal?" Dan continued complaining.

Shaking his head, Walker rolled his eyes. He knocked again.

Man, Dan was morphing into Tessa. Even nagged like her. Being with Tessa softened his midsection and hardened his personality. He could pressure Dan to break up with the harpy bitch. Dan had always been susceptible to peer pressure, even at twenty-three that remained true. But he wouldn't. Apparently, being a cold-hearted, mean-spirited bitch equaled freak in the sheets. According to Dan, Tessa was a very freaky girl. Walker wouldn't deny his oldest friend ass. At least one of them got it on the regular.

Save one crazy-ass experience a few weeks ago and again a few nights back, Amelia had him on the celibacy track. Before that, they hadn't had sex in so long he couldn't remember what being inside anyone, let alone her, felt like.

Ooh... but when she did give him the gushy stuff. Not even thinking about sports kept him from knocking one out of the park in less than three seconds. The night of the anniversary of her parents' death, Amelia had been wild, like a different person. Amelia 2.0.

Of course, Amelia 2.0 wasn't around long. After sex, her expression had been one of mortification, not happiness or satisfaction. It hurt, but he knew why she acted the way she did. She thought she hid her true feelings, which was why he cut her so much slack. More than the others, her parents' death killed an integral part of her.

Amelia kept everyone at arm's length in a misguided attempt to spare them a fate she couldn't possibly be responsible for. But he knew deep inside she remained the girl he loved. She cared for people to her own detriment. It was why he loved her and why he hoped his daily reminders, text messages, and surprise visits assured her he would always be there.

Speaking of always being there—he'd barely spent any time with her in the past week. Odd, since he rarely went two hours without at least texting her. Matter of fact, he couldn't remember the last time they spoke. Weird how that only occurred to him now. His normal MO would have been to show up at her house and stay there whether she liked it or not.

When her parents died, she'd shut herself in her room for a week straight without food or drink. She'd refused to see anyone. That didn't stop him from forcing his presence on her, which resulted in a fight between him and his one-time best friend. Evan wouldn't let him in the house, so he'd broken in through her bedroom window. After that, she couldn't shake him, and he had no remorse or regret over the incident.

Had he not gone to extreme measures, they wouldn't still be together. New Amelia put effort into nothing other than waking up, shopping, and breathing. He despised new Amelia. But he'd wait her out. His Amelia was in there somewhere. He had faith Amelia would snap out of... whatever funk she was in, and he'd be there when she did.

"Dude... I'm sweating balls out here, where're your fuckin' parents?" Dan whined.

What's with this guy? The fat bastard had lived in Arizona his whole life.

"Chill, bro. You're really bitch made, aren't you?" Walker asked, knocking again.

"Hey, yo, fuck you, bud. I just—"

The door opened, interrupting Dan.

Walker's whole world stopped at the sight of the only person he deemed more precious than Amelia—his little sister, Rebecca. His pride and joy. Being an older brother was the only job no one could say he didn't do well. He adored this chocolate-eyed, brunette angel. People thought he was possessive over Amelia, but they ain't seen nothin' until they saw how possessive he was of his sister.

When his parents had kicked him out, he'd promised to bring her gifts every time he stopped by, which was why she stared at him now with a Kool-Aid smile plastered to her face.

"Hi, Wall, I missed you." Rebecca beamed over his shoulder. "Hi, Danny boy," she crooned in a love-struck singsong voice, pissing Walker off.

The crush his ten-year-old sister seemed to develop overnight on Dan made him see red and worried him a bit. In Dan's glory days, he'd been something to look at, but since being with Tessa—yeah, not so much. Man, if his sister's tastes geared this way now, he'd hate to see who she married. Provided, he allowed her to marry.

"Hey, little mama, how many hearts you break today?" Dan flirted.

Rebecca blushed and giggled. "You're silly, Danny boy. I can't break hearts yet. Nobody likes me."

She opened the door wide and backed out of the way. He and Dan entered, then shut it behind them.

"That's because boys are stupid right now. You wait, you'll be breaking 'em soon enough. Trust me," Dan assured.

"What took so long for you to answer the door?" Walker asked, recapturing his earlier aggravation.

His parents ignoring his knocks didn't surprise him, but Rebecca was a different story. Hopefully, his dad hadn't been filling her head with trash talk about him.

"Mommy said if you wanted to come in so bad you'd find your key. I snuck and answered the door anyway 'cause you shouldn't have to wait. It's hot. I didn't know if tattoos sweated off."

God, his parents' indifference toward him grated on his nerves.

Rebecca gave him a curious once over, then walked a full circle around him before stopping in front of him. Her face fell into a lip-jutted-out pout.

Walker and Dan exchanged amused glances.

"What's wrong, pumpkin face?" Walker asked, feigning ignorance.

Rebecca's brows crinkled, and she sighed dramatically. "Nothing," she answered, dragging out the word.

Unable to stand her unhappiness for a second, Walker dug into his pocket, pulled his fisted hand out. He made a fist with his other hand, rolled his clenched fists around each other, then extended them to Rebecca. "Pick a hand."

Her entire face lit up, and she squealed. "Umm..." Big brown eyes rolled as she deliberated. "The right—no, no, the left." Before Walker opened his left hand, she changed her mind again. "No. Do both."

Smirking, he gave her an arch stare. "That's not an option, silly. One or the other."

"Can I have a hint?" She smiled, hopeful.

Walker cut his eyes at his little sister; she was lucky she was cute. He cracked open both outstretched hands.

Rebecca peeked between his fingers, then laughed. "The right. Open the right."

Walker opened his right hand; a ten-dollar bill and a silver mood ring sat on his flat palm.

Rebecca grabbed the money and the ring, threw her arms around his waist, and hugged him tight. "Thank you, Wall. I love you. You're not the best brother you're the bestest big brother."

God, he never wanted to let her down. Her genuine unconditional love warmed his heart. Looking into her eyes, he didn't see the judgments his parents and the world passed on him for his appearance or his delinquent past. He saw pure adoration.

"If it isn't my bastard son the human doodle." Jason Palmer's greeting was belligerent.

His father had such a way with words...

Nothing says lovin' like reminding him he was born out of wedlock. Degrading him in front of company was one of his father's favorite pastimes. Ranked right up there with degrading him in private and... wait for it... his other favorite wouldn't be far behind.

Rebecca released him from the death grip she had him in and admired her ring. "Pretty. What kind of ring is this, Wall?"

Walker spared his father a grimace before returning his attention to his sister. "A magic ring that predicts what mood you're in," he said, making his voice deep, spooky. "It's called a mood ring. It changes colors based on your mood."

Jason raked a hand through thinning blond hair. "Guess you're adding fruity to that long list of shit, aren't you, boy?" He smiled without humor. "First, you dye your hair like a fruit, then write all over yourself, then pierce your—"

"Did you get Amelia a pretty ring, too?" Rebecca interrupted—on purpose. "I didn't see one when she was here with Talon the other day. Why was she with Talon?"

Good fuckin' question!

Heat flooded Walker's body, scalding his face at that news. He didn't know why he wasn't pissed before at the lack of contact, but he sure as hell was now. Was his cousin making moves on his woman? And why did she make time for Talon but not him?

He spoke through clenched teeth. "What'd they do while they were here?"

Please don't let anything like "closed doors" or "weird noises" come out of my sister's mouth.

"Nothing. They weren't here long. Amelia waited by the door while he got his stuff."

Thank, God. Killing his long-lost cousin wouldn't help endear his family to him. Didn't matter that Talon was an over-muscled giant; Walker still would've chin-checked him. Still might if Talon continued to screw around with a good thing. He'd been waiting for Amelia to come around for too long to let his cousin, or anybody else, swoop in and take his woman.

"Still goin' with that colored girl, huh?"

And there we have it.

Jason Palmer's other favorite pastime. The reason he fought his father and got kicked out a year ago.

"She still freezing you out?" his father continued, wagging his eyebrows. "As far as colored women go, I'd say she's the prettiest. Easy enough to tolerate, too. Not loud like them other ones. Like a white girl trapped in a black girl wrapper."

Walker ground his teeth. If Rebecca wasn't standing here, he would've busted his father's lip. Couldn't the asshole ever just let it go? Nooo... Every time he saw him, he had to say something racist.

Dan crooked his finger at Rebecca. She skipped over to him, grinning from ear to ear. He bent down to her level. "Why don't you go show your mom your pretty ring, sweetie? Tell her to come say hi, okay?"

Rebecca flashed him a serious tight-lipped smile. She'd seen this scene between him, and their father more than any child should. She nodded, then skipped off through the great room and disappeared.

Once she was gone, and out of earshot Walker hoped, he laid into his father. "What the fuck is your problem? Is your life so unfulfilled that you gotta bring other people down for shits and giggles? You can't go one day without saying some shit about my girl?"

Stepping so close to his father that their chests touched, Walker shook with rage.

At five-ten, Walker had a two-inch height advantage over his father, but what Jason lacked in height, he more than made up for in weight and muscle. If it came to pass, this fight wouldn't end well. He hated the idea of fighting his father—again. Over the same bullshit. If only the Dog the Bounty Hunter clone learned to keep his mouth shut.

The last time they'd fought Walker ended up with a busted nose and a broken arm. But, that wasn't what got him kicked out. The trip down the stairs he sent his dad on a week after the fight did. Jason broke both his legs, his right arm, and received a mild concussion. Wasn't pretty. His mom agreed to it thinking distance would fix their relationship. It didn't.

Dan pried them apart, standing between them in his typical peacemaking position.

"Rebecca's in the kitchen. You really want her to see this again? Split her loyalties like this? You really wanna do that?" Dan asked, alternating his glare between them.

Neither one backed down. They were stuck in some sort of who-can-make-the-meanest-face staring contest.

"You keep this up, and one day, she'll walk away from both of you," Dan scolded.

They both eased back, a step.

Dan stayed put.

Just then, dressed in gray sweatpants cut off into shorts and a white tank top Shannon Palmer stepped into the archway, separating the foyer from the great room. Brunette hair in a messy bun bobbed as she shifted narrowed green eyes on him and his father.

She pulled the black tea towel draped over her left shoulder off, wiping her hands on it. "I see I missed the good stuff," she said in a calm tone. "You think you boys could ever act like family. Like you like each other just a tad?" Throwing the towel back over her shoulder, she leveled her eyes at her husband then her son.

"This wasn't me this time, Mom. You need to take that up with the KKK's grand dragon over here. You asked us to come for dinner. We came," Walker reminded her.

Shannon ignored him and smiled at Dan. "Hello, Daniel. How are you? How's Tessa?"

"I'm good. Tessa's... good," Dan replied.

His mom seemed to be holding back laughter or a knowing smile. Took her a second to find her voice. "I love that girl. She's exactly what you need. I still remember you running around here—both of you—cocky little shits, even in sixth grade. You needed someone to knock you off that high horse. Why didn't you bring her? I told Walker the invite was for both of you. Even Amelia if she wasn't working."

Right, like he really wanted to invite Satan into his family home. Please!

"Where's Talon? Becca said he took his stuff somewhere." Walker glowered at his father. "What? You kick him out, too?" He glanced back at his mom.

"He said he was thinking about staying longer, so he rented a place of his own. I tried to talk him into staying, save his money, but he said he'd be around. He stopped by with Amelia earlier," Shannon informed him.

Hmph. Why the hell was he with Amelia? Again. Looked like he and his jolly white cousin needed to talk.

"Alright boys" — Shannon clapped — "go wash up." She shooed Walker and Dan with the wave of her hand. "Jason, go in the kitchen and make sure your daughter hasn't chopped a finger into the salad."

Jason did as directed. He and Dan went upstairs to his old room.

When Shannon Palmer said jump, anybody within earshot asked how high. She had this way of being patient and gentle, yet able to send a man's balls back up into his body. Like, the more soothing her tone, the worse off you were. Scared the crap out of most people. No one dared defy her.

Dan made himself comfortable on the bed while Walker went into his bathroom to wash his hands.

"I don't get how your parents are married," Dan mused aloud. "They're the exact opposite of each other."

"They got divorced," he reminded him.

Dan scoffed. "Yeah, only to get remarried, like, what...? Two weeks later."

Walker poked his head through the open doorway. "Try a year, ass-wipe."

Dan plucked a football off the floor and tossed it a couple times. "Whatever. I'm just sayin', inquiring minds wanna know."

After a long lull in conversation, Walker exited the bathroom.

Dan tossed the football to him, heaved himself off the bed, and went to wash. "So, how'd your mom expect you to get in if you didn't have a key?!" he called.

Walker dropped into his big cushy soccer ball chair. "I had a key. I gave it to Talon when he got to town."

"Let me get this straight. First, you let him borrow your house key, which he didn't give back even though he's not staying here anymore. Now, he's borrowing your girlfriend?" Dan's voice rose with snide curiosity. He entered the bathroom doorway and leaned against the door jamb. "Dude, since when do *you* share your girlfriend?"

The whole situation had a headache building behind his right eye. He didn't share his girlfriend, shit, he didn't share anything. Walker got his jealous nature from his dad.

Whenever he thought to object to Talon seeing Amelia, or started to call or text, he didn't. Couldn't. He physically *couldn't* do anything about it. It didn't make sense. Fuckin' infuriated him. No way would he cop to bitching out. Not to Dan, or anyone else. "I don't share. But it's my cousin, man. I can't do anything to him." *But I want to.* "Simmer down, bro."

Dan arched a brow. "Simmer down?" he repeated. "You almost rolled your dad for calling her *pretty for a colored girl.* But your scary ass, gigantic cousin, you don't know from Adam, who—let's be real—could double as a Greek god statue. No, you let him spend whole days alone with her and shit. What happened to you?"

Walker let his head fall back. His eyes closed, and he counted to ten. He didn't want to fuck up another friendship by killing his best friend. But fuck! He'd gut Dan if he didn't shut the hell up. He already felt punked, shit!

That's it! Come rain or shine, he would see his girlfriend tonight.

No, tomorrow.

Shit!

Chapter Seventeen

"**E**w! What is that horrid smell, brother?"

"Bianca, please," Calin grumbled exasperated.

Irritation boiled over into pissed as he and Bianca stepped off the curb outside of Super Saver Cinema and crossed the lot. Since the night in his room, he'd seen Amelia every day. Met her for lunch, dinner, and her breaks at the theater. She was supposed to be here today but called in for some insane reason. He assumed it'd been to spend time with the menace guardsman. He'd been wrong.

"Please, what?" Bianca whined. "First, you cage me like some rabid animal. Now you expect me to endure his stench. Don't think I won't seek retribution. His odor is an affront to my delicate nature."

He snorted. *Delicate nature, my ass!*

Just before they visited the theater, she was covered in blood, entrails, and other mortal innards from her so-called breakfast.

"Well, well, well..." Calin drawled as the new bane of his existence met them in the middle of the parking lot. "If it isn't my BFF. If you're looking for our scrumptious little caramel apple, she's not here."

Calin enjoyed watching the male's jaw tense and his posture stiffen. He did not enjoy the proprietary flash in the VRG's blue eyes. Amelia was his, dammit! Whoa. Not like that. She was his mark. He had plans for her. The mortal laying false claim to her presented no challenge. The Vampire Royal Guard? Yeah, he'd relish destroying the prick. The one and only reason he hadn't done so already was because it would look suspicious and might upset Amelia.

Shit! Not upset Amelia. He didn't care what upset her as long as he achieved his ultimate goal. That's what he didn't want to upset, his goal.

"When you speak of Amelia, you will do so with respect," the lapdog bit out. "Otherwise, you will refrain from speaking of her. That's your only warning."

"I will *refrain*, huh?" he mocked in the douchebag's uppity tone. Only a douchebag wore leather pants and a long-sleeve button-down when they were supposed to blend in with mortals, which Calin assumed was the errand boy's MO. "Who are you to tell me what I should and shouldn't do? You don't look like Amelia's father, and as far as I know, she's of legal age according to mortal standards."

"Brother, we mustn't dilly-dally—the sun," Bianca reminded him, stomping a patent leather-shoed foot.

The VRG's attention shifted to her. He scrutinized her with sharp suspicion.

Fuck! Of all the days to run into the glorified guard dog. Calin might not be able to read minds, but he knew what the vamp was thinking.

Millennia ago, when the Vampire Royals were slaughtered, The Fates forsook the supernatural. Ceased communication. Permitted the chaos that had breeds of supernatural on the brink of extinction. Due to their silence, White-witches, whose duty it'd once been to spell vampire females' bodies, allowing them to conceive, no longer participated in vampire procreation. Besides The Fates, the Vampire Royals were the only other beings capable of giving consent to procreate. Other than the rare Dhampire popping up, a part mortal part supernatural Halfling—more often than not, part vampire—there shouldn't be any vampire fledglings.

His age wouldn't be obvious. But Bianca's...

"What are you?" the guardsman demanded without taking his eyes off Bianca.

"You really must think I'm stupid," he teased, in hopes of getting the guard's attention off his sister's origins. "Well, don't hold your breath. I haven't decided to sell the rights to my E! True Hollywood Story just yet. When I do, you'll be the first to know." Calin thrust his hands into his jeans pockets.

"Why must we waste time with this—bitch? Isn't that the term males use to taunt one another?" Bianca asked in a haughty tone.

A low growl emanated from deep within the vampire's chest. Blue eyes flashed fire.

"You touch my sister, and the universe won't be big enough for you to escape me. And as far as Amelia is concerned, I won't be leaving her world anytime soon," Calin said, letting the unspoken threat hang between them.

The guard knew as well as Calin did what they both waited for. The *Awakening*. The rise of their queen. More than likely the VRG presumed Calin wanted to stop her rising. Rogue factions might seek to prevent it, if they were even aware of the *Awakening*. Not him. No, for his plan, he needed her to become queen. For a minute.

"What. Are. You?" the guard repeated, stepping toe-to-toe with Calin.

Their chests bumped. His was wider, but the guard's was no less muscled. The sheer size and obvious strength of him would've intimidated anyone other than Calin. As it were, the open act of aggression and assumed dominance incensed him, and was funny as shit.

Without breaking eye contact, Calin reached to the side, hooked an arm around Bianca's waist, and shoved her behind him.

She snarled but didn't fight.

"Allow me to introduce myself," the VRG said through clenched teeth. His funky arctic breath washed over Calin's face. "I'm Talon Cantemir, Vampire Royal Guardsman, son of the chief of all Guardsmen. You don't want to tangle with me. I'll end you."

Fuck me!

How did he not recognize the cocky son of a bitch? The inflated sense of self-worth, he should've known. Oh, he couldn't wait to battle this male.

"What makes you so sure you know how to end me? You have no idea what I'm capable of when properly motivated."

"I'm giving you one last chance. If I have to find out what you are on my own, the consequences will be worse. And I'll deliver the justice myself," Talon spat. "Now, what are you?"

A silver Audi sped past them behind Talon. Damn, he'd give anything to have mind control abilities. He would've loved to mow down the asshole. The male had balls of iron to threaten him. He didn't know who he was dealing with, and unlike him, Calin didn't intend to introduce himself. Let it be a surprise.

"My lips are sealed." Calin picked a pretend piece of lint off the collar of Talon's shirt. "But consider me adequately warned. Tell me, what do you think Amelia will say when she finds out about our little meet and greet? How you threatened her poor new friend's life? Might blow your cover," he stated in a singsong voice.

"If you don't stay away from Amelia, I'll hunt down and destroy everyone you ever cared about. Then you," Talon gritted out. He glanced over Calin's shoulder at Bianca.

"Lucky for me, there isn't much I care about."

Bianca harrumphed behind him.

In one abrupt, fluid motion, the vampire turned and stormed off in the direction he came. Without glancing backward, he said, "Because of Amelia's affection for you I won't harm you—yet. Once she sees you for the abomination you are... I'll destroy you. And your little demon sister, too." From beside a dark grey Chrysler, he turned. "By the way, my self-worth isn't inflated. I'm *that* important. Learn to guard your thoughts." On that note, he got into his vehicle and drove away.

"I don't care for him, brother," Bianca commented several minutes later outside Calin's hotel room. "However, he is quite the sight."

Calin wanted to burn his ears off. He dug through his front and back pockets in search of his keycard. Didn't matter how fast his sister aged or how old she got; he didn't ever want to imagine her with a male. Any male. Especially a Royal Guardsman and absolutely not a Cantemir. If he never encountered another prick from that bloodline, it'd be too soon.

Fed up with hunting for his damn card, he glanced left then right. No one other than Bianca. A wave of his hand turned the light on the keycard reader green. Unlocked.

He opened the door, held it for Bianca.

She strutted past him and gasped. Halted just inside the room.

Instantly on high alert, Calin cleared the threshold in one step. He screeched to a stop and glared.

Long, leather-encased legs crossed at the ankle stretched out on his bed. No shirt covered a lean, pale chest. One hand rested behind a head of mussed black hair. The other stroked an expertly trimmed goatee. Sapphire eyes gleamed with mischief and demented humor. "Hey, precious," he said to Bianca. Then to him, "Hey, buuuddy. You surprised? No? No matter. I'm happy to see you—over the moon, in fact. After little precious here called Balkan to report the less than stellar treatment she'd been receiving, he thought I should come check things out." He pointed to the bed. "I hope you don't know mind. I did a little mind trick, and the maid let me in. Your bed is super comfy."

So, this was the brat's retribution. Calin ground his teeth hard enough to grind them to dust.

Fucking, Emilio!

"**S**ince when do you call me this much," Amelia groused into her cell phone, which was cradled between her ear and shoulder. She sifted through her overstuffed closet in search of something to wear.

"Since my little sister started giving me the slip," Evan snapped. "And what's this I hear about you runnin' around togged to the bricks with two tree-sized schmucks?"

Arrgh! "Why do you talk like that?"

"Like what?"

"Uh... like a nineteen-thirties gangster. Our conversations would go a lot faster if I didn't have to take ten extra minutes deciphering your code. You give me a headache."

"Be straight with me, Nugget. What's really going on with you?" Evan asked, all teasing gone.

God, what could she tell him? Since their awesome conversation almost two weeks ago, he'd called every day and asked the same inane question. She'd been able to get Kasey to smooth out the mess she'd made with her hypothetical question, but Kasey couldn't fix everything. Evan was bound and determined to find out what was "going on" with her.

But how did she answer a question *she* didn't know the answer to? Life had somehow taken a weird, unexpected turn. She went from a virtual zombie, a shadow of her former self to—what? A girl who'd cheat on her boyfriend? Not that she'd done anything with Calin, but his daily visits to the theater could be construed as emotional infidelity.

When she worked a double, he had lunch and dinner with her. When she worked normal shifts, he sat with her on breaks. Sometimes, he brought Bianca, and sometimes, he brought his guitar. They'd sit outside the pizzeria next door, and he'd play for her. He didn't sing often, but the one time he did, Cicely just so happened to catch the tail end of a song he wrote for his sick mom. That moment transferred Cicely's crush on Talon to Calin.

Talon. Her personal giant. He'd officially taken on the job of being her shadow. Where she went, he went. He reminded her of one of those guards in front of Buckingham Palace. Always stone-faced and serious. Always standing watch and asking a million questions. It was like a never-ending game of twenty questions. Yet she didn't want him—or Calin—to go away.

How fucked up was that? She had Walker. He was loyal. When she gazed into his eyes, she knew without a doubt he loved her. But she didn't love him. Not that way. Amelia cherished him, his friendship. The way he forever saw her as she used to be. She never wanted to hurt him. But wasn't that what she was doing? Holding on to him when she didn't feel the same? No wonder he kept forcing her on Talon.

Maybe he'd gotten tired of her. Her moodiness and depression. She wanted to be better for him. Couldn't. So much death and heartbreak changed a person. Changed her. No one understood that. And the part she hid? The part that loved him and everyone close to her was willing to sacrifice her happiness to keep them safe? That part didn't want to take the hope away from him. And it wasn't fair.

None of this was fair. Her being drawn to Calin, who never expected anything from her, didn't know her to expect the bright shining Amelia. He gave her freedom. Freedom to just be.

Talon's annoying ass somehow provided a tangible sense of security. Like nothing bad could touch her with him around. The way he made her lash out invigorated her. With him she felt safe to laugh and taunt. For years, many close to her tried to get her to open up. Yet somehow, two strangers did the impossible.

And she'd lose them.

Once Walker found out about the baby.

Hanging out with them offered an escape. An escape she couldn't afford. All vacations ended. As this one should. Calin would leave. Talon, too. She'd be the girlfriend and mom that Walker and the baby deserved. She'd talked to Wall earlier, scheduled a dinner to tell him in a couple days. Her respite was over, but first, she needed to get through this call.

"I'm being straight up," she insisted. "Nothing's going on. And you don't need to know who I hang out with. I dress up regardless of who I'm out with, you know that."

"Did you and Wall break up?" Evan asked, sounding way too enthused. "Please tell me you dropped that nutty Moe."

Just when she thought she missed him, he had to go and be...Evan. "God—"

"Yes."

"Shut up," she snapped at her brother's poorly timed joke. "You need to get over your beef with Wall. You used to be best friends. Kiss and make up already."

"Uh... not gonna happen. I got something for Walker to kiss—my big, fat, hairy nutt."

TMI. "Well, sorry to disappoint you, we're still together. And if memory serves me correctly—which I'm sure it does—you've got your own little crazy factory to deal with."

Yes, it was a cheap shot at Kasey, but it was all she had at the second.

"Touché. But, umm... FYI, when a dame's crazy, it's adorable. Means she's a tomcat in the sack. When it's a guy—especially one I've known since the cradle—it's if-I-can't-have-you-no one-will, news channel three worthy."

Amazing.

Evan always seemed to know just what to say to make her want to stab him in the eye. "Okay, Evan. Gotta go. Bye." She hung up without waiting for a response and finished looking for an outfit.

Ten minutes later, Amelia emerged from her bedroom, dressed in a black, long-sleeved V-neck, four-inch pumps, and designer jeans. No sooner than she entered the hallway, she was greeted by the sounds of a show she called, *That's So Ike and Tina*. Starring Tessa as Ike and Dan as Tina.

Tessa laughed. "In the great words of 50 Cent, *I talk a lot of shit 'cause I can back it up*. And anyway, the first step to conquering an addiction is admitting you have a problem."

Careful not to interrupt, Amelia tiptoed into the makeshift dining room.

"Shut. Up!" Dan growled. "Maybe I'm gaining weight because I deal with your scrawny ass all the time. Ever thought of that?"

Clucking her tongue, Tessa shook her head. "Oh, no! That's another symptom of addiction—blaming others for your problems. Why are you so testy, sugar?"

Dan shot Tessa a flat stare. "Gee, I wonder."

"We should go jogging."

"Tessa!"

"What? I want to go jogging," Tessa whined.

"Right! I've never seen you walk at a brisk pace, let alone jog," Dan pointed out.

"So, is that a no on the jogging?"

Dan blew out an agitated breath. "No. It's a fuck you, Tessa! Why are you with me if you don't like the way I look?"

"I do like the way you look, baby. You jump, I jump, right?" Tessa crooned, saccharin sweet, before bursting out laughing.

"Shut up," he snapped. "You're gonna push me too far one day and, love or no love, I'll leave you."

"Oh, Romeo, Romeo, Romeo, thou mustn't write checks with one's lips that thine ass can't cash," Tessa said in a poor British accent.

"I swear to God, woman, one day I'm gonna—"

Simultaneously, Dan and Tessa turned and saw Amelia standing mere feet from their spot on the loveseat.

Dan's face flamed in embarrassment. Tessa gave no reaction. So, Tessa.

"Where are you going, puddin' pop?" Tessa asked, noting her purse and outfit.

"The mall. Why? You writing a book?"

"Jeez, what's up with everybody and their stink attitudes? Is it me?" Tessa asked in mock innocence.

"Which boyfriend you taking?" Dan asked.

She cut her eyes at his stupid question. Although, if she were being honest, it kind of felt like she had three boyfriends nowadays, which was why she took the day off work. To be alone.

"Ha. Ha! Mr. DiCaprio. Been a while since *Titanic*, huh? A glacier sunk the ship—my ass! I know what sunk it." She quirked an eyebrow at him.

Yes, yes, she was being bitchy, but her stomach was knotted with anxiety. In a few days, her life would change forever. She'd apologize later. Maybe get him something at the mall.

Dan pinned her with an icy glare, then flipped her off.

"I'm gone. Have fun fighting," she said, turning. "Don't break my shit," she called, making her way through the front room.

"Hey!" Dan's shout halted her before she twisted the doorknob.

She swiveled around. Met dull, solemn green eyes as Dan entered the front room.

"Talk to Wall lately?"

"This morning. Why?"

Hefty shoulders lifted in a lazy shrug. "Just wondering. You're always so busy with his cousin, I had to check. Gotta look out for my boy."

She rolled her eyes, sighing. "Not that it's any of your business, Daniel, but we're having dinner in a couple days so—"

"You going to tell him about the—"

"Shut up, Tessa," she said hurriedly, cutting off her best friend.

"What? I wasn't going to mention the one thing in the one place. That he—as much as I hate it—has a right to know a—"

"Goodbye, nosy people," she snapped, flinging open the door. Sunlight blinded the couple for a brief second before she slammed the door in their faces. Oblivious to her surroundings, and fuming, she stomped down the broken stone path through her yard. And ran smack dab into a brick wall.

So much for my day alone.

She didn't look up or argue, just switched directions and headed toward the dark gray Chrysler.

Chapter Eighteen

"**I**n coming! Something wicked this way comes—ten o'clock."

From where she swept inside the concession stand, Amelia's head snapped up at Cicely's announcement. As irrational excitement fluttered in her abdomen, and anxiety had her gripping the wooden broom handle so tight she heard a *crack*, she prayed.

Please don't let it be Talon.

She'd endured a very long, weird trip to the mall with him yesterday and couldn't handle more Talon time. He normally respected Heidi's ordinance that he and Walker not visit, but things had ended strangely between them last night.

First, he'd acted as if he'd never been to a mall. Bright-eyed and antsy, like a kid in a candy store. It was the most animated she'd seen him be about anything. She'd tried to coax the same reaction from him when they went to the castle to ensure the specially ordered imported Italian leather furniture arrived, but got nothing.

He was totally indifferent to the impressive furniture she had a small hand in designing to accommodate his large frame. Beds, sectionals sofas, dining room tables, and chairs—each piece had to be custom built so he didn't break it with his freakish strength or make it look like doll furniture when he sat down. Did he so much as crack a smile? No. But that's not why she didn't want to see him.

While putting away some barware—every bachelor pad needed a bar—curiosity got the better of her. She opened his crate. The giant guarded the thing with his life, but he'd gone to talk to some friend and left her inside with it. Big mistake. Amelia could be trusted with a lot, but the temptation of the forbidden... reeled her in. It's how she "accidentally" stumbled upon Evan's *Hustler* magazines in a lockbox under his bed at thirteen. Plus, Talon was always so serious and tight-lipped. She wanted to know something deeper about him. Nothing prepared her for what she found.

Thousands of plastic wrapped...

Comic books.

Fantasy comic books. He had hundreds about different types of mythical creatures. When she went to open one, he magically appeared, and the comic disappeared. One second, she was sitting alone, and the next, he had her on her feet across the parlor far from the crate. He'd stammered through some explanation about collectors' items.

Whatever.

Sounded like nonsense boy logic to her, and she got it. But it also showed her a different side of him. A softer one. Now things were more... complicated.

Yesterday, her resolve seemed impenetrable. She knew what had to be done. Continuing any sort of relationship with Talon and Calin was wrong and disrespectful to Walker. Anyway, they were men. Once she explained the reason why she couldn't see them, they'd be out like sauerkraut. Guys didn't hang with pregnant chicks. Should be easy. She was the kind of woman who made decisions, and no matter how painful, stuck to them. Except, she was scared. Frightened to the core of her being of never seeing them again. Why? They were just men.

Yeah, men with looks to die for and abs hard enough to knock on.

Okay, there was that. Shit! Why did this have to be so hard?

"Which one?" she asked, incapable of unraveling the ridiculous threads of apprehension in her stomach.

Cicely bounded behind the concession counter and locked her purse in a drawer. Her pigtailed micro-braided hair flopped against slight shoulders. "Tall, built, and nasty," she replied with a mischievous smile.

"I'm not hearing this," Gordon chanted from where he stood counting down one of the registers.

Ignoring him, Amelia asked, "Nasty?"

"Umm... Yeah. Because of all the nasty thoughts that run through my mind when he's around. Gurl, him coming up here makes this crappy job bearable."

On a head swiveling roll, Cicely missed the sideways glare Gordon threw her way. Amelia didn't.

The lobby doors opened. Early evening sun illuminated the male perfection filling the doorway.

A sigh escaped her and Cicely in unison. She despised the way something snapped into place inside her at the sight of him. As if he was the missing piece to her, an incomplete puzzle.

Another white T-shirt, jeans, and unnecessarily large, skull belt buckle ensemble. Who would've thought this would be this season's sexiest look? On anyone else it wouldn't be. But, when Calin wore it with his shaggy brown hair, black wraparound sunglasses, and five o'clock shadow, he made it hotter than a Versace original.

Calin grinned in her direction. She clutched the broom for support. He checked his watch, then crooked a finger at her.

Not missing a beat, or an invitation, Cicely hooked an arm through Amelia's and pulled her out of the concession area. The broom fell with a clatter.

"Excuse me!" Gordon called after them.

"What?" Cicely snapped, barely sparing their manager a glance, and not stopping.

"Where are *you* going? You just got here."

"Break," the too eager young girl barked. The girl had some cojones. "Just cuz I just got here don't mean I don't need a break. I woulda got one sometime. Might as well be now."

Calin held the door for them. He smirked at the disgruntled frown she sported. Cicely refused to keep her hands to herself. Once outside, Amelia yanked her arm from Cicely's grasp. They went to the pizzeria next door to the theater. She and Cicely sat across from each other at one circular plastic table. Calin scooted another table beside theirs and sat on top of it.

It never ceased to amaze her how he did that. Calin was six-three, built like John Cena in his prime, yet the table held his weight. He reminded her of a black panther: big, agile, and able to balance himself on anything.

"So, I've been thinking," Cicely said, batting her eyelashes at Calin.

"Have you now?" Calin drawled in his interesting accent. One thick brow peeked over the rim of his sunglasses.

"Yeah. I think I can help you with your girlfriend problem."

The corner of his sinful mouth tilted. "Girlfriend problem?"

"You know, you don't have one," Cicely explained. "See, I was thinking you could tell people I'm your girlfriend. It'll help keep the ladies from bum-rushing ya."

Calin tugged the end of her ponytail and gave her a look that, even though Amelia couldn't see his eyes, she knew they were alight with amusement and curiosity.

She shrugged.

"Just a suggestion—help me, help you," her coworker rushed to clarify.

"Look what the fuck we have here."

Oh, no! This can't be happening. Amelia's stomach somersaulted. The heavy scent of Axe Body Spray and sweat hit her like a fist to the face. She, Cicely, and Calin turned simultaneously toward the snarky voice.

Walker, Dan, and Talon, looking the part of some mismatched gang, strutted their way. Towering over the other two men, Talon appeared to be the leader with his imperious stride and black-on-black outfit, leather pants, button-down, and fingerless gloves. Dan in a T-shirt and jean shorts, and Walker in a wife-beater and Dickies, were unimpressive flunkies.

Amelia tapped Calin's shoulder. When he looked at her she murmured, "You should probably leave."

He shook his head. "Not likely." Then he stood—in front of her.

Sonofabitch! This wouldn't end well. Her hand was caught in the proverbial cookie jar. She stayed seated. Tried to convince herself it was because she didn't want to get in the middle. Failed. She kept her seat because she couldn't bear the betrayal sure to be in Walker's expressive brown eyes.

Amelia glanced at Cicely to gauge her response. Cicely's eyes were glued to the scene, her expression awed. She seemed ready to burst out of her skin with giddy anticipation. Of course, the teenager loved drama.

Turning back to—Calin's wide back—Amelia struggled not to be sidetracked by his unique, clean, dark, autumn night scent.

"A," Dan said, easing her distraction. Given the nearness of his disapproving tone she assumed they reached the curb in front of the pizzeria. "This doesn't look good for you."

Dick. He was probably still pissed about the Leonardo Di-Caprio dig. Sheesh! You'd think that was the worst thing he'd ever been called.

"Shut up, Daniel," she snapped. Yeah, she sounded tough; behind two hundred and fifty-some odd pounds of Calin.

"*Signorina*," Talon's steel, resonant, voice crooned, "come here to me?"

Before she could comeback at his question-veiled command, Calin answered. "I appreciate the offer—really, I do—but she won't be going anywhere with you. Now, or ever."

This couldn't be happening, this soap opera, *90210* bullshit. She'd spent her whole adolescence being ridiculed and basically ignored by the opposite sex for her weird hair and eyes. Now, all of a sudden, guys were fighting—over her?

"Who the *fuck* are you? Answering for *my* girlfriend? I'm the only man who answers for her."

Oh, no he didn't. "Excuse me?"

"Be quiet, Amelia, I got this."

Be quiet, Amelia?

"Wall, the last time I checked, slave days were over," she bit out, glaring at Walker around Calin's torso. "And why are you here? Didn't Heidi ban you from coming up here?"

"So now I need an invitation to visit my girlfriend?" Wall asked, glowering at Calin.

"Are you guys gonna fight?" Cicely chimed in far too chipper for Amelia's liking. "If so, hold up. Let me get popcorn."

"I don't think a fight would be wise. Do you, Talon?" Calin asked, which was weird since as far as she knew, they didn't know each other, and she'd never mentioned Talon.

She wasn't trying to hide him from Calin. They'd met in passing before, kind of, but the whole thing was again... complicated.

"Step away from, Amelia. Now," Talon ordered, further proving her complicated theory. "Come to me, Amelia."

Not in this lifetime, Talon. Why were people suddenly treating her like a bad poodle or something? They all knew—Talon and Calin included—she wasn't the you-say-jump-I-ask-how-high type of woman. Them bossing her around and thinking she'd come to heel, pissed her off.

"Maybe we should table this conversation for another time," Dan suggested.

Oh, now he wanted to play peace-keeper. Wait until she told Tessa about this. He'd be lucky if his hand wasn't too afraid to satisfy him after she laid into him.

"Did you not hear me, dick weasel? I said get the fuck away from my girlfriend." Walker closed in on Calin, stepping shoulders to chest with him, given his disproportionate height.

Seriously?

Calin could demolish Walker's boney tattooed ass. He'd better hope Talon stepped in. She loved him, she did. But she'd warned him that one day he'd get his ass handed to him.

Guess today's the day.

Calin glanced past Walker. "I would get your pet, if I were you."

"Walker," Talon said in that stern way of his.

Busy eyeballing Calin, Walker paid him no heed.

"Daniel," Talon said, in the same commanding tone.

Dan met Talon's gaze.

"Take your friend and go to the car," Talon instructed.

Not to Amelia's total amazement—Dan had an eager-to-please personality; it's why he and Tessa got on so well—Dan grabbed Walker by the shoulders. "Let's go, bro. He's not worth it."

"That's right, listen to your friend. I'm not worth it... bro," Calin said, meaning to antagonize Walker, but she sensed more behind his words. Like he believed he was somehow unworthy.

Walker shook off Dan's hold and got in Calin's face.

She tried hard not to laugh at the fact that Walker had to lift onto tiptoe. Cicely, on the other hand, wasn't as successful in her attempt—if she made one. She giggled behind an open hand.

This was Amelia's fault. If she'd done as Walker requested and stayed away from Calin, they wouldn't be ready to fight. She didn't pretend to understand this intrinsic need to be with Calin, nor could she fight it. It was thigh bone connected to the hip bone; hip bone connected to the backbone—necessary. She'd never felt anything like it, and it was equally as strong with Talon. Yep, com-pli-cated.

And she couldn't stop this. Couldn't jump up and get in between them in her fragile state. God, this suck—

Before anyone guessed his intent, Walker struck. Balled his fist, and threw a left hook. Caught Calin square in the jaw. A loud *crack* ripped through the air.

Blood splashed, gushed, from Calin's mouth. His head lolled on his neck. He righted it so fast the movement was near imperceptible. A low rumbling, guttural sound shook the ground, the pizza parlor windows, her ribcage. It resembled a revving motorcycle engine. She half assumed it came from her. But she saw the unmistakable vibration in the back in front of her.

Calin. Growled.

Calm. Too calm, he advanced. Walker backed farther into the street. Amelia wished she had a clear view of his face. Whatever Calin's expression, it transformed Walker's prior cocky satisfaction to terror. He was petrified. His usual, rich brown "come-hither" stare had changed its tune. Now it shouted, "Please go anywhere but hither."

Calin proceeded to force Walker's retreat.

Talon flanked Walker on the right—sort of. He appeared to be standing guard, yet not. His sapphire eyes looked almost calculating, torn between wanting to join in and caution.

Dan, on the other hand, looked ready to piss himself. He didn't wait until he was cornered. He got way back, like near the car.

Amelia's stomach quivered. Something deep within her stirred, something shameful. The craving. Anticipation raced through her entire body. She shivered.

Not anticipation to see how things played out, but for the fight to begin. Something inside her craved... bloodshed. Hungered for it. Wanted to go over there and punch Walker—or Dan—just for a chance to have their blood on her skin. In her hand. In her...

Mouth.

She stood quickly. Her chair crashed to the ground. No one so much as batted an eye in her direction. A crowd had congregated, and their attention was otherwise engaged.

Not hers though. She was repulsed by her desire. Her gums began to throb.

What's wrong with me? This was her boyfriend and friends. She didn't wish them harm, even if they deserved it for being testosterone-filled fucktards.

Her heart pounded, begged for freedom from her chest. Anticipation turned to full-fledged desperation. She was desperate for bloodshed. Needed it like her next breath, which she'd gladly do without if it meant blood would spill.

She stared, transfixed, at the fray about to unfold. Without warning, Talon's gaze swung to hers. Concern replaced his previous caution or indecision. He stared as if he saw inside her. Knew her struggle. Then he did something she'd never expected the ever-composed Talon to do.

He tucked his head, crouched low...

And piledrove Calin. Knocked him clear off his feet. Calin's back hit the ground. Hard.

Cicely screamed.

Passersby had long since stopped to watch the affray. Of course, no one thought it'd be a good idea to—*oh, I don't know*—stop the fight. However, when they saw the impact of Talon's head driving into Calin's abdomen, collective gasps rent the air.

She would swear the earth moved from the force of the blow. The tables and chairs jumped in response. Incredible.

Incredibly scary!

Nevertheless, it broke her out of whatever trance had rooted her to the spot. Did she care about Calin's well-being? Yes. More than she should. She also cared about Walker and Dan. Amelia didn't wish them bodily harm. It defeated the purpose of her apathy affected specifically to protect them from her curse that would see to their untimely deaths. But she couldn't focus on those concerns right now. She was too scared. Scared for them and scared of herself. So, she took a page from Forrest Gump's book and...

Ran.

Chapter Nineteen

"**A**re you okay?"

Shit! Too concerned. Hating the hysterical edge in her tone, Amelia threw her purse on the passenger's seat of the Mustang and closed the door. Guys, especially rebel without a cause types, scared easy. Her mother hen act probably freaked him out.

Calin shut the driver's side door of his Rolls and headed in her direction.

Oh, this was risky, being outside her house. Thank goodness no one was home. Of course, that didn't mean they couldn't arrive at any minute. Amelia didn't feel like defending her friendship with Calin. He'd been through enough today.

Amelia inspected him. Not a scratch. How had he escaped the brawl without injury? She bit her lip; her breathing grew shallow. The man's very existence should be outlawed.

He'd changed in the hours since the fight. His damp brown hair appeared black in the fading sun. A snug carbon t-shirt stretched to the limit under the strain of restraining his massive, chiseled chest. He wore a fresh pair of dark blue jeans and black combat boots.

They met between their parallel parked cars. He leaned against his trunk. She sat on her hood.

"My jaw's not made of glass," Calin replied, rubbing his stubbled chin. Cocking a brow, he grinned. "Were you worried about me?"

Damn, his smile lit his entire face. He looked years younger than the twenty-five years he claimed. Gazing into his pale blue-green eyes, Amelia felt the urge to run to church and confess. The man was sin incarnate.

"Maybe a little worried." No sense in denying her concern, but she'd admit nothing more. It'd come off sappy and further blur the lines of their friendship. "Sorry I took off. Shouldn't you be lying down or icing something? You got hit pretty hard."

"Wasn't as bad as it looked. You worried for good reason though—for Walker. I would've killed him."

Not a comforting thought. Especially, given the murderous glint in his eyes as he said the words. Plus, he outweighed Walker by at least a hundred pounds. He *could* kill him. Walker's jealousy bullshit might annoy her, and they might be together for the wrong reasons, but she didn't want him dead.

Calin grabbed her hand. Held it in his much larger one—a new thing he'd started doing in the last week when they were alone. Felt wrong, and right—kind of. Either way, she never pulled away. Friends were sometimes affectionate, weren't they? Tessa went through a whole two years infatuated with slapping her on the ass whenever the mood struck.

"Coming or going?"

"What?"

He nodded toward her car where her purse could be seen on the seat through the windshield. Calin played with her fingers. He stroked them, cracked a couple knuckles. With his other hand, he ran his thumb from the hollow behind her ear to her right shoulder bared by her off-the-shoulder white tee.

Amelia gulped. This felt far too intimate for friends. Yet, she couldn't bring herself to move or tell him to stop.

"Were you leaving or coming back from somewhere?" he asked, clarifying his question.

"Leaving. I wanted to get in a little alone time. Apparently, the universe is conspiring against me." Crap! She didn't mean that how it sounded.

"Want me to leave? Let you meditate or journal, sacrifice small animals... chant."

"Shut up!" She laughed. "I don't chant. Who chants?"

"Sure, you don't." He smirked, brought her hand to his sexy, full lips.

The kiss he placed on her knuckles was chaste. Tender. If she were a girl who swooned she'd be a puddle on the ground. Tingles radiated over the spot his lips touched and shot up her arm.

Calin dropped her hand. Backed away as if he felt it, too. "Go. Have your alone time. I'll hook up with you tomorrow. Be at work."

Like a bursting dam, a dose of sheer panic flooded her system. "No," she nearly shouted before he reached his car door. "Come be alone with me."

Headed east on the US-60, the sun drooped below the mountain line. The darkening sky turned a hazy blue-purple-orange hue. Day morphed into a marvelous night for dining under the stars. Calin frowned.

He was hungry. It'd been a while since he fed, and the small portions of mortal food he consumed weren't cutting it. He needed blood. The mango-almond aroma wafting to him from the passenger seat didn't help. It beckoned him to do... things. Made it hard to distinguish between sexual hunger and blood hunger. Calin suspected Amelia might take issue with either remedy to slacken his thirst. Molesting her outside her house was where he drew the line.

He would not pull over, drag her across the seat divider, and force her to straddle his lap. No matter how delectable she looked in her cropped, off-the-shoulder shirt, which exposed creamy brown skin, an innie belly button, and teal shorts.

"Ooh, ooh, ooh," Amelia said, bouncing in her seat. "Get off here." She pointed out the window toward the Alma School Rd. exit.

Calin deserved an award for the strength it took to follow Amelia's directions to a complex of townhomes and not drive them into a tree. Inviting breasts that defied logic, given her size, and gravity jiggled. Was she wearing a bra? *Focus, dammit!*

If he ran into one of these rotted trees, it'd disintegrate on contact. Shrubs were bare, resembling tumbleweeds rather than actual shrubs. Wooden gates to the units were spray painted with graffiti. Stucco on most of the homes was chipped. Charming.

Note to self: Bring Bianca here to feed. One of these bums goes missing, and no one would find out for weeks—if ever.

"It's actually a good thing you're here," Amelia said, as he parked outside a grouping of townhomes and they got out. "Usually, I have to stack a couple bricks to get up here." She stopped outside one of the few not vandalized wooden gates. "I'd get a ladder, but I don't want people thinking I'm breaking in."

Somehow, he doubted anyone in this neighborhood would care. The only thing she risked would be interrupting a robbery already in progress.

"What are you doing?"

"I need you to open the latch on this." She pointed at the top of the gate.

Reaching up and over the gate, he unhooked the latch. Must take a lot of bricks for her to do this alone. The gate was at least nine inches taller than her and hooked on the inside. For reasons unbeknownst to him, his mind rebelled against the notion of her doing anything this strenuous. Her doing this alone agitated him—ah, hell, who was he kidding? He didn't want her doing this type of activity without *him*. Crazy.

And very unlike him.

He didn't give a rat's ass about anyone. No one cared about him. If anything, the world owed him.

Once open, they entered the small dirt backyard of a vacant townhome. Amelia walked over to a square, beige metal structure, a utility box. She climbed on top of it. Before he realized what she meant to do, she grabbed hold of the roof, planted a foot on the wall for leverage, and pulled herself onto the roof.

"What the hell are you doing?" he asked, rushing over to the box. Uncaring who saw, he used supernatural agility to leap onto the roof in one jump.

Her eyes widened to the size of saucers. "Holy, shit! Who are you—Superman?"

"No. I'm Batman," he teased to draw attention away from his blunder.

Why he did, he didn't know. What would she do? Cry vampire? Not likely. If mortals did that, there'd be an overpopulation issue in insane asylums, not prisons.

"Sit with me." She motioned to a corner of the roof, too close to the edge for his comfort.

Fuck! What was with these protective instincts he felt toward her? This irrational fear he had of her falling? The last thing he should feel is protective. He would kill her, soon. Twice.

They sat in companionable silence. Time passed. Bright stars sprinkled the sky. This must be the sole stretch of unpolluted Arizona sky. In the distance, blue lights lit the contours of a tall, glass building.

Amelia broke the silence. "When I was little, before Dad got a better job, we lived here. I could see that building outside my window. I thought it was a castle. I'd make up all sorts of stories about me being a lost princess. Of course, Evan—my big brother—ruined it by telling me it was a bank. I come here whenever I need to... I don't know—breathe. It's my favorite place in the entire world, which isn't saying much since I've never been anywhere."

She turned and smiled. Twin dimples indented her cheeks. Something inside him shifted. He captured the hand closest to him that rested in her lap. Her fingers curled around his, and for a moment, everything in his world was right. Then, she tugged her hand away.

"Walker." Amelia clung to the name like a talisman capable of stopping whatever *this* was between them. When it didn't work, which he knew it wouldn't, she dragged her knees to her chest.

Wrapped her arms around her legs. Chin resting on her upraised knees, she turned her sad gaze on him.

"So, your idea of a castle is a glass building with blue lights? I can show you castles, Duchess. There's no shortage of them in Romania or Europe."

"I was a kid, stupid. I don't believe in castles or fairy tales anymore. Nothing but hard facts for me now. Anyway, I come here because of my parents."

"Why?" He couldn't imagine visiting any place for his parents. Eliza might think he was here for her, but it served his goals. The fact it cured her—an undesired bonus. "Do they know you come here?"

Color drained from her face. "My parents died three years ago—I thought I told you. I usually lead with that." The next time she spoke, her voice was low. Even with his preternatural hearing he had to strain to hear. "Do you think a person can be cursed?"

He scowled. "Why do you ask?"

Amelia's eyes glistened with unshed tears. Grief vibrated from her every pore. Calin's protective instincts charged to the surface. His need to help reached primal proportions.

She swallowed hard. "Because everyone I love dies. Trust me, I know how stupid or juvenile that sounds, but it's true."

Didn't sound stupid or juvenile to him. He knew firsthand about curses. *Thanks, Mother.* Suspicion gnawed at his gut. There was more to this story. "Who's died?"

"Both sets of grandparents, my best friend." Looking at him, she clarified. "My guy best friend, and the folks who started it all... my adoptive parents."

"Grandparents age and pass on. That's not abnormal."

"It is when all of them died tragically trying to get to me. And all within the span of three years."

That was strange. Calin kept his features neutral. His mind was another story. She was right, although it didn't sound like a curse. It sounded like systematic elimination. Someone had exterminated those who'd miss her or prevent her from moving on. She lived a strict mortal life. Talon was the only supernatural close to her. He doubted the douche's moral code would allow him to perform such a cleansing.

Who would orchestrate this?

The prophecy of her birth came only twenty years prior. From his intel, the prophecy outlining her transition appeared three months ago. Someone would have to have known about her longer to hatch a plan that spanned three years. He gazed into her sullen eyes. His chest tightened. Damn, soul! He'd solve the mystery later.

"I was just a baby when they adopted me. Evan was two. Most adopted kids have issues. Wanna know where they came from. Not me. My parents kept me grounded. Now everyone expects me to just... get over it." She shook her head. "How am I supposed to do that, continue to live, when the ground's been knocked from under me? It's been three years. I'm *barely* functional."

Amelia would be the death of him. She really would.

He should stop touching her. Continually feeling her warm—well, not that warm since she was further into the transition—satin skin under his palm. Really, he shouldn't touch her, but dammit he couldn't help himself. A greater force demanded it. He peeled one of her hands from around her leg, enclosed it in both of his, and held it in his lap.

She didn't pull away.

Feelings weren't his forte. He cleared his throat a couple times. "Build a new ground. A new foundation to stand on. It takes time. I did it when my father died."

When his mother abandoned him, the callous bastard, no matter how insufferable, had been all he'd known. His only family. Calin took care of his father when he was sick and arranged a private funeral in the family plot when he died.

"Easier said than done," she muttered under her breath.

"Don't I know it? But you move on. Never forget, but through it."

Startling him—something he'd never cop to—she laughed. A hearty belly laugh. He'd never seen her this open. She always shielded herself with sarcasm. An air of artificiality clung to her, but not now. It shook him on a level he hadn't known existed.

"I've known some of my friends forever—my brother my whole life. This is the first time I've ever talked voluntarily about this stuff. You know, like, *really* talked about it," Amelia confided over the roar of a car's bad engine in the distance.

Calin didn't even pretend to talk himself out of touching her this time. He put a finger under her chin, tilted her face toward him. When her gaze found his, he asked, "Why'd you talk to me?"

Her answer was important. In his experience, people didn't divulge weaknesses unless it was a strategic move. Some way to throw the enemy off-kilter.

"You didn't ask," was her solemn reply. "You don't hound me. Don't expect anything from me. You don't watch me like a China bowl in an earthquake."

Well, if that wasn't a swift kick to the gonads, nothing else would be.

An uncomfortable weight settled on his heart. A rock sunk to the bottom of his stomach. *Fuck!* He didn't do this—whatever *this* was—at all. He needed to go drain someone or fight something. Now.

"You let me be me, no matter who me is. It's nice. I guess," she finished and blushed.

I am a dick.

Damn pesky soul. Kicked in at the worst times. He lightened his tone, although he felt anything but light. "Good. Your secret's safe with me. I don't know anybody you know, and the few people I've met don't like me."

"Cicely would beg to differ." She laughed, pushing his arm playfully with her shoulder.

Throwing her a flat sideways glance, he went on, "Plus, I go back to Romania June twenty-seventh."

Amelia's expression brightened. "Hey! That's my birthday. I'm turning twenty-one. I'll be legal for everything, at least for everything here. What's the legal drinking age in Romania?"

"Oh, that's what you're after," he drawled. "You don't care about your birthday, you just want to drink." He laughed, nuzzled their joined hands on his whiskered chin. "I hate to break it to you, *ma douce*, but you were legal to drink at eighteen in Romania."

"Ma douce?" She gazed at him with clear innocent eyes.

"It's French. I'm from France originally. It's nothing." The last thing he wanted to do was explain to her—or him—why he'd called her "my sweet."

"You should come to my party," she offered, curiosity forgotten. "We can make a special bon voyage toast to you and Bianca. Where is she anyway?"

Saying he left her with some psychopath rogue at his mother and grandfather's behest wouldn't work. Didn't work for him either, which was why he left when they went to feed.

"She's out with a friend. It's nice out here," he said, changing the subject. *Smooth.*

"It's why I come here."

Inspiration struck. He stood, extending a hand to her. "Dance with me?"

Eyebrows scrunched; her mouth turned down. "There's no music." Yet, she took his hand, trusting him, again.

He pulled her to her feet. Her softer body came against his—hard. Calin willed himself not to pitch wood. Her breasts pressed into his chest. Nope, no bra. She felt good. He took a moment to collect himself before wrapping an arm around her waist and taking her other hand in his.

He sang, "*'Oh, you must've been a beautiful baby. You must've been a beautiful child.'*" The ladies loved Bobby Darin's "You Must Have Been A Beautiful Baby." Calin bounced and swayed them to the beat he created.

She giggled but went with it. "This is your idea of dancing, huh? You're lucky you sing so pretty, or this would be fruity."

"Masculine, not pretty," he corrected, interrupting his song but not the dance. "Nothing about a man should be pretty." He continued singing.

Something about her ethereal, tinkling laughter and general happiness brought him joy. A feeling he'd never experienced before. He felt empowered. As if with her in his arms he could do anything. If there were a way to bottle this moment and keep it forever—glancing down at her blissful face, her shining, stunning eyes—he'd find it.

"Spin," he instructed. Latching onto one elegant hand, he spun her outward and slammed into a nightmare.

He lost his grip. Amelia slipped off the edge of the roof.

No, not slipped. Fell.

Not fell, plucked. She was filched from his arms and pulled off the roof.

Calin catapulted himself from the roof, landing in a crouch on the ground. He rose to his full height with slow deliberation. He didn't give a fuck who watched now. No one stole from him. His predator's eyes cast light, allowing him sight in the darkness. He zeroed in on the male kneeling over the unconscious descendant.

"You played long enough; find your own prey," slurred a thick German accent without sparing him a glance. "This one's mine now."

Insane with animalistic, homicidal rage, something about the snarling rogue's voice managed to penetrate Calin's blind fury. Inching closer, he took a second to focus on his unexpected foe.

White-blond hair, wearing jeans with holes in the knees, stained black T-shirt... He knew this vampire. Once upon a time, he'd hunted with this rogue, taught him to fend for himself against the VRG. "Friedrich?"

The rogue's head snapped up. "Calin?"

Calin stepped closer.

"What has it been—a decade? What are you doing here?"

Hearing expanded, Calin checked Amelia's vitals. He had to. It was an undeniable compulsion. Her heart beat steady and strong. She couldn't die before the *Awakening*, at least, that's what he tried to convince himself was the reason relief swept over him at the sight of her chest's rise and fall.

His gaze slid to a bump and gash above her left brow, traveled to a cut on her arm. Blood bubbled from each wound. The scent of her blood filled the air, alerting all who wished to do her harm to her whereabouts. Ire punched through his relief.

Assured Amelia would be okay, he switched his attention to the topic at hand. He moved closer, scant feet separated him and the vampire. "This is far from Germany, Friedrich."

"I know this. Thought I'd take a vacation. There are quite a few fillies here in this Valley of the Death."

Sun, death, all the same for a vampire. Who cared if the nimrod got it wrong? Calin prowled around Friedrich who was still hunched possessively over his prey.

"You into horses now, Friedrich?"

Friedrich chuckled. Descended blood-stained fangs revealed the rogue had been on a recent feeding frenzy—not that his blood-encrusted shirt didn't also tell the tale. "I am equal opportunity feeder and breeder. Try everything once, I always say, eh?"

Calin nodded, distracted, completing a third lap around his former acquaintance—a shark circling quarry. "How does my grandfather feel about you being this far from your assigned territory?"

"You know, Herr Balkan."

"I do." Another lap.

"I handle him with kid gloves. What he does not know won't hurt him."

So, true.

"What brought you here?" Calin asked, feigning interest.

"The smell. I was ten, fifteen, miles away when scent on the wind caught me. I track it here."

"Hmm... a scent on the wind?"

Friedrich's nod was enthusiastic. Blond hair flopped into blue eyes. "It was delectable, true delicacy."

"That she is," he mused, stopping behind Friedrich. "Now, when exactly did you scent me?"

The rogue turned at that precise moment. Calin conjured his favorite weapon, a silver-plated Kung Fu sword. A whistle sounded as he drew the sword back, Friedrich's only warning before one swift slice...

Decapitated him.

The rogue's body continued to hover where it leaned over Amelia. Its head slid off its shoulders, down its back, leaving an oozing trail of slimy, fetid blood on the black T-shirt. The severed head fell to the ground. Bounced. Dirt sullied ice-blond hair. Pale blue eyes stared sightlessly.

Calin marveled at his work for a moment, knowing that—

As if on cue, the body and head popped, burst apart in a puff of ash like flour-covered hands clapped together. They disintegrated.

No muss, no fuss. Just how he liked it.

He approached Amelia's supine body with caution. He bent, dusted the ash remains of his brethren from her clothes. She'd be dirty, but alive. He'd concoct a good cover story when she came to. Being so far into the transition, her cuts and scrapes were already healing. The only evidence left would be an easily explained small bump. Calin lifted her into his arms. She weighed nothing, less than a feather. More than he should—shit, he shouldn't at all—he relished the feel of her snuggled against him.

No need for pretenses now. He blinked them from the backyard of the abandoned townhome to his Rolls. She was out, and anyone who saw him would chalk it up to some drug-induced hallucination. Calin opened the back door with his mind. Settled Amelia on the seat, then closed the door.

Bet Friedrich never expected what he didn't know to hurt him.

Chapter Twenty

T alon gazed at the little nymph passing through the paneled door he held open.

She glared daggers at him.

Be as mad as you want, milady. I'm not going anywhere.

"I don't understand why we're here," he groused aloud. "How can you plan a meal yet not know how to prepare what you've planned?"

"Quit your bitchin', you weren't invited," Amelia snapped, jabbing him in the stomach with her bony elbow. "Oops, my bad."

Yeah, right. Accident—his ass. She was pissed he'd shown up at her house just as she was about to leave again. Apparently, she planned to prepare dinner for Walker tonight. He didn't give two shits about her plans. On Gawain's advice, he'd given her one day to cool down after the fight. She'd stolen the extra two by avoiding him. Three days was his limit.

Amelia didn't comprehend the favor he'd done her. Her eyes had begun to glow, and she'd been salivating with the desire for bloodshed. It was either play on her ridiculous affection for the rogue and hit him or kill the mortals. No one noticed her rapt interest, glowing eyes, or the slight descent of her pre-transition baby fangs. If someone had, she would've attacked. She wouldn't have been able to control the instinct.

Talon didn't know much about the transition. In all honesty, no one did. No mortal had ever transitioned to immortal. One of the few pieces of intel he'd managed to glean was that she could not feed before the *Awakening*. Her digestive system would remain mortal until she transitioned. Feeding would cause great pain; her body would reject it.

Similar to the ten-year reprieve The Fates bestowed upon *Natural-born* young, Amelia's demon lay dormant—for the most part—and couldn't influence her. Meaning, her blood hunger would remain at manageable levels. Provided her demon wasn't tempted. The nearer it got to her twenty-first birthday, the easier her demon would be to tempt. If roused, it could rise to the forefront and cause her to experience dissociative moments.

He prevented causing her pain by forcing her demon to retreat. Her response to the damn *Daywalker* infuriated him. She'd gone from bloodthirsty to lucid in seconds. Amelia treated him like he had the Ebola virus while treating Calin as if he were a delicate flower. Talon had gone out of his way to keep her safe, was created for her, and she hated him. He wasn't jealous, just painfully aware of the double standard.

Amelia glanced at him. At that precise moment, several mortals seemed to materialize from nowhere to enter the bookstore, forcing him to hold the door for them all. She flashed him a haughty smile, and then sashayed deeper into the establishment.

Talon clamped down on the impulse to release the door, let it bash the entitled mortals in the head. He watched the sway of her hips, liking the way the acid-wash denim maxi dress caressed her curves. She could run but not hide. Her cherry blossom scent was etched in his brain. He'd find her anywhere.

In any event, he needed to make headway with her, and he'd be damned if she continued this infatuation with a *Daywalker*.

Her behavior was unbefitting of a queen. He didn't know Calin's game, but he wasn't playing. Talon would've destroyed him, but he was curious about him. Better to know one's enemy. Something was different about Calin. Talon intended to figure out what. Anyway, it would be suspicious if Calin disappeared.

Given Amelia's inquisitive nature, she'd not only notice but assume his guilt. The *Awakening* was too close to alienate her in that way. Plus, for some reason, Calin didn't seem to be interested in the *Awakening*, if he knew about it at all. He'd had ample opportunity to kill her if he were trying to stop it. He knew they spent time together. It irked him each time he smelled Calin's dark, evil scent on Amelia. Made him wonder if Calin wasn't waiting for the *Awakening*...

What was he waiting for?

Speaking of questions needing answers... Where did Amelia escape to? After the last mortal took advantage of his unintended generosity, he went in search of her. He found her in the cookbook aisle.

"What happened to your forehead?" he demanded.

The bruise above her left brow wouldn't be noticeable to most people. Talon wasn't most people. His superior vision clearly saw the fading purple bruise. Ten to one said the *Daywalker* had something to do with it.

Rich, earthy red mottled Amelia's cheeks, but otherwise, she ignored him and continued browsing the shelves.

Ooh... she was difficult. "Amelia, I apologized."

She turned hard eyes on him. "You said *I said I was sorry*," she corrected in a deep voice he assumed was her impersonation of him. "That's not the same, and I'm not the one you should apologize to. You beat up an innocent man. Didn't your parents ever teach you to keep your hands to yourself?"

Yeah, he wouldn't touch that. His parents had taught him to destroy first and ask no questions.

"Why do you do that?"

"Do what?" he asked genuinely curious.

"Act so amazed by everything. Although, weird, I could believe you'd never been to the mall before. Some guys aren't mall guys. But you're looking around here like you stepped into the Twilight Zone."

Damn, she was observant. He *hadn't* ever been to a mall. It'd been an experience, to say the least. He likened it to the grocery store she'd taken him to. He'd been repulsed. Animal carcasses were sold in a plethora of forms: Frozen, sliced, nuggets...

nasty. Going to the mall had been *Raj* on Earth. If a natural disaster occurred, the mall would be a vampire's grocery store. Mass amounts of mortals in all different varieties locked in with him...? Yum!

The bookstore provided another type of awe. Books on a multitude of topics filled shelves against walls and set in the middle of the store. They were everywhere. The *compound* could use a facility such as this—without mortals, of course. White-witch Advisors kept the supernatural's historical tomes in a communal palazzo guarded by lion-shifter Royal Guardsmen.

"I don't get out much where I'm from," he finally answered.

She nodded and started away.

"Where are you going?"

"Nowhere. I wanted to look at another book."

If she thought to ditch him, she thought wrong.

"I'm not ditching you," she said, giving voice to his thoughts. "I'll, literally, be two aisles away."

Getting to know her got harder every day. Time was of the essence, and he was nowhere near ready to explain her destiny to her. If he skipped getting to know her and told her anyway, she'd think him crazy and more than likely jeopardize her safety. He somehow needed to break through the fortress she'd erected around herself.

Not really seeing the books, Talon wandered through the aisle behind the one Amelia disappeared down. He'd give her one more minute of solitude. Fine hairs on the nape of his neck rose. Something was off. He didn't want to risk being inundated with the scent of blood, so instead of expanding his olfactory senses, he reached out telepathically. He searched for any hint of a rogue mind. Found nothing.

On his second pass through the aisle, a book caught his eye. He frowned at the intertwined naked male and female bodies. Turning, he found himself staring at a fuchsia book with two stick figures in a compromising position against a wall.

What section is this?

He looked up at the placard above the shelf...

"Relationship."

Holy, hell!

Wretched, depraved mortals! How could they publish such private matters? He didn't pretend to understand their need to sell possession at every turn. Strip clubs, prostitution, porn... *Jersey Shore*. He wasn't a prude, far from it. Training had always superseded his carnal urges. But like any virile male, he had needs. A mental list of things he wanted to try—with Amelia.

Shit, no! Not with her. This section corrupted his mind.

Other mortal media for possession at least had enough decency to warn a being instead of thrusting itself on them unawares.

"Amelia," Talon said, trying to employ Her Majesty's idea of a whisper. She seemed to think he had a problem modulating his tone. He couldn't help it his voice carried. "A-mel-ia."

She rounded the corner. "What?" she asked in an exaggerated semi-whisper.

"Did you know they have books on possession here?" He pointed to the offending material.

Her expression blanked. "What?"

"They have books on possession here," he repeated exasperated. Dammit! Why couldn't she ever respond the way he expected. Females were usually outraged by things of this nature. She didn't seem to have a clue. He tried again. "You know...?"

"What?" she asked again eyes narrowed. "You mean, like, demon possession?"

"No." He rolled his eyes. "I'm well-versed on that. I mean *possession*," he said, deepening his voice an erotic timbre. "When a male claims a female...?"

The laughter that burst forth from her mouth stroked his dick like a hand. Fuck!

"Talon, you're a weirdo. I can almost forgive you for—"

A ghost. Couldn't be. Why would he be here? Talon grabbed Amelia by the hand none too gently.

"Hey," Amelia protested. "Now, I don't forgive—"

"We need to leave. Now."

Amelia huffed but allowed him to lead her to the checkout counter. Despite her protest, he paid for her book and got the hell out of there. He all but threw her in the car, slammed the door, and hurried around to the driver's side.

Once behind the wheel, he yanked out his cell phone, hit speed dial number "3". Skipping the niceties, Talon uttered four words as soon as the male answered. "Gawain, Emilio is here."

At the sound of the buzzer, Amelia grabbed two black and white cow-designed potholders off pegs hung on the wall above the stove. She yanked the stove door open, reached in with protected hands, and pulled out the glass casserole dish. Baked Ziti. Walker's favorite.

"Mrs. Brady, eat your heart out," she said aloud in the empty kitchen. Tessa was somewhere with Dan. She'd have the house to herself to ruin Walker's life. Wasn't every day a girl got to be the anti-Ed McMahon. Instead of making his dreams come true with a whopping Publishers Clearinghouse check, she was about to saddle Walker with a huge dream-crushing responsibility.

Loathe didn't cover how she felt about this, but it had to be done. She'd delayed as long as possible, and her period hadn't magically appeared. Time to put on her big girl panties and deal with the consequences of her actions. Walker would want to do all the right stuff. Go to doctor's appointments, move in, get married, and she'd let him, knowing full well it wasn't fair to him. She'd be faithful and good to him while depriving him of true happiness with a woman who returned the love he gave. Wasn't she great! Yep, ranked right up there with Lorena Bobbit.

Ding... Dong!

Shit! Her stomach dropped. She looked at the microwave clock. Of course, Walker would be on time. Never in his life was he on time. The night she had to tell him news that made her want to vomit with nervousness, he popped up right on time.

Amelia set the casserole dish on top of the stove. Dessert would be her famous vegan chocolate cake. She wouldn't be able to eat. Break dancers were battling inside her tummy. Careful not to mess up her ponytail, she removed her mother's vintage, red lace bib apron, folded it, and put it away in a side drawer.

Thanks to the giant butt-munch—aka Talon—she was running behind. Not only did she not have time to change out of her maxi dress, but she hadn't put the topping on the Grape Tomato Bruschetta appetizer Walker loved. Damn tree!

Pausing at the door, she took a deep breath, which did bupkis to settle her nerves. *Walker Palmer, this is your life...* She opened the door.

"Hey, baby, how was your day?" Walker smiled. His heated gaze roved her body.

Score one for the maxi dress. The guy had sex on the brain 24/7.

Dressed uncharacteristically professional in tan khakis, a white button-down with sleeves rolled just above the wrists, a navy-blue silk tie, and, of course, his trademark Chuck Taylors, he looked good. Must've just gotten off work.

Walker enveloped her in a bone-crushing embrace. Kissed her hard.

Amelia sucked in a quick breath. Not from the force of the hug, but from the delectable scent that hit her like a linebacker. *What is that smell?*

He better not have eaten already. She'd told him this was a special dinner.

"Better now that you're here," she answered, using the cutesy voice he liked. "I missed you, stranger." Before he let her go, she kissed his neck—and damn near licked it.

Whoa! Pregnancy hormones must be kicking in hardcore. No Axe and sweat smell tonight. He smelled wonderful.

She stepped back before she followed through with her crazy impulse to lick him. To sidetrack herself she went to check on the cake. It had baked fast—that could be what she smelled.

"Somebody's been busy, I see," Walker commented, entering the dining room as she entered the kitchen. "Did you have fun with Talon today?" Shuffling noises hinted that he pulled out a chair and sat.

Amelia grunted.

How to describe her time with Talon? He frustrated the bejeezus out of her. One minute he barked orders, the next, he was scared she'd find his secret comic book stash, then back to being demanding, then he was skittish about sex. For someone who looked like sex personified, it was hard to believe he got shy around sex books. Talon baffled her.

"What'd you guys do?"

God, didn't he understand the universal grunt for "I don't want to talk about it"? "Nothing. Just walked around, looked at books." Seeing that the cake had a few more minutes, Amelia took the bowl of dressed tomatoes out of the refrigerator. She placed them on the island next to the plate of toasted bruschetta.

As she'd suspected, Walker had loosened his tie and sat at the dining table in front of one of the settings she'd put out earlier. Tonight was a good china night. She even used the Vera Wang Princess Crystal wine glasses Talon had bought her as a thank you for decorating the castle. Walker might not be impressed with the glasses, but his favorite Chianti would bring infinite joy. He loved wine.

"That's good. Now you've got someone to do all that boring shit with." He smiled when she scowled at his snide comment. "What're you doing in there?"

Amelia spooned tomatoes onto the bruschetta.

I will not ruin this night by arguing.

"Umm... Tessa's somebody."

"Yeah, if you consider a soulless harpy somebody then... I guess. I kinda thought you'd like somebody to hang with who didn't have to hide a 666 brand under a boy's haircut."

The spoon clanked as she dropped it into the metal bowl. She pegged him with a frigid glare. Why was he trying to argue with her? If anyone had the right to be testy, it was her. He seemed to forget his unprovoked assault on an innocent man a few days ago. "That's fucked up. And who are you to talk shit about somebody's hair?"

Abashed, he lifted his hands in surrender. "Touché. I'm sorry. What're you doing?"

"Making appetizers," she answered, happy for the subject change. She didn't want to argue. They'd have enough time for that later. "It's supposed to be a surprise. Go look at something."

Walker got up and wandered over to the old school stereo and stack of CDs on the shelves built into where the wall stuck out a bit from when Evan's room had been expanded. "You look hot. I like when you wear your hair like that. So... what's up with dinner? I thought you were pissed at me for mangling your little friend."

What a gloater! She should tell him Calin didn't have a scratch, but it'd be a low blow. "You shouldn't have done that. He didn't do anything to you. It was my fault."

Snorting, Walker put a CD in the CD player. "What? You think he would've backed off if you asked him to?" He cocked an eyebrow and shook his head. "I had to handle it."

So annoying. She finished the appetizers. "Okay. You can sit down. I have grape tomato bruschetta appetizers and wine."

"Red?"

"Of course."

"You know me so well." He sat in his previously vacated seat. "I hope you don't mind, I put some mood music in."

"Fine with me." She brought corkscrew, salad, appetizers, and lastly the wine to the table. This felt awkward. They hadn't been alone together in what seemed like years. Uncomfortable tension filled the space between them. Like they were both guarding against offending the other. Maybe it was her. She was stalling. No matter how much had changed about her in the last three years, one thing hadn't. Amelia didn't beat around the bush. Tonight, she did.

Amelia sat the wine bottle down and peeled the black wrapper off.

"Want me to do that?" Walker asked, extending his hand for the bottle.

She jerked it out of his reach. "No, I can do it," she said, placing the coil in the center of the cork and drilling it in. With the hinge on the neck of the bottle, she pulled. The cork slid out a few inches then refused to budge.

"You're so stubborn. I'll do it, babe. I don't want you to break your pretty nails." He reached for the bottle once more.

Dick!

Rage ripped through Amelia. On a foolish whim, she lifted the bottle, put her mouth around the small bud of cork she'd wiggled free, gripped it with her teeth, and yanked. The cork popped out.

She tossed him a smug, tight-lipped smile. Although inside... she freaked the fuck out. Wall's comment had pissed her off, but not to the point of super strength. Pulling the cork shouldn't have been that easy. She didn't even spill any wine.

Playing it cool, she moved to Walker's side. She reached for his wine glass. The same mind-frazzling scent from before attacked her. Of their own accord, her eyes drifted closed. She dragged in a breath so deep it touched her toes. The bittersweet scent hit like a sledgehammer to the gut. Saliva pooled in her mouth as an odd, yet familiar, taste settled on her tongue. Tasted as if she'd sucked on a penny. Her stomach growled. Loud.

Walker chuckled. "Hungry?"

Not really. She was a bundle of nerves. When she'd checked the cake, her stomach turned. Now...

She was famished.

An uneasy chill raced down her spine. Setting the wine bottle aside, she muttered, "I'm gonna get the rest of the food." Intuition told Amelia she needed to get away from Walker. She took their dinner plates and went into the kitchen. "I thought you put mood music on?" she asked, dishing out the sauce and cheese-coated pasta. The aroma of cooked onions nauseated her.

"I did. Let me check." Amelia heard sounds of him moving. A second later, he said, "My bad, forgot to press play."

A cacophony of crickets chirping, sticks, and rocks being driven over, and other night sounds permeated the room. Finished preparing their plates, she turned a droll stare on Walker.

Mood music, huh?

"What?" He shrugged. "Some people get in the mood to John Mayer or Bruno Mars. I prefer Limp Bizkit."

Amelia rolled her eyes as Fred Durst uttered the words, *"You're gonna love this,"* from the song "Eat You Alive". Somehow, this put her at ease, Walker being Walker.

She loved that about him. He wasn't afraid to be him, and he didn't apologize for it. Reminded her of why she got together with him in the first place. Wasn't the fact that he tattooed her name down his ribcage before she ever agreed to go out with him, but his conviction? His certainty? Confidence? No one agreed with him or his choices. And he didn't give a shit.

Electric guitar and a drum riff tore through the room as she sat his plate in front of him then sat her own in the space across from him. She took her seat. Walker dug in with zest. She picked up a forkful, got it halfway to her mouth, and gagged.

"What's wrong?"

Shaking her head, she lowered her fork to her plate.

Following suit, Walker reached across the table and grabbed her hand. With the other hand, he stroked her cheek. Love shone in his brown eyes. She missed this. Maybe that was what was with her lately. She couldn't have feelings for Calin or Talon; they were strangers. It'd been so long since she'd accepted any affection from anyone close to her.

Leaning into his comfort, she said, "Thanks, I'll—"

The smell was back with a vengeance. Kicked her square in the solar plexus. Mouthwatering didn't cover it. It was orgasmic. She swallowed several times to keep from drooling. Where had she smelled this before?

"Having a senior moment?" Walker chuckled and moved to drop the hand rubbing her cheek.

"No!" she shouted near panic. He kept his hand in place. "I like that."

Reminiscent of a kitten, she snuggled closer to his warm hand. Much warmer than her skin as of late. She nuzzled back and forth against his palm, sliding her nose up and down his wrist.

Mmm...

Her eyes drifted closed. Then popped open as if guided on instinct. She saw it. "What happened to your neck?" she asked, staring at the white square stuck to Wall's neck to the right of his bulbous Adam's apple. A red haze clouded her vision.

As if called forth by her gaze, a small spot of red formed in the center of the tissue. Crept toward the edges. Summoned her.

She was transfixed.

Not sure when she moved, she found herself crouched, balancing her weight on the balls of her feet on her chair. She leaned over the table and stared at the square up close.

That smell...

Amelia licked her lips.

Walker drew back. His new position highlighted the thick, blue veins under his tattooed skin. Beautiful. She ran her tongue over her top teeth. Her right and left incisors were longer. Sharper. The canines were longer and sharper than those. Hmm... That should worry her. It didn't. Her give-a-damn didn't seem to be working.

A switch flipped inside her. She tore the tissue square from Walker's neck. The stunned widening of his eyes urged her on. Thrilled her.

Scrambling to rise, Walker pushed his chair back. And fell backward.

With grace she hadn't known she possessed, she lunged. Shot up and over the table like a lioness pouncing on prey. She landed on his chest. Her now clawed nails pierced his shirt, digging into the butter-soft flesh of his shoulder. Red crescents of blood sprung to the surface. He struggled. It was useless. She was stronger. Something inside her awakened. Roared to life.

Walker was terrified.

When the chair tipped, he'd half expected her to laugh and help him up. No such luck.

This wasn't Amelia anymore.

She'd transformed into an animal. A lithe, agile creature that moved with impossible speed and possessed startling strength. And let's not forget the glowing eyes.

He blinked several times, hoping to extinguish the nightmare. No such luck. When he looked up, he saw her staring down at him. Her head turned this way and that as if curious about his reaction. No recognition.

Walker had to save himself. "Amelia, baby...? Please stop."

Yeah, that worked as well as aspirin for a bullet wound.

She smiled. A harsh savage showing of—fangs? They were beautiful in a frightening way.

His heart stuttered, then took off. Beat faster than the fastest drum blast beat. Turned the drum riff of one of his songs—what he thought would be mood music—into an ominous soundtrack for his living nightmare. Why had he put it on repeat?

Although it seemed trivial, given the seriousness of the situation, he couldn't help noticing an enticing cherry blossom perfume emanating from Amelia. It relaxed him. He stopped struggling. Not because he wasn't afraid—he was ninety-nine percent sure he'd pissed himself. Walker couldn't move because, like a chemical nerve agent, her scent paralyzed.

She speared him with her luminescent stare. Her gaze dropped to his neck. As if aware of being watched, his carotid pulsed, tapping out a frantic tattoo.

Amelia's eyes met his. She traced her top lip with her tongue. Licked each of her unbelievable fangs. No doubt checking their sharpness. Her gaze bored into him. Through him. Stole his will.

He loved her so much. Been infatuated with her since the first moment he spied her deep, honey-brown skin, awesome eyes, and red hair. Walker didn't delude himself. She didn't love him, and he knew it. Oh, she might have at one time, but not now. With every death she'd endured, Amelia changed. He saw the irrational fear that stayed in her eyes. The way she died inside when her surly attitude and purposeful verbal diarrhea, meant to put people off, did just that. He got it. Just held out hope that one day her feelings would return.

She'd never understood the depths of his love for her. He'd do anything for her. Give anything to give her peace, see her happy again, including his life.

Cobra quick, she struck.

His last conscious thought... *I love you so much, Amelia.*

Chapter Twenty-One

T he night was warm. Almost as hot as it'd been during the day. How did mortals handle this weather? Calin doubted *Pakao-Brava* was this... consistent. Deathly hot all day, oven warm all night. Heat wouldn't bother any other vampire. Unluckily for him, he wasn't any other vampire. His Dark-witch and mortal halves felt heat just fine. His vampire half merely kept him from succumbing to heat stroke or other heat or cold-related mortal ailments.

Vampire hearing made it possible for him to hear banging pots, pans, children refusing baths, couples bickering. All sounds of the typical suburban neighborhood. *Her* peaceful neighborhood.

She'd warned him she wouldn't be at work today, and he was okay with that. Until nightfall. For reasons unbeknownst to him, his mind revolted against going twenty-four hours without seeing her. Could've been residual anxiety from the whole Friedrich incident. Had to be. It was the only reasonable explanation. He wanted to ensure no one else tried to take out his... cash cow—for lack of a better term. Or power line. Whatever you called it, it explained his decision to walk through her neighbor—

A gut-wrenching wail stole Calin's thoughts. Disturbed the night.

"What was that?" Bianca asked. "Sounds like one of my snacks before a feeding."

Another shriek pierced the air. Amelia.

Grabbing Bianca in his arms, he said, "You wanted to walk faster, right?" Her solitary warning before he blinked. They disappeared. Left an empty sidewalk in their wake.

They reappeared on Amelia's doorstep.

Bianca squirmed out of his arms, swaying on unsteady feet. "Keep your hands off me!" she shouted, smoothing the wrinkles in the metallic, frilly blue dress she wore. She fluffed her long blonde curls. "We could have run! You know the blinky, teleporting thing hurts my stomach. Just wait until I mature. I'm gonna blink you back to France."

Dogs barked and car alarms sounded as another woeful scream came from the house.

Now wasn't the time to point out the flaw in Bianca's logic. She couldn't strand him anywhere.

Without hesitation, Calin kicked in the door. It swung open, hitting the wall. The scene that greeted him was straight out of a horror film.

A bloody massacre.

Amelia sat on the floor in the middle of the front room. Walker's head lay in her lap. His face was ashen, and his pupils were fixed, dilated. Dead. Fresh blood covered her hands, chin, and cleavage. Saturated her denim dress and lap.

Was it wrong that he was proud of her?

"What are you waiting for? Get in there and shut her up!" Bianca shouted, hands covering her ears.

A glare over his shoulder had her shrinking back. "I can't. I haven't been invited."

He couldn't take his eyes off the gore. Two puncture wounds pierced Walker's carotid artery.

Impressive.

She got it right without guidance. And was a bit of a messy feeder.

Calin couldn't care less about her killing the pompous jerk. Her head snapped up. The anguish in her beautiful, dimly lit eyes screamed she didn't share his sentiment.

Her eyes found his. Waves of panic and fear shot out of her. Bulldozed him. Throwing her head back, she screamed her torment to the heavens and anyone else in the state.

Desperate to quiet her, Bianca pushed past him. Tried to enter the house. Her body seized. Then it bounced off the invisible veil meant to keep vampires from entering mortals' homes. The force hurled her through the air. She landed in the street. Under different circumstances, that would've been hilarious. But he'd have to give it a good laugh later. Amelia's profound misery oddly called to him.

For the second time in a week, he was compelled to help her. Amelia was perfect. Even with blood dripping from her retracting fangs and chin. It made her more beautiful.

"Duchess!" Calin called, trying to get her attention.

She continued shrieking.

"Amelia! You have to listen to me."

Still nothing.

"Amelia! Do you want to be arrested? The police will be here soon. You'll be arrested if you don't let us in. Now!"

That got her attention.

Her eyes returned to normal, fangs retracted completely. Tears spilled over the brim of her eyes. "What did I do?" she asked voice raw, pitiful.

"Let me in. I'll help you, *ma douce.*"

"Do what you want," she said flatly. "Let the police get me. I don't care. I deserve to be arrested." She shook Walker's lifeless body, spreading blood everywhere. "Walker, baby, please wake up—what did I do?"

"Amelia, you've got to listen to me."

"I don't care what you do!" she yelled; tears streamed down her face. "Wall, baby, please wake up."

Things were going to be a lot harder to engineer from outside the front door. Adding to the shitload of complications, he heard police sirens. They were miles away but coming fast. Shit! If he sweated, he'd be soaked. Fuck the *Awakening;* if anyone saw this she'd be put to death. He had to conceal this.

"Amelia, you have to invite us in."

Her gaze lifted slowly, a question in their tortured depths.

No time to be cryptic. He had to be honest. "We're vampires. We want to help you. But can't until you invite us in—by name—okay?"

"Calin and Bianca Luca... please come in," she said, shockingly asking no questions.

He grabbed a recovered Bianca by the upper arm.

"Hey, what are doing? I don't want to go in there," Bianca said.

If Calin didn't know better, he'd say his little hell-raiser was scared. One zap from the veil seemed to mellow her ass out. Store that for future reference.

"Calin, stop, no," she complained.

Ignoring her protests, he yanked her over the threshold. Then became a blur of action. He left the food—it'd further validate the cover he orchestrated.

"Bianca, close the front door. Go throw around and mess up as much as you can. Break a couple things while you're at it," he ordered.

A devious smile brightened her face.

This was how she drew prey to her. That adorable smile got 'em every time. Shit! Almost made him forget she was pure evil—almost. "Wipe your fingerprints off of anything you touch," he reminded her.

Bianca blurred into motion Tasmanian Devil-style and was just as, if not more, destructive. Good. Now, to fix Amelia...

He approached with caution, knelt beside her. "Alright, Duchess, I'm gonna move his head, okay?" Calin reached for Walker.

"No!" she shouted, pulling his head farther into her lap.

Calin sighed. "Amelia, there's nothing we can do for him now. I'll help you fix it though."

Shaking her head, she stroked Walker's hair. Stared at his pale face.

He wasn't good with feelings, but he needed her cooperation. He gentled his tone. "Will you do something for me?"

Bloodshot eyes gazed at him.

"I need you to lick the bite marks."

She blanched.

Shit! Too much to ask.

"Lick his neck?" she rasped.

"You need to seal the wound. Lick it, and the bite mark will go away."

"What? I don't even know how I did this," she snapped, yet her voice lacked affect. She was going into shock.

Placing a hand on either side of her head, he turned her face toward him. Their eyes met. "I promise I'll explain everything when this is all over. Right now, I need you to believe me. Do you trust me?"

Amelia nodded.

An indescribable pang of some emotion stabbed his heart. She trusted him. For a moment, he considered not letting go. Her dark caramel skin was smooth as silk, and her eyes held such vulnerability. But the sirens were getting closer. Allowing his hands to slip from her face, he nodded his encouragement.

She bent and licked the puncture wounds. They waited.

Nothing happened.

Shit! She wasn't far enough into the transition for her saliva to carry the healing agent needed to close the wounds. Bending, he licked the wounds. Under their watchful eyes, the wounds sealed. Disappeared.

Amelia gasped. "What the heck?"

He shook his head. "Remember, I promised, later. I don't break promises."

A gust of wind blew past them, tousled strands of Amelia's crimson locks that'd come loose from her ponytail.

In its wake, Bianca stood at the front door. A smug smile flirted with the corners of her mouth. "The house... is trashed," she said in a mock grave tone.

"Go outside. Listen for the sirens. When they're two minutes away, come get me."

For once, Bianca didn't complain just nodded and did as instructed.

Relief swept through him. He didn't need an audience to his treachery. Bad enough Amelia would be in the room with the monster that was him.

"What about these?" she asked meekly, holding up Walker's wrist.

Two puncture wounds were there as well. Calin's chest tightened. Why did she have to be his assignment? Her first kill, and she'd drained him dry from all the best spots. She was truly ravishing. He had a lot to consider. Later. He bent and licked the wounds. They disappeared.

Now for the hard part.

Placing his palm on Amelia's forehead, he recited a quick incantation. Being a hybrid, he might not have the ability to compel, but he had a few witch tricks up his sleeve. The blood on Amelia's face and chest vanished. Her gaze unfocused, she stared through vacant eyes.

"You won't remember a thing, Duchess. See you soon," he whispered. A kiss to her forehead implanted new memories of the night's events. She'd believe vandals broke into her home and killed Walker.

A wave of Calin's hand sent Walker's body flying into the hallway wall. His head slammed hard against it, making a loud *crack*. Walker's spine broke. His skull fractured. What blood was left in the useless mortal's body splattered, painted the white wall. He levitated Walker's body back to the position it'd been in, head lying in Amelia's lap.

"Calin! Two minutes!" Bianca shouted.

Chapter Twenty-Two

Walker was fading. One second he was there, running toward her locker in B hall, or the Fresh Meat Hall, as the junior and senior boys of Durango High referred to it. The next, he was... disappearing.

This was a dream. Or more accurately, a memory. The day Walker had convinced her to go out with him. Amelia squeezed her eyes closed to keep from waking, but the dream wasn't playing out right. This was how it should go:

Amelia stood at her locker with Tessa between fourth and fifth periods.

"Wanna hear a dirty joke?" Tessa grinned, twirling a strand of long brown hair around her index finger.

"Oh, yes, tell me your joke, pervert." She smiled, pulling her biology book out of her overstuffed backpack. She tried to stuff it into the too-small space between two other books.

"Billy fell in the mud." Tessa giggled, pulling a pack of gummy bears out of her jeans pocket. "Wanna hear a clean joke?"

Still struggling, she groaned. "Fine, Tessie."

Tessa squealed in delight. She never kept it together when telling a joke. Just watching her try not to laugh before she got to the punch line made the joke funnier. "Billy took a bath with bubbles. Wanna hear a dirty joke?"

How the hell long was this joke?

Amelia wiped sweat from her brow, turned toward her best friend, and pegged her with an arch stare. She renewed her fight with her textbook.

Taking the hint, Tessa hurried on, "Bubbles is the girl next door." She burst out laughing so hard she snorted, making Amelia laugh harder.

Glaring past Amelia, Tessa sobered. She leaned against the locker beside hers and groaned.

"What happened?" Amelia chuckled. "You run out of steam, Porky?" Observing Tessa's disgusted face, she frowned. "What?"

Ripping her candy open with her teeth, Tessa jerked her chin toward the hall. "Swoon, here comes your boyfriend."

"My, what? I don't have a..." Her sentence trailed off as she followed Tessa's glare.

Dressed in black baggy jeans with a silver chain hanging from his front pocket to his wallet in his back pocket, an open white button-down over a black wife-beater, and combat boots, Walker headed in their direction.

All the freshman girls were jealous because a senior guy was enamored with her. Little did they know, it wasn't that simple.

Walker, Dan, and Evan had a three musketeer's deal going. Walker had been around since she was in third grade; dating him would not only be hella awkward, but damaging to his friendship with her brother. She didn't want to be the reason her brother lost a friend, plus he was like a member of the family.

But damn, he made it difficult to refuse him. He whipped out all the stops. Bought her jewelry, stuffed animals, chocolates, and roses. He even volunteered with her at the senior center.

"God, could he be wearing any larger clothes?" Tessa mused, chopping on a gummy bear.

"Shut up, Tessie!" she warned between gritted teeth. "It's cute in a punk sort of way."

"Whatever," was Tessa's haughty retort. "He looks like a pile of dirty laundry."

Walker sidled up to Amelia. "Hey, Miss Lady." He grinned at her, then inclined his head toward Tessa. "Broom Hilda."

Tessa flipped him off.

"Oh, no thanks, sweetie. I heard the line was *really* long for that ride." Leaning in, he pretended to whisper, "I hear it's like throwing a hot dog down a hall."

Amelia alternated her wide-eyed gaze between Walker and Tessa. She was speechless. Didn't know whether to laugh or be afraid for Walker.

"Just wait," Tessa threatened, glaring murderously. "You just friggin' wait. Payback's a bitch."

Ignoring her, he turned bedroom eyes on Amelia. "I got you something."

"Wall, you don't have to keep getting me stuff," she said, exasperated partly at him and the other part at the stupid book that wouldn't go into her locker. "I can't be your girlfriend. And I'm out of places to put things."

He snatched the book she'd been fighting with, shoved it into the slot like a piece of paper. Then started taking off his over shirt...

She and Tessa exchanged wary looks.

"Is this a naked gift?" Amelia asked bemused. She didn't want to see him naked—okay she did, but not in the hall.

Walker smiled but otherwise ignored her question. "Fine. You can't be my girlfriend, but what about a date?" He untucked his wife-beater. "Just one date?"

"Walker," she stated in trepidation, "I don't think that would—"

He lifted his shirt. Amelia and Tessa gasped.

"Oh. My. God!" Tessa shouted. "What is wrong with you? Were you dropped on your head or something?"

Amelia stood stupefied, mouth gaping. She stared.

"You don't have to find a place to put this one." Walker winked. "I already did."

She had no words.

Tessa didn't suffer the same ailment. "First, you shave your hair into that god-awful mohawk—on a bet. You pierce your *penis* because someone said you wouldn't. Now, you brand yourself?" Incredulity heightened her voice. "You have no impulse control."

After several heartbeats, Amelia regained the ability to blink and close her mouth. Even once Walker fixed his shirt, she continued to stare at the left side of his body. For the rest of his life, her name would be tattooed vertically down his ribcage in Old English letters.

"Don't you know branding yourself is the kiss of death for a relationship?" she breathed.

Walker wagged his eyebrows and smiled. "We're not in a relationship. So, see, it could have the opposite effect. C'mon, one date. Then I'll leave you alone—promise."

Tessa snorted unladylike.

Although his rationale was crazy, she couldn't help being flattered by his antics. They were the stupidest, sweetest things anyone had ever done for her. She sighed in resignation. "How can I turn down a guy with my name tattooed on him?" She smiled. "I would love to go out with you, Walker."

Amelia tossed in her sleep. That was how the memory/dream was supposed to end.

Not this time.

Instead of his footfalls growing louder as he ran down the hall toward her, they grew fainter.

Walker stopped running. He stared at her for long minutes.

Tears stung her eyes as realization slipped into her unconscious mind. He'd never come running again. The dream would never end the same. Walker would never barge into her life—which irritated her to no end—again. Now, watching him fade away, she discovered too late that she wouldn't have preferred it, him, any other way.

How could anyone not appreciate such blind devotion? She'd been a fool. And now it was too late. Why did everyone she loved die? What was it about her that summoned death? The saying was true... she didn't know what she had until it was gone.

"*I forgive you.*" Walker's voice reverberated through the dream hall. People and things around them moved in slow motion. Chatter became an echoic white noise.

Amelia's throat tightened. Dropping her Biology book, she ran toward him. Reaching for him all the while. But as often happened in dreams, she found herself barely able to move. And him fading faster.

Her heart battered her chest. She wanted to speak. Beg him to stay with her, but something wouldn't let her. Could have been the lump in her throat or the dream itself. All she knew was she couldn't speak. There would be no final goodbye, no apologizing. He would never know how much he meant to her.

Moving at a snail's pace, she continued to reach for him.

He mouthed the words, "I love you."

Inches away from him, she thought she might reach him in time. But as she went to grab him, her hand clawed at empty space.

Walker was gone.

Amelia screamed.

"Nugget? Nugget!"

Amelia started awake. Prying open sore, swollen eyes, she rolled to her back toward the concern laden voice. Worried cerulean eyes met her surely bloodshot ones.

Evan. He'd come home a few days ago. He brushed his thumb underneath her right eye then the left. It wasn't until then did she realize she'd been crying in her sleep.

"Hey." His voice was low, gentle. "You okay?"

Ugh... The dreaded question.

Of course, she wasn't okay. Why did people ask that question after a tragedy? Did anyone really expect her to jump up, smile, and be like, "Yeah, I'm cool. Let's get the day started"? What if she did do that, would they assume her nutty and insensitive? Or would they prefer she slit her wrist right here in front of them? Honestly, what answer sufficed for this asinine question?

"I'm fine," she answered, vocal cords raw. Probably best not to rip her brother a new asshole. He suffered, too.

His black hair was mussed, sideburns untrimmed. White tank stretched and loose, as if he'd slept in it and his black Dockers. Eyes red-rimmed. Walker and Evan might not have been friends anymore, but that was because they were stubborn. Didn't mean they didn't care. This was as much Evan's loss as it was hers.

Sitting up, Amelia flung her arms around her brother's neck. Hugged him tight. "I'm so sorry, Evy," she whispered in his ear.

He stroked her hair, sniffling once, but didn't cry. When he pulled back, he cleared his throat twice before speaking. "We gotta quit meeting like this," he joked, offering a weak smile that didn't reach his eyes.

Oh, that was so her big brother, always strong. The never-let-'em-see-you-sweat, tough guy. He'd much rather joke than break down, especially not in front of her. She wanted to be like Evan, trying to smile. Joke. But she couldn't.

"Shannon called. Asked Dan and I to be pallbearers." He hesitated before continuing. "They're trying to get things done as fast as possible." More hesitation. "Umm... Mr. Palmer specifically requested that you sing."

Huh? Though sitting, she felt like someone had knocked her down. It was common knowledge Jason Palmer didn't approve of her relationship with his son—or her. The idea he would go out of his way to request she do anything that didn't involve her death was a stretch. Plus, she didn't sing anymore. After singing "I'll Fly Away" at her parents' funeral, she'd sworn she'd never sing again.

Old Amelia sang, not her. Permitting herself to listen to music felt like a betrayal of her oath. But she couldn't eradicate music from her life totally. It kept her soul alive when she had to shut out her emotions. No way could she sing again. Not when she still couldn't imagine a world without her parents, Jon, her grandparents, and now Walker. She wouldn't do it.

"Okay, I'll do it," the words slipped out so fast they shocked her.

"Aces! I knew you would." Evan patted her hand, smiling tight-lipped. "I already told him yes. The funeral's next Tuesday." He stood. On his way out, he turned to her. "Oh, hey, some wrestler lookin' Joe's at the door for you. I think he said his name's Caitlyn."

The sun was fierce today. Calin would swear steam rose from the asphalt. He focused on that instead of the un-characteristic anxiety plaguing him as he stood outside Amelia's front door.

Why the hell was he here? Testing himself—his resolve?

He'd done some introspection in the three weeks since finding her with her dead boyfriend. Distance from Amelia provided him much-needed insight. Walker's death was good. One less obstacle for him to overcome in his quest to gain Amelia's trust. The *Awakening* was what mattered. His end game.

Her killing her boyfriend meant Calin wouldn't have to. He was one step closer to the *seal*. Soon, he'd call the shots with the *Daywalkers*. Emilio, the psychopath, wouldn't bust his balls about his humanity anymore. Not that he gave a shit what Emilio Cantemir thought. Once he became king, and after he imprisoned those who doubted him, his second order of business: Destroy all Cantemirs. The cocky, maniacal bunch of vamps needed to be obliterated before they further procreated.

Grandfather would exsanguinate, not in a dungeon. No, Calin wanted him somewhere special. Somewhere he could watch him reign. He'd achieve everything Balkan never could. A devoted *eternalmate* who wouldn't hesitate to bear him young. Loyal *retinue, vassal,* and guards would serve him. The supernatural would thrive under his rule, while Grandfather Balkan hung, drying out on a wall in some common room of the castle he'd construct for himself.

Calin stared at the door in front of him. Oh, yes, his endgame was reaffirmed.

Amelia was the enemy—fucking amazing—but the enemy, nonetheless. A means to an end. The farmer never got caught making goo-goo eyes at the cow before slaughter. And neither would he. No more romantic bullshit. He still might bone her, but that's where it ended.

So, why was he here?

Million dollar question right there. His intentions and desires wouldn't align. Some fundamental force dragged him here to check on her. Now he knew how his mother felt when the curse reared its ugly head. Ridiculous.

Decision to beat feet made...

The door opened.

Calin was blindsided. Amelia stood in the doorway. Her short, white halter dress with sweetheart neckline and flowing crimson locks—although, damn!—wasn't the cause. Her dull, puffy gold, emerald, and brown gemstone eyes were. She gazed at him in expectation.

He was torn—literally. The mortal part of him knew why her eyes swam in unshed tears. His demon didn't get it. Wanted to pick at the open wound. She lifted a hand to shield her eyes from the sun. Pain lanced his heart. It was obvious to the protective male in him that she'd spent considerable time in the dark. More than likely alone. His desire to pull her into his arms and comfort her warred with his intention to focus on his goals.

Leaving was the best choice. He had no business being here. This was his mark.

Then why did you erase the knowledge of what she did?

Calin didn't know. Nor did he comprehend the overpowering urge to protect her. She made him... He needed to get away. So, he turned and walked away.

"Calin!" Amelia called before he reached his Phantom. "Where are you going?"

Away from you, devil woman.

Against his will, he stopped and turned.

She stepped barefoot over the threshold. Her petite hourglass figure held him enthralled. His cock hardened.

Yep, time to go.

Hand on the driver's door; he took one final look at her. She appeared lost, vulnerable. Not surprising, given his erratic behavior. Amelia deserved more than this. No—shit! Damn. What was she doing to him? Why was it so hard to keep things straight around her? One look from her had him reevaluating his whole plan. His existence.

Calin raked shaky fingers through his hair. He had to say something. Seconds passed. They stared at each other. "I wanted to see how shitty you were doing," he said, after a minute. "Cicely told me what happened."

"So... were you hoping I'd siphon that information from your head?" she asked voice hoarse from crying he assumed. "Or were you gonna shout it out the window as you drove off?"

No escaping now. He'd have to persevere. Keep his objective at the forefront of his mind. Calin trudged up the walkway, stopping a few feet from Amelia. He thrust his hands into his jeans pockets.

"Now, why were you leaving?" she asked, pulling the door behind her closed a crack.

"I wasn't."

"Oh, no?" Her voice rose in disbelief, brows arched. "So, walking to your car and almost getting in isn't the universal signal for 'I'm leaving' anymore? Good to know." Amelia nodded.

The female was a pit bull when she locked on a theory. Of course, she was right, but he'd prefer to suffer his stupidity in silence. Amelia would have none of that. "Sorry, I'm no good at this."

Her brows drew tight. "Good at what?"

"Caring."

Amelia's expression fell.

Damn. This was why he didn't do this. Emotions, physical displays they weren't his—

Omph! Amelia threw herself at him. Foreign instincts made him catch her. He wrapped his arms around her petite frame as if the move were choreographed.

Fates! She felt good—right.

Her touch wasn't hesitant. She wanted to touch him. At once, his warring natures abated. Or maybe they were stunned silent. Never in his existence had anyone hugged him without reservation, snuggled against his chest as Amelia did. His father loved him but didn't hug him. He excused his lack of affection by saying men didn't embrace as women did or as man does with woman. Every time Eliza touched him she looked like she'd rather be staked.

But Amelia...

Her affection was free. He felt it. She wanted to touch and be touched... by him. That knowledge caused warmth to envelop his seldom-beating heart. This was a new emotion, not entirely bad, but new. Different than his constant companions, rage and resentment. He tightened his hold, careful not to crush her. This was nice. So much so, he didn't try to hide his growing erection. She should know what she did to him.

Calin closed his eyes, savoring the unexpected moment. He stroked her lustrous hair. Let the waves glide through his fingers. When he reopened them a minute later...

An average-height male with black hair, an impressive set of sideburns, and blue eyes glared at them from the doorway. Someone must've raided Elvis's wardrobe. Black slacks, an unbuttoned retro black and silver DaVinci dress shirt exposed a white tee underneath.

The male cleared his throat. Loud.

Calin tensed, fought to keep his shit together.

Amelia must've felt him tighten. She gazed over her shoulder. Spotting the male, she wiggled out of his arms. Smoothed out her dress and hair.

He felt bereft at the loss of contact. It was... disconcerting. What was happening to him? He'd only held her twice. This was the second time since the roof, but his body recognized hers. Mourned her absence as if an appendage had been amputated. Calin didn't condone this shit at all. He struggled not to yank her back into his arms. As it were, he did hook an arm around her middle and pull her back against his chest.

"Amelia, what are you doing?" the man asked, censure lacing his tone.

"Who. Is. That?" Calin demanded.

Amelia gazed at him through narrow eyes. "That's Evan—my brother. Didn't he introduce himself when he answered the door?"

Evan had no idea how lucky he had just gotten. If she hadn't said he was her brother... "He didn't open the door." Calin ground out, still salty from Evan's interruption.

"I'm sorry," Amelia said, "my brother's a huge jackass." She made flat introductions, "Evan, Calin. Calin, Evan."

Her kitten-size temper made him hard as stone. Damn, he needed to get away from her before he drilled a hole in her back. She had to feel it.

"I'm gonna go." Relinquishing his hold of her waist, Calin backed away. He hid his erection under his waistband on the sly.

"Wait." Amelia spun around and grabbed his hand. "Umm... Walker's funeral is next Tuesday. This is—I mean—I know it's not. Anyway, I'm singing. My friends will be there. I can give you directions."

Evan coughed, exaggeratedly. He and Amelia turned toward him.

"Nugget." Evan sighed irritated. "You can't invite people to—"

Calin stared into Amelia's wide—sort of, given how swollen they were—imploring eyes. There it was again. The compulsion to soothe her woes.

Even if she hadn't confided in him about the pressure she felt from her friends, Calin saw the struggle in her gaze. She wanted to allow Walker's family their privacy, their grief, yet she craved the solace his indifference afforded her. To say that didn't stroke his ego would be a bald-faced lie. A decent man would refuse her. He was neither decent nor a man.

Calin grinned. "I'll be there. Call me with a time and address."

Again, the day was unseasonably warm. But as was starting to be normal, Amelia was chilled to the bone. Though, she wasn't entirely sure if the chill was real or mental as she approached the apartment door. The dead inside feeling had returned tenfold. She traced the brass apartment numbers on the door frame.

Three. Two. Zero. Five.

A lump formed in her throat. She didn't think her tear ducts were capable of creating more tears. Tears burned behind gritty lids. Wrong.

Why did I agree to do this?

Originally, she'd refused Shannon and Jason. It was too soon, coming to Walker's apartment. Packing his belongings... made it real. In the end, guilt won. Weeks of no communication, hiding a pregnancy she now didn't know what to do about, grief over her curse striking again. Remorse for each issue suffocated her. It hadn't taken much prodding to get her to capitulate.

She might not have been in love with Walker, but she loved Walker. That love contributed to the home invasion, which resulted in his death. Add that to her regret over the lack of time she'd spent with him... Packing his apartment was the least she could do. Shouldn't be too tough; he hated being alone and rarely stayed here.

Amelia dug through her Louis for Walker's keys.

For the life of her, she couldn't figure out why they'd grown apart. It made no sense. Speaking of things that didn't make sense—Calin and Talon. Those two had become her new Walker, or how Walker used to be. One of them was always around. If she were a conspiracy theorist, she'd say they were to blame for Walker's recent distance. Ridiculous, she knew.

Why would they care how much or how little time she spent with her boyfriend? Not like they forced her to choose them over Walker. Walker had chosen not to be around on his own. A more attentive girlfriend would've hunted him down and made him tell her what was wrong. Instead, she'd clung to the distraction of Calin and Talon. Now, it was too late.

Something wet hit Amelia's cheek. She looked at the sky. Crystal clear. If it wasn't raining what—she swiped at her cheek. Tears. When had she started crying? Great. Now she cried without her knowledge? She was a basket case. Her perfectly constructed world, shields were fall—

A heavy *thump* from inside the apartment captured Amelia's attention. She brushed the wayward tears away with a rough hand, shaking her purse. Keys scraped the bottom. Found 'em. She stuck her key in the lock. It was locked?

Duh...Amelia, robbers are good with locks. You don't hold the market on being able to lock a door behind yourself.

Okay, so grief had her on bobblehead duty.

She unlocked the door and stepped inside. Immediately, Walker's unique scent—Axe body spray and butt—assailed her. Funny, the things we miss.

Outrage ignited her blood. For once, she didn't resent the influx of extreme emotion. If someone was in here, they were in for a battle. She was sick, sick, sick of this shit. The universe kept bending her over without the courtesy of putting a pillow under her head. Amelia was forever on the periphery of danger. Either a smidgen too late or a tad too soon.

How dare someone burgle a dead man? Walker hadn't even been laid to rest.

Dropping Louis on the kitchen counter, Amelia scanned the open floor plan. Her gaze devoured the living room, office space, and dining room. All clear—if clutter and garbage counted as clear.

Amelia soundlessly pushed closed the front door. A loud crash came from the rear of the apartment. She jumped. Her heart took off at a dead sprint.

Fight or flight? Fight or flight?

She worked to steady her breathing. Oh, no, she wouldn't play fate's bitch today. She took self-defense. Amelia could subdue a criminal. Jab to the eyes, palm thrust to the nose, kick to the crotch if it's a boy...

Piece of cake.

She leaned her head to one side then the other, cracking her neck like they did in the movies. Pulling her fingers, the way Calin did, she popped her knuckles.

Fight it is.

Chapter Twenty-Three

Peeking through a slight crack in the bedroom door, Amelia saw a black and gray camo pants-covered ass bent over Walker's king-sized bed. She couldn't tell if it was a man or woman, but whoever it was had an ass that wouldn't quit. Please, don't let it be a woman. That would raise a whole new set of issues Amelia didn't need.

Rolling her eyes at her wayward thoughts, she refocused on the task at hand.

Subdue the burglar.

She burst through the door. Sprinted into the room. Kicked the thief in the butt. Hard. He or she face-planted on the disheveled bed. Straddling the perp, she grabbed both beefy hands and twisted them behind its black tank top-clad back.

"Ow!" the robber yelled.

One mystery solved. It was a guy. A really big, muscular guy she didn't know what to do with. This was not a well thought out plan.

The burglar squirmed beneath her.

Amelia smashed his blond head into the mattress. Oh, for the love of all that was holy, why hadn't she thought first? Damn, adrenaline. Nobody knew she was here, and she hadn't even had enough sense to call the police first. *Shit!* If she got out of this eight seconds without getting bucked off the bull she was bitch-slapping that self-defense instructor who left out what to do after you defend yourself.

"Amelia, get off me," a familiar, muffled voice demanded. "Don't make me throw you."

She'd know that thunderous, accented bass anywhere.

She looked down at his hand. Confirmation, big ole pimp ring right ring finger. Amelia let go of his hands but didn't move.

"You throw me, and I'll have you singing soprano, buddy," she threatened. "What are you doing here?"

Talon flipped over so fast he didn't even jostle her. *Impressive.* But now, there was a huge problem... she straddled his front.

"Considering you ball-checked me from behind with your heel, I should be singing soprano now." He grinned.

Wow! He *so* didn't do that enough. The man's smile was far more threatening than his commands or height. He had to have the straightest, whitest teeth in the world. Someone should thank his orthodontist. Heaven help her, he was gorgeous. Like pinch-me-I'm-not-sure-I'm-awake gorgeous.

Please, God, forgive me. What am I thinking?

Having ascertained he wasn't a burglar, she should move. Minutes ticked by.

His biceps were much larger than she'd assumed. He always made sure to wear a shirt that covered most of his arms and his gloves. Now, all his pale, corded muscle was open to her perusal. What the hell was she doing? More time passed. She didn't move.

Why wasn't she moving?

Talon arched a thick golden-blond brow. "Are you okay, milady?"

No, I'm burning up, and if you have the hose I think you do, then only you can prevent this forest fire. Damn voice.

Heat crept up her neck, burned her cheeks. "I'm fine. Why are you here?" she snapped.

"I thought I'd help pack. Figured you might need a friend."

"Why are you always everywhere I am? Are you stalking me?"

Smiling, Talon grabbed her waist on either side and wiggled his hips. "Right now, you're everywhere I am." Hewagging his eyebrows. "Am I wrong?"

Amelia gasped. Talon never acted so... playful. Suggestive. Would've been a welcome change of pace if the circumstances were different. Since they were what they were, she felt... Whoa! She felt... She checked to see where his hands were. Both hands were on her hips, which meant...

Good Lord, the man is hung like a friggin' stallion.

Her stomach tightened. She grew uncomfortable, in a very hot, wet way. This was not okay. Not in the least. Amelia hopped up, moved across the room as if Satan himself was after her.

She covertly patted her pleather pants, making sure she hadn't lit on fire. Although she had a white tank top on, she was starting to rethink the thin, black, off-the-shoulders sweater she wore over it. Her core temperature had heated to hell fire with Talon beneath her and wouldn't cool.

They needed to get out of the bedroom. ASAP. "Well, shake a leg if you're gonna help. I don't have all day," she ordered, exiting the room.

Four hours later, Amelia wrapped mismatched sports-themed plates in newspaper. Packed them in a box filled with a hodgepodge of other glassware. She didn't know what Walker's parents planned to do with his stuff. The kitchenware wouldn't be of any use. It was the typical bachelor's random assortment of dishes. She'd had to throw out several pieces of silverware and cookware because food—or what used to be food—had begun to procreate on them.

Talon packed the makeshift office area just off the living room. Shockingly, besides their awkward moment in the bedroom, the last four hours with Talon hadn't been bad. It was strangely comforting having someone here with her, although she'd never admit it to said someone.

At lunch, she wasn't hungry, and for once, Talon didn't press the issue. At home, Evan and Tessa force fed her. Okay, maybe it wasn't force-feeding, per se, but close. They watched her eat every bite then took the dishes when she was done. Time and time again, she explained that she didn't eat much when she was depressed. They never listened. They pressed the issue, which was why she was shocked when Talon didn't.

He'd said, "You'll eat when you're hungry."

Those words went a long way to soften her toward him.

Nobody ever let her grieve at her own pace. She believed it best to live in her emotions, riding them out until they subsided naturally. In everyone else's minds, there was some limit to sadness, anger, or even unhappiness. When that imaginary limit was reached, people began to worry and use fancy terms and phrases like: "You need to get help." "Inpatient behavioral health center." "Manic depressive." And one of her favorites: "Mood stabilizers."

What a crock of BS...

Since when did drugs ever help anybody? Yes, some had a nice temporary effect, but in the long run, even those were addictive. Then, after all was said and done, the original mood the drug was meant to fix was still there, lying dormant. Waiting for insurance to lapse or the prescription to run out. No wonder the directions said not to abruptly stop taking the meds. Wouldn't a prisoner, beaten and shackled into submission jump at the chance to be let loose in a locked room with a gun and their defenseless capture?

What made emotions meant to be expressed any different? Of course, they turned their hosts crazy once set free. That was why she preferred to deal with her emotions head-on. Ride the wave as her hippie cousin, Caushion, taught her.

"Hey, look what I found," Talon said, breaking into her mental tirade.

She placed another plate in the box, looking through the opening to Talon at Walker's computer desk. She didn't want to see anything. Being here with Talon, albeit nice to have someone here, felt wrong. She'd rarely come here. Walker usually opted to hang at her house, but this was his place. As much as she wanted to deny it, there was chemistry between her and Talon. Anything other than contempt between them here felt traitorous.

"Whatever it is, leave it alone. Pack it," she said curtly, joining him at the desk.

Sometimes she liked him, other times she treated Talon with disdain. She shifted between these two responses constantly and for no discernible reason. As if she deplored his existence. But other times...

He smelled excitement weeping from her body.

Mortals confounded him—her more than most. Vampire emotions were intense, hard to deny. When a feeling hit, it hit hard. Consumed. And most times, the vampire went with it.

Amelia's fickle moods were his worst enemy. Talon stared at the long, rectangular, black velvet box he'd planted in the desk drawer. The real reason he was here.

Thank The Fates, he had the good sense to compel Walker to write the note weeks earlier. Not that he'd known the idiot mortal would die. That'd been a serendipitous shock. Walker out of the picture made things easier. If only Calin were that simple to dispose of. Talon's only concern was Amelia.

He'd given her space over the last three weeks. Saw her whenever she left her house, which wasn't often. No, that wasn't conducive to his plans, but circumstances warranted finesse. Talon would like to give her more time to grieve. Unfortunately, time was of the essence. The *Awakening* was barreling toward them, and her safety was paramount. He'd asked Anton, but no one knew when sun sensitivity kicked in. Side effects of transition were unpredictable. They only knew it would. Talon didn't want to find out when Amelia's skin caught on fire. That'd be difficult to explain. She needed an amulet to allow her to walk in the sunlight.

She also deserved to know the truth. And he needed to tell her. But, he couldn't when things between them were so adversarial. Something had to change.

Talon turned, faced Amelia. "Why the hostility, milady?"

Amelia folded her arms over her chest. "What were you looking at?"

Change wouldn't be easy. "I'll show you in a second. But first, answer me one question."

She glared at him with those amazing eyes. "No. Pack whatever it is and let's go."

Amelia turned to walk away.

Grabbing her arm, he spun her around. The glare she bestowed upon him was murderous. His mamma often gave Sebastian a similar look. It meant one of two things: cover your jewels or...

Cover your jewels.

Okay, so it only meant one thing, but that one bore repeating. Talon didn't have to be told twice. He dropped his hand. Females were dangerous.

"Hey, now," he said, stepping back and bumping into the desk behind him.

"What, Talon?" She sighed.

"Am I really that unpleasant to be around?"

"Yes."

Ow!

"No." She sighed, defeated. "I just—there's just..." She expelled a long-suffering breath. "You're a lot to deal with. Anybody ever tell you that?"

No. No, they hadn't.

In truth, he wasn't around a lot of "people". To Amelia, he was the average mortal, which meant he went out, dated. But those things had been denied him. Even if they hadn't, he doubted any experience compared to this mortal in front of him.

"Well?" Amelia prompted.

"You're the first person to say that. Maybe if you tried to see me as a friend and not something slimy you stepped in, it could work?"

Amelia seemed to take the bait, or at the very least, consider it.

Time for full-court emotional press. "Walker would've wanted us to get along—be friends."

He smelled the salt of tears a second before her eyes watered.

He kicked himself mentally. If it wasn't of the utmost importance that they break down the wall between them, he wouldn't have stooped to such tactics. Though he couldn't deny that her features softened as she considered his words. The urge to listen to her thoughts overwhelmed him. If she were any other mortal he would have, but he tried never to scan her. He'd violated her enough. Whenever possible, he refrained from taking her only escape from him, too.

Long silent moments passed. "Okay," she acquiesced at last, "we're friends." She held her hand out palm up. "What'd you find?"

He narrowed his eyes in suspicion.

"Truce—I promise." Amelia smiled.

Talon knew it for an act, but she showed bravery and courage amid a tragedy. He admired her strength.

He turned her proffered hand palm down, lifted it to his mouth, and placed a chaste kiss on each knuckle. His dick nudged his zipper.

Damn, he was sleazy. Here she offered him a truce, and all he could think about was kissing his way up her arm. Her collarbone. Her neck. Then making his way to those full lips.

Not wanting to offend Talon, Amelia lightly tugged her hand away. He was right. Walker would want them to be friends. In all honesty, she didn't *not* like Talon. In fact, the opposite was true. She liked him too much, which made things harder. All his weird manners, his presence, did things to her that she dare not examine.

She cleared her throat. "Uh... so, what'd you find?"

Reaching behind him, he retrieved a black velvet necklace box. He offered it to her.

"I believe he planned to give this to you, for your birthday," he said voice sullen, deeper than usual.

She took the box with shaky hands. God, she wished there wasn't an audience present for this moment. Tears sparked behind her eyes. Blinking several times, she held them at bay. This felt surreal, eerie.

Should she open it or wait?

After what felt like hours of indecision, she took a deep breath and opened the box.

Her breath caught. Lying on a black satin pillow was one of her favorite symbols: A yin-yang. Instead of black and white, the circular pendant was diamond and ruby. A tad bigger than a silver dollar strung on a gold chain.

Dozens of small rubies formed the typically black yin side. Diamonds comprised the usually white yang side. A solitary diamond was placed in the center of the largest part of the yin. In the largest part of the yang, a singular ruby. Heart-stoppingly beautiful. Rubies were her favorite precious stone and also her birthstone. Walker wasn't this considerate.

He treated her well, fantastic even, but this...? This was extreme even for him. Unless he had GPS installed in it. That wouldn't be out of character for him at all.

Jeez, cynical bitch, be grateful.

Here she was holding a gift that had easily set her dead boyfriend back a couple grand and she was being negative. When had she become this jaded? Tears for the loss of not only Walker, but herself, welled in her eyes. She didn't recognize herself anymore, and it wasn't because of her new ashen skin and mercurial emotions.

"Here. Let me help, milady," Talon said, reminding her of his presence.

"Umm... okay." She sniffled.

She plucked the necklace from its pillow, handed it to Talon, and turned. Talon's muscular chest made contact with her back. It took immense strength to not be affected by the chill of awareness slithering down her spine. Strong, sure, masculine hands swept her hair to the side. A shock of sexual tension imbued the space between them. It took saintly concentration to ignore the zing of electricity that danced over her skin as the tips of his fingers grazed her nape. Her breath hitched. She used every ounce of willpower not to lean into him as cool, solid arms caged her in and gathered each end of the necklace behind her.

"Oh, I forgot. This card was with it," Talon said, handing her a small white card.

Thank God he spoke when he did; it cold-watered their mounting situation. Talon clasped the necklace. She read the card to herself.

I know how much you like the dark, but I thought you could use a little bling to light your way. Keep this close to your heart at all times. Love ya, babe. Wall

Chapter Twenty-Four

T he church service wasn't long. Walker's family was non-practicing Catholics, so they opted for a smaller service. Evan, Dan, Walker's dad Jason, his sister Rebecca, and a couple of Walker's other friends spoke. To Amelia's astonishment, his father's speech was the most heart-wrenching.

He and Walker's relationship had always been tumultuous at best, patricidal at worst. Everything Walker liked—tattoos, piercings, Goth/Punk style—her—his father hated. Or so everyone thought, but today, she saw a side of Jason Palmer no one, including Walker, knew existed.

Gazing at the sea of mourners through humble brown eyes, Jason stood tall behind the podium. Big body shoved into a black three-piece suit, long dirty blond hair in a ponytail, Mr. Palmer gushed over his baby boy.

He praised his son's courage to live life on his terms. Confessed that he envied Walker and should never have taken out his anger at his own shortcomings on him. He wished aloud that he could have been a better father, the type who deserved a son as amazing as Walker. One who wouldn't have waited to tell his son he loved and was proud of him. Then, as if his heartfelt confession didn't have everyone bawling, he turned sincere eyes on her. A single tear fell as he apologized for any hurt he'd caused her and said he didn't blame her for what happened to Walker.

The squeeze of Rebecca's small hand in hers brought Amelia to the present. A present she prayed with all her soul wasn't real. But it was. And they really were in the limo heading to Land Grove Cemetery, Walker's final resting place.

From the corner of her eye, Amelia glanced at Rebecca. Her long brunette hair was spiral curled and half up in a pearl clip. She wore a black, ruffled, satin and taffeta dress and a stone expression on her face. That light squeeze was all she'd done—besides walk when told—the entire day. Well, that and stick to Amelia like glue, which was why, instead of sitting with her parents, she was wedged between Amelia and Tessa.

When Shannon had tried to coax her into sitting on the other side, the look of panic and desolation in Rebecca's chocolate eyes touched an empathetic place in Amelia. Rebecca was lost. Without her big brother, her anchor, the world no longer made sense. Amelia understood completely. She'd felt the same when her parents died. Clung to anyone and anything for safety.

Today, her black, Diane Von Furstenberg, wrap dress was her armor, holding her together on the outside while inside she fell apart. All day, she refused to meet anyone's eye out of fear she'd break down. She couldn't do that. Rebecca needed her to be strong. So, to keep her grief in check, she kept her gaze out the tinted limousine window.

They were close to the cemetery. She turned away from Rebecca, rested her hand on the door handle, and returned her unseeing stare outside. A funny "how fucked up" not funny "ha-ha" thought came to mind.

As a little girl, she'd loved watching celebrities arrive at award shows in luxurious black limos. Vowed to herself she'd ride in one, one day. Including today, she'd ridden in a limo five different times, each time for a funeral. Fate really had a shitty sense of humor.

Lush green grass, black iron gates, and the tops of headstones came into view. Her heart clenched. Walker didn't like being alone. He'd spent most of his time at her house, with Rebecca, or at Dan's. Now, he'd rest alone, indefinitely. She wasn't sure if the afterlife existed. If it did, she hoped a lot of people would be waiting in the light for Walker.

At the cemetery, pallbearers Dan, Evan, Talon, Walker's cousins Anthony, Rick, and Jeff, carried the maple casket to the burial grounds, placing it on the lowering device. Everyone took their seats or places. She, Shannon, Rebecca, and both sets of Walker's grandparents sat while everyone else stood. The priest, a white-haired man with flat gray eyes and a withered face, dressed in a plain black suit at the family's request, stood at the head of the casket.

No sooner than he'd taken his place, clouds moved across the sky, covering the sun. Overcast. Fitting.

"We gather here today to say farewell to Walker Jonathan Palmer and to commit him into the hands of God. Before we go further, the family has requested that Walker's girlfriend honor him through song." The priest gazed at her and gestured for her to come forward. "Amelia."

Her stomach knotted. Her breath caught, and her heart slowed way down.

I can't do this. I can do this.

I don't want to do this.

She wasn't good with goodbyes, and this was goodbye forever.

From their positions behind her, Evan and Tessa patted her shoulders in comfort.

She forced herself to stand. Walk.

Her heartbeat resounded in her ears. The priest offered her a sympathetic smile. He squeezed her hand and then stepped aside. The heels of her Manolo's sunk into the ground. Yes, it was a trivial thing to notice, but it was necessary if she wanted to stop her knees from knocking and betraying her anxiety. She scanned the crowd. No Calin.

Why she cared, she didn't know. Maybe because that strength he seemed to have in spades would've come in handy at the moment. What she saw was a lot of people who loved Walker.

In tribute to Walker, those closest to him who had tattoos made sure they were visible. Evan had his left suit sleeve rolled, revealing a spider web tattoo on his wrist. Dan's barbed wire tattoo along his collarbone showed through his open collar. Tessa's strappy heels showcased the ladybug on her right ankle. Rebecca had a temporary heart with a dagger through it on her hand. Amelia's dress stopped at her knees, displaying her vampire fairy, which now had an extra drop of blood coming from its mouth in Walker's memory. Shocking everyone, Walker's parents had fresh matching tattoos of dice rolled to snake eyes with Walker's DOB and date of death inside them. His dad's was on his upper arm, which explained why he'd changed into a black wife-beater in the limo, and his mom's was on her exposed shoulder blade.

Amelia took a deep calming breath. Didn't help. Looked to Talon. Couldn't explain why. Maybe because he couldn't be hurt by her curse. Or because in a sea of people falling apart, he stood proud, stoic. He anchored her with a curt nod. This was the last thing she would ever be able to give to Walker. She would not fail. After another breath, she sang—changing a few words—an acapella version of Brandy, Tamia, Gladys Knight, and Chaka Kahn's song, "Missing You."

Talon skidded past floored and right into stupefied.

Locking his knees prevented him from falling and crushing little Rebecca, whose chair he stood behind. Amelia had the voice of a—shit, nothing compared to her gentle, ethereal voice.

Originally, he'd thought this ceremony was another barbaric mortal custom. Why would anyone bury their supposed loved one's corpse in a box underground? Vampires turned to dust when destroyed. Box not required.

What happened when one patch of Earth got too full to store these boxes? Did they stack them? And what about the smell? Mortal blood stank after the body died or if out of the body too long. Really, the whole idea of a funeral seemed ludicrous...

Until now.

He could listen to Amelia sing the ingredients for anthrax and be just as captivated. Her melodious voice pleased the ear in a way nothing else could. As a Royal Guardsman, his duty was to protect her above all else, including his existence. Before today, that was his job, but after hearing her sing...

He'd cut his own heart out on the spot if it pleased her. He'd take off his ring; walk into the sunlight if it'd make her smile.

Whoa! Wait. Where'd that come from?

Yes, his feelings for her were headed into dangerous territory, but at the moment, they were obsessive, psycho-style. Her song continued. His head swam. Something wasn't right, and he had about a minute to figure it out before she usurped his will.

What was happening?

Talon surveyed the mourners. No sniffles. The intermittent sobs had died. Every gaze latched onto Amelia. Their eyes glazed. Mass hypnosis? Realization, a swift kick to the nuts... struck. They were all enthralled.

Out of his peripheral vision, he saw groundskeepers and people visiting elsewhere in the cemetery shuffle woodenly toward Walker's plot. No. Not the plot. They were drawn to the one who commanded them, their master...

Amelia.

Thrall broken, Talon saw with his preternatural sight what was happening. Thin wisps of vapor emanated from Amelia's mouth. Millions extended as far as twenty miles. The strands roped around anyone in the vicinity, leading them to her. Even birds, dogs, cats, and other creatures migrated to this spot.

Amelia was oblivious. She sang as though her heart were breaking. Her song came from the depths of her soul, and yet she stood tall.

Talon's admiration for her soared. Not only was she the most precious, beautiful being on two or four legs, but she was coura-geous, strong. A survivor. He couldn't have designed a better female than her. Why keep lying to himself? She was everything he would ever want in an *eternalmate*...

And she could never be his.

Acute pain pricked his dead heart. Would've dropped him to his knees if two things hadn't happened simultaneously. One, something ten miles off caught his eye. Two, he knew what else Amelia was.

"**W**hat a waste of perfectly good parts," Bianca complained, stomping her foot. "Brother, we must kill these mortals. Their ignorance knows no bounds. You take half and I'll take half. We'll bathe in their blood."

Calin glared at the top of Bianca's dirty blonde head. Why he'd brought the little hell-raiser, he had no idea. Simply another, among many, stupid decisions he'd made in the last week. Why the hell had he agreed to come to this Fates forsaken place?

Oh, right... because he was a special kind of moron who forgot there'd be a priest officiating the service. It was the same reason he'd had his father buried in a special plot near their home in Paris with no one in attendance but himself, two maids, and a butler. That was one hundred and forty-five years ago, but the facts remained the same: Wholly evil beings couldn't go near sanctified people or buildings. Due to his three natures, he'd never been sure if he was exempt from that or not. Bianca wasn't, and after her veil experience, she wouldn't test the funeral.

So affected by Amelia's touch when she'd asked him, he hadn't stopped to consider the ramifications of such a request.

Gazing across the wide expanse between him and the cemetery, Calin spied Amelia sitting next to a young, ivory-skinned girl with long brown hair. Holding hands, they stared straight ahead. Amelia's wavy almost waist-length, red hair hung loose, blowing in a light breeze. Dark tinted sunglasses, like many of the guests wore, covered her eyes. A black, collared, V-neck dress hugged her petite curves. She looked divine.

"Brother, I'm bored. If we're not going to feed, then why are we here?" Bianca asked. She gazed at him, light brows furrowed quizzically. "Are you staring at that putrid blood sack of a descendant?" Her lip curled in disgust. Disgust transformed into a wicked grin. "I can't wait to kill her. Her teeth will make nice earrings for me. Or maybe a bracelet for Mum."

Calin felt his eyes heat. Glow. He snatched Bianca off the ground by her throat. Lifted her to eye level with him. Her eyes bulged, and her face reddened. She struggled to breathe and clawed futilely at his hand to loosen his grip.

He was torn. He knew what he had to do. The only way to accomplish his goals was to end Amelia's life. It would give him indisputable power. He had to do it.

No, you don't. Become king consort, rule with her.

Not that simple.

He didn't care that his mother would remain cursed. What didn't sit well was the knowledge Grandfather Balkan and his army would come after him in earnest. He'd be hunted for as long as he lived. Bianca might anger him, but she was his sister. The prospect of one day battling her, or any of his family, didn't appeal to him.

Damn humanity.

Others wouldn't think twice about sacrificing him, yet he stood there holding his sister by the neck for threatening a mortal. A tiny, insignificant, useless *mortal* who... touched him in a way no one ever had. Treated him as if he meant something, as if his presence brought her joy. The war in his mind raged. He squeezed Bianca's throat tighter. She kicked and hit him. Then the voice of a goddess reached out to him.

He dropped Bianca like a hot rock.

She coughed and sputtered, trying to regain her ability to breathe. Calin was only aware of it with the lesser part of his mind. His gaze fastened on Amelia. Like an angel, soft white light enfolded her. She pushed her sunglasses up to rest atop her head. Her eyes held a faint white luminescence as she sang from the very core of her being. Lugubrious expressions on the gatherer's faces were replaced by awe and adoration. Her voice called to him. Ensnared. He wanted to obey.

How could he not go to her?

So what if he couldn't go near a member of the clergy without being electrocuted? Amelia was worth the agony. If he could, he'd lay the world at her feet. He'd endeavor to secure the moon and stars for her if that was what she wanted. Whatever Amelia's will, he'd kill to ensure it was done.

Calin shuffled forward. He bumped into Bianca and—

What the fuck am I doing?

He grabbed Bianca's shoulders. Turned her to face him. Eyes vacant, expression stuck in the same awestruck mask everyone at the funeral wore, she kicked him. Or tried. He sidestepped the attempt. She jerked against his hold. That's when he saw it. White cloud-like wisps wound around Bianca and everyone in a twenty-mile radius. For those who couldn't hear, the warm glow of Amelia's eyes and the soft white light she was encased in enthralled them.

Like a caged animal, Bianca fought his hold—hard. What was going on? He glanced across the cemetery and caught Talon's eye. Concern shone through malice.

It happened at the same time; he could tell because the second it dawned on him he almost saw the light bulb above Talon's head. They needed to stop Amelia before she inadvertently exposed the supernatural and brought Armageddon down on all their heads. Across the way, Talon's rigid stance mimicked his own. The one difference?

He was fighting to restrain a five-year-old Hybrid who not only kicked but also tried to bite to get away and go to her master. Truth be told, he'd be in a similar state if it weren't for his age and will. They had to stop Amelia.

Horns honked and tires squealed as motorists swerved their cars through traffic to reach Amelia. Her magnificent voice converted everyone to mindless drones. Their life's mission: Serve her. While this ability might come in handy as queen—when she could control it—right now it'd serve as the catalyst that restarted modern-day witch trials or vampire slayings, depending on the circumstances.

Calin planted his feet, gripping Bianca tighter. The draw grew harder to resist. He couldn't believe this. The Fates had ordered the race terminated. Used them as an example of what happened when supernatural didn't follow the Most High's law: Remain inconspicuous. A handful of the stubborn, narcissistic, prideful race was pardoned by The Fates, but only if they agreed to conform. These beings could bring down mortals and immortals alike with nothing but their obscene beauty and voices. No one had seen neither hide nor hair of them for centuries. They were assumed extinct.

Clearly, the saying about people who assume was true, because here in their midst, making an ass out of them all was a real, live, descendant of a...

Siren.

Chapter Twenty-Five

A melia barely made it through to the middle of the song before tears choked her. She couldn't finish. This was one goodbye too many. Everyone stared at her. God, she hated people seeing her weak. But she was, and not just emotionally. Physically, she was drained. Exhausted.

Underneath her, the Earth moved, swayed—wait—maybe that was her. Before she passed out, Talon caught her. Her Superman. One minute she wobbled the next...

He was there.

He whispered in her ear, "Are you okay?"

No. But this was Walker's funeral and not about her. She might be light-headed and weary, but she was alive. She nodded.

Talon led her back to her seat. He stood beside her. The look of relief on his face hurt.

Judgmental asshole.

Sorry her singing wasn't up to snuff for him. Let's see him sing acapella while dying inside. Had it not been highly inappropriate, she would have punched him right in the junk.

What's with the violent outburst?

Her moods were growing more unstable and intense by the minute. She'd always had a long fuse, but now, a sideways glance or ill-timed smile was a death sentence for the giver. What was going on with her?

Before she could examine that thought too closely, the priest approached the unofficial speaking spot.

"If everyone will bow your heads." He paused, allowing everyone time to comply. "Lord, our God; you are the source of life. In you, we live and move and have our being. Keep us in life and death in your love, and, by your grace, lead us to your kingdom, through your son, Jesus Christ, our Lord. Amen."

The casket lowered, and with it... another piece of her heart.

The priest bent, grabbed a handful of dirt. "God, our father, we entrust Walker Jonathan Palmer into your hands." He dropped dirt on the casket as he spoke. "We, therefore, commit his body to the ground, earth to earth" —he picked up more dirt and let it fall — "ashes to ashes"— he picked up a final clump of dirt, dropped it onto the casket — "dust to dust, in the sure and certain hope of the resurrection to eternal life."

At his final words guilt, grief, and sorrow collected their toll. Everything went black.

Amelia fainted.

Talon and Evan traded glares across the limo. Beside "The Idiot" sat Kasey and Dan. Evan could glare until his eyes stuck that way. Talon would not relinquish his hold on Amelia. The mortal might do something stupid, like drop her.

Never in his existence had Talon witnessed someone lose consciousness so quickly. One second, Amelia sat straight in her chair, the next—lights out. He caught her a nanosecond before she hit the ground. The idiotic mortals hadn't even attempted to catch her. Thank goodness the service had ended then.

The Palmers were holding a reception at their home. Since Amelia showed no signs of recovery, they'd opted out. Now they were headed to Amelia's house. The tension in the limo was thick enough to cut. That Talon hadn't had his daily allotment of donor packs, amplified it.

He smelled the tangy, sweet, copper scent of everyone's blood. Tessa's was the strongest, given that she sat beside him. Talon not only saw, but heard, blood rush through the thick artery in her neck. If he weren't holding a still-unconscious Amelia, he would've gone rogue and killed everyone in the vehicle. Lucky for them, he tempered their scent with Amelia's hardly mortal one. When their scents overwhelmed him, he dipped his head low or lifted her minutely and took a discreet whiff of her cherry blossom fragrance.

Twenty minutes later, they reached their destination. Talon nearly flew out of the limo. He needed to get away from all these temptations.

Evan scrambled around the car, blocking his path to the walkway. "You can scram. Give me my sister," he demanded, holding out his arms.

Talon glared at the skinny arms. He yearned to rip them off and beat the fool mortal with them. The boy had no idea how close he was to the lion's den.

Tessa ran to where they were. "Really!" she shouted, narrowing moss-green eyes at both of them. "You're really gonna do this, huh? Fight over who gets to hold Amelia after we just laid" — glaring at Talon — "*your* cousin and" — pegging Evan with a similar glare — "one of *your* best friends to rest. Calm the fuck down!" She scrunched her face, disgusted by them both. Her eyes came to rest on Amelia's serene face, and her features softened. She brushed a tendril of hair from Amelia's forehead and spoke softly. "You don't deserve this. I'm so sorry." Louder she added, "These guys are bastards. Get her inside," she ordered.

Elbowing Evan out of her way, she stormed up the walk, unlocked the house door, and disappeared inside. She left the door open behind her.

Reminiscent of a well-trained puppy, Dan followed. Before going in, he turned to where Talon and Evan mean-mugged each other. "You'll have to excuse her she's—"

"Daniel!" Tessa shouted from inside. "Bring your ass!"

"...grieving," Dan finished, then hurried inside.

Kasey started up the walk. Hard brown eyes appraised them. During the funeral, Talon hadn't really taken time to notice her. He saw her now. Nice! Tall, dark hair, olive skin, exotic features, clingy black dress—she could be a model.

"Get inside!" Kasey barked at Evan. "You don't need to be out here in that suit—checking out girls."

Evan rolled his eyes. "Kasey, I'll be in when I get in."

Her eyes widened; mouth gaped appalled. She spun, flipped her hair, and grumbled as she went in, "You'll be in when I tell you to be in. See if you get any tonight. Get in when you get in....? My ass!"

Evan refocused on Talon. "Put her inside and leave," he ordered, then plodded inside. His faster stride suggested he might talk a mean game, but Kasey ran that show.

After the Awakening... I feed on him first.

"Come in, Talon!" Tessa yelled.

Thank The Fates! He would've gone in sooner if he didn't have to wait for a formal invitation. Now he could come and go as he pleased—finally. He carried Amelia inside and lightly kicked the door closed.

Eating some sort of crushed ice treat with a plastic spoon, Tessa met him in the front room. "Just put her in bed. Down the hall, double doors on the right. Reach a room with a toilet, and you've gone too far."

Acknowledging Tessa's orders with a sharp nod, he followed her directions. The first door he passed had a poster of a 1930s gangster in a pin-striped suit holding a Tommy gun. He guessed it was Evan's since he wore an almost identical suit today. After Evan's room, a set of double doors were cracked open.

The master bedroom, atta girl.

He pushed open the door with his elbow. What had to be close to six hundred pictures of Amelia and obviously her adoptive parents plastered the walls. In the middle of the room, burgundy and gold sheets topped a queen-sized, black, four-poster medieval bed with a sheer black canopy.

She might not know it, but the mortal inherently had a queen's tastes. Her room was decked out in the royal colors. All she'd missed was the royal tilde *seal* embroidered on the sheets.

He pulled back the comforter and top sheet—damn they were soft, at least fifteen hundred thread count Egyptian cotton. Of course, it was Amelia. Talon laid her in bed and covered her.

Now, to go feed.

"Talon?"

He turned to see Amelia looking at him. "Yeah."

"Stay with me."

How could he decline such a sweet plea? Those words ignited a fire so fierce inside him it could burn the house down. She wanted him to stay...

Dammit! Why didn't he feed earlier? "I can't. Your brother already wants to kill me." He couldn't, but it was a better excuse than the real reason.

She frowned. He felt an unfamiliar tightening of his unbeating heart. Fates, he wanted to stay, but he couldn't.

"My brother has Kasey to play with. I don't have anyone anymore. Get in bed," she said, throwing the comforter back and patting the space beside her. "Please. I don't bite."

I do.

With a groan, he toed off his shoes and left them next to the door. He slid in next to her. He assumed a rigid half-lying, half-sitting position, grabbed a few pillows, and shoved them behind his back.

To his amazement, Amelia wrapped her arms around his waist. She laced her fingers behind his back and laid her head in his lap.

Please don't get hard...please don't get hard.

If he got hard, he'd drill a hole through her temple. He tried to think of things to keep his nether brain in check.

"Do you know the song 'Smile' by Michael Jackson?"

"Trust me, the last thing you want is for me to sing."

She sniffled and sighed. "Okay."

They were silent for a while. Something Anton told him popped into his mind. "You want to hear a joke?"

"King Tight Ass knows a joke? I'm shocked."

"I don't know how good it is. If you don't want to hear—"

"Go ahead," she interrupted.

"This kid—we'll call him George—walks into an ice cream parlor."

"Ok."

"And the guy behind the counter—we'll call him Frank—says, 'Hey, George, what can I get for you today?' George studies the board behind Frank. Finally, he says, 'Hmm... I'll have one scoop of chocolate ice cream in a waffle cone.' Frank says, 'Sorry, George, we're out of chocolate ice cream. Pick something else.'—You following so far?"

"Yep, got it. George wants chocolate ice cream; Frank says there isn't any."

"Right. Anyway, George studies the board again. After a minute he says, 'Alright just give me a small cup of... chocolate ice cream.' Frank rolls his eyes then says, 'George, man, we're all out of chocolate ice cream, pick something else.' George says, 'Oh, okay, sorry about that. Umm... then... let me just have a regular cone, double scoop of... chocolate ice cream.' Frank groans, thinks for a minute, then says, 'George, take the van out of vanilla, what do you get?'" Talon paused.

"Oh, you want me to answer?" Amelia asked, snuggling up to Talon's groin. If he could've had heart failure he would've been dead. "Illa," she responded.

Clearing his throat, he went on, "Then Frank says, 'Now, take the straw out of strawberry, what do you get?'" He paused again.

"Berry," Amelia answered without hesitation.

"Then Frank says, 'Now take the fuck out of chocolate, what do you get?' George thinks about it for a second then says, 'There is no fuck in chocolate.' 'That's what I've been trying to tell ya,' Frank exclaims, 'There is no fuckin' chocolate!'"

The vibration of Amelia's laughter on Talon's dick wreaked havoc. He envisioned her lips wrapped tight around his shaft. This was equal parts torture and heaven. She was so soft and smelled so good. He ran his fingers through her hair—might as well have been touching a cloud. He didn't want this moment to end.

Something wet soaked through the fabric of his slacks. Amelia's laughter turned to sobs. She sniffled. "Sorry."

"For what—weeping?"

Amelia nodded.

"You don't ever need to apologize to me for anything, least of all, weeping." He stroked her hair with a tenderness he didn't know he possessed.

Unsure how to help, he listened to her muffled sobs. Talon hated feeling powerless. He was a male of action, yet, since meeting her, it'd been a lot of inaction. Continuing to smooth her hair, he savored each stroke. This was the first time Amelia had let her guard down with him. It was nice. She was so... female.

After some time, she quieted. He thought she'd fallen asleep, but then she asked in a raspy voice, "Do you think I'm cursed?"

He tucked a stray strand of hair behind her ear. Voice thick with unexpected emotion, he answered, "Not in the least. Why would you think you were?"

She dabbed a tear with the corner of her blanket. "Everyone around me dies."

His heart ached for her. "No, *cara*, that has nothing to do with you. It was their time."

She nodded. More tears soaked through his slacks.

At that precise moment, an electrical shock pierced his heart. Like someone shocked him with defibrillator paddles. An odd mixture of pain and pleasure coursed through him. He clutched his heart.

"You okay?" Amelia asked.

"Yeah," he lied, voice strained.

This couldn't be fuckin' happening. It should've been impossible. He was a Royal Guard. She, a Vampire Royal. Possible or not, he felt it. This surpassed the feelings he fought having for her. This was more than love. That shock was the *Centripetal Impulse*.

This meant one thing. Amelia was...

His *eternalmate.*

Chapter Twenty-Six

"No, Kasey, he just left. I wouldn't cover for him. I promise."

This girl is frickin' insane. Amelia loved her like a two-dollar hooker, but the girl had a serious insecure, stalker mentality. She sat at the island on one of the barstools. "It's been ten minutes. There could be some bitch between here and there. You don't know."

"Really?" — *What a nut* — "Let me get this straight. It takes fifteen minutes to get to your house from here. Evan left ten minutes ago, and you think that gives him enough time to cheat."

"You don't understand, A," Kasey whined. "He doesn't have the same blind devotion to me as..." Her sentence trailed off.

"...*Walker does to you*" hung in the silence between them. Amelia's heart constricted. Salt, wound—rub, rub. There was no more Walker. Her logical mind understood, but the words made no sense to her heart and soul.

Obviously, like Amelia, Kasey didn't know what to say. Silence reigned. Finally, she said, "I'm so sorry, A. I shouldn't—I should—someone needs to rip out my tongue. I never should've—"

"It's fine, Kasey," Amelia interrupted. No use in Kasey castigating herself for telling the truth.

Walker had given Amelia blind devotion. Devotion she never appreciated and wasn't worthy of. Had she been a person worthy of someone like him she would've freed him to find his real soulmate. She was damaged and dragged him along for the cataclysmic ride that was her fatal life.

A knock at the front door surprised her. She jumped. Who the hell? Everyone she cared about was accounted for. Tessa was staying at Dan's because she couldn't stand being in a house where someone died, though she wouldn't admit it. She only came back to check on Amelia and sit with her for a few hours each day to spread some of that old Tessa charm. Evan was en route to Kasey's, and Kasey was at home. Everyone was where she preferred them: away from her and her shitty luck.

"Hey, Kase, I gotta go. Somebody's at the door."

"Are you just trying to get off the phone with me? I'm sorry," she said, full of contrition. "I didn't mean to say what I did. Did I hurt your feelings?"

"No. I really gotta go. Call me back if Evan doesn't show up. I'll hunt him down for you."

Kasey let out a loud exasperated sigh. "Fine. Go. But, be safe, okay? Ask who it is. God forbid anything happen to you, Evan would never get over it."

Oh, yeah, God forbid her cursed luck actually hit the right target for once. "I'll be careful. Kick Evan for me."

"Will do and... I'm sorry."

Amelia pressed *End* and went to get the door. Why did people keep apologizing to her? Was she the one whose life was cut short? No. Was she the one who'd lost her son or brother prematurely? No. Yet everyone kept saying sorry to her. She was the one who hadn't spent any time with her boyfriend in the last month. Hadn't told him, or anyone else, she was pregnant. Let's not forget her lustful feelings for two guys she barely knew. One of which happened to be her late boyfriend's cousin.

Yeah, sorry was the last thing people should feel for her. What she needed to do was focus on keeping her loved ones safe from her. Figure out what to do about her unexpected bundle of joy and stay the hell away from Talon and Calin.

With that, she opened the door. Shit! Should've asked who it was...

"Well, well, well... Look who finally decided to grace me with his presence," Amelia drawled, leaning against the open door.

The plan had been to come here and vanquish his crazy obsession with her. Calin also needed to pry some information out of her. Figure out where in her family tree sat a Siren. Wouldn't hurt to get this show on the road either. He had news to break and an *Awakening* to plan. That's why he stood here with guitar in one hand, a plastic bag containing a packet of microwaveable popcorn, and a DVD in the other, ready to conquer temptation and chant down Babylon.

Best laid plans, huh?

This was so much more than temptation. There she was in all her fucking mortal perfection. Every time he was near this insignificant female, strange things happened inside him. Things that made him want to touch her skin, press his body into hers to test if it was as inviting as it seemed. Taste her like he'd never wanted to do with another mortal. Mortals were sustenance, but that's not what he wanted from her. He wanted to savor her, cherish her...

Protect her.

That thought scared him most. Where was his fucking resolve? Probably skipping through a damn field of daises with his end game.

She could be yours. Rule together.

Why was his demon playing with him? He was a smart Hybrid, smarter and more powerful than most. Not around her though. He got lost in those jewel-colored eyes that were currently narrow and staring at him, waiting for an explanation. What could he say to soothe her disappointment?

"Amelia, I'm sorry I didn't make it to the funer—"

She held up a hand, silencing him.

Well, that didn't work.

General rule of thumb: Calin didn't soothe. He might have a smidgen of mortal blood, but it wasn't enough to give him arcane insight into females of any species. Her standing there with her hair twisted up in a clip, wearing a gray wife-beater and short black shorts resembling men's briefs, didn't help bring the right words to mind.

Dayam!

The mortal was hot as fuck. And oblivious to it.

If she turned around he was sure he'd glimpse a caramel ass cheek. Made him want to drop the bag he held just to watch her pick it up. Tiny and sexy, she had his full attention... and he was definitely giving a standing ovation.

Amelia threw a hand on her hip. "Do you remember about—oh, I don't know—a week ago? We were kind of in this same situation, but we were both outside and it was daytime?" she asked, sarcasm drizzling from each word.

Calin didn't know how to answer, and apparently, she didn't expect him to because she plowed on. "You were all sweet and made it seem like I could count on you, but nope." Her voice rose. "Turns out I couldn't. Weird, huh?"

His first instinct was to sink his teeth into that succulent neck of hers and drain her dry. Who the hell did she think she was? Talking to *him* like *that*? She wasn't queen yet.

He leaned his guitar against the open door jamb, cupped her chin with his palm. Caressed her soft cheek with his thumb.

Given the mood she was in he thought she'd pull away, but she leaned into his touch.

Her skin was like nothing he'd ever felt before. Satin. Silk. Velvet. Not one compared to her so-soft-it-did't-feel-real skin. She was—

An electrical shock, a cross between pain and pleasure, blazed a trail up his arm. Seized his heart. Said organ stuttered. It felt as if he'd been struck by a bolt of lightning. What the—?

Centripetal Impulse...

Chapter Twenty-Seven

Amelia stood speechless as Calin gazed into her eyes and rubbed her cheek. She should put some distance between them. But right now, she couldn't move if someone paid her to. Some unseen force seemed to have her rooted to the floor.

This was wrong. Her boyfriend had just passed. She had no business letting a guy Walker hated touch her.

"*Calin...*" Damn, that was supposed to be a stern reprimand, not all breathless. Let's try again. "*Calin...?*" Whatever. Breathless it was. "What're you doing here?"

Turquoise eyes lit like a kid's on Christmas. The sight literally stole her breath. That lopsided grin thing he did... sinful.

Dropping his hand, he reclaimed his guitar and raised the plastic bag in his right hand. "I come bearing peace offerings slash apologies—if you'll have me?"

What a loaded question.

Color crept into Calin's cheeks. Wow! Calin blushed! He shook his head. "I mean, if you'll have them?"

An hour later, Calin had wormed his way back into her good graces. True to his word, he sang and played. She hadn't known the song off the bat. He added quite a few embellishments. Once he started singing, her heart melted as she recognized Jason Mraz's "I Won't Give Up". When he finished, she offered him a tentative smile.

Although wonderful, something seemed off about his song choice. It was as if he were sending her some sort of a subliminal message. The last few times he'd sung for her it was incredible, to say the least, but there was an innocence to it. This time was... more somehow.

She hadn't wanted company, but this was nice. He didn't play couch commando with the remote. Barely ate any of the pizza she ordered because of *tummy issues*—his words, not hers.

Now, it was movie time. She put it in, turned out the lights, then got comfortable lying on the loveseat. Calin sat on the floor in front of it and leaned against it. He said it was in case she got scared, but she thought it might be more for his benefit. Wouldn't that be a sight, a big masculine guy like him scared of a movie? She laughed at the thought.

"What's so funny up there?" he asked, turning to look at her.

Damn! Turquoise eyes scintillated in the dark. Her mouth went dry just looking into them. She bit her lip, used the pain to remember how to speak. "I was just wondering why you're so fascinated with vampires," she lied.

"And that made you laugh?" Calin asked eyebrow raised.

"You want the truth?"

Calin flipped around to face her.

Amelia's breath caught in her throat. No one had the right to be this raw masculinity, dangerous, and sexy blend. The searing gaze he trained on her made her wish her clothes were of the breakaway variety.

Must. Get. Him. Turned. Around. Or she was gonna burst into flames.

"Of course, I want the truth, Duchess," Calin answered solemnly.

So serious, in fact, it made the hairs on the nape of her neck stand on end. Suspicion tunneled through her mind. Was he not telling the truth about something? Impossible. What would he have to lose or gain? In a matter of weeks, he'd be gone, and she'd be a memory.

"Fine." Amelia sighed. "I was thinking it would be funny if the movie scared you."

He laughed. "I'm never scared remember?"

"Oh, excuse me, Bone Crusher." She snorted. "I forgot *you're* the scariest thing out at night."

"Bone Crusher?"

"Haven't you ever heard the song 'Never Scared'? By a rapper... named Bone Crusher?"

God, he probably hadn't. Calin seemed to listen to soulful artists who wrote meaningful lyrics. Such a contradiction to his badass persona and size. That was one of the most intriguing things about him.

Calin shot her an arch stare.

Damn. Those eyes. She shouldn't have let him in. Somewhere deep inside, she hadn't wanted to be alone tonight. At the same time, she hadn't wanted to deal with anyone waiting for her to "break down" or "want to talk about it". She needed to... *be* for a while, no pressure, or expectations. Calin was her usual go-to for that, but tonight, in his saran wrap-tight black T-shirt and faded blue jeans... Her libido couldn't cope.

He needed to turn around before she did something stupid. "Never mind. It's not funny if I have to explain the joke. Turn around; you're missing the movie," Amelia directed.

Calin complied without protest.

"So, *Interview with the Vampire*, eh? Never pegged you as a Brad Pitt man. But, whatever. I'm a Brad Pitt girl so... why not? To each his own."

"Whoa! Are you insinuating I might not fly right?" he asked offended.

"Hey, I'm no one's judge. You can fly whatever direction you want."

Turning, his mouth fell slack. The look on his face... priceless. "What makes you think I'm gay? This movie's good. The closest mortals get to getting it right. Plus, you can't tell me that little girl doesn't bear a striking resemblance to Bianca."

"Mortals? As opposed to what—immortals? Please tell me you're kidding about this whole being a vampire thing."

"Would it be bad if vampires existed?" he asked.

Sheesh! Him and his vampires. Guess hot guys were geeks, too. "I don't know. I don't think about nonsensical things. I'm a realist."

He chuckled. "Humor me for a few minutes. Please?"

"Fine. What was the question?"

She couldn't believe she was actually entertaining this craziness. The only reason she agreed was to discern how worried she should be about Calin's mental health. Not that she wouldn't visit him in the loony bin. Crazy people needed love, too—and padded rooms with barred windows. Anyway, this kept her mind from lingering on her sorrow and guilt.

"Would it be bad if vampires existed?" Calin repeated, chuckling. "Why don't you think it's possible?"

"Well, for one, vampires eat people. So that'd be bad. For two, if they existed, they'd be pretty easy to spot. I mean, they'd be the ones who came out at night talking all, where for art thou, in the twenty-first century, wearing clothes from a Jane Austen movie."

Calin made a noise in the back of his throat. He nodded. "So, what, you don't think vampires can adapt to the times?"

"According to your favorite movie here" — she gestured toward the TV — "no. Brad Pitt's all weird and uncomfortable talking to Christian Slater. Most people don't have such a serious, constipated look when talking to others. He looks like he should be on the toilet, not giving an interview."

Chortling, Calin shook his head. "Okay, let's not use Brad Pitt as a reference. You really don't think a vampire could dress and talk like... me, or your friend Talon?"

"What does Talon have to do with this? I thought we were talking hypothetical?"

"We are. I was just giving you true-to-life examples. Plus, he talks weird, doesn't he?"

"Talon talks funny because he's from all over. Anyway, neither one of you are vampires. I've seen you both during the day. You have cars. Vampires wouldn't need a car. And you have a sister that resembles you—and surprisingly Kirsten Dunst in this movie. Vampires can't have babies. You always look like you were mugged by Ed Hardy. You don't have fangs, or a widow's peak, and you don't dress in all black," Amelia stated, proud of her rationale.

Calin was silent for so long she thought he'd conceded. For no reason at all she felt like apologizing. But for what, she didn't know. She was about to speak, but he finally did.

"I guess we know which one of us is racist and prejudiced. Should I go pick the hangin' tree, or is that your favorite part? You got your lynchin' rope," Calin said, using a dead-on hillbilly accent.

Offense and hurt were evident in his tone. She actually felt guiltier than earlier. "I'm sorry, Calin." —Why was she apologizing?— "I thought we were playing around. I'd never be like that against a real person. I mean, look at me. I'm a mutt. I can't be prejudiced or racist."

God only knew why she felt the need to explain, or why she wanted to comfort him, but she did. Scooting into a half-sitting half-laying position, she massaged his shoulders—and almost suffered from heart failure.

Calin's back was ripped. Muscle upon muscle. Ripped. Supreme effort went into resisting the urge to lean down and bite him. Her mouth watered.

Without warning, he leaned his head to the side, captured her hand between his whiskered cheek and shoulder. Amelia yanked her hand back as if he'd burned her. Truth be told, she felt like she was on fire. And not the kind the fire department dealt with.

"You alright?" Calin asked, looking at her.

God, those eyes!

They were hungry eyes she wanted to see in the—no! Not hungry eyes. They were normal eyes she shouldn't focus on.

"Yeah, I'm fine. Watch the movie," she ordered flatly.

Calin shrugged, a lazy lift of powerful muscular shoulders. His attention shifted to the TV.

Now it was too quiet. Sexual tension arced between them. Quiet time gave her time to think. Thinking led to dirty wet dreams while awake. She needed some way to keep herself under control. Inspiration hit like a cement truck.

"Let's say I buy into this vampire theory—I don't—but let's say I do for argument's sake." This had to be better than thinking about different sex positions.

"Ok. And…" Calin prompted.

"Explain how I've seen you during the day."

"So, I'm a vampire?" Calin asked, amused.

"Hey, you said it, not me."

He nodded. "True. I'm a vampire. I'd answer your question by saying there are different breeds of vampire."

"Uh-huh. That's evasive. You should've been in a coffin or a pile of ashes long ago." She laughed.

"Commoner, Natural-born, and Convert vampires would be in ashes. But why would anyone want to sleep in a cramped coffin? Being a vampire doesn't mean you like tight spaces. There are ways to keep a bed out of the sun. Is your bed outside?"

"Ha. Ha. What's a commoner vampire?" This conversation was getting weird.

"Vampires born without nobility and no more ability than the superhuman strength, speed, heightened senses, and mind manipulation capabilities all breeds of vampires have—save two," Calin explained as if they were talking about something as normal as the stock exchange.

Though it was dumb to encourage him, she was oddly curious. "And which two would those be?"

"Hybrids. They're supposed to be forbidden, but for every person who abides by a law there are at least ten people who seek to break it, so… there are Hybrids."

Well, that was totally unhelpful. God help her, but she wanted to understand. "And what's a Hybrid—who forbids it?"

Calin laughed as if her question was funny. Strange, given the fact he was rambling ridiculousness. Where did he get this crap—Vampire Mythology-R-Us?

He went on, "Pretend for a minute that vampires, witches, shape-shifters, werewolves, demons, fairies, and any other things you don't believe in are real." He turned and winked at her.

Her heart almost stopped.

Good thing he went on without a prompt. His salacious gesture left her winded.

"Now, envision all those things living lives like you or me. Working, getting along, for the most part, as well as people of different ethnicities do. Only they're ruled by a monarch, like in England. Vampires are forbidden by The Fates from procreating with any other being—"

"Who are The Fates?"

"Hmm... They're angels. A triumvirate God bestowed with the power of creation shortly after Lucifer fell. Do you know much about Christianity?" Calin looked at her.

She nodded, then averted her gaze before dirty thoughts crept in. This conversation was ridiculous, but if it kept her hormones in check... She'd ride it until the wheels fell off.

Calin went on, "They created the supernatural—all those things you don't believe in. There were four, but as with Lucifer, one fell. He became BFFs with Satan. Now he's The Dark Majesty, like a devil for supernatural."

Amelia's eyes glazed. This was worse than listening to her brother talk. *Either this or sex.* "How does this explain me seeing you in the morning?"

"I'm getting to that. Hold on. A long time ago, The Fates prophesied the king vampire and his wife would be destroyed. Because they didn't have heirs, the metaphorical crown would go to the vampire king's distant female cousin. Neither the king nor his subjects wanted that. So, the king decided to bump uglies with a bad witch to create heirs, thus creating the first breed of wholly evil, crazy powerful Hybrids. They possess magic and most vampire abilities."

Wow! By the way he explained it, she'd think he knew these creatures personally or at least wrote the book on them. "What are the other Hybrids? You said there were two kinds."

Check me out, pretending to give a shit.

Calin nudged her knee with his elbow playfully. "You listened. I'm shocked," he said. "The second type was created by one of the king's Hybrid daughters. She conceived them with mortal men. Because they have a bit of mortal blood, they can be out during the day, provided there isn't prolonged direct sun exposure. So, if I was a vampire, I'd be a Vampire-mortal-Dark-witch Hybrid."

Nuts, but made scary nutty sense. "And you'd drink blood or eat food?"

Calin laughed, a rich earthy sound. "Vampire-Dark-witch Hybrids drain their prey's blood then eat the corpse. If a Vampire-mortal-Dark-witch Hybrid turns wholly evil, they do, too. If I'm a Vampire-mortal-Dark-witch who retained his humanity, I only drink blood. I also eat small amounts of food, but my digestive system processes slower than mortals."

Good thing this conversation was complete bullshit, otherwise, it'd be a tad freaky. Sitting in the dark, watching *Interview with the Vampire*, talking about vampires... a little spooky for her tastes.

Time to lighten the mood.

"Tell me, Obi-Vampire Kenobi, are all vampires' masters of seduction like these ones?" She pointed at the television. Tom Cruise was in the middle of seducing a whore while Brad Pitt brooded on the balcony.

Calin stood and paced across the room. "Some vampires have quite a few extra abilities. The Vampire Royals—" He glanced over his shoulder. Catching her blank expression, he explained, "Vampires chosen to rule the supernatural by The Fates because of their angelic lineage." He resumed his leisurely stroll.— "They have powers unique to the specific individual and their familial line." At the television, he stopped the movie.

The room plunged into almost complete darkness. A soft glow from the blue-screened television provided the only light.

"Some vampires are handpicked by The Fates to possess greater strength, speed, and psychic ability." Calin's voice grew gravelly.

Amelia's breath quickened. Her mouth went dry. Something about Calin's absurd explanation set her blood on fire. Or maybe it was his voice. The low accented lilt. Focusing on his words, and not what she wanted him to do, became difficult.

He slowly swiveled around. "But all vampires are filled with the innate power to seduce. They have infinitely more pheromones than mortals. Their attractiveness, a gift from their once angel-turned-demon creator." His voice deepened. "Do you find me attractive?"

How to answer that? He was so far past *attractive* it wasn't even a dot in the rearview. The lecherous blue-green look he offered rendered her mute. Her stomach fluttered. She felt flushed with fever.

Except for his hooded pale gaze, he didn't look so much affected as arrogant. Like he knew his effect on her. He grinned, devilish.

Moisture rushed to the juncture between her thighs. She squirmed, uncomfortable in her damp panties. This was wrong. Walker's body wasn't even cold, and she already contemplated sleeping with the enemy. What's worse, she couldn't bring herself to stop him.

Calin's eyes drifted closed. He inhaled deeply. His nostrils flared. A groan escaped barely parted lips. His eyelids lifted. Luminous, beguiling eyes stared at her. Amusement danced in their hypnotic depths. As if he had a secret. His tongue snaked out between full lips to drag in his bottom lip. He bit it.

Fuck moisture, she was soaked. Liquid. Her clit throbbed. Never in her life had she felt such an untamed pull toward a man. That's why she couldn't stop him, even with guilt riding her hard. Her need for Calin was elemental.

Scary.

Eyes steady on hers; he lowered himself to the ground. First to one knee, then the other. He dropped onto his hands and knees. His pupils dilated.

Her heart hammered her chest.

And he moved. The muscles of his wide back rolled, rippled, and flexed under his black T-shirt. He crawled, prowling. Sensual. Approached like a feral beast stalking prey.

Fear and anticipation spiked within her. Apparently, there was a thin line between turned on and scared shitless.

This had to be the rawest sensual moment of her entire life. Her breasts felt full. Heavy. Her nipples pebbled. The lace fabric of her bra stimulated the sensitive peeks, sending electric jolts through her. Gulping, she nodded in answer to his forgotten question.

Her breath became ragged. She reached to run her fingers across his stubbled chin, but he rose to a kneeling position. He lowered the top half of his body over her. She reminded herself to breathe. No matter what he did, he never released her gaze.

Resting one arm on the back of the loveseat and one on the armrest next to her head, he caged her in. He smelled of dark spice and Calin.

Face mere inches from hers; he playfully nipped the small space separating their lips. Given her extreme cotton mouth, her answering smile was weak. His grin tugged at something inside her. A foreign, aching need pulsed through her.

The air between them thickened with sexual tension. She struggled to hold onto her guilt. This wasn't right.

He dipped his head to her collarbone but didn't touch. Her mind short-circuited. Why hadn't he touched her yet? The flesh his lips hovered above heated. Her stomach muscles quivered. He blew a blazing trail along her collarbone, up the column of her throat. To her ear.

Goose bumps peppered every square inch of her body.

"What makes you moan, *ma douce*?" he whispered in her ear.

That... Shivers raced down her spine. Her eyes rolled back in her head. Calin blew in her ear. The contrast of his cool breath on her overheated skin... A moan escaped, unbidden.

She wanted to touch him. Run her fingers through his hair, but the way he bent over her pinned her arms to her sides.

His hand, which had been resting on the back of the loveseat, lowered. Hovered millimeters from her abdomen. Electrical currents popped, sizzled, sparked between his palm and her stomach. It didn't hurt. Just made her painfully aware of the fact that he hadn't touched her. Her heartbeat grew erratic the longer they stared into each other's eyes. Electricity built. Their shared gaze felt magnetized. She arched her body, desperate for his touch. His weight.

Ho-ly, shit! This was happening.

And she would let it. God only knew why. She'd freak out later. For now, she wanted him to lie on top of her. Kiss her hard and feel his cock deep inside her. He could make her forget everything. Healthy or not, she wanted that.

She shivered, moaning. "Please..."

He smirked. Pearly whites gleamed in the dark. "I don't want to crush you, Duchess."

Why did that sound like, "Better to eat you with?" He could steamroll her for all she cared. *Touch me.* This was unbearable. Shaking her head, she breathed, "You won't crush me."

Calin tsked, cocked his head to one side. He looked her up and down, crown to toes. Up again. His gaze rested on her mound.

Said mound purred like it'd been caressed.

He groaned. "What do you do to me?"

Boy, did he have it backward. He wasn't the one close to combustion. She bit her bottom lip to keep from saying that. Blood bubbled from the tiny self-inflicted wound. Amelia nearly moaned from its tangy-sweet taste. What was with her?

Calin licked his lips...

Then swooped in.

He crushed his lips to hers. She gave herself mad props for not buckling under his firm lips. His tongue forced her mouth open and made a thorough sweep. He sucked her bottom lip. His low groan reverberated through her. The combination of his cool tongue thrusts against her hot probing ones, arousal at its most heightened. Decadent. Warm chocolate drizzled over vanilla ice cream. She tilted her pelvis, desperate to get close to the obvious bulge in his jeans. The bulbous head was huge and unhindered. Was he commando?

Curses to whoever made zippers.

Working a hand between their bodies, she wriggled her fingers to the waistband of his jeans. He pulled back. Amelia affected her best sheepish grin.

Calin smirked. He knew she felt his erection. Good. He wanted to feel her, too. Feel her pussy swallow his cock. What would her pussy taste like? Calin groaned.

Mine.

This adorable, fragile, honey-skinned goddess was his *eternalmate.* Corny as it sounded, he reeled from the knowledge. She was his to do with as he pleased. He could summon a High Priest or Priestess and have them *bound* before dawn. By tomorrow, he could be feasting on her thick femoral blood—as well as other things between her thighs.

But what if she wasn't his mate? Fated to be her mate and executioner? It contradicted the whole purpose of a mate. Feeding off another vampire would poison him. Of course, she wasn't vampire yet. That delicious token bit of blood from her lip wouldn't do anything. Except make him long for a more substantial taste. It also provided a connection. He'd be able to find her anywhere. Were The Fates stoned when they decided this?

He studied the beauty beneath him.

Amelia's eyelids, two drooping curtains, hid her marvelous, glazed gaze briefly before they lifted to half-mast. Her coy smile stole his heart.

Fuck...

This was wrong. He knew she thought he'd told her some vampire fable. Revealing the truth to her was more than important now. As her mate, he shouldn't keep things from her. But he was beyond the stopping point. His baser instincts were all predator.

Calin dipped his head away from her soul-stealing gaze. Kissed her collarbone. Sprinkled kisses up her neck. He took a deep drag of her almond-mango scent. His balls drew tight. He dragged his nails up her ankle, over her satin-smooth calf. She gasped.

He moved to her ear, sucked the lobe.

She shuddered.

"You beg so prettily," Calin said around the flesh trapped between his teeth. He lifted his head, met her eyes. "Did you like that?"

She nodded.

"*Tell*... me you like it," he growled.

Her eyes widened. Pupils dilated. Breath hitched. "I-I l-like it," she stuttered.

Calin grinned. Nipped her earlobe. She yelped.

It made sense now. His soul. He'd always viewed it as inconvenient. Annoying. Not anymore. His puny, insignificant soul recognized her. Her musical laugh. Her big heart. It needed her soul to complete it.

I will have her, details be damned.

He returned to her lips. His tongue drove past hers. Pushed his steel hard cock against her cloth-covered core. Ground it into her. Her loud moan vibrated their joined mouths. He broke the kiss. Kissed her forehead. Amelia's hand squished between their bodies, reaching for his zipper.

"You're mine." He groaned. "I want your name branded on my chest."

The temperature in the room dropped.

What the fuck?

One second, she'd been about to unleash The Terminator, the next... She went rigid. He leaned back. She slid off the loveseat. What happened? Calin felt... uncomfortable, alone. A bewildering ache built in his mid-chest region. Oh, he did not do this shit at all.

He would've asked her what was wrong, but when she turned... The pain behind her icy stare was a rusty nail driven through his temple.

"You have to go," she said. She removed the movie from the DVD player and put it in its case. On her way back to the loveseat, she grabbed his guitar. She thrust both items at him. "I'm sorry."

Accepting his belongings, he stared dumbfounded. "What happened?" he asked, floored by her abrupt dismissal. "Did I do something?"

She tugged his hand. Still thrown, he stood. Let her lead him to the front door in silence. She opened the door and pushed him out. He turned to find her eyes swimming in tears. Grief and tart guilt vibrated from her. He got it. Didn't like it. But understood.

"You didn't do anything. Sorry about your blue balls." She winced in imagined sympathy. "It's me, I'm the slut. Sorry."

"You did nothing wrong. Talk to me, Duchess."

She shook her head. "I need to be alone. Call me tomorrow, okay?" She shut the door.

In his face.

Raw emotion tore through Calin like a tornado. Remorse, uncertainty, confusion... concern. How did mortals cope with such unpleasant feelings? Calin sauntered toward his car. Three houses down and across the street, an elderly woman in a loud floral moo-moo checked her mail.

His mouth watered. Fangs descended. He put his guitar and movie in his Rolls Royce, then cast a spell to cloak his vehicle. The corners of his mouth curled. Mortals could deal however they wanted. He much preferred his way. Calin strutted across the street.

Chapter Twenty-Eight

"**Y**ou're sure!"

Talon corrected his Chrysler before he ended up on the wrong side of the street. This pretending to be mortal bullshit pissed him off. If he sublimated or ran, he would've been done with his nightly check-in. He hated driving.

"No, not at all," he answered dryly. "I've only known the male—hmm... my entire existence... yet never managed to catalog his actual description."

"Sorry, shit!" Anton swore on the other end of the phone. "You'll have to excuse my shock. I can't believe Emilio would follow you and the descen—Amelia—and not make contact. It's not his shtick."

"Believe it."

"Maybe you're only seeing what you want to see. You've been acting weird since you got there. And that's saying a lot. You were already weird."

The fledgling refused to believe there was no deeper meaning behind his indifference toward his brother. "Why would I *want* to see my brother? He's a psychopath on his best night. Trust me; there are things I want to see. He's not one of them."

"Oh, no? So, what is playa?" Anton asked full of amusement.

Talon would not indulge him. "Did you find out anything about the Daywalker? He's got young with him, about five—give or take—out in the daylight, too. No governess. There's something with her. She seemed..." Talon paused, searching for an accurate descriptor.

The stunning little female's demeanor confounded him. She seemed evil, rogue. But that was impossible. Part of the mercy The Fates took on The Dark Majesty's "experiments" was the ability to procreate through their previous mortal means. As further reparation, they gifted vampire young with ten years reprieve. Young would have as normal an accelerated childhood as possible with no demon interference. Concepts of good and evil, right and wrong, should be to her as they are to mortal children—taught. Balkan's Hybrids were the only exception to the rule. They were born of two soulless beings. In all honesty, she shouldn't exist. But she did, and she seemed...

"...hollow," he finished. "Evil. I thought she might be a new Hybrid of Balkan's, but she had that odd fledgling, erratic heartbeat. Get me information on her too."

"Yes, sir," was the fledgling's sardonic answer.

Talon almost heard the young's eyes roll. Luckily, they weren't face-to-face. If they had been, Anton would get to feel what it was like to actually have his eyes roll—out of his head. "What do you know of Sirens?"

"Oh, we're changing the subject? Let me catch up," Anton groused sarcastically. "Uh... I just read about them—among other things," he grumbled under his breath. "Umm... Let's see. Popular myth says they're ugly, female-headed creatures with bird bodies. But in truth, they're humanoid, beautiful, and immortal. No one can resist their song or beauty. They have the power to enslave millions—human or supernatural. The effects can be temporary or permanent."

"So, they can create unlimited *vassal*? What about weaknesses?" Talon asked, horrified.

Surprises never ceased, did they? No wonder prophecy dubbed her *Most Powerful*. When mortals were compelled, too often they became permanently enthralled, *vassals*. Mindless servants to whichever supernatural last compelled them, only dying when their sire did. What would that do to an already immortal supernatural? He shuddered at the thought. Immortals treasured their power and their free will. Superiority. Having it taken away...

"Why would The Fates create them if they could do that?" he queried more to himself than Anton.

"I don't know. Do I look like one of The Fates? Why would the Most High let the four of them create the supernatural when he knew one would break off and become best friends with Lucifer? Shit happens."

Talon rubbed his temple. No, vampires didn't get migraines. Amelia seemed to get them a lot when they were together. Described them as severe pain in one's brain. Dealing with Anton always made his brain hurt. Maybe vampires weren't as impervious to mortal illnesses as he thought.

Gripping the steering wheel tight enough to pop his knuckles and crack the steering column, he snarled, "Quit your shit and answer the question."

"Jeez, take a fuckin' joke." Anton sighed, put-upon. "I guess The Fates originally thought they'd be good at policing the supernatural, keeping order, playing buttboy. Apparently, they short-sold the value of a good mirror. Sirens got cocky. Like most of us, their immortality comes with limits. The Fates out clause with all of us, if you ask me. They're probably harder to kill than werewolves, the guards, and VR. But where there's a will, there's a way. The Fates sentenced them to death but were merciful to those who agreed to keep a low profile. Thee end."

"No, not thee end—thee beginning. What are the chances Amelia is part Siren?"

"Slim, I'd say. Real slim. Why?"

"We only know her maternal family line. Couldn't her father have been one?"

"No. First, the prophecy said, 'a descendant of *pure* noble blood.' Second, males can't be Sirens. They carry the gene that makes their daughters Sirens. Either way, they're Sirens from birth. Even their infant cry is beautiful. And they're extinct, so this is all moot."

"I guess Amelia's moot then because she is one." He hadn't meant to tell him, but the little guy said he wanted to help... "I saw it with my own eyes. Get on that. We need to find her paternal line. The *Daywalker* saw it, too. Who knows what he'll do with the information."

"You know, *please* and *thank you* would be nice additions to your vocabulary," Anton complained.

"Goodbye, Anton." Talon hung up abruptly and tore out the earbud to better distinguish the sounds of the evening.

A block away, a male and female argued about who'd forgotten to pay the electric bill. In another home, a husband slammed drawers and muttered angrily about a lack of oral attention. Neither was the sound that enraged him, forced him to hang up on Anton.

There.

Muffled sobs. He'd know that voice anywhere.

Talon slammed on the gas. Took a corner so fast he nearly went up on two wheels. Why was she crying?

He'd never understand mortal emotions. They laughed one minute, cried the next, yelled at odd times. Maddening. Mortal emotional... stuff... freaked him out. Except Amelia's.

Hers stirred emotion in *him*. Warm emotions, causing him to reminisce about the night of the funeral a week ago. Following some rare, useful advice from Gawain, he'd implemented nightly drive-bys and check-ins but hadn't spent any real time with her to allow her to grieve. Although, to be honest, he needed the time, too.

Riding the denial train worked for a few days, then his rational side kicked on. He'd felt the *Centripetal Impulse*. No matter if it was *The Fates* or a trick of *The Dark Majesty*, she was his *eternalmate*. He had no idea what to do with that. But he did know what to do if someone hurt her.

His stomach knotted with fury. He fought to keep his fangs retracted. If someone had hurt her, he'd rip the beating heart from their chest, drink from it, and spit it back in their face. Throwing his car into park in front of Amelia's house, he was out and at her front door in under a millisecond. Who cared who saw him?

Hearing her sobs through the door, he bypassed the doorbell and knocked hard enough to dent the wood. The door yanked open.

"Talon?" she asked hoarsely.

Her always raspy voice revealed nothing. The dulling of her brown skin was an expected attribute of transition. When her heart stopped, it'd pale a small amount more, acquire an inner radiance. Another anticipated side effect of transition: unstable body temperature. Explained the black velour tracksuit—a designer brand, knowing her. What didn't he expect? How worn out she looked or the reek of saltwater emanating from her.

She cleared her throat. "What are you doing here?"

"Are you hurt?" he demanded gruffer than intended. "Who's here? What happened?" he asked in rapid succession, barging past her and into the house.

Excuse me, Your Highness.

"What are you doing here?" Amelia repeated, pissed at the intrusion.

She should've slammed the door in his face. Couldn't she have a breakdown in peace? Was that too much to ask?

The last time she'd tried, Calin showed up and... Yeah, not going there. It wasn't that she didn't like it. She *really* liked it—until the one part. Too much too soon. Despite that, she didn't want to lose Calin. She couldn't lose Calin. For unclear reasons, she needed him. The whole fish-to-water, moth-to-flame, deer-to-headlights theory—needed him. And she needed this time to sort through that and the events of recent weeks.

Talon sniffing around like a dog freaked her out; it wasn't an exaggeration either. He literally searched her house and sniffed. She hadn't spent any significant time with him since the funeral. He'd stayed with her all night, tweaked her total opinion of him. They'd lain in her bed, which he hung off of because he was a giant. He told her about his strained relationship with his parents. She elaborated on being adopted.

Nope, she didn't fear losing *him;* he stuck like glue.

Closing the door, she turned to glare at him. "Has anyone ever told you you'd make a great police dog? You know, one of those drug or bomb-sniffing German Shepherds. Seriously, what are you—a member of the secret service?" When he continued to search, she snapped, "I'm alone, Talon."

He got down on all fours, looking under the daybed. "Why are you crying?"

"How did you know I was crying?"

"Why—milady?" he asked brusquely.

"Oh... I don't know, let's see. Your cousin—my boyfriend—was murdered by criminals who broke in and ransacked my house. That tends to make me a tad emotional. Why are you here?"

"I don't understand. You shouldn't be alone when you're... emotional."

Actually, that's exactly what she needed. Getting Tessa out of the house wasn't hard. Evan had taken to staying at Kasey's whenever her roommate was gone. One "I'm okay" from Amelia, and his divining rod led him out the door.

She sat on the daybed. "Hey, Cujo, when you're done you, wanna sit for a minute, or do I need to let you out back to do your business?" She tried to laugh, but it felt wrong.

If she'd thought everyone watched her before, she was wrong. Hawk-eye didn't begin to explain the eye kept on her since the funeral. Any time she looked on the brink of tears, Evan gave her valium or some other mind-numbing prescription drug and put her to bed. That made tonight doubly important. She needed to think and grieve. The walls tumbled down when she confirmed she'd be alone.

"You're funny," Talon said flatly, sitting on the opposite side of the daybed. "Your safety is paramount. The suspects in your home invasion haven't been found."

She snorted. "Paramount, huh? That's the same crap Tessa and Evan keep saying. Like whoever it was is coming back. Honestly, I'm surprised it happened at all. Peoria, Arizona, isn't a hotbed for random crime, especially not this neighborhood."

"Where are Tessa and your brother?"

"Are you ever going to tell me why you're here? I've asked like eight times. Shouldn't you be digging a moat or pacing the halls of the turret?"

"Hey, watch your tone. Talon not asshole; he friend," he said, doing a Tarzan impersonation. He smiled.

Wow, he should do that more.

Damn it! The floodgates were opening again. Her throat felt swollen, tight. "Sorry, I'm not having a good day." She glanced away from his enervating blue gaze. A tear rolled down her cheek. Shit! When did that start? "You can leave if you want."

She tried to keep it together, but some fundamental part of her was broken. The dam had a crack, and she couldn't uncover her usual sarcasm or anger to patch the fissure. Tears kept coming. Amelia felt Talon's eyes on her. She didn't want to look and see the horror sure to be on his face. Guys didn't do well with crying chicks.

She'd seen this scene in movies before: Woman sits bawling, a broken mess. Guy stares, wondering if she'd notice if he left. Amelia swore she'd never be that girl. Now, look...

Talon shifted.

Figures he'd capitalize on her offer. She gazed at him. Attempted to glare, but it probably didn't come off that intimidating with teary eyes. Their eyes met.

Nothing felt warm to her in weeks, so she was completely caught off guard when a warm rough hand touched hers. She started.

Talon moved. She was looking at him, yet didn't see it. But he did. He'd been at the other end of the daybed. Now, he sat right beside her.

No one had touched her with such—tender—affection in so long. You'd think she had some sort of contagious skin rash. A zing raced up her arm.

Yes, Calin touched her—oh... did he ever. It was the literal equivalent of sexual healing, all hot and erotic. Others touched her, but theirs was of the "there-there" pity variety. Talon's strictly consoled. A soothing balm to her battered soul. Involuntarily, she scooted closer and collapsed into his open arms.

Chapter Twenty-Nine

Led by some dormant male instinct, Talon draped an arm over Amelia's shoulders and tucked her head under his chin. He stroked her hair, ran his fingers through the silken strands. Bringing a few strands to his nose, he sniffed. Inhaled the scent of almond, sunflower seed, and mango oil.

She burrowed closer.

He bit back a moan.

The female was destroying him. And she was sobbing. Hard. Tears stained his T-shirt. Good thing he didn't care about his clothes.

Amelia lifted her head, sniffling. "I know this sounds all 'poor me' and whatever, but why me? My parents were good people. Jon never got a chance to live. My grandparents... all four" — she drew a shaky breath — "Wall made me his world—did you know he got that tattoo before we were together? You know the one common denominator in all their deaths?" she asked, then answered her own question. "Me. Death stalks me. I just want the people I care about safe. I'd keep Tessa away from me if I could, but she's too damn stubborn. Part of me's happy Evan stays on campus at NAU. If he lived here, it'd be on borrowed time."

She believed that? Mortals weren't his specialty. But beneath her quips, Amelia was special. Honestly, her quick wit and edge were part of her charm. How could she think herself deserving of tragedy? Her problem wasn't her inability to care. She cared too much.

Brows knitted, he stared into her eyes, perplexed.

"You better be careful," she said in an ominous tone. "You could be next." Wide, moist eyes gazed back at him.

And he was lost.

Something snapped inside him. Unraveled the last vestiges of his honor and duty. He had to have her. Just a taste. Enough to chase the despair from her eyes. Careful of his strength, he grabbed her right leg. God, her velour-clad thighs were soft and smaller than one of his biceps. No time to dither on the details now. If he thought, he wouldn't act.

Spurred by her accelerated heart rate, he yanked her leg up and around his waist. Lifted her to sit astride him. Amelia's eyes widened. She hadn't expected that, but her shallow breaths said she'd expected something.

Their eyes collided. This was it. The moment of no return. Stop or go. She sucked her bottom lip into her mouth. Square, white teeth nibbled plump flesh. Talon wouldn't mind doing that. He'd never had one, but he'd love to introduce her to a blood kiss. Damn, he couldn't. Yes, she was his *eternalmate*—for now—but taking blood under false pretenses...

He wasn't that far gone.

She wrapped her arms around his neck. Long dainty fingers caressed his nape and slipped through his hair. Tingles spread through his scalp. Talon ran a hand up and down her spine. Reveled in the fact that, for this one moment, he had the right to touch her. He weaved his fingers through her hair. Crimson locks cascaded over his pale hand.

He'd never thought of finding his *eternalmate* on this journey—didn't want to. But holding her in his arms, his shaft hardened under her round ass. Talon couldn't imagine not knowing her. He tugged her hair. Tilted her head, providing access to her creamy brown throat.

His fangs throbbed, begging for freedom. One bite. No. He couldn't. But he could do this. Wrapping his large hand around her frail neck Talon retained eye contact. He forced her mouth to his. Crushed his lips to hers... *Sanctuary*.

In unison, he groaned, and tremors racked Amelia's frame.

Talon wasn't sure he'd done it right. He'd never kissed anyone before. If her fervor were an appropriate gauge... she liked it. Ardor oozed from her pores. Vibrated from her spirit. It was peculiar having his cold, hard, lips pressed intimately to her warmer petal-soft ones. Feeding had been his only joy for... ever. Now it was her. This insolent slip of a female, who acted in none of the ways a female of breeding should.

Supple breasts smashed against his chest. Damn, he wanted her naked breasts on his bare chest. Their weight in his palm. They were disproportionate for her size. More than a handful. Amelia clenched the fabric of his over-shirt in tiny fists. As if she never wanted to let him go. Rolled her slim body against his. He struggled to keep his eyes open. The friction her movement created—delicious. He gritted his teeth behind his closed lips. Ooh, he wanted to fuck the shit out of her. He growled. Adjusted his grip on the back of her head. Clutched a bit rougher.

Amelia grabbed his bicep. Dug her nails into his tough flesh through his clothes. She wanted more. Of what, he wasn't sure. His dick was granite. He'd give it to her. But it didn't seem to be what she wanted.

Something slick and wet lit a hot trail across the seam of his lips. Why would—? Tentatively, his mouth opened. Her tongue slid in. Confident, meaty flesh stroked the top, side, and underside of his. It felt like fire. She was still so warm compared to him. She sighed into his mouth, content. He opened wider for her. Plunged his tongue deep inside her moist flaming cavern. Amelia tasted sweet, divine.

Their tongues tangled. Caught up in passion, and sensation, their eyes drifted closed. No responsibility, no concept of right or wrong, touched him in this place. For once, he was just a male, enjoying his female. Coppery, tangy blood particles in her saliva had his fangs close to descent. He sucked her tongue.

She moaned.

The musky scent of her arousal hung thick in the air. Of their own accord his fingers dug into her hips. Reminding himself of her fragile mortality, he loosened his grip. But didn't let go. She undulated against his shaft. Holding tight, he moved her back and forth on his turgid length. His eyes rolled behind his closed lids.

Amelia hissed.

The corners of his mouth quirked. He broke the kiss and looked into her eyes. "What?" he asked, amused at her dazed wide eyes. "You thought I was a small male?"

She shook her head.

He may not have the sexual prowess of Gawain or Anton, but he knew what he had. "There's a lot you don't know." Talon winked.

Pulling his mouth back to hers, Amelia deepened the kiss immediately. She gyrated on his straining hard-on. And that was all she wrote.

It happened quickly. One minute, Amelia straddled Talon's lap. The next, she was cradled in his arms and moving, fast. Without breaking the kiss. She'd swear only a second passed before she found herself lying on her bed with him perched above her.

Heavy-lidded midnight-blue eyes gazed upon her with un-masked desire. She shivered. The feral look unnerved her. Her breath faltered. He wasn't breathing hard. Wasn't flushed. But she knew he was affected. She traced the lines of his strong, defined jawline with the tips of her fingers. Baby's butt smooth. As if hair had never grown there.

He lowered himself on top of her. Balanced the bulk of his weight on his forearms. Blond locks skimmed his brows. Dipping, he captured her lips with his.

Mmm...

He tasted scrumptious. Like kissing a York Peppermint Patty. Sweet and cold. He'd been so hesitant when they first kissed. Now, like everything about Talon, he dominated. Took complete control. His tongue sank into her mouth. Explored every nook.

She was dripping wet. A slow burn started low in her pelvis. His thick erection pressed into her belly.

Finally, her soul sighed. An odd sense of calm washed over her. Amelia shuddered. Wound her arms around his neck. Held him to her. She should feel like a tramp, kissing him and Calin within days of one another. She didn't. This felt... right. It settled something inside her. Like recouping after the tilt-a-whirl ride at the fair, her world righted.

Deep tongue thrusts contrasted with butterfly brushes of his lips. She wrapped her legs around his lean waist. He ground his cloth-covered erection against her. Damn. What would that be like with nothing between them? He broke the kiss. Stroked her swollen lips. The awe in his eyes was astonishing. He should be scared? She'd told him everyone who got close to her died, and here he was. This was Russian roulette at its finest. Minutes passed.

Was that it?

He shook his head as if answering her thoughts. Okay...

She tossed him a wanton smile, reaching for the zipper of her hoodie. Unzipped. His eyes bulged as black lace was revealed. Thank you, Victoria's Secret, and foresight to not wear a shirt. The halves flopped open. When he stared immobile, she crooked a finger. He stepped back. Tore off his black button-down. Grabbed the hem of his gray T-shirt, and in one fell swoop pulled it over his head and tossed it to the floor.

Good, Lord! Amelia's heart stopped.

Talon didn't have a six-pack. Oh, no. He took it to the next level with a well-defined eight. Glorious. A sinful smirk stretched his lips. Chills enveloped her.

He eased back down on top of her, pressing against titillated nerve endings she'd never known she had. Talon raised and winked. Licked his long index finger, ran it from her throat to her navel, and like magic... Her bra was undone. Weird part? It clasped in the back.

She dragged her nails roughly down his chiseled chest, and his muscles flexed. A bestial, bone-rattling growl came from deep within him. Amelia traced the well-worn path to the front of his pants. Cupped him.

Wow!

The walls of her sex contracted. Talon's large hand slipped into the loose cup of her bra. He squeezed her breast, eliciting a moan of sheer ecstasy from her. Circled her puckered nipple with the palm of his hand. Her eyes closed. Her heart pounded.

It felt so...

Gone.

What the—

Amelia lifted onto her elbows. Saw the impossible. Talon was across the room, clothes pristine. "What the hell?" she asked winded, confused.

The expression on Talon's face was harsh. Cold. "This isn't right. I shouldn't—We shouldn't," he stammered, which was the only sign he felt anything. "I've gotta go."

Before she caught her breath, he was gone. Stunned, she zipped her hoodie robotically. She stared through her open doorway, baffled. How did he go from hot to cold so fast? Was it her?

Seconds later, Evan sauntered up to her doorway. If the harsh sting of rejection wasn't gnawing at her, the way her big brother had his arms crossed and his bottom lip poked out like a petulant child would have been comical. "Uh... She wanted to talk instead of doing what I planned. I said some things. She said some things... I'm sleeping here. Nite, Nugget." He stormed to his room.

Chapter Thirty

"In a bid to prove The Fates incompetence to the Most High, The Dark Majesty sent his Sanguinary Demons to wreak havoc on Earth. This violated two of the Most High's commandments to The Fates: No harm shall befall his Beloved (humans) at the hands of supernatural, and supernatural shall not reveal thy true nature to his Beloved.

Battle ensued for a decade. The Fates dispatched their strongest supernatural to combat the demons, but in the end, the country Deria fell. Blood flowed through the streets, painting dwellings. Bodies drained of blood were strewn about. No creatures stirred. Not even a mouse—"

"Anton Isaac Liakos!"

Anton tossed the leather-bound history book. It plopped onto the charcoal granite coffee table. Six weeks of reading the same bullshit over and over. He needed some spice—shit!

He grinned at Vanessa.

Sitting behind her executive desk, she pursed her lips. Swiveled side to side in her high-backed leather chair. Bony, pale elbows propped on top of the desk. Chin rested on interlaced fingers. "You are reading your race's history. Take it seriously," she admonished.

"I can't. I just can't." Anton threw himself back, lying flat across the cherry-red leather sectional.

He could have it worse, he supposed. He'd seen mortal classrooms on television, crowded, boring little rooms with wood-topped metal desks and uncomfortable, hard plastic chairs.

The learning annex his father commissioned Lea to decorate years ago was nothing of the sort. It was close to one thousand square feet and boasted three equally spaced identical sectional sofas ringing the coffee table. Black velvet blackout curtains covered large windows outlining the room. He shouldn't complain, but... since when did he do what he should?

"This is boring as hell," he groused. "Shit's like reading a damn fairytale."

"It is your lineage," his governess pointed out in exasperation, "and your punishment. Therefore, you can and *will* read it."

This was stupid. How could rehashing crap from before even his father's father shot his first load teach him not to eavesdrop? He shook his head. "Naw, I can't. This shit's booty. Don't you have some Playboy back there? I hear the—*articles*—are amazing. Full of knowledge." Anton turned and winked at her.

If looks could kill, the "keep testing me" glower Vanessa shot him should've skewered his heart. "Anton, I will put you in the sun if—"

"All right, all right," he grumbled. He picked up the brown book. In the same martyred, dispassionate tone he used when feigning interest in one of Lea's shopping stories, he continued reading. "Fearful the Most High would destroy them and their cherished supernatural, The Fates panicked. They cursed the Sanguinary Demons to forever be incorporeal. Thus returning the insubstantial demons to *Pakao-Brava*.

"Furious his most loyal were rendered useless; The Dark Majesty hatched a plan. He summoned his second-favorite demon, Hasher Demons. With their uncanny ability to draw humans to them in order to feed on their energy, they served The Dark Majesty's purposes well. Hashers lured six humans, three males and three females, at the height of their youth, twenty-one years of age, to a specific spot on Earth where the veil between *Pakao-Brava* and Earth was thin.

"Once in his clutches, he placed the humans in stasis, stopping all bodily functions. With an enchanted dagger, he made two points of entry. One in the humans' hearts and one in their heads. He gathered the strongest and most powerful incorporeal Sanguinary Demons and spliced the beings.

"The newly created beings would no longer age or change. They would remain at optimum health and gain the demon's abilities and extraordinary beauty. These beings would be his most lethal weapon. The ultimate predator. Able to assimilate among mortals, further his agenda of ruling Raj, and deliver mortal souls to Lucifer.

"Excited for the next phase of his plan, The Dark Majesty woke his creation.

"Although they awoke, their circulatory and respiratory systems ceased functionality, and their digestive systems no longer processed human food. More shocking, the human soul proved a formidable foe. Refusing to vacate the body, it suppressed the demon spirit. Reduced it to a dual conscience. Disgusted by his failure, The Dark Majesty cast the defective experiment to Earth."

"**W**ho orders cheeseless pizza?" José Padilla griped into the silent truck cab, checking the receipt for his next delivery.

One more stinking semester, then he'd have his bachelor's degree and could quit this stupid job. First to graduate college in his family, he'd get a better job and start sending money to Mami and Papi in Mexico. They were proud, would never admit it, but he knew they needed help.

Speaking of people who needed help... José parked in front of a shabby, red brick house with a dingy brown door and a badly painted two-car garage. The lawns of nearby homes were well maintained. Probably kept up by some underpaid Mexican immigrant-owned and operated landscaping company. Obviously, no one was taken advantage of to care for this lawn.

Dusty, brown interior shutters were closed over a window to the right of the door. The house looked eerie. If it were in black and white, it would be some scary shit. No, fuck that, if it were night it'd be scary, too. But the people living here must have money, a brand new, royal-blue Ford Mustang was parked in front of the ugly garage.

José slapped on his black cap, grabbed his warmer bag with the weird pizza inside, and got out of the truck.

"This better not be a prank," he muttered, following the cracked, red, stone path.

He rang the doorbell.

Dang! They must've been starving. The echo of chimes hadn't subsided, yet the door creaked open to reveal...

A frickin'—angel!

José didn't care if fuckin' Casper or the spirits from *Poltergeist* lived here. He'd gladly deliver here anytime—for free.

The petite, brown sugar-skinned goddess dressed unseasonably warm in a black, mid-thigh length, off-the-shoulder sweater dress was beyond description. At first sight, he assumed her long hair swept into a high ponytail—showcasing a long, eloquent neck—was black. A sliver of sunlight hit it and disclosed its true deep red hue. The *chiquita* had striking, jade-green, honey-brown, and bright-gold eyes.

Her adorable button nose wrinkled as she stepped forward hands out. She eyed the warmer like it insulted her mother.

"Careful, it's hot," he warned, taking the boxed pizza from the carrier, and extending it to her. When she only nodded and took it, he couldn't hold his curiosity, especially not when her sensual lips spread into a peculiar, wicked grin. "Something wrong with the pizza?"

Stepping back, she shook her head. "Uh-uh. I guess I'm not in a pizza mood anymore. But something else smells good. Are you wearing cologne?" She shrugged off the question, expression looking abashed. "How much?"

"Thirteen fifty-four."

"Alright, umm" — she glanced side to side — "let me sit this down, then I'll get you your money. I'll leave the door open, so you don't think I'm trying to stiff you." With that, she rushed away on bare feet toward the back of the house.

Oh... yeah!

This was too good to be true. He'd seen this scene play out in porn dozens of times. Scantily clad woman, home alone, orders a pizza. Innocent pizza boy gets and gives more than he bargained for. Yeah, buddy!

José stepped inside the front room. In the far corner was a desk. Underneath the shuttered window he'd spotted from outside was an overstuffed navy-blue armchair. Against the far wall, a white wicker daybed with threadbare, floral, pastel covering. Not exactly the black satin sheet fantasy, but it'd do. He tapped the door. It slid almost closed.

His honey-skinned angel returned. Coming right up to him, she proffered a twenty-dollar bill. Damn, he didn't want to leave yet. There had to be a way to get things poppin'. He reached for the money. Fingers curled around the bill, he went to pull away and found his hand immobilized. Freakishly strong fingers gripped his wrist.

Damn! She didn't want him to leave either. He was so down.

About to run a smooth line to get the party started, he gazed at her face to find her focus on the gauze-covered wound on his left wrist. Helping cut vegetables, he'd damn near taken a chunk out of his wrist. Bleeding stanched before his deliveries, a dot of red managed to seep through in the interim.

She stared at the spot as if the secret to life was written in it. The angel turned his wrist this way and that. "What happened?" she asked, voice taking on an airy, echoic quality.

He shrugged, which caused his wrist to move. She about yanked his arm out of its socket to hold it still.

Fuck Wheaties! This *puta* must eat whole cans of spinach. Can included. This was getting weird. He wasn't with that dominatrix shit. "Umm... Ma'am?" he stammered when another attempt to extricate his arm from her death grip failed.

Her head snapped up at the sound of his voice as if she'd never heard him speak before. A slow seductive smile inched across her face. She put a finger to full lips. "Shh..." No sooner than the sound slipped past her lips, her crazy eyes lit like a cell phone in a dark theater.

What the—?

"*Ay dios mío, el Diablo*," José breathed in part horror and amazement. Her words had a magical effect on him. No matter how hard he tried he couldn't move. Every bone in his body knew he should run, but he couldn't. He was paralyzed.

Chapter Thirty-One

Talon hoped Amelia was in a better mood. When he rose this morning, he'd called her. To say he'd gotten a less-than-friendly reception would be the understatement of the century. She'd been mighty frosty. After an hour of groveling, she reluctantly agreed to let him come over to talk. Happy with his small victory, he'd told her he'd be there in half an hour—three hours ago.

While he flatlined, Gawain stole his ring. He'd been forced to wait on the elder guardsman. When he finally did arrive, Talon was angry enough to spit fire. Now, breaking more than a couple traffic laws, he sped toward Amelia's home.

He wasn't skilled in the ways of females, but one need not be a genius to know walking out right before penetration was a faux pas of grand proportions. The need to possess her rode him hard. But his conscience wouldn't allow him the privilege without first telling her the truth. Anyway, he couldn't take all the credit for his ability to walk away. The roar of a car pulling into her driveway had helped clear his head.

The more distance he'd put between them, the more clarity he'd gained. He couldn't have her. Too much was at stake if he slacked this particular thirst. His family.

The supernatural. They were counting on him.

The Fates abandoned them for over 1000 years for an unprovoked war. There was no telling what they'd do to him, a guardsman, trying to claim the queen as his *eternalmate*.

He turned down the street to her house. Today, he would tell her the truth, tell her everything. This would not only change her life but take it. Introduce her to things no mortal truly comprehended. Things that would take the thin veil of what she thought was reality and blow a hole in it. She'd hate him. He hated him.

Talon rolled down the window. A malodorous gust of wind hit him. His senses went on red alert. Fear vibrated the air in explosive shock waves. Somewhere, a mortal was terrified to an immeasurable degree. Unease tightened his gut.

Expanding his senses, he caught whispered words in a thick Hispanic accent. "*Ay dios mío, el Diablo.*"

Oh, shit!

Talon reached Amelia's house in seconds. With preternatural speed he was out of his car, through her door, a gust of wind past the pizza delivery man, and standing behind Amelia. The scene he burst in on alarmed and aroused. Interesting.

As it'd done at the funeral, soft white light hugged Amelia. Complemented her glowing eyes. Her fangs were descended, and her mouth hovered close to the radial artery in the man's left wrist. Gorgeous.

He pressed intimately close to her backside. Each inch of his hard length snuggled against her. Had the situation not been dire, The Fates themselves couldn't have stopped him from possessing her. Sex: the ultimate vampire distraction. Talon forced himself to focus.

Clearly, her Siren ability held the man in immovable thrall. He wasn't struggling. Just staring dreamily into her eyes with his head cocked to one side. So focused Amelia didn't even flinch when he entered, or maybe she hadn't noticed.

Damn, she was sexy lethal... and still mortal, which meant this couldn't happen.

Stooping to her level, he pressed his lips to her ear. "You don't want to hurt this man, milady," he said in the even tone he used for compulsion. He hoped it would break through the fog of bloodlust. If it didn't, he'd have to use physical restraint. The idea repulsed him. He couldn't hurt her.

A full minute passed. She shifted her gaze to him—without releasing her prey. The impact of her radiant eyes devastated. So much so he had to concentrate hard or be lost in them. "Let him go, *cara*. He may have family, friends. You don't want to take him from them, do you?"

With deliberate slowness, Amelia shook her head. Her fangs retracted. Bewildered glowing eyes cooled to their natural beauty. The glow encasing her body extinguished. Big, fat tears welled in her eyes, threatened to spill over.

Talon wished he could wrap her inside himself to stop her from feeling the pain and fear radiating from her. Or maybe it came from the delivery man now paralyzed by terror since her powers had dissipated. Horror warped his expression.

Hands at her waist, Talon steered Amelia toward the daybed. He urged her to sit. When she did, he knelt in front of her. Stared solemnly into her eyes. "Will you do something for me?"

She shook her head. A tear escaped her right eye.

He wiped the tear from her eye with the pad of his thumb. In complete shock, she stared straight ahead, into his eyes but not seeing him. Only one tear might have fallen, but any fool saw that inside, her soul cried. Shouted its anguish and confusion. He needed to get this over with so he could attend to her.

Peering into her eyes, he softened his tone. "I know this doesn't make sense right now, *cara*, but I need you to do something for me so we can let" — he stole a quick glance at the delivery man's name tag — "José go home. Will you help me?"

That penetrated her haze. She ran her tongue over her top teeth then the bottom as if to assure herself that what happened wasn't real. Satisfied, she worried her bottom lip between her teeth. After a long pause, she rasped with a slight nod, "Okay. What do you need?"

He glanced at José. Her eyes followed his gaze. Looking back at her, he said, "I need you to go over to José and erase his memory."

"I-I-I," she stuttered. "I don't—I don't know—I can't."

Talon caught her chin between his thumb and forefinger. He gave an encouraging, tight-lipped smile. "You can. I'll show you."

Taking both of her cool, dainty hands in one of his and rising, he tugged her to her feet. Led her the short distance to where José stood petrified. They stood face-to-face with the delivery man. Positioned behind her, Talon placed his hands on her waist.

Somber, concerned eyes turned to him. "Did I hurt him?" she asked, voice cracking.

Lifting one hand from her waist, he pushed her head to his chest, smoothed her hair. Kissed the top of her head for momentary comfort. She was so precious. He reassured her in earnest, "You didn't do anything wrong, milady. This will help him."

Nodding, she returned her attention to José.

He returned his hand to her slim hip and resumed instruction. "Look into his eyes and concentrate like... you're trying to decide which purse to carry." As suspected, his lame joke didn't breach her terror-fogged mind.

Amelia took a deep breath. Sweat beaded on her exposed shoulders from the extent of her focus. All of a sudden, she gasped. Tremors racked her frame.

He understood her alarm. The first time he'd manipulated a mortal's mind, it rocked him to his foundation. Mortals' eyes truly were windows to their souls. José's black eyes became small television screens, replaying scenes from his day, his life.

Talon rubbed her goose-pimpled arms. "I know. It's okay," he crooned. "It's frightening at first, but it gets easier. Focus your intent on the moment before you grab him. If you go too far, concentrate on bending the picture to your will. Make your desires his. It'll rewind or fast-forward as you wish. Be careful," he warned, "you could damage his mind by tampering with too much. Mortals are easily broken. Focus on only what you need."

The mortal's eyes blanked as Amelia struggled to control her emotions, and in turn, José. Talon continued to stroke her arms, trying to provide solace.

Under his attentions, her breath evened. Pictures restarted in José's eyes. Talon renewed his guidance. "Focus on the moment you wish to erase, then let your mind go blank. The scene will, too." It did. "Great. Lower your voice to a steady, gentle caress. As if calming a hysterical child, yet keep your tone firm, authoritative. Then suggest a different memory to replace the first. You don't want to leave your prey" — she flinched at the term, and Talon barreled on, knowing there'd be time to explain later — "with missing chunks of time. It's known to be uncomfortable for mortals—maddening even."

She experimented with the memories, rewound, stopped, and fast-forwarded them several times. He watched as she took the pizza from José, placed it on the dining table, retrieved money from her purse, and approached him.

Inexperienced, and mortal, Amelia hadn't been able to identify the scent that distracted her when she first answered the door. Her demon had. It zeroed in on it and took control the moment José extended his hand. Scent identification and control were taught from birth. Amelia would undergo on-the-job training. Could take decades to learn control enough to repress her demon's primal urge—wait, money?

The delivery man wasn't holding anything now. Talon scanned the immediate area. A torn twenty-dollar bill lay at the male's feet. Mystery solved, he watched the man's eyes. Amelia replayed the scene once more before it stopped as she reached for the pizza and faded to black. His little queen-to-be was good. She might have halted it a bit soon, but she successfully erased the memories.

"What do I do?" she asked in a panicked whisper.

He whispered in her ear. "Never talk while replacing memories. It's akin to recording something and capturing background noise. You don't want to confuse the memory. Remember, make a soft, stern, believable suggestion to fill in the gap."

She nodded. "José, you're exhausted. It's been a long day. You're waiting to accept payment, but you don't feel well. When you leave here, you're going to call in sick for the rest of the day."

"You need to release him. Blink or bat your eyes. I clear my throat," Talon murmured.

She coughed.

Life returned to José's face. Confusion crinkled his dark brows. Talon figured it was due to Amelia's failure to explain his presence. "That'll be thirteen fifty-four?" José said, voice rising, making the statement more of an uncertain question.

Talon dug his wallet out of his back pocket, retrieved a fifty. Reaching around Amelia, he handed the bill to José. He slid his wallet back into his pocket.

"Umm... I don't have change for—"

"Keep it," Talon interrupted.

"You sure?" José's eyes went wide in disbelief.

"You earned it" — he snorted — "trust me."

José snatched the money and dashed out of the open door like a scared bunny crossing the highway. He might not know why, but the lingering adrenaline in his system and self-preservation instincts did.

As soon as the sound of a truck being started and tearing down the street faded, Amelia whirled around. Her nostrils flared with each exaggerated exhalation of breath. He reveled in his proximity to her petite frame. The way she looked vamped out. The rush of delicious blood pumping through her veins...

Smack!

She slapped him across the face. Surprisingly hard. If his pale skin changed there would be a small red handprint seared into his right cheek. Good thing she wasn't at full immortal strength.

"What did you do to me?" Amelia growled.

"And here I thought you'd say thank you," he teased.

She wasn't amused. Her eyes remained cold, flat. Even irate, she amazed him, like an adorable angry chipmunk.

This was absolutely not how he'd planned to tell her the truth. He wanted to ease her into things, but the situation fast-tracked the inevitable. "Have a seat, milady." Intending to guide her to the daybed, Talon reached for her hand.

Amelia flinched away. Sat on the desk chair. "Quit with the *milady* bullshit and tell me what you did," she screeched.

Talon ran his fingers through his hair and sat on the daybed. "This is not how I wanted to do this."

"I don't give two shits about what you wanted. Talk!" she shouted. She shivered and wrapped her arms around herself.

"I'm trying very hard not to black out here. I knew you were hiding something, but I let it go. I should've known..." Fire flashed in her eyes. "How close was I with my weekend serial killer theory? If you're gonna kill me, stop stroking me and do it!"

He cringed at the accusation. She had no idea. "I'm not a serial killer. I try not to—"

"Kill people!" she cut in. "Is that what you were going to say?"

"It's not what you think." He shook his head. "My moral compass isn't like yours."

"Neither was Jeffrey Dahmer's." She chuckled without humor. "Didn't make what he did any less wrong—what's your point? Is this, like, the big confession before the kill?"

"No!" How could she short-sell him this way? He might not be mortal, but his honor, his integrity, was all he had. With all the time they'd spent together, he thought his core had been apparent. "Amelia, I'm not like you."

She threw her head back, and a strangled, fear-tinged laugh tore through her lips. He hated it.

"Are you gonna point to the ceiling and tell me you're an alien who's capable of molecular manipulation? If so, be forewarned, it's been done before on an old show called *Roswell*."

"I'm a vampire."

This time her laugh was all humor. "What are you and Calin doing—reading from the same book or something? He already used that line, and you're not any closer to getting in my pants than he w-wa-wa—"

Amelia's breath caught. Her smile fell. Its replacement, mouth gaping, dumbstruck, fear. One minute, Talon sat on the daybed feeding her bullshit. The next, he cleared his throat... from the kitchen. Before she could scream—or wet herself—he stood beside her.

What the fuck!

Why couldn't she pass out? From the moment he'd come in and this nightmare began that was all she wanted to do. And it wouldn't happen. She was known to faint at times of extreme stress. This *had* to qualify.

Amelia didn't want to look at him, but something demanded she verify he was real. Gazing sideways at him, she poked his arm through his white button-down. Yep, definitely real.

He smiled at her. "Satisfied?"

She yanked her hand back. "Not at all. I don't believe you. Crazy people come off as normal all the time until one day they show their true colors. Clearly, the crazy done trickled right out of you. Lucky me to be here to share it with you," she said dryly.

Glancing at her through soul-scorching eyes of the deepest blue, Talon offered a morose grin. He mouthed, "I'm sorry." Then hissed pulled his lips back from his...

Fangs!

Holy shit! Fangs descended and his eyes were literally aglow. Was there such a thing as the men in black? What about the X-files? She didn't know, but she was about to find out.

Moving faster than she thought capable, Amelia jumped to her feet and ran.

Chapter Thirty-Two

G ood thing Talon decided to monitor her thoughts because...

She was off.

Amelia dashed through the open dining area. Bumped into
a chair and reached for the telephone hanging on the wall near
the kitchen. He had to give it to her—she was fast. But he was
faster. Talon anticipated each move before she made it. Amelia
dodged right. He went left. She stepped left. Talon went right.
She climbed onto the short counter to his left. Grabbed for the
phone. Talon covered the receiver and base with his back.

She tried for the phone several more times, screeching
each time her hand clutched him instead of the phone.

"Amelia, you don't want to do this," he spoke calmly.

"Yes, the hell, I do!" she hollered. "Something is wrong with
you. You're all *28 Days Later*. Is this contagious?" She gasped.
"Is it airborne?—I'm pregnant!"

He knew she believed that. The suspicion and indecision
regarding it had been present in her mind on several of their
outings. Her symptoms were from the transition, her body's
way of preparing her for the *Awakening*. "You're not pregnant."

"What're you—a part-time gynecologist or something?
How would you know?"

Amelia reached, again, for the phone. He leaned, blocking her path. Dejected, she climbed off the counter. Never taking her eyes off him, she backed out of the kitchen. When her butt hit the far wall between the back of the loveseat and dining table, she slid down to sit on the floor. She drew her knees to her chest. Careful to pull her dress so her panties didn't show, she wrapped her arms around her legs.

Helpless would be a good word to describe how she looked. Maybe vulnerable was better. If nothing else, she definitely appeared lost, and he was about to set her further adrift. Talon wanted so much to go to her, comfort her, but her mental state was fragile. He heard the incoherent ramblings in her mind. She might have said she didn't believe him, but a greater part of her did, and she was terrified.

"How. Do you. Know?" she shouted, bringing him back to her question.

"Because of the heightened sex drive, difficulty eating, lack of menses, cold and hot flashes, blood cravings... Those are transition symptoms."

Amelia's mouth opened, closed, opened, and closed. Her eyes watered and tore at his heart. She shook with disbelief. "So, you did do this to me." Her voice a mere whisper, she sounded resigned, betrayed. The face she made was one of utter revulsion. "*You* did this to me. I let a million-year-old dead guy kiss me and infect me with the mother of all cooties," she babbled. "Why in the world didn't I pay more attention to Buffy? Or Blade...? Shit, I'd take Crocodile Dundee at this point. I need a stake. He may be delusional, a serial killer even, but everything dies with a stake to the heart. Shit, shit, shit!"

Great. She was hysterical. He didn't know what to do. Why hadn't Gawain or his father prepared him for this? All his existence he'd trained to protect her and the one person he couldn't protect her from was herself. *Idiota!*

"I don't mean to interrupt, milady, but I'm nowhere near that old nor am I dead," he said dryly as a diversion. "And I didn't do anything to you."

"So, is this the part where I beg you to make me like you? Tell you I can't possibly carry on without your vampy charms?" she asked the last part in an impressive southern drawl. "Don't hold your breath. I'm not a stupid vamp tramp from TV—oh wait, you don't have breath. But okay, I'll bite—pun intended. If I'm not pregnant what am I?"

"You're dying." His answer was. "A mortal death. I don't have to do anything. It's genetics."

Mouth agape, she stared up at him, moist eyes widened. "Dying? Like, dead, dying? Like you? How's that possible? I know your thousand-year-old mind might understand all this, but I'm new. What's genetics?"

"Stop it!" he ordered because he felt like a pervert with the way off age references. "I turned one hundred and twenty February twelfth. And once again, I'm not dead."

"Do you have a heartbeat?"

"No."

"Do you breathe?"

He shook his head, and her eyes bulged. Bugged to the size of golf balls.

Amelia gagged. Clutched her stomach. She lurched to her feet and staggered. "Move! I'm gonna be sick."

Talon didn't immediately catch on. He glanced behind him. In addition to blocking the phone, he also blocked the quickest entrance to the kitchen and double-sided stainless steel sink. He didn't put it past her to do a fake out. "Are you trying to get the phone?" he inquired with a healthy dose of skepticism.

The chilly glare she fixed on him confirmed the gravity of the situation. He moved. Fast.

She pushed past him, leaned over the sink, and retched.

This wasn't his area of expertise. Solid mortal food disgusted Talon; he had no desire to see it regurgitated. Out of the corner of his eye, he saw the end of her ponytail slip past her shoulder. He might not know how to help, but he assumed no one liked vomit in their hair. He fisted the wavy locks. His gaze slid to her scrumptious ass. Leaning over the sink as she was, her sweater dress crept up soft, toned thighs. Just another inch or two, and creamy brown a—

Whew!

Rancid, old blood burned his nostrils like battery acid. That wasn't recycled mortal food. Dragging his attention to the sink, he froze. As if a pipe burst, blood spewed from any available orifice in her face. Mouth, nose, the corners of her eyes. Sweated out of her pores. Her face turned deep rouge as she heaved uncontrollably.

In spite of the red-hot fury coursing through his veins, he rubbed her back in wide gentle circles. This was what he was here for, to prevent this shit. Yet somehow, he'd missed something. Dark clouds rolled in, further souring his mood as exactly what "something" came to mind.

She'd fed. The problem: she was mortal. Her demon might crave blood, but it wasn't compatible with her mortal digestive system. The pain she must be in—excruciating. Violent tremors racked her body. Blood poured from Amelia for what seemed an eternity. Minutes ticked by. Yacking turned to dry heaves.

She took several deep breaths. Head hanging in the sink, she turned sharp watery eyes on him. Blood stained her nostrils and trickled from her mouth. Her lip curled in a mix of anger and loathing. "What. Are. You?" she spat through clenched teeth, venom punctuating each word.

Now, she would listen and believe.

"Seeing The Dark Majesty's abandoned, emaciated creations from their dais in Raj, The Fates feared the Most High's wrath. While not responsible for the creation they were accountable. Responsibility for supernatural and supernatural happenings was theirs.

"Destruction of the creation would breach the Most High's commandments. To annihilate one (the demon) would kill the other (the human). In the end, The Fates felt mercy and compassion for the forever-changed mortals. With their limited omniscience, The Fates uncovered the cause of their weakened state. Like their demon, the creation required blood sustenance. Because the base of the creation was no longer demon, human blood provided nourishment.

"The Fates dubbed the creation; Vampire.

"Through the *Book of Being*, The Fates sent word to White-witches to retrieve the six vampires. The vampires were placed in a deathlike sleep and buried six feet underground. They were endowed with several supernatural abilities. Those which would help the vampire, the supernatural, and protect mortals—

"What if I was Atheist?" Anton mused in wry amusement, interrupting his reading for the umpteenth time. "Wouldn't that make the history null and void for me?"

"Excuse me?" Vanessa asked, voice rising. Narrowing hard bronze eyes on him, she dragged a hand through light brown tresses. "I don't recall that being part of your text. This is how you obtained the powers that protect you. The ability to compel, why the blessed Fates stole the vampires' reflection, these—"

"Umm... I have a reflection, thank you very much. And I'm one handsome, debonair playa if I do say so myself." Oh, how he loved fucking with her.

Vanessa's face went tomato red. "Anton!"

His smile was all innocence. "I'm just sayin'. I know it goes away after the Immortal Age, but for now, I have one—and FYI, I do accept cash gifts. By the way, not all their little gifts were for our protection, making the sun lethal, condemning us to the night? Those were to hide us from God's sight because *they* fucked up. And the stupid veil over all private mortal dwellings...? Yeah, that helps humans."

"Anton," his governess said, deadly calm, "if you do not continue reading I fear I may destroy you before you have a chance to reach the Immortal Age."

Damn, I'm good.

Chuckling, he picked up the book and continued. "Prior to waking the vampires, The Fates were halted by a startling revelation.

"They'd known Sanguinary Demons were charming, seductive, obsessive, possessive, agile creatures with retractable fangs and glowing eyes. What they didn't know was that they procreated through blood exchanges with their victim, thereby nullifying the human reproductive system.

"Having created the supernatural in their image, The Fates knew what joy creating life brought. They pitied the vampires and what was taken from them. The Fates reinstituted the vampires' reproductive organs. With the help of a spell, vampires would be allowed to procreate once every five years. Vampire offspring would age rapidly but be given ten years without interference from their demon conscience. For every human year, their young would gain two, ceasing to age at twenty-one.

"Once awakened, The Fates tested the vampires' nature. Several supernatural were sent to tempt them with evil. Vampires with weak characters or loose morals were more susceptible to the demon's influence.

"This fate befell two of the six vampires. Before the two were destroyed, Hasher Demons helped them abscond. Of the four remaining vampires, one remained strong, yet struggled daily to keep its demon caged. But The Fates found something extraordinary about the last three vampires. They possessed varying levels of natural psychic ability. These abilities made their souls more resistant to the demon's manipulations.

"Due to their unrivaled strength and indomitable character, The Fates dubbed these three, the Sanctioned. Of the Sanctioned, Grigori Dimir gained great favor with The Fates. An air of familiarity clung to him; a beacon only other angels sensed. Grigori descended from Armaros a human-angel hybrid known as Nephilim.

"Given their kinship with Grigori, The Fates decided he would make a suitable and trustworthy ruler. They gave him dominion over all Earthbound supernatural. The Fates had considered this role for the White-witches, but being their first creation, they were created too much in the likeness of humans. Although long-lived, White-witches weren't immortal as most supernatural were.

"Foreseeing opposition to the new order, The Fates chose the second strongest of the Sanctioned, a male, to act as protector, sentinel, to the king and his heirs. The male would recruit the biggest and strongest willing human males to convert into vampire guardsmen to increase their ranks. The Fates also dispatched the White-witch High Priestess Doreen to recruit the strongest of other supernatural breeds to form different branches of Royal Guard, all answerable to the king.

"In order to endue them with extra gifts, The Fates had the White-witches rebury Grigori and the male who would be the first Vampire Royal Guardsman. They branded Grigori and the male with seals that would identify them and their offspring, biological and converted, as either heir to the metaphorical throne or future guardsmen. All supernatural would sense their authority. Grigori's seal: an upraised tilde (~) on his heart and the inside of his left wrist to mark him as similar to The Fates. The guardsman's seal: an upraised infinity symbol (∞) on his heart and the middle of his right forearm to mark infinite servitude."

Finally! Anton hopped off the second step to the black and white checkered marble floor. Free at last! Free at last! Thank God Almighty, he was free. Fuck the mortal military or whoever else the mortal government used to interrogate and torture people. Vanessa was skilled in the art of torture by boredom. Once he got caught eavesdropping and she made him read the damn history book six million times.

Bullshit! Anton exclaimed mentally at the same time the word flew out of his father's mouth from behind his closed study doors.

What a predicament. Technically this wasn't eavesdropping, was it?

"*O engonós mou*, (my grandson)!" a thick, Greek-accented male voice pleaded.

Oh, c'mon! He was wrong. What Vanessa did was nothing compared to this torture. How could he be expected not to eavesdrop when his father and... whoever were making their private conversation public?

"I couldn't save your *patéras*, (father)," the Greek-accented voice shouted.

Oh, hell, this shit's getting good. Anton tiptoed to the door, leaned close, but didn't put his ear to it. He'd have to do some Hail Marys or something later if he didn't get caught, 'cause passing this up wasn't even kind of an option.

"Doesn't *couldn't* imply you tried to save him—which we both know you didn't? He was only a mortal and a bastard, right?" His father, Victor, snapped heavy on the sarcasm. "He didn't really need to be saved from a sperm-stealing bitch, did he?"

Damn, if it wasn't for eavesdropping Anton wouldn't know a damn thing. He went from knowing nothing about his family to having uncles and from what he could tell, a grandfather. Or he used to have a grandfather from the sounds of it.

The other voice answered the accusation calmly, "He was my relation, too, a grandson. I loved and protected him as I have you, your brothers, and your son."

"Right," Victor said dryly. He chuckled without humor.

"I've protected you all!"

Victor snickered. "Allow me to recap—if you will?" He paused, but then went on without an audible answer. "My father was violated twice by a Dark-witch, mad scientist, geneticist who knew he carried the dormant recessive vampire gene. Not only did you let her steal his sperm and work some freakish voodoo on it, but you allowed her to birth his children. Children she hoped would have active seals so she could turn them evil and hand them over to Balkan! Oh, Grandfather... you spoiled him. And I haven't even mentioned the vile depraved acts you *watched* him perform, but what do those matter? They were only against mortals—so you thought."

Whoa! Grandfather? What the fuck? He was having an information overload aneurysm. How was this man his grandfather? Apparently, his father knew him. Well.

"She's your *adelfí* (sister)," the Greek said, exasperated.

"Half," his father shrieked. "And what does it matter? She won't welcome me with open arms. Especially not when she discovers my true nature."

"That's not your nature. You resisted. She needs a brother, family. A protector."

"We're not puppets, Grandfather! You don't get to pull our strings and watch us dance."

"Wouldn't you rather have a family? A true sibling? Other than those twin miscreants, Lucian and Ivan."

"Again!" Victor wailed. "Another shining example of your well-planned protection detail. You knew they'd be evil if they killed their mortal parent, yet you allowed it. And as far as my wanting a family... You protected that right into oblivion, too. You knew my cunt mother would harm my mate, yet you allowed it!"

"I sent you here, have given you funds beyond your wildest imaginations, and got you and my great grandson protection," the other man defended.

Anton was way too shocked to consider referring to the man as *grandfather*.

"Protection? From beings who hate us...? Nice. Anton has lived a life of condemnation. Now, we're to be ripped from the only home he's known. Lea, the only mother he's ever known, will be taken from him after he reaches the Immortal Age. That's less than a month's time."

"It's of no import. Let the *courtiers* expel you. You have a sister who needs you. She can override their ruling. Go to this Ar-i-zona, be with her. Bring her home."

Anton had to fuckin' pinch himself. Actually, reach over, grab a hunk of flesh on his arm, and fuckin' squeeze.

He always thought it was an exaggeration or just an expression when people said they were so mad they couldn't see straight. Now, he knew better. As all the pieces clicked into place, he knew he'd been dead wrong because he was fuckin'... Pissed!

Cross-eyed, blurred vision, fucking pissed!

He stomped away from his father's study, not giving a shit who heard. They all owed him explanations of the size of Europe. His father's house-shaking bellow was the last thing he heard before leaving.

"Fine! I'll say it! She's my sister!"

Chapter Thirty-Three

"Who are you—really?" Amelia asked, sitting on the floor between the loveseat and the dining table. Looking up at Talon's forlorn expression, she almost felt bad for him.

That emotion dissipated posthaste.

This was her idea of Hell, not his. He was the soulless demon who'd manipulated her into caring for him.

"Clearly, you're not really related to Wa-Walker." She tripped over the name that was still painful to think and even harder to say. "What'd you use—a Jedi mind trick on him and his whole family? You're sick." She filled the accusation with as much disdain as possible. If his psycho ass played any part in Walker's passing... he'd pay.

Talon leaned against the wall, blocking the counter where her phone sat. Again. His stance was casual. As if springing ludicrous news on someone was an everyday occurrence. "My name is Talon Cantemir. I'm a Vampire Royal Guardsman, son of Sebastian Cantemir Chief Vampire Royal Guardsman to the Vampire Royals, which there haven't been any of in over a thousand years—until you. And I have no idea what a Jedi mind trick is."

Deep breath in. Slow, long breath out.

One thing at a time. She could deal with only one detail from Talon's gibberish spiel at a time. Otherwise, her head would explode and blow chunks of Amelia brain all over the wall.

Amelia rose. Lumbered to her feet, surprised her wobbly legs held her weight. "Let me see."

"What?" The stumped astonishment on Talon's face was almost comical.

"You said you're a Vampire Royal Guardsman. According to your fairytale, there should be some proof of that on your heart and right forearm, correct?" she challenged, brow arched. This had to be a lie. Things like this just... weren't real. Maybe it was some Criss Angel or David Blaine-type stunt. "Let me see."

She stepped forward, making small progress toward him.

Top two buttons of his white button-down already undone, strong fingers made to unbutton the third.

Amelia stepped back. Maybe he didn't understand what she wanted. Not that her heart didn't flutter at the idea of him shirtless again, but now wasn't the time.

He must've sensed her trepidation because he smirked. "Now, the thought of touching me repulses you? Funny, I didn't get that sense the other night."

Rat bastard! How dare he mention that? She cut her eyes at him, pursed her lips. Hopefully, she looked annoyed and not slightly embarrassed like she felt.

"I'm attempting to do as you requested. You might want to be able to see it."

"I don't need to see your whole body just your forearm. Leave your shirt on."

He rolled his eyes but ceased disrobing.

Thank, God! Her heart couldn't take it. In her current state of confusion, she'd either maul him or stake him. Each held equal appeal.

Talon unbuttoned his right cuff and rolled his sleeve. Since even his forearms were ridiculously muscled, it stopped just below his elbow.

She hated to admit it, but he was right. It would've been easier to see with his shirt off. Fortunately, she was defiant enough not to admit it. She suspected he knew by the cocky,

I-told-you-so, quirked brow. Sighing in agitated resignation, she closed the distance between her and the monster.

For the zillionth time today, her mouth fell wide open. Unthinking, she grabbed his arm. Yanked it, and by extension, him, to her for closer inspection. "What happened to you?"

The corners of his mouth kicked into a slight knowing smile.

She dropped his hand. Didn't take a freak of nature to know his thoughts. "Uh...don't even think it. I'm just curious. I couldn't care any less about what happens to you." She pointed to the upraised, flesh-toned, infinity symbol branded into the middle of his right forearm. "What is that?"

"What you expected. Stop trying to convince yourself this isn't real. It's as real as you or I." Talon rolled down his sleeve, refastened the cuff.

With an unladylike snort, Amelia retreated to her spot, never turning her back or eyes from him for a second. She stopped when her heel connected with the wall and slid down. A thought fought its way through her cluttered mind. "Stop trying to convince myself? You're doing your Jedi mind tricks on me, too, aren't you? Stay out of my head, Houdini."

"Milady, I have no clue what a Jedi—"

"What you did to the Palmers," she explained grudgingly. "To José..."

Understanding flashed in his eyes. "I implanted false memories in the Palmers' minds to build familiarity between myself and them. You erased José's memories then bridged the gap."

Get your jaw off the floor, she ordered herself. The Syfy Channel had always fascinated her. She'd even gone so far as to refer to herself as a closet Sci-Fi geek—always drawn to the possibilities of the unknown. But this, this was over and beyond her realm of understanding. "Have you ever done that to me?"

He shook his head, and dammit, the near smirk on his face could have been the cause of global warming. Tingles of electricity coursed through her. Jeez... there really was a thin line between love and hate.

"No. I've never done that to you. You're too far along in the transition."

Oh, his splitting hairs ass thought he was slick, but she caught the inflection on *that*. He may not have done exactly *that*, but he'd done something. A red haze clouded her vision as overwhelming anger set in. "You liar! Get. Out! You're so lucky I don't have a stake. Get out of my house!"

"You'll have to do better than that if you want to destroy me."

Damn curiosity!

"What makes you so damn special?"

"I told you. I'm a Royal Guardsman. The seal makes us stronger, faster..." He paused, seeming to search for another word. "More durable than *commoners* or *converts* and other supernatural."

Those names sounded vaguely familiar, but her head spun. She couldn't remember where she'd heard this before. This was too much.

"Maybe we should let this marinate for a—"

"Uh-huh, Gigantor. I'm checking into a mental institution later. Explain now. What do vampires have to do with me?"

Talon scrubbed his face with his hand. His lips smashed into a hard line. "This is where genetics enters the equation. Remember when I asked about your birth family?"

"Oh yes, mighty Quiz Master, let's reopen that can of worms. —Yes, Talon, shit! I'm not senile. Finish your damn story."

"As you wish." His tight, pinched features said it took the strength of God to leash his temper, which pissed her off.

What did he have to be angry about?

"Roughly, one thousand and twenty years ago it was said—and by your existence clearly true—Queen Ana-Marie Dimir and her *eternalmate* Victor Radulescu had a daughter. She was born two nights before a battle ended in their and their sons, Princes Nico's and Isaac's, destruction. Anyway, the rumor is Queen Ana-Marie sent the infant vampiress with her White-witch Advisor, Danae. Since all supernatural can sense royalty—because of the seal—it's presumed Danae somehow deactivated the princess's seal and raised the child as mortal. So, to answer your question..."

She didn't need an answer, she did the math. Amelia lifted her left wrist. Examined it. Nothing. This could still—

"No, you don't have one—yet."

"*Yet?* Oh, that's right... I have to be bitten, blood exchanged, buried with my maker? I know how it works. I streamed True Blood."

"I'm sorry." He shook his head. "I assume that's a television program. This is real, and that's not the way it works. Not for you anyway. According to our book of prophecy, you come from a pure line of royalty. Somehow you have Vampire Royals on both sides of your family tree. Both your parents possessed the dormant recessive vampire gene. Therefore, you don't need to be bitten. As long as you're buried alive by the time of your birth on your twenty-first birthday The Fates will ensure you rise three hours later as a vampire. Seals intact."

"Let's say I believe you—I don't—but for argument's sake, I do. I was born at midnight. What happens if I'm not buried?"

Sapphire eyes turned almost black. His rumbling voice went boulder-grinder deep, rough. "You die. A permanent, true death."

Good thing nothing was left in her stomach because it would have been on the floor. Ugh... Why couldn't she just pass out already?

"Oh, nice. A good incest story is so hard to come by these days. Especially one told by a dead guy you've made out with. Good times. Good... times... This is getting filed in the old Rolodex under—*Disgusting!*" A dry heave followed her outburst, the perfect emphasis for her point. Staring at him, she put the back of her hand to her mouth. "I've heard enough. Is your invitation rescindable?"

Talon arched a golden-blond brow. "Why? Are you still trying to call the police?"

Yes.

No.

She didn't know anymore. Amelia had an acute case of information overload, not to mention she was still so afraid she trembled. The line dividing reality and fantasy was smudged. Her actual brain hurt from trying to process everything. "This is too much," she said, voice dead, defeated. "Leave, Talon."

"Let me explain, please," he pleaded, hurrying on without permission. "I was created to protect you, Amelia. It's my duty. It was before I met you, and now that I know you, it's my honor. My privilege to guard you. What I feel for you is so much stronger than anything I—"

"Wait, wait, wait. Stop the camel." Amelia rubbed her face with her hand. "You were created to protect me? What does that even mean? Don't you have parents? I'm sure I wasn't on their minds when they were making you."

Talon groaned, frustrated.

Yeah, join the club, buddy. "Never mind, I don't care. Just leave. Don't you have to, like, do what I say or something?"

Midnight-blue eyes narrowed on her. "It doesn't work quite that way, *signorina*. You can't tell anyone about this. That's why we have to erase the memories of our prey we—"

"Could you stop with the pronoun bullshit," she interrupted, holding up a hand. "This is your delusion, not mine."

"It's not a delu—"

"Please, Talon." A sob she tried desperately to hold escaped. "Leave! Talon Cantemir you are no longer welcome in my home. I rescind your invitation."

With that, he was gone.

Shattered into a billion tiny particles of what looked like mist and... disappeared. The only sign that he'd been there: the absence of the phone. She hadn't seen him take it.

Not even a second passed before the tremors she'd tried to hide took over. They spread throughout her entire body as if she were experiencing her own personal earthquake.

Sob after sob bubbled up her raw throat and burst through dry lips. Tears and snot ran down her face. She wiped her nose on her sleeve. Childish? Yes. Ruined cashmere? Totally. But for once, she didn't give two shits about her appearance. *I don't want to die!*

How could this be true? It explained her symptoms, but didn't make sense. On some deep, deep level she was happy a defenseless baby wouldn't be sentenced to having her as a mother. Fucked up didn't skim the surface of what was wrong with her. But then, hope or relief from that burden meant the other was true.

Amelia ripped the ponytail holder from her hair. Crimson waves spilled free. She threw the traitorous elastic band with strands of hair wrapped around it. The idea had been to use the pain to wake her from this nightmare. It didn't. She still sat here on the floor in her ruined sweater dress... dying. Dying? Dead. How?

Her mind refused to believe it. Talon had to be lying. He didn't look like it. He looked serious. Pained. Like he regretted having to tell her the news. Maybe he was like that cult guy—what was his name? David Koresh? Hadn't he convinced all those people in Texas that he was God or something? Maybe Talon had done that. Convinced her she saw impossible things.

Then why did what he said sound so familiar?

Damn voice! What a fucking perfect time to reemerge. Unless it never left. Talon said it was her demon conscience. Oh, God... Arguing with herself. *I'm losing it.*

Her gaze ping-ponged around what little she could see of her house. Her parents' house. They expected her to look after this place. From the tacky navy-blue loveseat and couch set, the rickety daybed, to Evan. Tessa. Shit, even Cicely and Christopher were hers to care for. She wasn't ready to leave them. How lame was that?

She'd been a bitch to everyone she loved. They might be happier without her. No one knew the Ice Queen routine was an act. Her way to keep them safe from whatever it was about her that killed others. Losing everyone, being alone, were her biggest fears. Ironic that the way to avoid those was to drive everyone away. God, she was sliding all over the grief map, wasn't she? She needed to make things better. Wanted to make things better. Be better. *I don't want to die.*

After living the last three years as pretty much one of the walking dead, she didn't want to die. Not really. What a startling revelation...

Tears flowed unchecked down her cheeks. She needed something. A hug, maybe? *Talon.*

The name entered her mind of its own accord, which made no sense. She'd told him to leave. Revoked his invitation. Yet, some irrational part of her needed him of all people. She needed—

A knock at the door interrupted her musings.

Yeah, like she could answer the door looking the way she knew she did. Waterproof mascara only withstood so much. *Talon.*

His name shimmered in her mind, again. As if her soul cried for him. Uninvited or not. Pissed at him or not. Human or not. She needed him.

Talon!

A loud *crack* brought her head up. The bang of the front door slamming into the wall brought her to her feet.

Great, destined to be all *Shaun of the Dead*, and now her house was being broken into—again. The second break-in in less than two months. Neighborhood watch, her butt! More like the neighbors kept watching *her* house get burglarized. She trudged to the front room. The sight before her stopped her dead in her tracks.

"What're you—? I thought." Her nerves were shot. Stammering was all she had; clear thoughts be damned.

Talon stood at the threshold; expression morose.

Her heart skipped a beat.

"You called my name."

"I didn't—I was—I didn't."

Smooth.

He tapped his temple with his finger.

I knew he read my thoughts.

"I don't normally. You may not believe it, but I think listening to people's thoughts is rude. I heard you crying. I would've stood out here, waited until you fell asleep. But... you called my name." His sinful voice was remorse-laden, yet his jaw remained tight as if he were angry or struggling.

The day's events replayed in her mind. Right on cue, the waterworks started again. Fat tears poured from her eyes. When had she become the blubbering damsel in distress? She was beginning to annoy herself. But she couldn't stop, and Talon was right there. Her anchor. Always there. Yes, it was stupid, illogical. She felt stupid, and she needed him. It was visceral.

His stare pierced her with its feral severity. The flutter of a million butterfly wings flitted inside her stomach.

"Talon, please come in," she whispered. Her soul longed for him and though intellectually she knew this couldn't be, for so many reasons... She was loathe to obey her soul's desire.

Talon didn't have to be asked twice. He charged into the house and slammed the door behind him. Amelia gawked at the speed at which he moved. Startled disbelief and fear battled for her expression. Shock won. She didn't move. In time, she'd get used to his natural faster pace. It felt wonderful not to pretend anymore.

Before she changed her mind and forced him out again, he lifted her into his arms. Cradled her against his chest and carried her down the hall, to her room. Again. The third time in their short acquaintance. Funny. It seemed so much longer. Time had a crazy way of doing that, speeding up when you didn't want something to end.

Not that he wanted or enjoyed her in pain. Confused. Scared. He didn't. Especially not when he was the cause. No, what he liked, treasured? Being with her.

She challenged him. Kept him on his toes with witty retorts and sarcasm he didn't always understand. Amelia was strong. Embodied strength. What she lacked in size she made up for with character. Yet, beneath her rough exterior was someone not unlike himself. Someone who wanted to be needed. Not because they served a specific purpose like some handy tool. But needed for who they were.

Talon pulled back the gold and ruby sheets on her four-poster bed. He laid her down as if she were the most precious thing in the world. And to him she was.

"Lay with me?" she asked, voice rough from crying.

How could he not? He undid the laces of his steel-toed boots, took them off, and sat them next to the closed door. He climbed into bed beside her. As he'd done the day of Walker's funeral, Talon reclined against the headboard. Amelia scooted close.

Wrapped her arms around his waist and snuggled. Head in his lap.

Really?

His head fell back and hit the headboard. Hard. She was killing him. *Don't get hard, don't get hard.* "Do you want to ask me anything?" he asked, not so much to allay her fears, but for him. Distraction might keep little Talon soft.

Quiet minutes passed. "How old are you again?" Amelia asked, breaking the silence. The vibration of her larynx on his dick—torture. "Aren't vampires your age supposed to be all... *I vant to suck your blood*?" she asked, using an odd accent.

He lifted his eyes toward the ceiling, shaking his head. "I'm one hundred and twenty. And vampires don't talk like that."

"Wow," she breathed, sounding more shocked than he preferred. "One hundred and twenty. Much ass can be had in one hundred and twenty years."

If she only knew.

Talon chuckled.

"What?"

"Nothing. I told you I was created for you. I've trained every night for as long as I can remember. I was only permitted out to feed or learn from Anton or Gawain."

"Wait." She lifted her head, studying him through squinted, bloodshot eyes. He looked down his nose at her. A spark of understanding glinted in her eyes.

Talon pushed her head down. He didn't want to talk about this.

"No. Way!" Her head popped up. She regarded him through incredulous wide eyes.

Of course, true to form, Amelia pressed the issue and disregarded his "I don't want to talk about it" stare.

"You're a virgin?" her voice squeaked. "A mythical male virgin. I thought vampires were known for their virility and sexual prowess? This explains so much."

What did that mean? He'd be offended at her insinuation, but she was smiling. She hadn't smiled in days. He missed those dimples. His chest swelled with pride at the knowledge that he was responsible for the grin.

She seemed to realize what she'd done at the same moment. The light left her eyes. Her smile faded. She laid her head down. Remained silent for several minutes.

Talon resisted touching her. Until she sniffled. He could take anything but her tears. Sniffles came rapidly. What could he do? *You know.*

For once, he did.

He'd give into his damning need, willingly. Knowingly. Completely. For her. Who was he kidding? For him, too. For once, he would give and take comfort for himself.

He stroked her hair. Cherry blossoms enveloped him. Tethered themselves to his heart. Lustrous, silky-smooth red waves glided between his fingers. His hand slid from her hair, tracing the length of her spine. Moved to her hip. Absorbed the warmth of her skin through the soft fabric of her dress. Electric shocks raced through his fingertips as they skated over the dip of her narrow waist. He committed each curve to memory. Never would he have this time with her again. His misguided parents would be terminated for such a forbidden indiscretion.

He was a Royal Guard. She would be queen. He'd protect her. Watch her be mated to a suitable *courtier*. Protect her young. It killed him, but some things should never be. So this time, these touches, would last him an eternity.

Chapter Thirty-Four

A melia shivered. Being a virgin, he might not know it, but Talon was driving her crazy. His touch left an odd, yet not unpleasant, chill in its wake. White-hot desire blazed, started in her belly, and consumed.

She needed to stop him. One more glide of those strong, magic fingers, and she'd be a goner. Her emotions were fickle. Unreliable. For Pete's sake, she considered molesting a virgin demon of the underworld. That's after she kicked him out and then re-invited him in.

Strong hands gripped her upper thigh. Squeezed. Traveled to her ass. Meaty fingers dug into the flesh, providing interesting pressure.

Damn! She could orgasm from this alone. Time to stop.

A finger under her chin tilted her face up.

"It's only me and you. Just the two of us," Talon said when their eyes met. His covetous, luminescent gaze curled her toes. "Me and you. Show me what you like."

She'd meant to stop this. Really, she did. But the fervid look he speared her with obliterated the words.

He slid from under her in a deft move that should've been impossible and crossed the room to the door. If he left after riling her up, she would...

He didn't. Gaze unwavering; he unbuttoned his shirt slowly. Button by button. To inflict maximum torture.

This time, Amelia would cut her tongue out if she even thought about stopping him. Her gaze stayed glued to him as more and more of his muscled chest was exposed. His shirt floated to the floor. With the same methodical deliberation, he removed his fingerless gloves. Each fell to the ground.

Fathomless, hooded blue eyes bored into hers. A stutter-inducing grin spread across Talon's handsome face. He cocked a brow. "If what you're wearing means anything to you... I suggest you take it off."

Amelia's heart stopped. Totally. Then took off faster than a jackrabbit, thumping as hard and powerful as its hind legs. If she thought his V-card made him less potent, she was wrong. Talon was still his composed self, but different.

She saw the predator he claimed to be in his dominant shoulders back, chin up, legs shoulder-width apart stance. The feral gleam in his eyes. His commanding tone. Authority and supremacy clung to him. He owned the room, and at the moment, her. Without a single touch, he elicited responses only someone well-acquainted with her body should be able to bring about.

"What are you waiting for, *cara?*" Talon asked, crossing corded arms over his hard chest. "Take. Your clothes. Off."

She didn't know what "*cara*" meant, but the way he rolled the R had her wishing one of Victoria's secrets was breakaway panties. Wet didn't begin to cover how she felt.

Emboldened by some inner vixen—maybe?—or the fact that nothing about today seemed quite real, Amelia scooted back against the headboard. She kicked her comforter out of the way. Wouldn't want to obstruct his view. She shimmed out of her black thong. The musk of her desire wafted to her nostrils. Lace dangled from her index finger. Then she flung it at him.

Other than a quirked brow and ghost of a smirk, he didn't respond. However, the near-perfect outline of his erection bulging against his leather pants said more than words could. Dress rumpled from being carried, it didn't take much to hike it to her waist. She spread her thighs. Slow. Air brushed sensitive folds, and she shivered. Or maybe it was from the way Talon's incandescent eyes flared, pupils dilated. Zeroed in on her center.

His tongue made a sensual trek over his lips in what she was sure was an unconscious gesture.

Bringing two shaky fingers to her mouth she sucked them. Swirled her tongue through and around the digits. Talon's eyelids drooped.

This wasn't something she did, the sexpot routine. She left that to Tessa. Her dancer's body and naturally slinky gait were made to entice. But the way Talon's hot stare tracked Amelia's every move...

Urged her on.

She eased her thighs farther apart. Wet fingers spread her outer folds. Traced her inner lips. Chills tap danced over her skin at the sensation of her fingertip on arousal-slickened flesh. Her middle finger tapped at her weeping entrance. Never taking her gaze from Talon's, she bit her lip. Then sank the slim digit inside. She worked her hole. In. Out. In.

Talon's expression was severe. His jaw clenched. Joints worked overtime, standing stark against his skin. He groaned.

Her walls rippled around the slight intrusion. She wanted more. Needed to be filled. Unable to keep still under Talon's hungry watch, she rolled her hips. Mound met palm and clit met the base of her finger. She moaned. Talon's already pale face paled more. His features went taut. Tendons in his neck strained. Her breath became ragged.

Although his demeanor screamed, "I want you now and don't care if I have to kill to get you," he stayed put. Stood unnaturally still.

How hard must it have been for him to act human? Now that she knew his secret, she recognized the obvious contrast between his previous clumsy movements and his lithe, animal-esque, faster ones. Or lack of motion. No one should be that still. While the smaller part of her brain pondered that, the larger part wished—

He moved. Quick as shit.

Her heart pounded. The mixture of fear and excitement, erotic in a crazy way.

Standing at the foot of the bed, Talon squeezed his eyes shut. His shoulders rose and fell, but no breath accompanied the action. *Weird.* To her profound shock, rumbling like a souped-up engine built deep in his chest. Seconds later, a leonine growl ripped through firm lips.

It gave her pause but thrilled her, too. Amelia crawled to the end of her bed. Talon didn't move or open his eyes. Looking at his gorgeous face, she reached for his zipper. Her hand shook. A large hand covered hers. Stilled her actions. His eyes opened.

"Me and you," he said voice sandpaper rough.

She gulped at the wealth of meaning in his proclamation. They were crossing a line that once crossed, couldn't be uncrossed. Amelia understood the implications, did he? She nodded. And he released her hand.

Amelia lowered his zipper. An impressive erection sprang free. Her mouth watered. She licked her hand from palm to fingertip and wrapped it around his rigid length.

Damn!

She'd read an erotic book, or eighty, in her lifetime. Each described the hero's penis as velvet over steel; steel encased in velvet, huge iron rod, blah, blah, blah. The descriptions were laughable. But now....? She held a long, girthy, steel rod encased in velvet.

She stroked him. Worked his shaft in her small hand, wrapped both hands around it, and twisted them counterclockwise. He hissed. Groaned. Thrust into her hold. Pre-cum beaded on the tip. With the pad of her thumb, she captured the creamy liquid. Used it as a lubricant. She pumped faster. He bit out a sharp curse in a language she didn't know but understood nonetheless—he liked it.

"Stop," came his strangled command, several strokes later.

Amelia stopped but didn't let go. He throbbed in her hand. Talon stepped closer. Since she was kneeling, his penis came at her 3-D style. Threatened to turn a handjob into a blowjob. Lightning quick, her legs were yanked from under her. She fell backward. Before she hit the mattress, she found herself relieved of her dress. In only her black bra, she stared into passion-glazed sapphire eyes.

Maybe she should've rethought the whole strip panty idea because now she was wide open. And he looked. Stared like he'd just found Jesus' face on his tortilla. Self-conscious, she attempted to cover herself with a hand.

Talon shook his head. "Never hide from me. Ever." A cool knuckle skated along the seam of her nether lips. "You're wet for me, *cara mia*."

Her body convulsed.

"Cat got your tongue?" he teased, mouth quirking on one side.

No.

A bloodsucking demon had her cat. Good, Lord! The contrast of his cold skin on her swollen, sweltering lips was incredible. She would've told him as much but...

Talon disappeared.

One minute, he stood between her legs. The next, he was gone. At least, that's what she thought until she felt something fantastic. Talon's tongue delved between her folds. Darted inside her. An intimate French kiss. His tongue traced slow circles. The same way she'd done with her finger. Tingles enveloped her.

Then he added a finger.

Flicked her clit with his tongue, back and forth. Back and forth. She writhed against his mouth. Pinpricks of sensation shot up her spine. The gentle glide of his thick finger inside her had her moaning. He pumped in and out. She rode his finger like a woman possessed. Panting, she rolled her hips. He drew her clit into his mouth, and she cut loose. A dam broke, her feminine walls contracted. Fluid rushed to meet his seeking tongue.

Wow! How'd he know to do that? It was so... Talon. Giving what she needed without being told.

He stood, wiping his mouth. "You smell like *Raj*." Putting the finger that penetrated her to his nose, he took an exaggerated whiff and smiled. "And taste sweeter." He sucked his finger clean. Using freaky vampire speed, he undressed.

His legs were ripped, unreasonably so. What'd he do, lift apartment complexes for exercise? For once, his serious demeanor didn't bother her. In this instance, there was nothing she wanted more than for him to get down to business.

Stroking himself, his intense gaze bore into her. "Tell me you want me."

Shit! She'd tell him he was the president if he wanted. "I want you."

"Mean it," he gritted out between clenched teeth. "Only me. Tell me you want only me."

The severity in his eyes brooked no argument.

"Only you," she acquiesced, voice shaking.

He was on her then.

Talon meant to be gentle. But her ambrosial taste did more than wake his libido. It awoke the beast. The primal male part of him that was animal. Predator. He reached for her black strapless bra, a nail sharpened into a claw. He sliced the material in two.

Amelia squealed. He shoved her legs apart, positioned himself between her thighs, and thrust. The head of his dick barely breached her core. She was tight. Pulling out, he surged forward again. Met the same resistance.

He gazed into jewel-colored eyes. "Let me in."

Lust-glazed eyes blazed a bit at his command. She nodded and spread her thighs farther. Wrapped her legs around his waist, locked them at the ankle behind his back. Talon plowed into her. Impaled her. Amelia gasped. He moaned at the tight fit. Fluid gushed around him, drenched his cock. He gripped her hips to keep her in place for his thrusts.

Oh, now he understood why Anton and Gawain liked this. It was...

Indescribable.

He pistoned into her. Filled her over and over. Sharp nails pierced his back. Feminine walls pulsed around him in response to the marvelous assault. A shout stilled him. Had he hurt her? He never wanted to hurt her.

"What?" she panted. Sweat dewed on her forehead. "Why'd you stop?" Her chest rose and fell in rapid succession. Taut chocolate drop nipples grazed his chest. The rigid peaks did interesting things to the oversensitive skin. Made him want to slide out and hammer into her welcoming body again.

Amelia rolled her hips. Bucked and arched to egg him on. He knew what she wanted but wasn't sure she could take it. Hurting her would destroy him. When she dug the heels of her feet into his bare ass, he bit his tongue to keep from doing just that. Blood filled his mouth. Amelia whimpered.

"I can't. Please." He shook his head. Talon panted, not from lack of oxygen but from the sheer force it took to keep from unleashing his full strength on her. "I'll hurt you."

The frown she bestowed upon him undid his resolve, sort of. He didn't continue to pound her into the mattress, but he moved. Swiveled his hips. On each revolution, he thrust forward, hard. Deep. More warm liquid bathed his cock. Eased his passage. He doubted *Raj* would be more glorious than this. Lifting her leg over his arm he watched the delicious contrast of his pale shaft slipping between her brown lips and disappearing. His fangs descended. Sexual arousal triggered other desires. For instance, the desire to bond with his mate. Sink his fangs into the tender flesh of her femoral artery. Drink of her essence.

The impulse overwhelmed. Rode him. Talon closed his senses, shut down sight and smell. He focused on the sounds of possession. His skin slapping against her sweat-slickened skin. Bedsprings creaking under their combined weight. Amelia's mewls of pleasure, his grunts. His demon whispered to him, demanding he bind them. Claim her for his own, consequences be damned.

Fangs bared; he lowered his head toward Amelia's neck. Her body quaked under his. Fear vibrated from her. That provided the strength he needed to veer from her neck at the last second. He crushed his lips to hers. Their tongues dueled. Warmth clashed with cool. Her hips undulated. Pelvis kissed pelvis as she met him tit-for-tat. Short hairs of her neatly trimmed landing strip tickled his abdomen. Sent shocks of electricity through him, and by her cries—her, too.

Amelia pressed upward in a blatant effort to recreate the friction. He obliged, plunged downward until he was seated so far inside her they could've been one. Talon wished that were true. Instead of depressing him, the thought spurred him on.

He drove into her with blinding speed, forgetting his earlier decision to slow down. Lifting his head, he broke their kiss. She chanted his name. He gritted his teeth to keep from biting her.

Talon growled. Her breathing grew labored, her channel gripped his shaft. His cock throbbed in time with her pulsing inner muscles. His balls tightened. Bright ultraviolet light burst from his eyes, lit the room. Amelia screamed. Chilled semen spilled into her heated core. Jet after jet was milked from him. Radiant white light shot from her fingertips, traveling the length of her arms until it completely encased her body. The stranglehold she had on his dick rung another orgasm from him. Drained, he rolled off her. Flung his arm over his eyes.

They lay trying to regain their composure. He searched blindly beside him, patting the mattress until he encountered her hand. He laced their fingers.

"That was...Wow!" Amelia exclaimed through uneven breaths. "Is it always like that?"

Peaking under his arm, he met her awed glance. He arched a brow.

"Oh, right." She chuckled. "One hundred and twenty-year-old virgin. I forgot."

With his other hand, Talon reached across their bodies. Tickled her side.

She squirmed, giggled, and swatted his hand away. "Stop, stop, stop..." she begged, "I won't mention the big 'V' again.—Oh, oh, oh.—Promise. Promise."

"You better not. I think I proved it wasn't an issue."

She elbowed him in the side. "Yeah, don't let it go to your head," Amelia retorted. "Although... if I can get more of that...? Maybe being vampire queen won't be so bad."

Ugh! Her brain refused to comprehend her circumstances. He wanted to allow them to revel in post-coital bliss, but time was of the essence. "You won't be vampire queen, Amelia. You'll be queen, of *all* supernatural."

"Potato, potahto." She shrugged nonplussed.

"No, it isn't," he asserted. "You call all the shots; appoint different breeds of supernatural as royal representatives to police their breed in whatever region they reside in." Talon waited for her reaction. When she gave none he went on. "You're the supernatural's beacon in the night. The light at the end of the tunnel that will bring peace from the chaos they've lived in for centuries. Keep them from being exterminated and war."

"So, anybody looking to stage a coup or snuff me out has unlimited access to me? I thought you were supposed to make this queen business sound more appealing?"

"You misunderstood. Supernatural will only be able to feel the tie to you. To a force greater than themselves." Talon gazed down, into vacant eyes. How to explain? "Umm... Think of the way a zealot senses their God. They won't know your exact location, only that you exist. You, however, will know of their existence from their birth. You'll be able to identify all super-natural by face and name. And with focus, know their location as well."

Amelia propped herself up onto her elbow. Talon fought not to be seduced by the way her hair slid over her shoulder to cover one breast. "Shut. Up. Like a picture phonebook? I'll just *know* everyone?"

"I suppose." He didn't know. There weren't Vampire Royals to consult. "It'll work in your favor. Help gain fealty from *commoners*. Mind-to-mind communication with your retinue will help in that regard."

"The way you do?" she interrupted.

Shaking his head, he answered, "No. I don't communicate telepathically. I hear thoughts and influence minds. You'll be capable of projecting your thoughts into others' minds, have a mental conversation. With your Siren abilities, you'll possess great control over... everyone."

Amelia's brows crinkled in a most adorable way. Not being drawn into her unintended allure was getting harder. He'd love nothing more than to roll her underneath him and possess her again.

"Siren?" she asked, intruding on his musings. "Vampires are Sirens, too?"

Talon gently pressed her head down so she lay on his chest. With minimal resistance, she allowed him this, which said a lot about her mental state. "Vampires aren't Sirens. It's actually uncommon for supernatural to have dual natures. Seems you're more unique than we thought."

"So, besides incest, there's also a Siren in my family tree? Awesome," she said flatly. "Glad the wings skipped a generation and there aren't any sailors or boats around."

What the—? He laughed. "The whole luring men to shipwreck and half-bird thing is a myth. Sirens are humanoid with logic-defying beauty and heavenly voices that can enslave humans and supernatural alike. You'll have to watch how you talk and sing to keep from doing so accidentally."

"Right, beautiful! I must have misinterpreted all the teasing and insults about my skin color and funky hair throughout grade school. You might be off base about the Siren thing."

Talon ran his fingers through her hair. He'd admit—not to her—but to himself that her red hair, amazing gemstone eyes, and brown skin were shocking. He definitely hadn't expected them, but in no way did the oddity detract from her beauty. "No, *signorina*, you're a Siren. Remember your fatigue at the funeral? Had you not stopped singing when you did, you would've acquired the entire funeral party and surrounding neighborhood as *vassal*. Poor José was so bewitched he would've died willingly."

Amelia popped back up, yanking her hair from his hold. She scowled at him. "I fainted from stress, and I'm taphephobic. Seeing them bury Walk—" She choked on the name. Talon felt like a tool for rehashing the painful memory. "I'm not a Siren."

"You are," he said firmly. "It must have been latent like your vampirism. And it's beside the point. You'll have to learn to control all your new urges after the Awakening. It can take at least a decade to get the bloodlust alone under control."

With a roll of her eyes, Amelia flopped back down. Head on his chest, she drew lazy circles around his pectorals, reawakening his hunger for her. He sensed the absentminded gesture meant she was deep in thought. The desire to flip her over, surge into her, and listen to her thoughts warred inside him. Thankfully, she spoke.

"Can I ask you a weird question?"

"Of course," he answered, not letting worry seep into his response. With Amelia, it could be anything. She was far too curious and open about her observations.

"You have..."

Talon braced himself.

"...sperm, right? I mean... I felt it, I guess. How? You're..."

"I am not dead," he interjected. Why did she persist in this line of thinking? "I did not die. My reproductive organs work fine."

"Whatever." She sighed. "That's not what I really wanted to know anyway. You said you weren't that easy to kill. Aren't all vampires... durable, to use your word?"

He felt oddly vulnerable at her question. Earlier she'd threatened to stake him... He hesitated. "Yes. Mortal tales about vampire speed, hearing, vision, accelerated healing, agility, inability to walk in the sun are true. But the crosses, holy water, and such only apply to rogue vampires."

"Fascinating. Still doesn't tell me how to kill you."

No, it didn't. He should've known that answer wouldn't sidetrack her. "The Royals and the VRG are gifted with sturdier skin than other vampires. Piercing the heart paralyzes us but won't kill us. To destroy a Royal or Guardsman, the heart and head have to be removed. Burned separately from the body. Of course, sun exposure does it, too."

Talon rubbed her back, relished in the knowledge that for this moment she was his.

Amelia slapped his chest. "Wait, wait, wait." She looked at him, eyes narrowed. "I've seen you during the day?"

He held up his right hand, wiggled his fingers.

"The pimp ring?" her voice rose in surprise. "Good to know it serves some purpose. But why don't all vampires have one? I mean, it's ugly, but a lot less conspicuous than a bunch of pasty people walking around at night. Isn't the goal to fit it? Stay shrouded in secrecy?"

Ugh! This conversation would speed things up tremendously. Couldn't she ever be patient? "The idea for the day rings goes back to ex-King Balkan's concubine and mother of his hybrid children, Dark-witch High Priestess Lilith. She made sapphire amulets with dark magic for her children. Balkan forced her to create more for his army of rogue vamps, the *Daywalkers*. Balkan's *Daywalkers* attacked and destroyed his cousin, Queen Ana-Marie, your ancestor, during the day. We don't work with Dark-witches or black magic. We have White-witches and only a select few can make the rings. Ours are ruby. Without the use of dark magic, my ring and your necklace" —he tilted his head toward the ruby and diamond yin-yang she wore — "don't work for long and need to be taken off to charge daily."

Amelia stretched, yawned. She tossed herself onto the pillow beside him, stared at the ceiling. "Uh-huh... I now know what's past TMI—complete insanity."

He caressed the side of her arm with his thumb soothingly. "Don't try to understand too much. It takes time. After the *Awakening,* you'll have a White-witch Advisor and chief guardsman to help you adjust."

She turned toward him and grimaced. "Why would I need them when my boyfriend is head nacho, right? *Created just for me,*" she jested in a mocking male voice.

Talon stiffened. This is what he dreaded. Shit.

"Why did I say that?" Amelia asked then slapped a hand over her eyes. "God, now you think I'm some stage five clinger, don't you? That's supposed to be your role—you're the virgin," she rambled, twisting her head from left to right. Stopping abruptly, she turned. Peeked at him out of her left eye. "Why don't you want me to be your girlfriend? Being the queen's man's gotta get you some serious street cred."

Talon waited for her to take a breath before he spoke. When she glared at him, he figured he'd waited long enough. He swallowed hard. "Amelia, you are so...unexpected. Compound females are nothing like you. Their strength is quiet, subdued, elegant. You're opinionated, rude at times, but strong. I love that about you—shit, I love you. But we can't be together. VRG are forbidden to mate Royals. Our purpose is to protect and serve."

If looks could harm, Amelia's would've disemboweled him. His heart felt as if it'd been shredded. He'd take it back if he could, but this protected his species. His family.

Amelia sat, yanked the top sheet from under her, and wrapped it around herself. "You. Dick," she drawled. Potent rage vibrated from her, visibly shaking her. "I guess vampire or human, guys are all the same. You lure a girl into bed, then suddenly, she's not your type anymore. You're a piece of shit."

"Believe me, things will work out for the best. We'll go back to Italy. You'll receive your royal name, be bound to a worthy *Courtier* who will be your *eternalmate*." Those were the hardest words he'd ever say, but he couldn't permit them to delude themselves any longer. The needs of the many outweighed the needs of... him.

Sledgehammer strong waves of revulsion, hurt, and betrayal hit Talon, but the strike that hurt the most was regret. Amelia regretted what they'd done.

Holding tight to the sheet around her, she scooted away from him. "Get. Out!"

"It's not that I don't care. This meant more than words can say. It'll haunt me for—"

Eyes widened; her mouth popped open. "It'll haunt you?" she repeated deceptively calm. "Get the hell out of my house! Talon Cantemir I—"

Not wanting his invitation rescinded again, he moved with preternatural speed. He dressed, issued one final command, then left.

Chapter Thirty-Five

Alone and so far beyond pissed the word no longer had any meaning, Amelia could only think. Think so hard that stabbing, blinding pain gathered behind her right eye. Staring into space in the direction of her closed bedroom door, she pulled her ruby comforter tight around her naked body.

Moments ago, that door had been open, and the doorway filled with Talon.

Saying I love you, then walking out as if nothing happened...? Asshole! He seemed far too okay with the fact that the woman he supposedly "loved" would be handed to some other guy like a hand-me-down coat. That bit of knowledge should piss her off, but it barely registered a blip on her furious-o-meter. Not when Talon was slinging orders.

His words, stated in that rolling thunder voice of his, echoed in her head. *"And that wasn't a request. I've indulged your fondness for Calin, but no more. You go near him again, and I'll gut him. No stubborn or difficult shit—capisce? He's dangerous, and I won't tolerate you continuing to put yourself at risk so close to the Awakening."*

The *Awakening*. That's all he cared about, not her safety. He didn't love her. He loved what she could do for him, for the supernatural. She didn't allow herself to show emotions for her friends, but she was supposed to sacrifice her life for fairytale creatures?

She laughed aloud, a foreign sound with a hysterical edge. A deposed king killing his cousin because she was made queen? A vampire queen great, great, great, great—damn, how many greats should there be—grandmother? The Fates abandoning supernatural beings for 1000 years for disobedience? Vampires, Dark-witches, White-witches, Werewolves, Shapeshifters, and Sirens—oh, my!

This was the stuff of myths, legends—nightmares. Totally unbelievable. Could she be going crazy? Suffering from grief-induced psychosis? In her old life, back before everybody started dropping like live grenades around her, she'd wanted to be a psychologist. Wanted to help people through cognitive therapy. Now, she needed help.

She had to be crazy to even partially believe what Talon told and showed her. Maybe he was crazy. So talented a storyteller that he somehow dragged her into his delusion. Murder conspiracies? Awakenings? What difference did it make? They both meant death to her in the long run.

That thought chilled her to the bone, replacing whatever lusty remnants lingered from her tryst with Talon with pure unadulterated terror. Pulling her knees to her chest under the blanket, she wrapped her arms tightly around her legs. Chin resting on her covered knees, she rocked back and forth.

After a few minutes, outrage superseded fear, or at least melded with it.

What the hell am I doing?

Talon threatened her life. The guy was ginormous, scary as shit, and had basically admitted to having plans to kill her. She shouldn't be sitting here contemplating the reality of it. She should be calling the police. Where in the deuce did her self-preservation go? A sudden thought occurred to her, knocking some of the wind out of her bloated sails.

What would she say to the police?

"Umm... Hi. Some crazy lunatic thinks I'm the descendant of the rulers of all supernatural beings and, as luck would have it, fated to become the new ruler come midnight June twenty-seventh. Oh, what's the significance of that day you ask? It's my exact date and time of birth. Weird, right? Well, it gets weirder. If I don't let him bury me alive, so I can die and come back as a vampire, I'll drop dead—on my birthday."

Yeah, somehow she didn't see the police taking that call too seriously. Definitely wouldn't help convince her brother and friends of her sanity. They'd send a crisis prevention team to her and have her committed within the hour. Nobody would believe this...

The thought derailed as another struck like a brick to the forehead. She knew someone who'd believe her. Flinging the comforter off of her, she ran into her bathroom.

Ten minutes later, she emerged dressed in True Religion jeans, a V-neck Versace sweater, and four-inch Louboutin pumps. Who knew showers were so cathartic?

She grabbed her Louis Vuitton and car keys and left the house.

No psychotic man would dictate to her.

Calin sat on his bed, experimenting with different chords for a song he'd written for Amelia. A knock sounded at his door. With a wave of his hand, he unlocked and opened it while continuing to play his guitar.

"What the hell? How did you?—How did that?—Whatever. Can I come in?"

Shit!

Calin's head snapped up at the last voice he expected to hear right now.

"Can I come in?" Amelia repeated, agitated and fidgeting. "I might have been followed."

That put some fire under him. He sat his guitar behind him on the bed and rushed to meet her at the open door. Who the hell was threatening his female? Taking her gently by the arm, he ushered her inside. He peered out the door, looking left then right before shutting it behind her. "Who would follow you?"

"Talon," Amelia all but shouted breathlessly as if she'd run a marathon. She paced the room like a caged beast. "I ran all the way here from the car. He's crazy. I mean, like, really crazy—nuckin' futs, crazy."

Before she completed another lap, Calin caught her by the shoulder and turned her toward him. He pulled her into his arms.

Her soft body melted against his harder one. Breasts pressed into his chest as she settled into the embrace. She wrapped her arms around his waist and pressed her head against his abdomen as if she couldn't get close enough.

He smoothed her hair down. Raked his fingers through the damp strands. Whatever happened with Talon had her panicked. Rage burned in his gut, threatening to elongate his fangs. He worked hard to keep the edge out of his voice when he spoke. "What'd Talon do to you, Sweets? You're shaking. Tell me what he did so I know why I'm killing the bastard."

A myriad of conflicting emotions assailed Calin. Having Amelia in his arms was fantastic. Right. He rubbed his stubbled chin across the top of her head, inhaling her mango-almond shampoo. But while his carnal desires stirred, other more predatory urges lifted their heads. Foremost, outrage at what this "thing" Talon had done to his woman.

For several quiet minutes, Amelia trembled in his arms. Wasn't often he worried about another person. He'd never cared about a mortal. He saw problems and eliminated them. When he felt uncomfortable emotions, he killed something. There was always a solution—until now. With Amelia in his arms, he was helpless, truly helpless. As her *eternalmate*, it was his honored privilege, duty, and obligation to see to the health and well-being of his mate. Put her needs above his own. Standing here, simply holding her, couldn't be enough.

He wished Talon had followed her. It'd make destroying him a hell of a lot more convenient. He'd go in the hall, decapitate him, remove his heart, burn the body, then come back, and possess his female. Easy. Unfortunately, that wasn't possible. When he checked the hall, he expanded his senses. No frosty winter scent. Talon wasn't here. He could cast a spell, keep her here while he—

"Thanks for the offer, but I don't want you to kill him. He's sick," Amelia said, her sweet, raspy reply, cut into his planning.

"He's sick?"

"Yeah," she said, lips brushing his pectoral. Her warm breath penetrated the thin fabric of his grey T-shirt. The touch did crazy things to his body and hardened him to the point of pain. "You should've heard him. I know you believe in the whole possible existence of vampires, but you do it in a harmless nerdy way."

Gee, thanks.

"Talon took it to an insane level. He wants to kill me."

Calin's entire body stiffened. And not in a good way. Out of all possible ways for her to find out about him and why he was here... This was the worst. This wasn't how he'd planned to come clean. He had a new, intricate, calming spell he wanted to use. It would make her open to accepting him and what needed to happen. Her scared out of her mind wasn't conducive to making his plan work. He would terminate Talon for this, but not before torturing him.

Reluctantly releasing her, Calin pulled the chair from his workstation over to the edge of the bed. Led her by the hand and sat her at the end, facing the chair. He sat on it. Scooted close enough that their knees touched. He took her dainty hands in his. "Tell me what happened. If I'm going to keep you safe, I need to know exactly what happened. Don't leave anything out."

It took a while, thirty minutes, give or take. Amelia released a long breath and ran her fingers through her hair. She'd left the house in such a hurry she didn't blow dry her hair. Now it was wavy, afro'ed, wet in some spots, and tangled in others.

Calin stared at her in silence, holding her hands in his. He'd politely listened to the entire outrageous story without a peep or cracking a smile. Bless his heart. Of course, she'd left out the having sex with a madman part. Who'd admit to that?

She'd keep the lid on that one and let it be part of her own private, personal shame. Anyway, it didn't bode well for her; she had feelings for Calin. Admitting to knocking one out with her late boyfriend's mentally ill cousin did nothing for her image.

She had been right to come here. Repeating the story out loud helped. It sounded even more *Black Mirror* or *X-Files* than it had to her. Further proving how non-plausible the entire ordeal and sequence of events for the day were. Unbeknownst to her, Talon had probably slipped her something. A hallucinogenic, maybe?

God, he could've been high himself. Transferred it to her through the skin, like when he touched her when the pizza guy was there. It made perfect sense. She'd read that meth could be sweated out of the pores, thereby transferring it to others through touch. That was one of the main reasons she never let Tigger touch her—well, that and he smelled bad. That had to be what Talon did...

"Oh, my God," she breathed, not realizing she'd spoken aloud until Calin blinked.

"What?" he asked, stroking the inside of her wrist with his thumb.

Odd that'd never been erotic before. It was now. "I just realized Talon must've slipped me something. That's why I thought I saw his canines and incisors grow into fangs and his eyes glow. I was trippin'. Hallucinating. He touched me when he came into the house. Meth or something must've been coming out of his pores."

Saying it to someone else made it make more sense. Relief was an unexpected, but welcome, blast of fresh air. This was a good thing, a great thing... Although, if Calin's expression were anything to go by, one would assume she just nut-checked him. He bowed his head. Brown hair hung over his forehead and hid his eyes.

"Calin, did you hear me? Meth poisoning good; Amelia losing her mind, bad. I'm not losing my mind." She paused, considering her words. Okay, so none of it sounded great. At least she could recover from meth poisoning. Crazy was a whole other battle.

Amelia turned her hands in Calin's so hers wrapped around his. She gave a reassuring squeeze. He squeezed back but made no other move.

What was wrong with him? She'd think he was the one who'd been slipped meth.

She leaned in to get a look at his face. If the sullen expression he wore hadn't caused a knot the size of China to twist her intestines, it would've made her laugh. His strained face belonged to someone who should be in the bathroom. Alone. With the door locked. Reading a magazine.

She tugged her hands out of his. Ran her fingers through the thick strands of his unkempt hair. Pushed it off his forehead, out of his eyes. His hair slid right back down.

As she moved her hand, he lifted his head. Took her right hand in both of his and gazed into her eyes with piercing pale teal ones. Her heart clenched. Breath lodged in her throat at the soul-deep pain there. It echoed the pain she'd felt since her parents' death.

This wasn't sympathy. Even Chef Emeril Lagasse couldn't kick it up to this notch. Before she got a read on him, he hung his head. Maybe coming here hadn't been the best decision. He seemed to be going through something. She'd been so self-absorbed she hadn't asked or considered that when she barged in. Now that she felt better, she would comfort him.

They sat hand in hand, knee to knee for several minutes. Quiet. Every so often she felt a light squeeze on her hand as if he were reassuring himself she was still there.

Why he was silent, she had no clue. She kept quiet because she sensed it was what he needed. He still hadn't responded to anything she'd told him. Her body was still trying to process the excess adrenaline from the day. She'd come here completely confused, more than a little scared, and frazzled. Being here with Calin helped more than it should and confused her in another way.

She stared at his hands cupping hers. They were huge in comparison, like baseball mitts. He was a big man. All broad, wide shoulders, muscles upon muscles. It wasn't bulky muscle it was sinewy rope, smooth. His features made him ruggedly handsome. Yet his crooked smile held boyish charm. His presence intimidated other people. To her, his deadly air and raw masculinity meant safety. Protection.

When she felt threatened her first instinct—okay, so, her first instinct after considering calling the police—was to come to him. He'd never let anything happen to her; she was as sure of that as she was her own name. Calin always treated her as if she was the only person that mattered. So much so, he came off as an asshole to other people. But they didn't see what she saw.

Loneliness dwelled in the depths of his eyes, profound loneliness. The kind that lived inside her. He needed her. As much as she tried to lie to herself, explain it away, she needed him, too. Irrationally needed him.

God, it would be easy to love this man. On some level, she suspected she already did.

"I'm dangerous."

Calin's low voice yanked her attention to the present. "What?"

He cleared his throat. "Talon was telling the truth."

Chapter Thirty-Six

"**S**ort of... telling the truth," he revised. "I'm not sure how much of what he knows is fact or speculation, but he's right about one thing. I am dangerous."

Eyes wide, mouth agape, Amelia didn't realize she'd been holding her breath until her head started spinning. Only two options available: pass out or breathe. For once she didn't want to faint. She exhaled, loudly.

"I'm not dangerous to you," Calin rushed to assure her. "Anymore."

Tacking *anymore* to the clarification did nothing to allay her mounting fear. His words slapped her like a whip to the face. She tried to pull her hand free from his. He tightened his hold.

"Let go of my hand," she demanded when a second extrication attempt failed.

For the first time in almost ten minutes, Calin lifted his head. Her horrified gaze clashed with intense, bluish-green, and...

"Ho—ly, shit!" Glowing eyes—like Talon's.

If her hands weren't otherwise occupied, she would've pinched herself to ensure this was real. The chances of being confronted by two meth addicts were... Good in Arizona, but not so much for her personal life. Maybe she was still suffering the effects of Talon's touch. She thought she'd scrubbed herself skinless in the shower, but maybe some meth was left in her system.

Oh, no!

He came inside her. It was in his semen. Great! Perfect. What a fine time to have unprotected sex. She hadn't been thinking at the time. She'd needed an anchor in a storm of freaky make-believe. Shit!

Like an animal with its paw caught in a trap, she jerked. Tugged. Struggled to free her hand from Calin's, once soothing, now restraining, giant hands.

"Stop fighting. I'm not letting go until you listen."

Amelia eased her struggles. Fright wouldn't let her stop completely. "What exactly am I supposed to be listening to? Why can't I have use of my hand while I do it?"

She was shocked she spoke without her voice shaking. Especially since at her words the corner of Calin's mouth tipped into a wicked grin that exposed a hint of...

Fang!

"You remember the night we watched *Interview with the Vampire*?"

Dammit, she wanted to be all defiant. Not give him the satisfaction of answering. Unfortunately, the warm blush she felt rise up her neck and steal away in her cheeks appeared to be answer enough.

"Everything I told you was true. My mother is the daughter of the ex-king Balkan Dimir, and my grandmother was Lilith Luca, a Dark-witch. My mother was cursed to feel humanity by White-witch Gabrielle while attempting to flee persecution during the battle that destroyed the queen and her—"

Amelia stopped fighting his hold. Her face felt frozen as the blood drained from it. "Queen Ana-Marie Dimir?" she asked in a dead tone, not really needing confirmation.

Calin nodded.

"Of course, Queen Ana-Marie, your grandfather's cousin. My great, great—however many greats—grandmother. Awesome! We're related," she breathed. Bile rose in her throat. Good news kept on coming today, didn't it? Not.

"No," Calin said with an exasperated sigh. "We aren't related. Trust me, I checked. We're so removed, the line so diluted, you're more related to your next-door neighbor than me. Given immortal longevity, some still consider themselves related even if they're sixth cousins twice removed."

"So, how old does that make you—and F.Y.I. that doesn't make me feel any better?"

"Two hundred. And I know none of this makes it better. I'm sorry. My mission was clear. I had it all planned, then I met you, and the plan went to shit."

Amelia was barely listening after *my mission was clear*. Quite the feat since she'd only been half listening after *two hundred*. Something told her she wouldn't like this next part, but she had to know. "What mission?"

His grip on her hand tightened. "You remember what I told you about the type of vampire I am, right? Part mortal because my father was mortal and part vampire and Dark-witch hybrid on my mother's side?"

Amazingly, Amelia managed to nod when what she really wanted was to scream.

Calin went on. "Well, er—how do I word this? My mother and her siblings are the only vampire-Dark-witch half breeds. Born of two evil entities—a rogue vampire and Dark-witch—they're soulless. Psychopaths or sociopaths by mortal standards. Bianca and I are the only mortal, vampire, Dark-witch offspring. The only way for us to be as our relatives are is to kill our mortal parent."

The look on her face must have screamed terrified because he hurried to explain. "I couldn't do that. I didn't. Curse or no curse, my mother loved my father. I did, too. I couldn't do it. Not even after I reached the *Immortal Age* and my mother abandoned us. Bianca didn't have that same hang-up. At two weeks old, she killed her father. Five and a half years ago, my mother appeared at my door in Paris with an infant Bianca and persuaded me to move to Romania."

Amelia hadn't known her mouth was hanging open until he paused and smiled. Her stupid heart skipped a beat. She gulped. "Are you fucking serious? Bianca's only five and a half!"

"Accelerated aging, a trait from our vampire side. You said Talon explained?"

"He did. I mean, I don't know if he knew about you and Bianca, but he told me about the age thing and all the history. It's just one thing to hear it and another to realize I've witnessed it firsthand—kinda. So, what exactly is your mission? Why are you here?"

The pained, tortured, look came back full force in Calin's eyes. He caressed her hand with his thumb but didn't loosen his hold. "*Was* my mission, not is," he corrected. "Balkan's hell-bent on power and having it back in our family. He found out about you and the *Book of Being* prophecy—don't ask how because I don't know. A spy of his told him about a sort of... I don't know... grace period or loophole. If the descendant is destroyed as soon as it rises after the *Awakening*; the activated seal transfers to me. It'd cage my soul, make me like my family, and release my mother from her curse."

"It? You mean *me*?" she croaked in a near-soundless whisper. Tears filled her eyes.

Amelia was speechless. Sat perfectly still, trying to digest everything she'd heard today. Things clicked into place suddenly: her flat tires, the stuff Calin said walking to his hotel, his behavior since they'd met. How they'd met. The stuff he just said. What Talon said...?

It'd all been there. Right in front of her. A Jenga game teetering on the brink of collapse. Waiting for her to pull that one block that would send both Talon and Calin's plans, their lies, crashing down. She never would have foreseen which block to move, given the absurdity of it all... until the pizza guy. Her heart was lead in her chest. Talon and Calin weren't who they appeared to be. They weren't even men. Weren't human. They didn't care for her. This wasn't a dream or a hallucination.

She strained frantically against Calin's hold. Digging her heels into the carpet for leverage, Amelia worked to free herself. All she wanted to do was get far away from Calin, Talon, and everything. She might as well have been pulling on solid steel chains for all the good her yanking did. Calin barely acknowledged it.

Meanwhile, she felt like her arm was going to pop out of the socket. That frustrated her more, increasing her fight.

"Amelia, stop. I won't hurt you," he said, not even out of breath.

A bubble of bitter laughter burst through her lips. "Yeah, right! Said the spider to the fly. Isn't it your job to hurt me, your *mission*, to quote you." Her voice quavered with panic.

Debilitating fear was setting in. She was a hairsbreadth from gnawing through her wrist to get free. This was too much.

Finally, he let go.

She hopped up like the bed was on fire and hauled ass to the door. Less than a foot from the bed, she saw Calin wave his hand out of her peripheral vision. A second later, she was pinned against the wall. And scared shitless.

With slow, deliberate grace, Calin rose. Prowled toward her. His hair hung over his glowing turquoise eyes. Inches in front of her, he stopped. "God, Amelia, what do you want me to say?" he asked, hitting the wall beside her head with his fist. "My instructions were to destroy the descendant. I didn't know you. Yes, I planned to do it, but when I saw" — he ran his nose down the column of her neck — "smelled you... I knew I'd never be the same."

Shivering under Calin's touch, speech should have been as impossible as the situation, but where there's a will... "So... let me get this straight. You were gonna get to know me... then ask me to let you bury me alive? And you expected me to say yes?" she asked with wide-eyed incredulity. "Clearly, you haven't been around a lot of humans. That's not a plan. What were you and Talon doing, reading from the same playbook? And how did he know what you were? Did you know about him?"

Calin, who'd been looking her in the eyes, averted his gaze, giving her all the answers she needed. They'd both played her for a fool.

"You're such a liar," Amelia sneered, finding courage from somewhere deep inside.

Calin's head snapped up. "I told you everything. If you feel made a fool of, it's your own fault. Nothing has changed. My personality, everything I felt for you—*feel* for you—is real."

"You lied by omission." Angry tears welled, unbidden, in her eyes. "You knew I didn't believe you—why would I?"

"None of it matters. All that matters is I have feelings for you, and I know you have feelings for me, too."

Low blow. "What you feel for me is based on truth. I've never been anything but me with you. You got to know me. The real me. But I never really knew you, apparently. You hi-jacked my feelings," she spat the words at him. The truth of her accusation broke her heart. A single, hot tear rolled down her cheek.

Calin caught it on the tip of his index finger. He put the digit in his mouth and sucked it dry.

To hide her awareness of the unintended sensual action, Amelia smoothed her features into an expressionless mask.

"As your *eternalmate*, it's my job to see to your happiness. It's predestined by The Fates. I know you feel it," he said with such conviction she almost believed him. "Do you have any idea what I'd do for you? What I'd give up or take on for you?"

She was flabbergasted, and not because Calin waved his hand and slid her up the wall. They were eye-to-eye. Okay, maybe it had a little to do with that too. But more so because Talon had mentioned the whole *eternalmate* deal earlier. Could Calin be it? Was that why when Walker asked her to stay away from him she couldn't? Why she found him so magnetizing? Why even now, when she felt betrayed, she... wanted him? She'd stopped believing in the idea of fate and destiny long ago. To believe in them meant those she'd lost were meant to die. Her brain refused to accept that reality.

Calin must have noticed her distraction because his body heat and the hand caressing her arm jolted her from her musings. He'd closed the distance between them. "I need you, Duchess. Touch me, please," he purred.

Everything inside her wanted to reach out and touch him. Run her fingers through his disheveled hair. Wipe away the anguish crinkling his perfect brow. "Let me down, Calin," she demanded through clenched teeth.

Frowning, he shook his head. Turned his back on her and paced a short distance away. "What can I do to make this better? What do you want me to say?"

"Tell me this isn't real!" Rage over the day's events and the twisted turn her life had taken made her snap. "That tomorrow when I wake up this will all have been nothing but a bad dream. That everyone I love will be alive, and I won't ever have met you or Talon!"

He whipped around so fast; Amelia wasn't sure she'd seen it happen. "You don't mean that!"

She lifted her chin in challenge. "Yes, I do."

Calin recoiled like she'd smacked him. Recovering quickly, he stalked toward her.

Now she felt the danger Talon had warned her about. He was mad, more than mad—hurt. Even if his fangs hadn't descended, she would have known it by the way his features pinched before he blanked them. Like the predator she now knew him to be, his luminescent eyes stayed locked on her with each step. His muscles, flexed, bunched, under the tight fabric of his T-shirt.

"You wish you never met me?" he asked, voice calm, dangerous. Hard turquoise eyes bored into hers. "I sacrificed my mother for you. Thought to disobey my grandfather for you, sought to rule by your side. Protected you. I destroyed one of my own for you and orchestrated a cover-up for... *you*. And you wish you never met me?" He chuckled humorlessly.

Feeling as trapped as she was, Amelia watched as fury burned in Calin's eyes. Fear formed a hard, cold knot in the pit of her stomach. Lithesome male elegance and power wrapped around each roll and ripple of his thick muscles. He was handsome. A beautiful monster.

Instinctively, Amelia flinched. Turned her head to get out from under the weight of his penetrating gaze. She didn't know what to expect. Would he hit her? Bite her? Sniff her again? No. That wasn't why she turned, and she knew it. She turned because...he saw too much. He knew she wanted him. Even now.

"Yes," was her belligerent answer to his question. "I wish I never heard any of this. I'm normal. Human. This is nonsense.

An intricate illusion." She didn't know if she believed what she said or not, but courage and stubborn defiance made her turn her head toward him.

Big mistake.

He was right in front of her. Nose-to-nose. Head tilting one way then the other, he examined her like a curious Rottweiler or Pit Bull. His mouth quirked into a harsh, sinful smile. "Is this an illusion?" Dipping his head to the crook of her neck, something razor-sharp skated from her earlobe to the top of her shoulder. It bordered on pain and pleasure. His dark spice scent engulfed her.

Iron will beat back the needful moan threatening to escape her lips. She couldn't stop the clench of her stomach muscles or the involuntary chills that caused her to shiver.

Lifting his other hand, he caressed her cheek. Something resembling an electrical current trailed each stroke of his large, calloused thumb. He dragged a fang—at least, that's what she assumed it was—down and up an invisible path from the top of her shoulder to her ear. Warmth bloomed low in her abdomen. Reaching her ear, he traced the shell with his tongue. Thank God, he had her pinned against the wall. The blast of arousal that hit her would've knocked her to her knees.

Nope, definitely not an illusion.

With him doing that, her anger got harder and harder to hold on to.

"Please... Calin, stop," she basically moaned, all breathless. Damn it! Real convincing.

"Touch me, please," he whispered in her ear.

She shuddered. Bracing a hand against the wall next to her head, he pressed his hard chest into her softer one.

Against her better judgment, she lifted a surprisingly steady hand and ran her fingers through the front of his hair to the back. His eyes rolled. The look on his face was pure ecstasy. Nuzzling her neck, he whispered, "Again."

Of its own volition, her head tilted toward his, so they were pressed cheek to cheek. His whiskers tickled her skin. Maybe she needed the closeness or maybe—she didn't know. Her brain was so fried from everything that had happened today. She couldn't craft a good lie to explain why she snuggled her cheek against his. Her mind screamed in protest, but she couldn't make herself stop.

"Touch me with your hand again," he growled. Firm, full lips moved against the corner of her mouth.

"No," she whimpered as he ground his jean-covered erection into her core.

"How could you want to forget this?" he muttered.

He moved his lowered body, and it took all her strength not to hunch hers to meet the bulge in his pants. Her willpower, however, wasn't necessary she discovered. He replaced the warmth of his groin with the palm of his hand. She gasped at his intimate hold. Whether in shock or desire, she wasn't sure.

"This is where I belong. Inside you. We belong together. Can't you feel it? Your pussy's hungry for my cock. Tell me you feel it," he ordered seductively.

Oh, yeah! I'm feeling something.

"We need to be together. *Eternalmates* can't endure long separations. It's mentally and physically painful. Mimics the withdrawal symptoms a hard drug user would feel. You can't be without me, and I can't be without you. I *won't* be without you," Calin said, kissing the left side of her face while petting her through her jeans.

Moisture rushed to that most sensitive part of her. Drenched her panties. She was on fire. "You're wrong. I'm not your mate. Let me go, Calin... please. I want to go home," she pleaded. Another tear fled down her cheek.

Calin licked it away.

"Don't cry, Sweets. I've allowed you a lot more freedom than I should have. I'll let you go if you promise not to see Talon again. His life depends on it."

Fine. She didn't plan on seeing either one of them again. "Okay."

Kissing his way to her ear, he shook his head. "Say the words," he demanded.

"I promise I won't see Talon again." *Or you*, she added mentally.

As the last word left her lips he placed a hand under each of her arms. Lifted her. He set her beside him on her feet. Without turning back, lest he discover the anxiety and resolve in her eyes, she walked to the door.

"Hey, Duchess, I'll see you tomorrow."

Home free.

"Amelia."

Almost. "What?" she asked, hard-pressed to keep agitation out of her tone. She grabbed a firm hold of the doorknob.

"Could you turn around please?"

No! Working her features into an unreadable mask, she faced him. Without letting go of the doorknob.

"I know it seems crazy, but I do love you," he said, voice low, sincere.

Turning the knob and opening the door a crack, prepared for a quick getaway, she said, "You know, that's a popular sentiment tonight. But... I just can't seem to care."

With that, she was out the door faster than the roadrunner escaping Wile E. Coyote.

Chapter Thirty-Seven

"Oh, she didn't *accept* the truth?" came the sarcastic question from the other end of the phone. "Of course, she didn't. I don't know why any of you thought this plan would work."

Talon sank onto one of two black Italian leather sectional couches in the den—or as Amelia called it, the man cave. Cell on speaker phone, he placed it on the overstuffed arm to his left. He gritted his teeth, fighting his annoyance with Anton's uncharacteristic hotheaded attitude.

Scoffing, Anton went on. "Befriend her, then tell her the truth…? Wh-what kind of plan is that?" he asked, disbelief raising his voice. "That's not even a plan!"

Oh, yeah. Something was off here. Anton was a natural jokester. Light-hearted. Nothing fazed him for too long. This new-found biting sarcasm, rude shit… unacceptable.

Kicking his booted feet up on the coffee table in front of him, Talon conjured his favorite push dagger. "T" handle clutched in his right fist, the short blade protruded from between his second and third finger. He performed some practice jabs.

The fledgling was lucky he wasn't here. With the way Talon felt about the monumental fuck-up, which was this supposed "cake" mission. His stupidity in dealing with Amelia and what should have been a beautiful experience the other night coupled with her subsequent silent treatment. He was on edge. By the way Anton acted, one would think he was the one sentencing his family to death for his failure.

No. Talon hadn't technically failed yet, but he wasn't stupid. He knew Amelia's silence didn't mean she would agree to the Awakening. He didn't want to contemplate the mess he'd made of things or how he would regain her trust. What had taken almost two months to build had been destroyed in a total of forty-five minutes. His control of his temper was hanging by a thin string. The new combative Anton plucked at the threads of that string.

He spoke with lethal calm. "I didn't hear you complaining or making any worthwhile suggestions during the planning stages, *fledgling*," he snarled.

"Ha!" Anton's laugh was acrimonious. "Like anybody would've listened to me. Y'all think I'm beneath you. Yeah, I got you, though. We'll see about that—in due time," he muttered the last part. "What you guys came up with wasn't a plan. It was barely an idea. It was what you think about before coming up with something better. Shit! Why do you people hide the truth? How the fuck did you think she'd respond?" he asked rhetorically, given the fact he waited not even a second before raising his voice an octave to mimic a woman's, "Oh, this is so great. All I have to do is let you *kill* me, then take me away from everyone I know and love to rule beings who'll more than likely rebel against my rule or try to destroy me? Oh, boy! Sign me up."

Talon was stunned. A full minute passed. He had no idea how to respond to Anton's nonsensical, insubordinate tirade. The fledgling would've been begging for his life if he were in front of him. "First off, *youngblood*, you need to remember who you're talking to. Second, what the fuck are you talking about?"

"Nothing." Anton sighed. Talon pictured the golden-eyed vampire scratching his auburn-haired head in irritation. The reason for said anger remained a mystery. "What you should've done is told her everything right out the gate, dawg. Then you could've used your time beguiling her, and shit, with your bibbi-di bobbidi boo. She would've been so mesmerized she would've let you lop off an arm if you asked."

"Trust me, it wouldn't have been that easy." Picking his fingernails with his dagger's blade, Talon rolled his eyes. Things were never simple with Amelia. If he said the Earth was round she'd argue its symmetry just to be difficult. "You don't know her like I do she's..." He paused in search of a word to describe the insufferable mortal who'd wormed her way into his heart. "Complicated."

"That's just fuckin' it!" Anton yelled, voice cracking. "I should know her. I should be her! That's what's fucked about this. All because of some fluke of fuckin' inbreeding bullshit, she's her and I'm me. I've lived this shit, dealt with this shit day in and day out. She didn't even know any of this existed. I'm knee deep in this game, feel me? I should be there, not here. Shit! I don't know how to help you with this one, *patna*. But you gotta get it done, cuz if you don't... there's a million mutherfuckers ready to take your head if you fuck this up—and hers! Peace." He hung up.

Talon stared dumbfounded at his cell phone. Yes. Definitely something wrong with Anton. If he didn't have a stubborn mortal to transition into a reluctant queen, he'd delve into Anton's problems. But he did, so he couldn't. He just hoped the fledgling straightened up his act quick. He'd hit the *Immortal Age* July thirteenth. With the way he'd just acted, his demon would cage his soul, turn him rogue in seconds. After that, it wouldn't be long before Talon was ordered to destroy him. If Victor or the *courtiers* didn't tag the little shit first.

Resting his head on the back of the couch, Talon shoved a hand through his hair. So much to do, so little time to do it. Amelia was treating him like the enemy. If only she knew her buddy Calin was the real villain.

Fates! He wanted to shake her. Make her see being a vampire wasn't bad. She seemed to be more worried about feeding and what she perceived as the "monster" aspect than being queen. Anton had a point.

If he'd told her in the beginning, he could've spent time preparing her. Showing her the more exciting parts of vampirism. Training hadn't prepared him for the culture shock of America, Arizona, and mortals. Sebastian's stupid idea to starve him only hurt, not helped. He'd spent considerable time controlling his desire to feed. And Amelia? No one could've prepared him for her.

Mistakes had been made. No use dwelling over what should've been. He had a suicidal princess on his hands, the fate of his family and all supernaturals on his shoulders, and a fuckload of rogue beings lined up to take out the female he loved.

The female I love.

An issue in and of itself, wasn't it? Even if she agreed to the *Awakening*, which he'd be willing to bet she wouldn't, could he serve her feeling the way he did? Watch her be *bound* to an uppity *courtier*? Worse still, he'd told her he loved her. Shit!

What he needed to do was devise a plan. Get back down to basics. His mother accused him of being an investigative thinker, and he was. He'd lost sight of himself from moment one. Now was time to be the guardsman he'd trained to be and protect his queen. Seventy-two hours before he needed to conduct the *Awakening*, he had shit to do. Wallowing in self-pity never got anybody anywhere.

"Gawain!" Talon shouted.

Sparkling, aquamarine mist drifted into the den, stopping near the other black sectional. Amelia had not only picked out both couches but designed them online and had them rush-ordered. She said if she didn't have a hand in designing everything she couldn't be sure they were big enough and sturdy enough to accommodate a "big boy" like him—her words, not his. She'd even designed his solid oak, medieval king-sized bed.

Damn, just the thought of her and his bed made him as hard as iron-coated brick.

Since apparently today was his day to be a bitch, might as well admit that he missed her. Before he could dwell on his admission the mist swirled, stacked. Congealed. Formed his six-foot-five, two-hundred-and-fifty-pound mentor and elder VRG.

Gawain's black hair hung in his greenish-blue eyes. He wore a navy, velvet smoking jacket over his bare chest. His signature black silk, drawstring, lounge pants, and black leather slippers brought the look together.

"You bellowed, My Liege." Gawain smirked.

Talon gawked at his supposed mentor's attire. Gawain went around to the waist-high hidden bar behind the sectional. According to Amelia, anybody who was anybody had a hidden bar, named because to others it appeared to be a cherry wood credenza. In reality, it contained a mini fridge and freezer, barware, and a hundred different bottles of top-notch wine and liquor.

Taking out two crystal rocks glasses, Gawain put two cubes of ice in one then looked at Talon. Brows lifted in question. Talon shook his head. Gawain put the second glass away and retrieved a bottle of Black Label Johnnie Walker. Poured it over the ice, then retrieved a glass flask filled with dark liquid. He mixed a large portion of the contents into his drink. After putting everything away, he reclined on the chaise part of the other sectional.

Sure, take all the time you need—asshole. Talon stared for several speechless moments.

"What can I do you for?" Gawain asked, kicking up his slippered feet then taking a sip of his drink. "I'm conducting a little business in my quarters—if you know what I mean. Got a hot blonde falcon shifter and a red-headed succubus I wouldn't want starting the party without me." Wagging a black brow, he swirled his drink with his pinky finger. "I'd offer you one, or ask you to join, but the thought of crossing swords with another male makes me sick. Plus, you got that whole... destined-for-greatness-must-be-celibate thing going on." He sucked his finger dry.

Talon gave a slight, almost imperceptible nod. Stared blankly. A long minute passed before he spoke. "Three questions?"

"Yeah, whatever, bruh. Shoot." He lifted a piece of ice, sucked it. Dropped it back in his glass, oblivious to Talon's anger.

"What the fuck are you wearing? Why are you drinking my damn blood? And how did you get females inside without Amelia inviting them in?" Talon snapped.

Gawain shook his head unfazed by his ire. "For one, this isn't your blood. I got a personal donation from a sexy sun monster last night." Off Talon's arch glare, he added, "Don't worry, I fixed her. She won't remember a thing... except for unbelievable pleasure. Second, Amelia was here for a minute to check on a delivery while you were out. She invited them in happily. Third," he said, emphasizing his point with a tug at his partially open smoking jacket, "I wear this... for easy access, baby."

Nasty. Talon wished he was deaf. "Don't make plans for Saturday night. I'm gonna need your help—"

"What?" Gawain interrupted with a chuckle. "You finally figure out what your dick's for? Need me to help you catch a sweet young thang?"

Talon let his push dagger dematerialize. Gawain might appear relaxed, but it was deceptive. With a good thirteen hundred and eighty-some-odd years on him, he was impossibly strong and fast, which was why Talon didn't attack. Circumstances as they were, he settled for moving fast, grabbing Gawain's drink, and flinging it at the wall. The glass shattered into a million tiny pieces.

"Don't worry about where I stick my dick," Talon growled, leaning over Gawain. "You offered to help, right? Well, there's a party I must attend. So, come Saturday you need to suit up. *Capisce?*"

Talon turned to leave. A thought had him turn back around, "Man up your entrance. The shimmery, droplet thing is fruity." He stalked out.

"Woo, baby!" Kasey hollered toward the road. Four guys, clad in full riding gear, zoomed by on Ducati crotch rockets. "How about gettin' some real power between your legs?"

The sun shone bright. The temperature outside, and in what Amelia now knew to be her transitioning body, was set on Hell sauna. Against her protests, Tessa still insisted on throwing her a birthday party. Even after she'd claimed miscarriage to explain away her pregnancy that never was. Right now, she, Kasey, and Tessa were down the street from Tessa's "sanctuary," also known as Dan's house, sitting outside Starbucks. They were making final decisions for a party she couldn't care less about.

Amelia pinned Kasey with an arch stare. "How is it that you're allowed to do *that*, but Evan can't turn his head when another girl is within a twelve-mile radius of you?"

Kasey flipped her mahogany mane over her shoulder, tossing an annoyed glare at Tessa and then Amelia. "I'm a girl. I don't cheat," she said imperiously. "That was just appreciating attractiveness. Nothing else." She sipped her caramel Frappuccino before continuing. "When a guy looks at another girl he doesn't just appreciate her assets, he wants to touch... her assets. I ain't gon have some bitch take my man from under my nose." Crossing her legs, she sat back in her chair, complacent with her ridiculous explanation. "You feel me?"

Somewhere, there was a straitjacket with that girl's name written all over it. Kasey was crazy. The scary type that would cut a bitch for looking at her sideways. People that type of crazy were the scariest because they had nothing to lose. The sad part was Kasey used to be the sweetest person until she got cheated on one too many times. Now, she was whatever was past jaded. She and Tessa remained friends with her because... well... crazy people needed love, too. The one reason Amelia never pushed Kasey? Crazy people fought dirty. She didn't want to test how fast a friend turned foe. Tessa on the other hand...

"No, but I smell you," Tessa retorted, waving her hand in front of her nose at an imaginary odor, "and you're full of shit." She put her hand down. "Haven't you ever heard the saying 'what's good for the goose is good for the gander,' or, in your case, what's good for the gander is good for the goose?"

Kasey's answering cutting smile was full of deadly intent. "Have you ever heard the saying, 'my foot and your ass need to meet'?"

Had Amelia not been facing her own mortality, she would have laughed at their badinage. Tessa and Kasey were what was referred to as frenemies. Friends who talk mad shit about each other but hangout. Why anyone wanted a friend like that, she had no idea, but it worked for them. Who was she to mess up a good thing?

"Bring it, bitch," came Tessa's vapid taunt.

Better break this up before the shoes came off and the hair went flying. Amelia banged her caramel Macchiato cup on the table to get their attention. "Guys, I thought this was about the party?"

Tessa's mood instantly lifted. "It is. You can't get all the details, though. It's your party. But we got you one thing we can tell you. It's something you've always wanted..." Her voice trailed off mysteriously.

"A tiara," Kasey blurted.

The acerbic glare Tessa threw Kasey was priceless. "Thanks," she said dryly. Recovering some of her previous exuberance, she turned to Amelia. "It's got diamonds, A. Real effing diamonds."

Amelia offered her friends a smile she hoped passed for happy. There had been a time she would've fainted from the joy of wearing a diamond-studded tiara. When they were kids she used to dream she was a princess. Every Halloween she dressed up as one. One year, she even went trick-or-treating as a vampire princess. If only she'd known then what she knew now.

Only Tessa and Kasey were privy to her one-time wish. Now that they were trying so hard to make her dream come true, she wanted to run. This was all too much.

Physically.

Emotionally.

Mentally.

Too... much.

Though sitting outside, Amelia felt closed in. Trapped. She couldn't breathe. "Thanks, guys, I'm stoked. Can't wait to see it. I need to walk." She rose and started away so fast there should've been skid marks.

"Uh... okay. You want us to come with?" Tessa called after her.

Mustering as cool a face as possible, she stopped and turned toward her friends. "No, wait here. I'll be back." Before they objected, Amelia speed walked to the shopping plaza across the parking lot.

The more distance she put between them, the easier breathing became. Acting normal was becoming harder to do. She needed time to think. Being around people she might never see again, who she couldn't tell the truth to was too much. Even if she told them, it wasn't like they'd believe her. Part of *her* still didn't believe it, and she'd seen evidence to the contrary. Belief in what Talon and Calin told her meant her days were numbered.

How did she say goodbye without saying... goodbye?

She had no answer, which was why, as stupid as it was to have a party while death pounded at her door, she let Tessa talk her into it. It was the only way to say, *"Goodbye, hope I don't eat you next time I see you."*

Hindsight really was twenty-twenty. Had she known what would come of her, she would've done so much differently. How had she let her grief get this far out of hand? Albeit a stupid answer, she did know. At the time, she'd thought eternal grief would be the ultimate gift to her lost loved ones. Never changing, never moving forward, just existing kept their memory fresh and alive. To her, change meant forgetting, and she didn't want to forget. But now, facing imminent death, everything was crystal clear.

Her parents had never liked her to experience grief or unhappiness. How could she be dumb enough to think they'd want her to grieve for the rest of her life? The answer was so simple it was complicated: Emotions. Emotions didn't have rationale or reasoning powers. They were irrational. The person hosting said emotions needed to use their brain to figure them out. Too bad her mind took so long to clue in.

The only way to honor her parents' memory, make their life and death not be in vain, was to live. Show them all those lessons they'd tried to teach her didn't fall on deaf ears. Be better. Do better. Go to college. Become a psychologist. Get married. Pass on everything they instilled in her to her...

Walking past Safeway, the mailbox store, and Big Lots, she watched mothers shepherd their rambunctious children into stores. A tornado of grief whipped through her. Destroyed everything in its path and unearthed the thought she dreaded. She'd never have children to pass anything onto. That fact brought reality slamming to the forefront of her mind harder than a kamikaze bird flying into a newly cleaned window.

She'd wasted her life. Instead of living it to the fullest, she'd merely survived it for the last three years. And not well either. She'd been vicious, cruel, and distant to those who did nothing but care for her. It was too late to make amends. Death, or rather, undeath, waited to claim her.

She couldn't do justice to her parents, grandparents, and friends by becoming a vampire. For three years, that'd been what she was, one of the walking dead: cold and emotionless, except with a heartbeat. How could she continue on that way but without a heartbeat? Or a soul? Would her parents want that for her instead of death?

How could she be queen of the supernatural? From what Talon had said, she wouldn't have proper control of her abilities or her bloodlust for a decade after the *Awakening*. If the supernatural were in chaos, what good would an out-of-control queen do? He'd told her another guardsman or a White-witch could teach her to control her abilities. In all honesty, she didn't want any part of them and their world of deception.

Speaking of things, she didn't want, her cell phone vibrated. Probably more apology calls from Calin or Talon. For the last week, they'd been blowing her up. She never answered. Calin even sang Robin Thicke's "All the Stupid Things" to her voicemail. It was beautiful—as always. But this wasn't a musical, it was her life. Yes, she sort of missed them both, but she couldn't get past the fact that they'd both lied to her. How could anything about supernatural be good, worth preserving, if the only way to usher in her—their queen—was to lie?

Nothing says, "We need you. Join us," like a lie, and a terribly flawed one at that. They didn't understand humans if they thought she'd be excited to die and become queen of the damned. Yeah, those weren't scary, unattractive, bullshit options at all—not!

Anyway, not everyone wanted her to join. Apparently, tons of beings would be out to destroy her after the *Awakening*. Lucky for her, as queen, they wouldn't be able to track her, but she could track all of them.

Yay! Not really.

She had no desire to be a walking talking police scanner for things that go bump in the night. Amelia didn't want to watch the cadence of her voice or monitor her singing because of her Siren charms.

Thinking about all this gave her the heebie-jeebies and a migraine. She felt trapped in an episode of *Black Mirror*. This was very—chimerical? After Talon and Calin's show of power, there was no denying it was real.

The Fates seemed to want to give her a lot. All they wanted in return? Her life.

Was that too much to ask?

Yes!

No matter how much either *vampire* reassured her, she couldn't believe she'd still have a soul or feel like herself if she went through with this.

Talon and Calin had each gained her trust and, as much as she hated to admit it, a piece of her heart. Against her better judgment, she'd cared for them and foolishly thought the choice was between two men she had inappropriate feelings for. She shouldn't have been making the choice so soon after Walker, but she'd considered it. Until she found out it was a lie.

They'd both engineered the situation for their own self-serving motives. She didn't want to think about those motives since both included her death. The ability to come back from one form of death or not didn't matter. The fact remained; she'd be dead with no choice in the matter. That pissed her off royally—pun intended.

Life constantly took her choices from her. At birth, she'd been given away by her birth mother, not that she'd trade her adoptive parents for the world. That was just an example of her lack of choice. She'd had no choice when it came to the loss of her beloved parents. No choice when her best friend Jon died. No choice when she'd lost her grandparents or Walker. Now,

The Fates were ordering her to be queen, a vampire, and lose her brother and her friends...

No more. She would have a choice. Amelia refused to continue being a victim of circumstance. There was only one way to do her parents' memory proud. And in the end, they'd all rest in peace.

"B rother!"

Now what? Calin shut off the shower. He stepped out, grabbed a towel from the rack, and wrapped it around his waist.

Whenever The Holy Terror, sounded this happy it never led to anything good. He dried his body and hair then pulled on a pair of gray sweatpants. Rounding the corner of the bathroom/vanity area, he watched Bianca's bright white smile turn into a frown.

"Really, Calin!" she exclaimed. "I'm going to go blind. Please put a shirt on."

"Nuh-uh." He shook his head. Water droplets flew everywhere. "I changed to adjoining rooms for a reason. Don't like what you see... go to your room."

She sighed dramatically. "What crawled up your bum and died? Here I come bearing gifts for my poor downtrodden brother, and you rain on my parade." She pouted. "I ought to tell Grandfather of your sulky mood. Tell me, Brother, does this funk you're in have anything to do with that wretched descendant?"

Calin regarded his sister through narrow eyes. What did the brat think she knew? Luckily, she and Emilio had been out feeding when Amelia came and ripped into him. Unluckily for him, he hadn't been able to get a hold of her since that night. He'd set up a beautiful candlelit dinner for two on her rooftop and she didn't show. He'd sang to her voicemail repeatedly, but she never called back. He'd even stooped so low as to flirt with her irritatingly perky co-worker, Cicely, to get her to call Amelia. Amelia hadn't answered or been back to work.

She was irrational and ungrateful and pissing him the fuck off.

He'd shared parts of himself with her that he'd never shared with anyone else. The night she callously left him blue-balled, he didn't kill her neighbor, only drained her *close* to death. He was even willing to spare her life and rule *with* her, which meant he'd have to do battle against his own family—for her. Had she appreciated his efforts...?

Nooo...

He'd killed for her, covered a murder for her, and she wouldn't talk to him. She'd thrown his *I love you* back in his face.

To top it all off, his little sister had the nerve to stand there threatening him.

"Brother!" Bianca shouted, stomping her foot, bringing Calin to the here and now.

"What, Bianca?" he roared.

Instinctively, she stepped back.

He knew why, and what she saw: elongated fangs, glowing eyes...

Good. She should be scared; more people should fear him—soon they would. "Speak, Bianca," he ordered impatiently when she stood wide-eyed, stock-still, and quiet. "I assume you came in here for something other than to annoy me."

He knew she was afraid but true to form, she lifted her chin in defiance. Crystal-blue eyes met his glare head-on. "As I said, I brought you gifts." She clapped twice. "Emilio!"

Chapter Thirty-Eight

G reat, the other person I don't want to see.

Smooth and forceful as a gust of wind, Emilio entered and was gone just as fast. The door swung on its hinges behind him. In his wake, two gagged males sat hogtied on the floor. A middle-aged, heavyset, balding black man and an olive-skinned elderly gentleman with ebony hair and a thick mustache. Each wore a white undershirt and red boxers—*weird*. Fear and panic clouded both their dark eyes.

Another burst of wind blew through the room, stirring papers. The door hit the wall hard, nearly splintering it. Emilio entered sight unseen, the only reason Calin knew he'd been, the gagged and bound Asian woman in her early twenties seated near the men. She wore the same outfit as the men, except instead of barefoot, she had on brown cowboy boots.

Bianca tapped her foot restlessly. Looked out the open door. She uttered a sharp, unladylike curse, then murmured, "There'll be a little less in someone's paycheck this week." Louder, she said, "I'll be right back." She stormed out, leaving the door open.

Half curious half infuriated, Calin surveyed the abducted mortals. He crossed his arms over his chest. This, again, wasn't keeping a low profile. Emilio must be suffering from some sort of vampire retardation to let her do this. Not let—help—her do this. Bianca definitely gave the strongest mortal a run for their money, but she was a fledgling. She couldn't subdue these people and carry them on her own.

Emilio, the smug sonofabitch, really wanted to screw up this mission. Little did he know, the mission was fucked the second Calin caught a whiff of Amelia's unique fragrance. But what—

Calin lost his train of thought as Bianca dragged in a squirming, ball-gagged, and bound chubby man with brown crew-cut hair. He wasn't flummoxed because his, easily seventy-pound sister, in a frilly taffeta and satin baby blue dress and black Mary Jane's, almost carried a man triple her size. No, what shut him up was the fact that he knew the man wearing a white button-down, black silk tie, black vest, and black slacks.

This is not *good.*

Bianca beamed so bright and proud she should've been glowing. "Ta-da!" she exclaimed, dumping Matt, Amelia's co-worker, none too gently on the floor next to the Asian woman. "Now, I already told Emilio he can have one. But first pick is yours. I thought since you've been down you deserved some delicious take-out. See, I did something nice—right?"

Her innocent smile almost made him forgive her ignorance... *almost.*

Dealing with his own inner demons—figuratively, not literally—and bullshit, he'd snapped at the little monster. Told her she was selfish and inconsiderate before sending her to feed. Meaning, he was partly to blame for this killing spree—only partly. Emilio would bear the brunt of his wrath.

He raked a hand through his damp hair. "Bianca, what did you do? We talked about this. You can't go serial killing every night just because you're hungry. No one is *this* hungry," he scolded. "These are people who will be missed. Especially, that one." He nodded at Matt. "Remember, I said vagrants and streetwalkers. No people who could be traced back to us."

"But I didn't do this because *I* was hungry, Brother. I've already eaten. This is for you—to make you feel better. I was being considerate."

Yeah, right! As considerate as a freshly sharpened sword to the neck.

"And this one" — she kicked the chubby man in the ribs — "is the same one who laughed at us at the theater. He deserves whatever he gets. Mocking my brother..." She tsked, shaking her head at Matt. "Very naughty of you. Now your life is over. I hope you accomplished everything you wanted to."

The young male trembled and cried, drooling around the red ball in his mouth. Looked to Calin with pleading brown eyes. There was no saving him now. The nicest thing he could do was take his life quickly, spare him Bianca's torture.

"Where's Emilio?" Calin asked gruffly, his disgust undisguised. "I'm sure he wouldn't want to miss feeding time. The bastard."

Walking a slow circle, a vulture circling prey, Bianca gasped. "Calin William Luca, that's not a very nice thing to say. As far as I know, his parents were *bound* at his creation. Mother says a male of proper breeding should never spread slanderous gossip. Why, I told that very same thing to Emilio the other day when he told Uncle Hiram you were in love with the descendant and couldn't be trusted to destroy her. He even tried to get orders for your *immediate destruction.* But I told Uncle Hiram I'd be very put out if that happened. So put out, in fact, that I couldn't be held accountable for my actions."

Bianca bent and grabbed the chin of the olive-skinned man. Shaking it roughly, she cooed, "I sure did say that. Yes, I did...yes, I did." She dropped the man's chin. Blue eyes bored into Calin's, dead serious. "That was considerate of me too, Brother." Then, reverting to her cheery tone, she said, "However, should you fail? I can do nothing for you. Emilio's been ordered to destroy you and the descendant, should you not carry out your orders. On a brighter note, I've brought you food. Chicken" — pointing to the black man — "Italian" — pointing to the other man — "Chinese" — pointing to the Asian woman — "And Croatian" — pointing to Matt. "I've never had Croatian food before. Have you, Brother?"

Calin couldn't speak. Thanks to Bianca's theatrics, he had more to worry about. Icy comprehension ran through his veins. It all made sense now. Uncle Hiram might be a sick SOB, but he wouldn't have his nephew destroyed. His mistress? Yes. His nephew? No. No, that order came from the top. Grandfather Balkan.

Not wanting to lose the respect of his daughter and grand-daughter was the only reason he ordered the hit *after* he'd failed. He'd wanted to get rid of Calin since he found out he hadn't fully turned.

While Emilio may be the *defective* amongst the Cantemirs, Calin was considered the *defective* one in his family. Balkan didn't settle for less than the best. Calin didn't doubt for one minute that this hadn't been the plan all along. With Eliza so close, Balkan couldn't create a valid reason for Calin's destruction. This mission provided the perfect excuse. Either way, Balkan won.

Grandfather more than likely worried that if Calin got the *seal* he'd catch him on a double cross. Of course, that'd been the plan. Maybe the old vampire wasn't as dumb as he looked, walking around in a royal cloak that hadn't rightfully been his in over a thousand years.

Emilio sauntered in, a petite woman with a pillowcase over her head slung over one shoulder. "Hey, buuuddy..." He dragged out the word in his devious, chipper baritone. "Like your surprise?"

Judging by the self-assured gleam in the ex-guardsman's dark-blue eyes, Calin knew he wasn't just talking about the mortals.

"You know, at first, I was all, 'Can we do this?' Get all these mortals together like a sack lunch? I really didn't think we could. It was a tight fit in your car. We had to drive all around... yada, yada, yada. It took a lot of planning. But you see this girl right here." He pointed at Bianca with his thumb. Calin saw red. "She's a miracle worker, a go-getter—a visionary. There really isn't anybody quite like her. There isn't, there *really* isn't," he repeated, with a somber shake of his head.

Bianca, sensing Calin's anger, wisely stepped away from Emilio. "Don't bait my brother, asshole," she barked.

"How cute, she still worships you. If I know anything about siblings—and I think I do." Emilio lifted a dark, thick eyebrow. "Watch out! It'll all go to shit. Soon."

"Why would you help her do this? Our existence gets out and it's bad for all of us. Not just me." Calin glared at the vampire dressed like a BDSM catalog Dom in black leather pants and an untucked, white, silk dress shirt.

Emilio stroked his neatly trimmed goatee. Eyeliner made his white skin look extra pasty. The traitor laughed. "That's where you're wrong. The police find all these mortals drained of blood... they find you." A wicked grin crept across his face. "Don't you still have a heartbeat? That's right, you do. They won't think vampire. They'll think deranged mortal. You'll be the next big thing in mortal news. Bigger than Jeffrey Dahmer, the Unabomber, and Charles Manson."

"You can't set me up. I have more power than you could ever dream," Calin retorted, tone guttural. "You get my sister caught up, and there won't be anywhere on Earth for you to run from me, or my family."

"I never said I was setting you up, Houdini," Emilio said, knowing damn good and well that using the derogatory name used to reduce a true magical witch to a mortal illusionist wouldn't help him relax. "My plans for you are so much bigger." He dropped his cargo to the ground and pulled the pillowcase off her head.

Both he and Bianca gaped.

"Looks like someone we know, right?" Emilio grinned. "Caramel skin." He rubbed her cheek. The girl didn't flinch or acknowledge the touch.

"Red hair." Emilio fisted a handful of said hair, lifted it to his nose, and sniffed. Again, the girl didn't move.

"Nice, full, perky breasts." Emilio palmed one breast, squeezed it roughly.

A growl built deep within Calin's chest. Rose. Tore through his lips and filled the room. What the fuck had this crass bastard done?

The obviously compelled woman wrapped her arms around Emilio's leather-clad thigh. She rubbed her head on his muscular leg.

Wearing hip-hugging blue jeans and a black V-neck, she appeared to be of Native American or Middle Eastern descent. Her skin? Maybe a shade darker than Amelia's. Dyed red hair, not as long as Amelia's, fell just past her shoulders. Though definitely different, Emilio's goal was clear: duplicate of Amelia. From a distance, mortals would mistake her for Amelia.

"So what? Is that your plan? Somebody saw you bring her up here. Now they'll think I kidnapped Amelia, come up and find me with all these... hostages." Calin surmised with an arch glare and deceptive, unperturbed shrug.

His mind was in overdrive, trying to figure out Emilio's MO. If he questioned it before—he hadn't—but if he had, this removed all doubt that Emilio Cantemir was loony as fuck. Yeah, his grandfather's ace in the hole had one too many screws loose and a personal agenda Calin didn't fully understand.

Emilio chortled, a truly joyful sound, further proof of his lunacy. "This is not a movie!" he yelled. "I never did understand why the bad guy rattles off his entire plan. I always thought, 'What if you and your victim survive, bitch?!'" he shouted animatedly. "Then they gotta come up with a new plan. Well, none of that for me, fuck you very much. I'll let you bite your nails in anticipation."

"You can't do anything to me," Calin said with confidence he didn't feel. Emilio was unpredictable, his cage shaken far too many times. "I really don't have time for your cryptic bullshit. I have a lot to do. Take your..." He paused, searching for the word. "Smörgåsbord and get out."

"Ooh, that's right," Emilio crowed, absently rubbing the Amelia look-a-like's temple. "Somebody has a birthday tomorrow. I love parties, don't you? Oh, poo! I didn't RSVP. No matter, I didn't get an invite either." Jumping topic, he pointed to the bound hostages. "As our little sweetie pie mentioned, these are for you. Enjoy. I know I will." His voice dropped sensually low, and he stroked the doppelgänger's chin. "She's gonna provide sustenance on all sorts of levels. Mmm... I won't elaborate. Children are present. And..." He clapped his hands, then picked up his hostage, threw her over his shoulder. "I guess I'll get out of your hair." Moving to leave, he turned back at the last second. Faster than a striking snake, he yanked the Asian woman up and over his other shoulder.

"Hey! That's Calin's," Bianca protested.

"I know. And I'm sorry. But I've had a hankering for Chinese all day," Emilio said to Bianca. Then to Calin, "You let what I said marinate, and I'll see ya tomorrow night at the party. Be there or be square."

A squall of wind blew through the room, slamming the door shut. Left Calin and Bianca alone with the three remaining petrified hostages.

"What a jerk!" Bianca stomped her foot. "I knew I should've gotten an extra Chinese one. Sorry, Brother."

Calin shot his sister a droll stare. Emilio's disclosure took things from fucked up to Armageddon. If he didn't know what to do about Amelia before, he definitely knew now. Even the sight of a poor copy of her with another male made him insane. He could never allow her to be with another. She'd have him or no one.

Decision made, he blinked himself across the room to Matt. Damn, he wished the Asian woman was still here. He loved Chinese! He ran a hand down the plump male's cheek. Matt shivered. Beside him, the moist gushy noise of Bianca's immature fangs breaking through her gums sounded. Seconds later, he heard fangs slice through flesh and claws rend fabric as she feasted on the black man.

His fangs lengthened, filled his mouth, and pricked his tongue with their sharp points. Oh well, tomorrow night would be busy; he needed to power up. He sank his fangs deep into the juicy artery of his mate's co-worker.

Saturday, June 26th

Dear Mom and Dad,

I have no words to describe my feelings. Honestly, I don't know why I'm writing. When that therapist suggested I start this, I thought it was stupid. Now, it's my go-to move. Crazy, right?

Two months and one week ago, I was a silly girl stuck in a grief-stricken, zombie state. My biggest fear was turning twenty-one and being cursed to lose everyone I loved. It hurt to breathe. I counted every step to remind myself to live. And let's face it, I was a bitch. Took everyone for granted. Maybe this, me dying, is me getting my just deserts.

I never considered what anybody else might've been going through. Never asked. I was too busy making everything about me. I lost my way and myself. I forgot to smile like you always told me. Now, it's too late to make it right. Whether I deserve it or not, I'm scared. So scared. I don't want to die. It might've seemed like I did at one time, but I don't. I'll see you soon, or not. I've been pretty self-centered. If not, please know that I love you, always have, always will. And I'm sorry. Sorry for not being better, for blaming you for everything I couldn't do, for hurting everybody.

Forever yours,

Amelia Marie Keeler AKA Dead Inside

I t was time.

Amelia turned, appraising herself from every angle in the long mirror hung on the inside of her closet door. Wine-colored, front-fastening, back-lacing, taffeta corset? Cool. Matching full-length, hand-ruched skirt? Hot like fire. Black, strappy, four-inch Jimmy Choo's... perfect. Hair half up and topped with a diamond-studded tiara—stunning.

Go get 'em, girl! Today's a good day to die.

"Yep, nothing like a way morbid thought to get a girl ready for her birthday party," she said aloud.

Why did I agree to this party again?

To say goodbye?

How exactly did a person say goodbye without saying it? That was the million-dollar question. She'd have to be subtle. Dance with everyone. Thank them for putting up with her bullshit for the last three years.

Staring at her reflection for what seemed to be hours, she listened as Little Richard's "Tutti-Frutti" transformed into the Big Bopper's "Chantilly Lace" then progressed to Marilyn Manson's "Dope Show" to Willy Northpole's "Body Marked Up" to Eminem's "Going Through Changes". Stellar choices. Nobody could accuse her of not having eclectic tastes.

The party had been in full swing for fifteen minutes, but Amelia was forced to "make an entrance." The guest of honor never arrived early or on time to the party, even if it was at her house—Tessa's words, not hers. She continued to stare at her odd image.

Yeah, she knew she was weird-looking with her eerie eyes, brown skin, and red hair. She wasn't the average look for a part black, part white, part whatever else her birth parents were. Her features had been the source of her low self-esteem for years. Then one day, not long ago, she'd decided she didn't care. Being her would have to be enough for the world and if someone had a problem with it... tough.

Of course, that's when boys finally started to notice her. Funny, the things a person took for granted when they thought they had all the time in the world. She'd only barely begun to appreciate what God had given her, and as of tomorrow, she'd be toast—literally.

At least that's what she assumed.

Neither Talon nor Calin elaborated on the "what death would be like" details if she wasn't buried by midnight. And she hadn't asked since she refused to talk to them. She hoped it'd be painless and peaceful. Choosing death did not a masochist make.

A few hours ago, she'd parked her car down the street from her house, next to Montara Park, and walked home. When Evan asked about the Mustang, she lied. Told him it was parked in a neighbor's garage to give the partygoers more parking spaces. Inside her Mustang's glove compartment sat a notarized Last Will and Testament, leaving her possessions to Evan and Tessa. In the trunk, her duffel bag with her favorite black, velour sweat suit and a copy of Wilt Rhys's new paranormal thriller *Astrid Walker*. The yin-yang necklace she now knew Talon gave her so she could walk in the sun was snug in her jewelry box. Here. An hour and a half before midnight, when everyone was nice and drunk, she'd slip out. Drive to her Mesa townhouse and wait on the roof for fate, the dawn, or whatever to find her.

I will not be a monster.

"You ready?" Tessa asked, poking her head in the door.

Amelia's throat tightened at the sight of her best friend. Her best friend. She and Tessa had been through so much. First kisses, mono, broken hearts, funerals... now it was over. Pain so sharp its only rival was actually being stabbed with a rusty spike lanced her heart. To say she'd miss Tessa's brutal honesty, quips, and thoughtless ways would be an understatement of mass proportions.

She cleared the lump in her throat. "Umm... come in for a minute."

Pulling her head out of the crack, Tessa glanced to her right before entering. As usual, she looked fantastic. Her short brunette hair was in pin curls, framing her ivory face. Impeccable make-up made her green eyes pop. Silver-tone studs lined the pockets of vintage black pants. A black leather, midriff-bearing bustier completed the look.

"Is it okay if these *90210* rejects come in, too?" Tessa joked, stepping farther in to give the others room to enter.

Kasey was decked out in a form-hugging, floor-length black halter dress. Evan looked every bit the mobster with his over-gelled hair and black, pin-striped, zoot suit. Dan wore black slacks and a royal-purple, silk dress shirt. Lastly, someone who caused Amelia's eyes to bulge and her jaw to drop entered...

Caushion Rasmussen.

She hadn't seen her favorite cousin since her parents' funeral.

An inch shorter than Amelia, Caushion had the signature Keeler black hair, which fell to the middle of her back. Two strands on either side of her forehead were braided into thin braids. Instead of the Keeler bold blue eyes, hers were metallic gray. A fuchsia corset top, black mini skirt, and knee-high black boots with metal heels were magnificent on her bronze skin.

People who didn't know she was adopted would swear Amelia and Caushion were blood related. But, alas, no such luck. Caushion's dad, Bill Keeler—oh, excuse her, not Bill, Stone, which he legally changed his name to, to "fight the man"—was the wild hippie older brother of Amelia's father David Keeler.

Uncle Stone met Aunt Daphne—one of the most beautiful black women Amelia had ever seen—when they were seventeen. They got married two weeks later and were still going strong. Unfortunately, luck in love wasn't hereditary.

Only four years older than Amelia, Caushion had already had one failed marriage and a string of exes. Amelia couldn't understand why love eluded her cousin. Caushion was one of the sweetest, most genuine, airheaded people you'd ever want to meet. Now she would have to say goodbye to her too. *Greaaaat!*

"Surprise!" Caushion shouted, grinning ear-to-ear and arms open wide.

Plastering on her best fake smile, Amelia stepped into her cousin's waiting arms. "Don't squeeze too hard," she teased, "you'll mess up the effect I'm going for." Caushion released her from the bone-crushing hug. "What're you doing here? I didn't expect to see you until... I don't know—Christmas?"

Frowning, Caushion narrowed sparkling gunmetal eyes. "Miss my best cousin's twenty-first birthday...? *Puh-lease...* Like I'd really miss your first legal drink, especially since I was there for so many illegal ones. Oh! I brought some homemade aromatherapy candles and a free palm reading coupon."

Shaking her head and lifting her eyes heavenward, Tessa clapped her hands together. "Thanks, Caushion, who needs to bother with pesky wrapping paper when you tell people what you got them." She turned her attention to Amelia. "All right! Your theme songs cued, your entourage is here... let's party, beecheeez!"

No sooner than the words left her mouth the intro of Ludacris's "My Chick Bad" sounded. Her theme song. She took a deep breath, which didn't calm her nerves like she'd hoped. Amelia wanted to scream at the top of her lungs, "This isn't fair," but it wouldn't do any good. Months ago, she'd asked for help figuring things out, and this was destiny's twisted answer.

Taking a wistful look at the people she loved most in the world, she geared up to meet her fate. Something occurred to her. "Who cued the music if you're all in here?"

Evan clapped her on the shoulder with a firm hand and spoke in a tone meant only for her. "That would be our big cousin Caushion's new man, Ben." He glanced at her from the corner of his eye, smirking. Winked. "You dig?"

Ah... poor Caushion; another future ex in the making.

"Happy Birthday to you, Happy Birthday to you…" Everyone sang crowded around the island where Amelia stood in front of her three-tiered, white whipped cream-frosted, red velvet cake. Long, skinny, multi-colored candles ringed each tier until there was only one on top.

The night had actually been fun. She'd danced with almost everyone who mattered, and some who didn't. Tigger insisted on cutting in on her dance with Christopher and Cicely. She pretended to be into it for all of a minute before feigning exhaustion. Since then, she'd been ducking and dodging her twacked-out manager while keeping a secret agent eye on him to make sure he didn't steal her shit.

After trying with no success to keep up with him, she delegated the task to Christopher. She would've pushed the responsibility onto Matt, but for some reason, the pervert hadn't shown. When she inquired about him, Gordon, Heidi, and Cicely said they hadn't seen or heard from him.

Luckily, no one caught on to her "sort of goodbyes," shrouded in thanks and appreciation. Although, she hadn't danced with her brother yet. Saying goodbye to him without breaking down or spilling the beans would—

"Make a wish," Ben, her cousin's way too animated boyfriend yelled, interrupting her musings.

Caushion echoed his sentiment, "Yeah! Make a wish!"

I wish not to die. She blew out the candles.

"Alright guys and dolls!" Evan shouted above the clapping crowd. "Kasey, Tessa, cut the cake. I gotta dance with my little sister."

He pulled Amelia to the front room, the makeshift dance area, at the same moment Little Richard's "Lucille" started.

"So, how's my Nugget like her party?"

Amelia fought the tears threatening to strangle her. For as long as she could remember, she'd hated that stupid nickname. Now it was music to her ears. "It's great, fantabillastic. Thank you, for… everything. You're the bestest." She fought to keep her eyes from misting. "Oh, hey, make sure you keep an eye on Tigger and anything you want to keep," she joked half-heartedly.

"Yeah, I got my eagle eye on. That guy's a poster boy for how much meth is too much." Evan chuckled, then sobered. "Sorry this year's been crazy hard for you. I probably haven't been the best brother, but I'll do better. We're all we've got. I love you, Nugget."

Oh, God, what was he trying to do to her? Her stranglehold on her tears was close to slipping. She swallowed convulsively to relieve the thickness his words built in her throat. Glancing at Evan, she memorized his long sideburns, unkempt black hair, eyes as blue as the sky, the tattoos on his neck he tried to cover with his suit collar. This moment...

Keep it together, girlie. To him, these are birthday words, not good-bye.

Amelia took a deep breath. "Evie, you're the best brother. Wings and a halo material—promise."

He spun her away, then back into his arms. Something over her head caught his attention. Evan let out a hearty belly laugh. Gazing down at her, mischief glinted in his eyes. "Promise me something?"

"Name it."

"We'll always be close."

Damn it!

"You got it."

He grinned. "And you'll never hate me?"

"Couldn't if I tried," she vowed, unable to stop her voice from cracking.

"We'll see about that."

In the blink of an eye, he spun her around and right into the arms of...

Ben.

She glared at Evan. Laughing his ass off, he backed away and winked. Speaking of asses, her cousin's—obviously drunk—boyfriend seemed to take her momentary distraction as permission to grab hers. She moved his hands. "Is there any way you could keep your hands to yourself?" she asked, pasting on a smile.

"C'mon," Ben slurred, giving her a wicked whiff of Tequila breath strong enough to clear her sinuses, "make this count. It's supposed to be a birthday dance."

His hands crept to her ass. She jerked them to her waist. "Yeah, birthday dance. *My* birthday dance. Meaning, I should enjoy it. I'm not so much for the birthday feelski."

If it wasn't for the tight apologetic smile her cousin—standing a couple of feet away with Tessa gave her—she would've dropped the jerk with a knee to the junk. But with Caushion's mortified look and mouthing "I'm sorry, he's drunk," she let it go and continued watching her ass. Literally.

"C'mon, Amelia, don't be stingy with the booty. We're gonna be family."

Gawd, she hoped not. She didn't want to imagine the kind of mutants running around his family tree if this was how he thought family acted. Poor Caushion. Sadly, it'd be just like her to marry this dick.

Remorse-laden eyes sought her cousin; said cousin's eyes bulged. Her jaw slackened. Tessa's expression, although a bit annoyed, echoed Caushion's astonishment.

What are they gawking at? A lesser part of her mind wondered. A greater part struggled to keep Ben's hands off her butt—again. It was hard. Actually, he was hard and that was... disgusting.

Before she reprimanded him, he twirled her. She immediately saw what had Tessa and Caushion channeling Edvard Munch's painting *The Scream*. Her body stiffened.

Chapter Thirty-Nine

Talon stood on the fringe of the makeshift dance floor, watching the clearly inebriated, dark-blond-haired, mortal male grind on Amelia. He fidgeted with his ring. Yeah, fidgeted, like a pansy. Spun it round and round on his finger. Amelia would be—

Before he finished the thought, the male spun Amelia. The pointed glare she tossed his way held all the subtlety of a guillotine and confirmed his waylaid musing. She was pissed. Why wouldn't she be? He'd lied to her for months. Told her he loved her but couldn't be with her. Followed her—covertly—through a shopping plaza the other day, and he was crashing her birthday party. Oh, and he mustn't forget the nine thousand voicemails he'd left after she enacted the Great Freeze Out of the twenty-first century.

"Damn, what did you do to Her Royal Hotness?" Gawain asked, elbowing him in the side as he settled beside him. "She's giving you major stink-eye. Want me to listen in? Let you know what's good before she pulverizes you on the spot?"

"No," Talon hastily dissuaded Gawain, "don't. I know what's wrong, and it's a long story. I don't come off great... in it. Watch for the *Daywalker* and Emilio." In a sly reach behind his back, Talon conjured a CD. He shoved it at Gawain. "Give this to whoever's in charge of the music."

Gawain took the burned disc. Eyed it, then him with arch suspicion.

Talon knew his behavior was strange, but he was a desperate male. Not so much because he feared failing this mission—although, he'd be lying if he said it wasn't part of it. Millions of lives, including his and his parents' hung in the balance. However, what mattered more to him: A world where Amelia didn't exist. The idea turned his stomach. She could get through this. Become an amazing immortal. Be queen.

He needed to regain her trust. Fast. Like the next few minutes fast. All his time alone—when he wasn't stalking Amelia—hadn't provided clues on how to accomplish that or how to convince her to go through the *Awakening*. Force wasn't an option. When she rose she'd be bloodthirsty, in bloodlust, and angry. Uncontrollable. Put her reign in jeopardy before it started. No, her cooperation was necessary for things to go smoothly.

Talon hoped this CD helped things along.

Exasperated, he glared at his mentor. "Gawain, I'm lead on this. Do as I ask."

"All right, youngblood, just call me Jeeves." After a mock salute, he strutted away.

Gawain glided through the ocean of well-dressed mortals, oblivious to the lecherous female gazes and male glares. The males puffed their chests, lifted their chins, and wrapped protective arms around their dates. All while unconsciously stepping back from the danger their subconscious recognized that was Gawain.

Senses expanded, Talon scanned for potential threats. He'd be a fool to believe Calin wouldn't make an appearance. As long as he got to Amelia first, explained, and got her to agree, he'd let the imbecile have at the mortals. The song he chose expressed his feelings for her perfectly and...

The guitar intro to the song filled the room. Showtime. This had to work. Confident strides took him to his mate.

Approaching the dancing couple, he took a moment to admire Amelia's beauty. Dressed every bit the queen she was meant to be, she looked radiant. If he had breath, she'd take it. He tapped the mortal on the shoulder. As expected, the man turned and locked eyes with Talon. He scanned the mortal's mind.

"Benjamin," Talon said in a low voice reserved for compulsion, "walk away."

The male complied immediately. He dropped his arms from Amelia's waist and staggered toward the open back door at the rear of the house. Amelia stared after him. Talon used her moment of surprise to wrap one arm around her waist and pull her flush against him. Breasts pressed snugly against his hard chest. She felt good. Right. He took her other hand in his and swayed them in time to Garth Brooks' "Wrapped Up In You".

The scent of cherry blossoms filled his nostrils. Talon's contented smile was met by her narrow-eyed glare.

"Your vampire is showing," Amelia said in a snotty tone. "Kill anyone lately?"

Of course, she'd make things hard for him. "Actually, no." Talon smirked when she blanched at his response. "And what do you mean by my vampire is showing?"

"Let's see, you were across the room a second ago, and you did your fast-moving thing and now you're here. You did that eye-mind thing, too, didn't you?"

"What? Did you want to keep dancing with him?"

"Doesn't matter. It wasn't your decision to make," she said. Then muttered under her breath, "Like so many other things."

"I heard that. And, actually, it was, milady. You'd be surprised by his thoughts." He smirked. "Or maybe you wouldn't. Liquid courage had him ready to broach the topic of a torrid tryst involving you and your cousin."

Amelia took a minute to process that. *Poor... Caushion.*

"I know what you're thinking. You will go through with the *Awakening*. Everything'll be fine," Talon said, mouth at her ear.

Amelia hid her shiver, prayed he didn't hear her heart stutter. Why did his ridiculous thunder-rolling voice and forest-in-winter scent have such a profound effect on her? She wanted to hate him; part of her did. Another part settled at his nearness as if she'd missed him. Stupid, girly emotions. "You're dead. What do you know?"

"I'm not dead," he grumbled.

Meeting his gaze, she said in earnest, "I will be. That's what you're not getting. I will be. I'm human. Born mortal. You're asking me to *die*. That's a lot to ask."

They stared at each other, at an impasse. Talon continued moving them to the beat of the country song. She averted her eyes when what she hoped was sympathy flashed in his deep blues. After a moment, Amelia murmured, "I don't want to be a predator. You know I'm a vegetarian."

"I'm not a predator," he bit out between clenched teeth.

"Yes, you are. You hang out in the world, in hot guy camouflage, while people are completely unaware that they're your main course. I don't want to be a monster, hunting friends, neighbors, or... any person. You're a wolf in..." She paused, looking over his maroon dress shirt and black slacks, pretending not to notice how they hugged his lean muscles. Muscles she'd touched, knew intimately. "Calvin Klein's clothing."

He snickered. "It's not that bad, or that way."

"Yes, it is," her voice rose. Talon's jaw clenched. She lowered her tone. "It's like having a close gay friend that you didn't know was attracted to you stick his finger up your butt when you bend over in the locker room."

Talon balked. His upper lip curled. "Thanks for that image."

Who was she kidding? Amelia knew, on some level, he'd show up. The perpetual, dutiful bodyguard always did his job and no less. His being here would make escape difficult but not impossible. One last adventure wouldn't—never mind. One last adventure *would* kill her. Better to go down swinging.

She needed to think of something else before the eavesdropper tapped into her thoughts. Her cousin's raspy voice provided the perfect distraction. Amelia shouldn't have been able to hear Caushion and Tessa's already-in-progress convo. Especially, not over the music and distance. Just another weird vampy symptom: Super hearing. Great!

"He looks like that guy from all the fast angry car movies," Caushion said.

Brows knitted, Tessa's expression turned pensive. "Fast angry car movies?" she wondered aloud with a frown. Seconds passed.

Laughter burst from her lips, "You mean *Fast and the Furious?* Vin Diesel?"

Caushion waved the question away. "No! I know who that is. He's in that one movie—*Really Dark?*"

Impossibly, Tessa's brown brows pulled tighter in consternation. "What? There's no movie called *Really Dark?*" After a moment understanding lit her best friend's green eyes. She laughed so hard tears filled her eyes. Between breaths, she said, "You mean Pitch Black?" Tessa snatched the red plastic cup from Caushion's hand. "How much have you had to drink?" Scowling into the cup, she said, "You're cut off."

Caushion shrugged, unfazed. "Whatever. Not him. I meant the blond guy with nice teeth. Did you see the friend he came in with? Hello, Colin Farrell. If I wasn't in love with Ben..."

Amelia snorted. *Poor, poor, innocent Caushion.*

"Sorry."

Talon's rumbling voice brought her back to their dance. "What?"

"I'm sorry. I shouldn't have said what I said that night."

Oh, this was rich! "How sweet, just what every girl wants. A guy to say I love you then take it back." In mock delight, she exclaimed, "I'm such a lucky gal."

"I'm not taking it back, milady. What I meant is I'm sorry for saying it. Knowing I couldn't have you, I shouldn't have said it."

Wow! Did he think that helped? He really didn't spend much time with mortals, or women. Moron! Cutting her eyes, she asked, "Wanna know something else you shouldn't have done?" Then infusing her words with venom, she answered her own question, "Come here."

No sooner than the words left her mouth, Talon's body jerked as if shocked. Her gaze shot to his face. He looked anguished. His hands tightened painfully on her hand and waist before being torn away. As if they'd been pried apart by a crowbar. Talon's body was yanked away like someone was pushing him. His booted heels dug into the carpet. It did no good. He was pushed through the throng of startled partygoers. Bumped into those not quick enough to get out of the way. Then he was shoved back, back, and farther back. Talon hit the wall beside the fireplace in the living room. He stuck as if pinned there.

The music changed.

She recognized the artist and the lyrics, Prince's "Seven." With a sharp gasp, Amelia spun around...

And froze.

Calin gazed into his Amelia's big eyes. Beautiful. For the first time, she was dressed as a princess should be. With a diamond tiara to boot. *Fitting.* Her wine-colored dress accented the golden undertones of her skin to perfection.

The constant pain he'd been in for the last week slithered from his body. Replaced by an eerie peace, calm. The look in Amelia's peculiar eyes was anything but.

Fear shone in the gold, light-brown, and emerald depths. Fates! They'd be gorgeous all aglow. The night he'd cleaned the Walker mess, he hadn't seen them in their full blazing glory. And he never would.

He didn't have much time, but he would have this dance. Who cared what these mortals thought of him now? They'd be dead by night's end. Fisting his right hand, he used his abilities to drag Amelia to him. When her soft body collided with him, he wrapped one arm around her waist. Snatched her other in his left.

She lowered her eyes.

That wouldn't do. He wanted to spend every moment they had left looking into her eyes. Placing his index finger under her chin, he tilted her head. Forced her to look at him and close her open mouth.

"Why so scared, Duchess? You invited me, remember?" He smirked. "This is our song."

Amelia swallowed hard, recovering some of her bravado. "I thought my visit to your hotel and subsequent freeze out served as a disinvite."

He tsked. "It takes more than that to get rid of me, *ma douce.*"

"I wish I had a stake," she muttered. "Do you have to hold me so close? I can feel your... er... essence." She gazed down between their bodies then up again quickly.

He bet she could. His cock was rock hard from being so close to her. What would it feel like buried deep inside her? Probably, tight, warm... Dammit! No time.

"Hush... Don't be mean," Calin admonished playfully. "You know you like it. Anyway, I can't let you go—ever."

Her eyes glistened with unshed tears.

Shit! I'm fuckin' up. This was why he didn't do feelings. How could he explain what he felt without scaring her? She was everything he wasn't. The light in his dark existence. She put everyone's needs before hers when what she wanted to do was lay down and die. He knew because he felt her emotions as clearly as if they were his own. That's what the *Centripetal Impulse* did to *eternalmates*.

Amelia was pure. He would never be pure, good. But when he held her, he felt like he could be, do, anything. Anything, except lose her. "Stop being afraid," he commanded harsher than intended. She flinched. In a gentler tone, he revised, "Please, don't be afraid of me."

"Oh, okay," she said dryly. "Stop saying weird, scary stuff."

"Amelia, dammit!" he growled.

Her grin was sardonic. "No, the last name's Keeler, actually. But you're close. I do feel damned."

Damn, she wouldn't give him any slack. She didn't want to hear him—

"Ow!"

Fuck! He loosened his grip on her. Using his ability to hold her and Talon and control the music, which he restarted with a thought, was draining.

He stepped back with his right foot. Amelia stepped forward with her left. "Do you think I'll let you just ride off into the moonlight with Talon?" Calin ground out, stepping to the side. Repeating his step forward, he forced her to step back.

"I told you I didn't want anything to do with either of you," Amelia said through clenched teeth, stepping back with her right foot when he stepped forward again. She crossed her left foot over her right.

Feet together. "I told you I loved you," he countered, taking an aggressive step forward.

"I told you I don't care," she said. Forced to mirror his steps, she added haughty disdain to each move.

Stepping to the side, he ran his flattened hand up and down her spine. He drew lazy circles with a finger on her lower back. Calin slapped her ass. Hard. Rejoiced in her answering yelp. "Oh, but you should."

"And why is that?"

Bet she didn't know she could Tango. Just one of the many things he wished to explore further with her—naked—if there were more time. Midnight was an hour away.

"Because," he replied, hating the challenge in her tone. He squeezed her tighter. "I'll love you to death. Real. Death."

Chapter Forty

Amelia couldn't speak. Couldn't breathe. She stared blank-faced and open-mouthed at Calin. He continued to move them in what she suspected was a Tango. He mouthed the words to the song as if he hadn't just threatened her life.

Could eyeballs fall out of their sockets? Hers felt like they might. Was he serious? Would he kill her? He'd said he loved her, but following those words with a death threat didn't instill faith. Her body's unholy response to him also didn't inspire faith that if he did try to kill her she wouldn't roll over and submit to his will.

In a black blazer over a black dress shirt with the first two buttons undone tucked into black jeans, he was yummy. He smelled of autumn. Dark spice like the kind in pumpkin pie, and crisp, starry, fall nights. She inhaled deeply. For some insane reason, she'd missed it, him. Scary comments, inappropriate gestures, and all.

Where is Talon?

Gazing to the side, past Calin's thick, muscled arm, she intended to look for him. Then she caught sight of her friends. They watched her with a mix of horror and extreme interest. At that precise moment, she realized two things: While she'd been lost in her heated exchange with Calin, most everyone had gathered around them. Close, but not too close. Two, Calin wasn't lip-syncing anymore, but giving her a concert for one in his angelic voice.

He released her right hand. With the hand he'd been holding hers with; he made a gun with his index, middle finger, and thumb.

Amelia observed his actions through narrow, curious eyes. What the heck? She didn't wonder long. Calin positioned them so Kasey, Evan, Cicely, and Christopher were in her line of vision.

Singing of eliminating those who stood in the way of love, he jerked his finger gun as if shooting.

Each person flew across the room as if shot. Her eyes widened in utter horror. Anyone unable to avoid the projectile bodies was knocked to the floor like a bowling pin. Kasey, Evan, Cicely, and Christopher landed out of her sight. She struggled to break free of Calin's hold. The arm around her waist tightened, squeezed. Made breathing difficult.

He crooned about ownership. She was his. He was hers. All-encompassing love. Her head spun from oxygen deprivation as he shifted them toward the stunned faces of Tessa, Dan, and Caushion.

Tears stung her eyes, blurring her vision. Anticipation churned in her stomach. Like her, everyone seemed to suffer from fear-induced laryngitis. No matter. Screaming wouldn't help anyway. Calin's power was... immense. Greater than she'd initially thought. No one could stop him. As he and Prince sang, she prayed her friends would be all right.

Calin grinned and shot his imaginary gun.

Tessa, Dan, and Caushion were hurled across the room like so much trash. Partygoers crashed to the ground. Her friends' bodies crumpled. Amelia's heart raced. Her palms dewed. The implied threat wasn't lost on her. She tugged against Calin's crushing hold. She might as well have been yanking at iron shackles for all the good it did. Calin didn't seem fazed at all. In fact, he drew her impossibly closer.

"Shh... They're fine," he whispered.

She shouldn't believe him. After all, he was the guy who—for all intents and purposes—just assassinated seven of her loved ones. However, she trusted him—in this. It was that or stroke out. That couldn't happen right now. She needed a clear head to get through tonight, no matter the outcome.

"What did you do?" she asked voice tight.

"Just a little hocus-pocus," he said, wiggling the fingers on her back. "They'll stay fine as long as you don't try to leave me. We belong together."

A high-pitched, eardrum-shattering scream rent the air. Halted her snide retort.

Every head turned. Searched for the screamer and the cause. Calin's focus split. The music stopped. His grip loosened.

Well, she wouldn't look a gift horse in the mouth. Taking advantage of Calin's distraction, she extricated herself from his arms. She ignored the accompanying pang of loss. Another wicked scream ripped through the house. Thinking it might refocus him, Amelia jumped out of his reach. At that exact moment, a gust of wind blew past her. No, not wind. It, or he, moved so fast he hadn't been a blur. If not for the tail end of the navy-blue dress shirt and black hair, she wouldn't have recognized it as a person. Correction—not a person. A monster.

Talon's friend Gawain.

He rushed Calin. Came at him low and fast. Calin caught air as he was knocked off his feet. Gawain slammed him into the floor hard enough to crack the house's foundation. It'd surprise her if there wasn't a perfect indent of his head and shoulders in Calin's abdomen. Pain sliced through her heart. Sheesh! What would it take to convince her stupid heart to get over this sick infatuation? Her stupid ass was actually worried about him. Wanted to go and make sure he wasn't hurt. *Kill me now!*

Gosh, she was so stupid. Thinking Gawain was human? Apparently, all monsters were ridiculously attractive. How many gorgeous people were really monsters in disguise?

Why, oh, why did she ask that? Just the thought invited trouble. Literally. Amelia's breath hitched. The shit hit the fan.

Everything felt like someone pressed the fast-forward button and forgot to hit stop. Things changed rapidly. Yet, no moment was less important than the other. If you blinked, you would've missed something crucial.

Her tiny house became inundated with... things? Or did they prefer to be called supernatural? Whatever they were, there were a lot of them. They wore different-colored cloaks. Some were black, brown, charcoal gray, reversible maroon, and black.

Amelia didn't know how she *knew*, but she knew they weren't human. Okay, if she were being shallow, or honest, she'd admit these things were otherworldly attractive also. At least, the ones whose faces she saw were. By their broad shoulders, height, and wider frames, it appeared most were men.

What was the Woody Allen saying her mom used to quote? "If you want to make God laugh, tell him about your plans." He must be rollin' right now because her plans just went to shit. The craziest thing was, that while everything seemed to be going at hyper-speed, she moved in slow motion. Instead of being an actual participant, she felt as if she were a spectator. And no mistake about it, she was a participant. The catalyst.

Utter chaos reigned in her home. This place, which was all she had left of her parents, was overrun by things that bite in the night. Glowing eyes and fangs were everywhere. Screams and shouts pinged off the walls, filled the house. The number of supernatural versus humans was neck and neck. People tried to run and failed. Not for lack of effort, but because they were packed into her small house. Successful escape seemed impossible unless someone got brave and threw themselves through a window or something.

Every so often a loud *crack*, *bang*, or both in concert, reached her. She would've covered her ears if she wasn't paralyzed with fear. Bones were broken, crushed as people were trampled. Bodies hit walls.

Amelia scanned the area for her brother and friends. Then something occurred to her; she was a danger to them. The best thing was not to find them. They'd be better off on their own—she hoped.

Something hard slammed into her calf. The strength of the hit and height of her heels made her ankle bow. She teetered but managed to stay upright. Casting her gaze downward, she found a cap of greasy chestnut hair. Blood splotched what had been a salmon-colored button-down. Twin puncture wounds on the side of his neck trickled blood. The sweet-sour, copper scent tickled her nose. Did strange, disgusting, things to her. Damn vampire symptoms. Good thing Tigger appeared to be unconscious. Seems her unholy appetite abhorred easy pickings.

Shattering glass had her jerking her head up. Hooded things sliced through her guests like cream cheese. The sight brought an odd thought to mind. Talon and Calin said the Fang Squad needed a formal invitation from a human to enter a private domicile. Who would've invited these freaks into her house by name? Hmm...

A tall figure wearing a gold cloak entered her line of vision. Weird. His cloak reminded her of Talon's curtains. It's—and she referred to it as such because she couldn't see its face—hood was down. Wavy black hair reached the tops of its shoulders. Maybe it was a girl.

"Find the princess, now!" he, she concluded from the rich, unfamiliar accent, shouted.

Obviously some, if not all, the "things" were with him.

"I don't care what you do or who you kill. Plow through these mortals and find the princess," another accented man's voice growled from somewhere behind her.

Wait. Two things occurred to her simultaneously. First, the last accent sounded a lot like Talon's, but thicker and a bit higher. Given how deep Talon's rumble, tumble voice was the other was still crazy deep. Second—

I'm the princess.

Clearly, these things didn't know what she looked like, or she would've been spotted long ago. Standing in the middle of the room did not a perfect hiding spot make. Time to get the...

As if aware of her desire to flee, the gold-cloaked man turned. A strong, pale, angular face pointed in her direction. With his perfect aristocratic nose, the man defined masculine beauty. Their gazes met, held. His eyes were arresting. The right iris was honey-brown. The left, emerald-green. Amelia was so taken aback, she couldn't move.

"OMG!" shouted the bearer of the other accented voice. She hadn't noticed before, but the voice had an effeminate cadence. "Hello... She's right there!"

Something black moved in her peripheral. Amelia swiveled around to catch sight of the burly black-cloaked... thing... charging toward her. It wasn't a biting thing—well, okay, it had razor-sharp teeth, but it wasn't a vampire. Bushy, white-blond brows rested over feral onyx eyes. No glow. Oh, Gawd... she was going to disgrace herself right here if it got any closer.

"Where the hell did a bear shifter come from?" Calin shouted, literally appearing in front of her out of nowhere. "Stop!"

"Call them off, Emilio!" Talon bellowed from somewhere. She wasn't even tempted to look to see where he was. Not with Calin being the only barrier between her and a person-bear thing. Neither ranked high on her trust list.

Time to get the fuck out of Dodge.

With the bear-guy roaring, or whatever the sound was he made. No one was focused on her. Amelia hiked her skirt to knee level and...

Hauled ass.

For whatever reason, the front door was wide open. She dodged a few groping hands and ran outside. Although inside there was a literal war being fought, outside the night was quiet. Too quiet. Somehow none of the noise filtered outside, even with the door open. Crazy.

No time to ponder that issue. Amelia scurried down the walkway, ran to the corner. At the end of the street, she searched right, left. No cars. No people. No help. The compulsion to stop, check on her friends, was fierce. It almost won. But her protective instincts beat at her. Demanded she do the right thing. This would draw the bad things away. She needed to get to her car. Amelia ran.

She shouldn't have waited to leave. If anyone died tonight, it'd be her fault. Her feet fought the confines of her shoes. In the short work of a minute, she had them off and thrown. One stiletto embedded in a chain link fence, the other... she didn't care. For once it didn't matter.

The park felt a lot farther away than she remembered. She panted. Her heart raced. Her body shook, yet somehow felt numb, too. She'd never run this fast in her life. Her calves screamed in outrage each time her feet slapped the harsh pavement.

Another mile, and she'd be to her car, to relative safety. She loved scary movies, especially the ones that made Tessa yell at the screen, "Run, bitch, run!" Only this wasn't a movie. It was real, and she ran. Propelled herself so hard her chest hurt, and tears sliced her cheeks painfully before being whipped away. This couldn't be happening.

I'm a real person, dammit! Human!

If ever the question, "Can a soul cry?" was posed, Amelia knew the answer. Yes. Hers was. Not only crying, but screaming. Screamed for the absurdity, the unfairness, and because... someone was following her.

Lungs stinging, thighs burning, she hooked a left onto Desert Cove Avenue then a right on 64th Lane. At the far end of the curvy sidewalk, which bordered the large, lush green park, her Mustang waited. Her heart did a flip. Almost home-free, sort of. All she needed was to get there before whoever caught up to her. Something told her that's exactly what the person or thing wanted her to think. That she was getting away.

Well, she wouldn't be the stupid girl from the movies. Locking herself into a small space, becoming an easy kill. Umm... no thanks. Faking a left, like she would get into the driver's side of the Mustang, she switched at the last minute. Sprinted right, into the park. The wet grass felt wonderful against her battered feet.

Unfortunately, it made for a slippery get-a-way.

This area of the park had small hills and large trees big enough to hide behind. Ahead, a short, wrought iron fence. On the other side, the main road then a shopping plaza. Nothing was open. If she made it there, she could hop the fence. Supernatural were big on secrecy. If she got to the street, she'd be in plain sight. Whatever monster hunted her would have to—

Two large feet struck the middle of her spine.

Omph! Ow!

She face-planted in moist earth. Mud and grass dove into her nose, eyes, and mouth. Not giving her time to recover, her assailant rib-checked her with...

A boot.

The thing definitely had on boots. Steel toe, if the loud ping of what sounded like metal against bone meant anything. She hadn't realized how flimsy skin was. Shifting to the left, she attempted to shield her good side. It didn't help. A stomp to the already injured side cracked and broke ribs. Amelia coughed, wheezed. Excruciating pain tore through her side. She rolled onto her stomach.

Relying on an inner strength that surprised her, she wrapped an arm around her middle to hold her ribs together. With her other arm, she dragged herself away from the booted lunatic. Her attacker took this advantage to land several well-placed kicks to her spine. One connected with the back of the head. Her vision blurred. Her stomach roiled. Another well-timed blow broke the ribs on her right side. Jagged-edged bones threatened to puncture lung tissue. Amelia groaned. Hurt like a bitch! But she wouldn't surrender. One last, forceful kick catapulted her into the air. Images of the sharp-tipped, black wrought iron fence danced in her mind.

Lord, don't let me land there.

She landed. Immeasurable terror surged through her. She'd take a beating, impalement, anything over this. Amelia lay in a taphephobic nightmare. An open grave.

Chapter Forty-One

T alon ran at top speed. His strength seeped through his fingers, encumbering his progress. If his heart beat, it would be pounding. To passersby, he wouldn't even be a breeze. Not that he worried about discovery. The neighborhood was dead—no pun intended. Any mortals that would be out were at Amelia's, being compelled by Gawain and four other guardsmen, Roderick, Stefan, Adrastos, and Massimo. That, in and of itself, presented another problem.

The appearance of the four VRG was miraculous given that he hadn't requested backup and they'd been thought to be destroyed for over a thousand years. He'd worry about them later. Gawain vouched for them; if they weren't on the—

Shit!

He hurt.

Jaw clenched; he lifted the hand pressed to his chest. He glanced down. Tried, unsuccessfully, to stifle a groan. Pain gripped him as air rushed through the gaping hole scant millimeters from his heart. Whoever took the shot was stupid, but good.

Silver bullets killed werewolves, paralyzed shifters, and did substantial damage to vampires when left inside the body. This shot went clean through. Left a fist-size cavity in the hollow-point bullet's wake. Under normal circumstances, the tissue, muscle, and bone would've mended in seconds. With the power it took to protect the mortals, and move at preternatural speed, he was drained. Talon fought his body's natural response to *flatline* after severe injury. He struggled to remain conscious. He had to find Amelia.

With his waning strength, he worked to stretch his senses. Tried to catch even the barest scent of Amelia's cherry blossom fragrance while racing down the dark streets.

It didn't take a genius to deduce Emilio masterminded the attack that turned Amelia's birthday party into a gruesome massacre. What confounded him was why Calin went along with it. Calin had kept a low profile, until now. Why the change? The sudden devil-may-care attitude? Didn't seem his style.

Ugh! Massacres...

Blood splattered every available inch of Amelia's home. He didn't want to consider how long it'd take to conceal the scene. They'd have to trance everyone living there while they cleaned the house. There were several casualties. Luckily, none of the more serious were Amelia's family or close friends. He'd checked before leaving. When he found her, she'd want to know. And he would. Find her.

The alternative wasn't an option. If he reached Amelia late? Or worse, if she were murdered...? Talon wouldn't accept those outcomes. He'd walk himself into the sun if either happened. His passionate reaction would have nothing to do with failing the supernatural or his parents, but everything to do with falling for Amelia.

Why through tragedy was there always clarity?

Fuck the rules, or whether or not what he felt was forbidden. Fuck his parents; they should've destroyed Emilio—the dick—in puberty, and fuck the consequences. Talon loved and wanted—no, needed, Amelia. Wait!

Talon's nostrils flared.

Cherry blossoms. Faint, but there. Thank The Fates!

Expanding his senses, he nearly lost consciousness from exhaustion. He staggered but pressed on. Followed her scent left on Desert Cove. Right on 64th Lane. The scent trail ended. Not tapered off, but disappeared. As if it'd never been. He stopped.

Contemporary homes surrounded him on the left. It was too quiet. The neighborhood was darker than it should be. On his right, the sidewalk curved, extended five acres. Bordered a park. Eucalyptus and ash trees filled the lush green expanse. Cottonwoods encompassed the racquetball courts at the far end of the park. Shattered glass covered the basketball court where light should've illuminated it.

This shit was planned. Someone was toying with him. Had he not been unconscious from the shot for those precious seconds he would've gotten to her in—

A royal-blue Mustang parked near the far curb caught his eye. Putting on a burst of preternatural speed, he approached the vehicle. Amelia's car.

He suspected she'd try to outrun destiny. That's why he'd sublimated into fog and stole her necklace from her jewelry box two days ago. Stubborn Amelia seemed to be quite the strategist. Where had she planned to go? Wherever it was, she hadn't made it. The hood of the car was cold, but she'd come here. Difficult Amelia wouldn't detour from her plans.

Gazing at his wrist, he manifested a watch. A quarter past. He was too late. It'd taken too long to track her scent. He—

Saw a colorful—stone?—holding up a folded piece of white paper several yards away. In a secluded corner among a copse of tall pine trees, a freshly compacted mound of dirt. The stale stench of wet, disturbed earth drifted to him. A nanosecond later, Talon stood on top of the grave. He read the note.

My Sweetest Duchess,

Happy Deathday! Didn't I tell you I'd love you to death? You'll do well to remember I always keep my word. I know you're angry, but in time, you'll see this was for your own good. Loving someone means sometimes making hard decisions. I made this one for you. If you're reading this, then you've risen well and whole. I wish I could be there to welcome you to the first day of eternity. But, alas, I had to run. Had to keep moving. I'm a hunted male now after all. Shit explanation in a note is lame, I know. Don't worry. We'll see each other again, soon. I'll explain things better then. Thanks for the dance, Sweetest. I love you.

Your eternalmate,

Caitlyn

Her *eternalmate*? Impossible. *He* was her mate, not Calin. Talon resisted the urge to rip the note. Set it and the carved wax figure he discovered beside him, where he sat on the unmarked grave.

Time marched on.

He checked his watch. Three-thirty! Three and a half hours since midnight. The *Awakening* was a three-hour process. It hadn't worked. She would not rise. As much as he wanted to blame the vile *Daywalker*, he couldn't. Not entirely anyway.

At that moment, he blamed himself. He was a natural skeptic. How did a slight, mortal female with unusual eyes provide such a thorough distraction from him? Maybe he'd been wrong about a mortal being incapable of descending from vampires. *Dhampires*, while rare, weren't abnormal; it happened. In all his musings, Talon hadn't considered that the transition part of the prophecy could be wrong. To be honest, the transition wasn't prophesied. *White-witch Advisors* recommended it.

It'd been done to Queen Ana-Marie and her family after Balkan fell out of favor with The Fates. It was how The Fates activated the Radulescus'—their family name before Ana-Marie became queen—dormant seals. White-witches figured it'd work the same. They were wrong.

Amelia wouldn't rise. Maybe all *Dhampires* experienced un-predictable power surges the way she had. He'd never met a *Dhampire*. What if she had needed to be bitten? What had he done?

Talon slammed the heel of his boot into the soggy grass. He'd been good. Done his duty, accepted his fate without much complaint. He'd never asked for anything. Never been selfish. Until now.

Forbidden or not, she was his mate. He wanted her. Refused to give her up. In this, he would be selfish. Or would have if it wasn't too—

The earth underneath him rolled. He jumped to his feet. Dirt trembled. Quaked. Bucked. Talon stumbled forward off the grave seconds before it erupted. A large mass was expelled into the sky like a bottle rocket. Smoke and a wail followed the object. Shimmering gold mist swirled midair. Whirled like a cyclone, hovered inches above the open grave. For long moments, it spun, then slowed, condensed. Solidified.

A metallic gold cloak materialized first. Hung suspended in the air. Then, piece by piece, all that frustrated and intrigued him most formed underneath. Dainty feet adorned with black strappy heels. Toned brown legs. Talon grinned at the delectable petite frame with slight curves, wearing a clingy, cream-colored, satin camisole dress. Her long, graceful neck and red-painted, pouty lips begged for his kisses. Adorable button nose. Plum-tinted cheeks hardened him, and furious glowing eyes held murder in their depths.

"Why did you do this to me?!" Amelia shouted. She'd throttle the stupid SOB once she figured out how to get down from here. "You knew I didn't want this! You knew what happened to Walker, didn't you? Didn't you!"

Talk about an unhappy trip down repressed memory lane. While every bone in her body shattered like the fuzzy channel on TV and reshaped, she had been gifted with a warped version of *This Is Your Life*. Conscious, immobilized, feeling as if she were being shocked repeatedly with a defibrillator, she'd watched memories play behind her closed eyelids. She saw herself stalk Tessa. Relived her teeth tearing into Walker's neck. Felt his skin and bones give way under her stronghold. Witnessed fear swamp his expressive brown eyes...

"I suspected. I wasn't—"

"Oh, no! I know *who* was there." Damn, these fangs cut the shit out of her tongue. Hard to sound intimidating with a lisp. "And I know you did this! Admit it!"

"I won't lie," Talon said between gritted teeth. He staggered forward. White lines of strain bracketed his mouth. His hand rested awkwardly on his chest like he was about to pledge allegiance to the flag. "I wanted this for you, for me. For the supernatural. But not this way. You think I would've taken your choice? I may not have liked it, but it was yours to make."

She snorted unladylike. "Yeah, right! And I was born yesterday. Oh, wait! I guess technically I was, wasn't I?" Her fangs retracted of their own accord, punctuating her question.

"Listen, everything in my existence was chosen for me." He moved closer. "I was meant to serve you, born to help usher in the new queen and peace. Reared to believe nothing else mattered. No one ever asked what I wanted. My choices were taken before I formed opinions and desires of my own. How could you think I'd do this? I'm the last male on Earth and beyond who would do this." Talon extended what appeared to be a piece of paper wrapped around a rock to her. Written across the top in black ink: *Duchess*.

As if the desire to retrieve the object caused it, she drifted like a feather in the wind. Her feet touched the ground. She reached with her left hand. The cloak—which she had no idea where it or the new clothes came from—slid away from her arm. It provided her the first glimpse of her pale brown skin and the raised flesh on the inside of her wrist.

A tilde. Her *seal*.

She snatched the paper-covered rock from Talon's hand. Stiff, hesitant fingers unwrapped it. Orange wax face. Large, googly, white wax eyes, wide open mouth, thick black brows. Fuchsia and orange whiskers and fur. Big red nose. It wasn't a rock. It was Animal. Calin's wax figurine. She read the note.

Thick liquid filled her eyes, tinting her vision red. Why? Her hands shook. The paper disappeared.

She looked up at Talon, who, in her devastation, had moved. He stood in front of her. His jaw tight, harsh eyes aglow, he stuffed the paper in his back pocket. "Put that in your pocket and get behind me," he demanded in an urgent, guttural tone. "Someone's coming. You need to pronounce me as your chief guardsman so I can fully protect you—now!"

"Uh... pronounce you?" she asked, slipping the figurine into her cloak pocket.

Apparently, not moving fast enough for his liking, he shoved her behind him. He gave her his back. "You have all the knowledge you're going to need to rule. Think fast and pronounce me now! Unless you still want to die?"

Good point. She may have been on board with that plan earlier, but now that the deed was done...? Dying didn't hold the same appeal.

Pushing past her fear, she concentrated hard. Flashes of faces, names, and locations spun in her head. Made her dizzy. From among the chaos came words, ancient words. Not big on old-school, she paraphrased. "I name you, Talon Ezekiel Cantemir, my champion. My guard. I grant you authority to make decisions regarding my safety and to appoint others to protect me and mine. You are my chief guardsman. It is your duty, honor, and responsibility to put my existence above all else. So shall it be."

No sooner than the words passed through her lips, a crackle called her attention forward. That's also when she saw it. A hole. A hollow hole in Talon's chest, near his heart. Her stomach lurched.

From behind the tree in front of them stepped...

The man from her house? The one in the gold cloak.

Talon's back went ramrod straight. He dropped to the ground, knelt on one knee, and bowed his head, leaving her unshielded.

Some good the whole pronouncement did. Jackass.

"Prince Nico, My Liege," Talon uttered reverently.

From this distance, the man's features were even more beautiful. Not feminine, but strong and rugged. Coal-black hair hung in waves to the top of his shoulders. He wore black leather pants, boots, and an untucked, black button-down under his cloak. Long, inky lashes rimmed foreign eyes, yet they were familiar on some level and were fixed... on her. A fanged grin spread across the face of the man who, by all accounts, shouldn't exist.

"I know. That is a long story. I shall explain when there is more time. For now, I content myself with the privilege to gaze upon you. *I anipsiá mou, engoní mou, tin kardiá mou*, I have waited... a millennium to make your acquaintance."

Impressive, since she'd only been alive for the last twenty-one years. And what had he called her? Given the warmth in his mismatched eyes, it was sweet, but she had no idea what it meant or what language it was.

The man chuckled. "Forgive me, it's Greek. My native tongue. I called you my niece, my granddaughter, and my heart."

Weird, considering he looked to be her age, and a bit disturbing.

He laughed again. "Wit. So much like my mother—your great-grandmother. In *Raj*, she smiles proud. I've wished for you for so long."

"You're Prince Nico?" she asked, shocked her voice worked. "I guess you read minds, too. Should I... bow, too, or... curtsy?"

Prince Nico shook his head. "Please, call me *Pappoús*, or Grandfather, as they say in English. No. You do not bow to me. I relinquished that right. Forgive me. I bow to you." He sank to one knee, assuming the same position Talon remained in. Then he regained his feet.

"Why do the supernatural need me if—"

Prince Nico shook his head—yeah, she was so not calling him grandfather. "No. This isn't the time for that discussion. As your guard will inform you, there is much to be done. I must go. But, first..." He reached behind the tree nearest him. Came back with a white-haired, wide-eyed, elderly woman wearing a loud, floral nightgown. He held her by the arm, suspended a couple feet off the ground as if she weighed nothing.

Tears dripped from the woman's dull brown eyes. Her beet-red nose ran. Gazing between them all, she trembled, muttered repeatedly, "This is only a dream. Only a dream. Wake up, Cheryl." Her gaze collided with Amelia's. "Please, I have a family. Don't let them hurt me. Please, please, please."

Amelia's heart broke for the woman, thank God. She'd worried about waking up a mindless, bloodthirsty monster. Shockingly, she still felt human, and just as confused as Cheryl.

"The *Awakening* is not complete, *mou látreve éna*." My adored one. Prince Nico's heavily accented voice whispered in her mind, supplying the translation. How thoughtful. Not! Creepy, was more like it. "You need to feed. Do not drain her, but take her to the precipice of death. It's ritual." He trailed a sharpened nail down the column of Cheryl's throat. Red beads of the most wonderful sweet-sour, coppery—

Her eyes widened. Amelia slapped a hand over her mouth. What in the hell was she thinking? Blood smelled? Not just smelled, but smelled good. Fresh-baked chocolate chip cookies warm from the oven, fantastic. Running her tongue across her top and bottom teeth, she started. Fangs. Sharper than Kasumi knives had descended without her conscious consent.

"There is no cause for alarm, *kóri*." Daughter. Again freakishly supplied by Prince Nico. "You're famished. Feeding will complete the transition. I must go. There's much to do. Feed. Queen Amelia-Marie Belladonna Dimir, we shall meet again soon." He bowed his head. Then was gone.

The only sign he'd been—Cheryl. Curled in the fetal position, shaking.

Talon stood. Finally!

Somehow, she'd missed the vow of silence he'd taken in between the time she rose and Prince Nico's arrival.

He faced her.

"What the hell?"

"Sorry. I can't rise or speak in the presence of royalty until given permission."

"You seem to be doing just fine now," she pointed out. Her descended fangs pricked her tongue. The things seemed to have minds of their own. "Wanna explain that? I thought you said all the *Vampire Royals* were destroyed thousands of years ago?"

"Not thousands, one thousand and twenty—"

"I don't care," she interrupted loudly to block out Cheryl's whimpering. Amelia didn't have a clue what to do about that. Could she feed? Didn't matter; she didn't want to. Her stomach growled.

Talon smirked.

Okay, so her body wanted to, but this was time to employ the old "mind over matter" mentality because... Ew! How could this be happening to her and—

Talon's shrinking wound derailed her thought process. Ice-cold dread skittered down her spine. This wasn't just about her. She'd ruined more lives. The people at her party. Her family and friends. Calin. Cheryl. Talon.

"I'm sorry, Talon. I didn't mean to do this" — she waved her hand at his wound — "I just didn't want this. I still don't. It's unnatural. Where do you find meaning, learn to cherish people you care for, appreciate what's been given to you, when life is infinite?"

Talon lifted her chin, forcing her to meet his smoldering blue gaze. A zing of awareness traversed her body. "Remember what I told you? Don't apologize to me. Especially not for being scared or confused. Fates! I don't know what I would have done if I'd lost you."

He kissed her forehead. His lips lingered for a moment before he pulled back.

"You can't stop someone from apologizing. Trust me, it's something I haven't done nearly enough of in the last few years. I have a lot to be sorry for. Treating everyone like crap, getting you hurt—"

"Who cares about me getting hurt."

"Walker," she continued as if he hadn't spoken. Her voice cracked at the name, the bloody vision it evoked.

How could she? The guilt and agony she felt would be an acid bath eating away at her no matter how long she lived—existed. She needed to make amends with those who she could. Now that the deed was done, she felt relatively normal. She would fix things.

Her mother used to say "The difference between a good person and a bad one isn't who makes mistakes and who doesn't. It's what a person does once they realize they've made a mistake. That's what makes someone bad or good."

"You're hurt because of me," she continued. "The stress I caused you—everyone at my party—is because I was hell-bent on having my way. I ruined your plans and caused all this."

Shaking his head, Talon clutched Amelia's hands in his. "I heal fast. After I feed, there won't be a scratch left to indicate where I was shot."

Amelia's mouth dropped into an "O." Her eyes bulged. "You were shot! I thought you fell or something. Thanks for sparing my feelings," she said in a dry aside.

Talon smirked but otherwise ignored her outburst. "You're right. You destroyed my plans. You botched my entire mission."

Amelia frowned.

"You changed every idea of what I thought mattered. I never wanted a mate, but if I were forced to have one, I wouldn't choose a female like you. You question my authority, drive me insane."

Wow, pep talks—so not Talon's strong suit.

"You're my perfect distraction. The very idea of your existence has driven me crazy for over a century. And if given a choice between crazy and sane?" He stroked her cheek with his thumb. "I choose to be certifiable, completely *defective*. Drool-into-a-cup nuts. I never want to lose you. I'd be rabid without you. You're the most precious thing I never knew I needed." He squeezed her hands. "I'd be lying if I said I knew how this is going to work. I don't. What I know is that *you* give my existence meaning. *You* are what makes me appreciate who and what I am."

Tears pooled in her eyes. Amelia's mouth fell wide open. This was a lot to hear. A lot to deal with. None of it seemed real. She was adrift in a sea of the unfamiliar. Talon kept saying they were forbidden to be together. If so, then how could she believe he'd make such a sacrifice?

"You're worth the sacrifice, *cara*," Talon said.

Were none of her thoughts her own? Seriously, the mind-reading thing stayed on her nerves.

"What I'm trying to say—badly—is... I love you. Now. Forever. For always. I'll do whatever it takes to have you." Sincerity shone in Talon's eyes, layered his words.

He bent, capturing her lips with his in one of the tenderest kisses she'd ever had. She melted against his chiseled chest. He felt good and was the only thing familiar in her new, crazy world.

Reaching up on tiptoe, she wrapped her arms around his neck.

He lifted her off her feet. She held tight to him, her anchor. Held on for dear life, or whatever it was called now that her life had been greatly extended, provided no one destroyed her.

All different breeds of rogues would be after her from now to... eternity.

This was scary and overwhelming. Nothing was certain or guaranteed except two things: One, she loved this man in her arms. Talon would travel this road with her wherever it led. Two, a sick feeling in her gut told her this road was about to get mighty bumpy.

With a frown, she broke the kiss and turned toward Cheryl.

Amelia would need strength for this road trip. Time to feed.

Epilogue

/hree weeks later

A cruise? A freakin' Western European cruise! Who gives a girl they barely know a six-week cruise for her twenty-first birthday?

Calin. That's who.

Tessa blew a puff of air from the corner of her mouth. An attempt to get her overgrown bangs out of her eyes without touching her face. With a long-suffering sigh, she braced her left hand on the edge of the tub she'd just finished cleaning—again—and pushed to her feet. Her knees cracked.

Ugh... I'm getting old.

She frowned at her useless right arm. It'd been three weeks since the birthday party she barely remembered. Apparently, she'd gotten blackout drunk and jumped off the roof. Everyone said she did it. It sounded like her, but she couldn't remember it. She'd also missed a major brawl. From what she'd been told, it got UFC up in this bitch. People walked away with not only bruises but broken bones, too.

Whatever.

Nobody could say she didn't know how to throw a party. As the song went, "A party ain't a party 'til it's ran all through," and Amelia's party definitely was.

Of course, she wasn't worried about scrapes and cuts. Hey, party at your own risk. What had her cleaning like a dope fiend being paid in liquid cocaine was that she hadn't heard squat from her best friend in weeks. Nothing.

Nada.

Zilch!

Not a postcard, food stamp, smoke signal... nothing. In their entire friendship, she and Amelia had never gone this long without communicating in some way. Neither Talon nor Calin were answering their phones. Amelia's went right to voicemail.

Evan didn't think anything of it, but Tessa didn't share his newfound "no worry, no cry" attitude. She was worried as shit, and a worried Tessa was a clean Tessa.

This house was so clean surgery could be performed on any surface, which said a lot, given the fact that Talon had given Amelia a free home remodel for her birthday. Workmen were in and out on the daily, painting and whatnot. These foreign guys didn't seem to understand the idea of a card, flowers, maybe earrings. No, they gave cruises and remodels as gifts.

Must be nice!

Dan thought he was doing something by buying her a KitKat from the grocery store. Sheesh!

Speaking of candy bars, stress eating sounded pretty good right about—

Ding! Dong!

Doorbell.

At the sink, Tessa turned on the hot water with one hand and did her damnedest to wash off the cleanser. She really couldn't wait to get the cast and sling removed. It went from her elbow to her knuckle—Whoa!

Shutting off the water, she inspected her reflection. Turned her head right and left. Rough didn't cover how she looked. Normally lively green eyes were sunken in. Her pasty face bore no make-up. Bushy caterpillars replaced her usually plucked eyebrows. Her dark hair needed a cut, bad. The craziness of the last few months was kicking her ass.

Ding...! Dong...!

No time to dwell. She stomped on protective plastic and through tarp curtains hung from ceiling to floor.

Forgetting herself, she instinctively reached with her right hand to open the door. Was thwarted by the sling. Shaking her head, she opened it with her left.

"Does it usually take you an hour to answer the door, or were you getting pretty for me, baby?"

Waving her left hand, Tessa shooed the tall, wide-chested, broad-shouldered man out of the way. She leaned forward and poked her head out the door. She glanced right, left, up, down then straightened. Speech abandoned her.

"What?" the mystery man asked.

Tessa shook her head to clear it. "Is it raining you guys or something?" Who the hell would she open the door to next? First Talon, then Calin, and now Mr. Hottie McOhmigod...

The man was so hot the concept didn't touch him, which was the only conceivable explanation for him wearing black boots, jeans, and a thermal shirt in this heat. His long sleeves were pushed back to reveal tattooed forearms to die for. Muscled pectorals protested their confinement—so did she. Although his head was shaved, he had enough hair to tell it was auburn. The man was I've-fallen-and-can't-get-up gorgeous.

A quizzical dark red brow rose over one stunning golden eye. "Breathe, beautiful," he advised in a rich resonant voice meant for foreplay. "I'm, Anton. This is Amelia Keeler's house, right? Please, invite me in."

Of course, he was here for Amelia. They were all here for Amelia.

Dead Inside Soundtrack

1. Big Bopper – Chantilly Lace (Chapter Thirty-Eight)

2. Bloodhound Gang – Why's Everybody Always Pickin' On Me? (Chapter Five)

3. Brandy – I'm Missing You (Chapter Twenty-Four)

4. B.o.B ft. Hayley Williams – Airplanes (Chapter Forty)

5. Dem Franchize Boyz ft. Jermaine Dupri, Bow Wow, Brat – I Think They Like Me

6. Eminem ft. Dr. Dre – Guilty Conscience (Demon Conscience)

7. Eminem – Going Through Changes (Chapter Thirty-Eight)

8. Evanescence – My Immortal

9. Evanescence – Bring Me To Life (Chapter Two)

10. Evanescence – Sweet Sacrifice

11. Evanescence – Tourniquet (Dead Inside Soundtrack)

12. Gavin DeGraw – Follow Through (Chapter Fifteen)

13. Gun N' Roses – November Rain

14. Jason Mraz – I Won't Give Up (Calin's voicemail song)

15. Katy Perry ft. Kanye West – E.T.

16. Limp Bizkit – Break Stuff

17. Limp Bizkit – Eat You Alive (Chapter Twenty)

18. Linkin Park – Numb

19. Linkin Park – Crawling (Dead Inside Soundtrack)

20. Linkin Park – In The End

21. Lit – My Own Worst Enemy

22. Little Richard – Keep a Knockin (Chapter Thirty-Eight)

23. Little Richard – Tutti Frutti (Chapter Thirty-Eight)

24. Little Richard – Lucille (Chapter Thirty-Eight)

25. Ludacris ft. Nicki Minaj – My Chick Bad (Chapter Thirty-Eight)

26. The Bad Livers – Death Trip (Dead Inside Soundtrack)

27. The Black Eyed Peas – Just Can't Get Enough

28. The Gap Band – You Dropped a Bomb on Me (Movie Theater)

29. Pink – Split Personality (How Amelia Feels)

30. Prince – Seven (Chapter Thirty-Nine)

31. Rihanna – Unfaithful (How Amelia Feels hanging out with Talon & Calin)

32. Rob Zombie – Living Dead Girl (Chapter Thirteen)

33. Shakespears Sister – Stay (Chapter Twenty-Two Amelia's Dream)

34. Marilyn Manson – The Beautiful People

35. Marilyn Manson – The Dope Show

36. Ne-Yo – Never Knew I Needed (Chapter Forty-One Talon's Feelings)

37. One Inch Punch – Pretty Piece of Flesh

38. Willy Northpole – Body Marked Up (Chapter Thirty-Eight)

Acknowledgements

While writing Dead Inside I learned a lot about myself and writing. I realized being a writer doesn't mean you have to be a loner. It was actually impossible to be. After I researched my butt off, I went out a bunch—to gain personal experience to draw from, of course—received advice from so many friends and fellow authors it'd take an entire book to thank everyone individually. However, there are those that I feel deserve a personal mention for their contribution to my success.

First, I have to thank two dearly departed friends: Jon Tabler and John Witt. Both have made such an immeasurable impression on me and my life. Without them, I don't know who I'd be. Both saw me as more than I ever saw myself and helped me believe in myself. I will never forget either of you.

I'd like to thank Claire Ashgrove an amazing editor who helped whip Dead Inside in excellent condition. All of my beta readers. And special thanks to my author friends who also helped edit and read over difficult scenes without complaint: Buffy Christopher, Leslie Lee Sanders, and Nikki Prince. I'd like to offer an enormous thank you to author Gracie Cooper. She extended her friendship to me without hesitation, reservation, or judgment.

Another significant person I'd like to acknowledge is Cynthia Siqueiros. Your help over the last ten years has been invaluable.

There aren't enough words in the English language to express my thanks adequately.

Last, but certainly not least, thank you with all my heart to Téa-Bianca, Kayleigh, Nathaniel, and Jeremiah. Life has dealt a huge blow, but never one day have you been far from my heart and mind. There isn't one of you I could ever live my life without. You give my life purpose. I love you more than life itself. Without you, I'm Dead Inside.

Prologue

I. *Hate. You.*

Almond-shaped, medium brown doe eyes that were too big for the small, milk chocolate oval face they inhabited, shot a feral glare.

Respect had nothing to do with why she didn't speak the words to the emaciated woman standing before her. It was fear and loathing. This could be her scary future if she played her cards wrong. The fact she knew this at five years old said a lot about her life. Five felt like forty.

THIS is your brain on drugs. Way better than that egg skillet commercial. Somebody should hit her with a skillet, the little girl thought, glower glued to her "mother." The woman couldn't even stand still. She fidgeted. Picked at the tattered, black leather upholstery of the couch she stood behind. Shifted her weight from one foot to the other.

"Mama, we got one of them notices again," her twelve-year-old half-sister Kathy said from the archway separating the kitchen and living room.

"I paid rent yesterday, baby. Mama's broke," the woman rasped, now fingering a hole in the sleeve of the flashy sky-blue dress she wore. Not even noon, but she looked ready for a pageant. Or the club.

With cat-like onyx eyes, Kathy took after her father instead of their so-called mother. They might not be full sisters, but their clothes—two sizes too small, and so threadbare they were nearly transparent—and fed-up glares, were identical. "Mama, that was two months ago. They gon' make us leave," Kathy reminded. Frustration deepened skin a couple of shades darker than her own.

Yep, she loathed this *woman*. The self-centered, she-devil didn't deserve respect. She'd wasted enough tears on her and her lost childhood. She wouldn't waste words. Their mother had left two months prior, with the promise of grocery shopping only to return this morning. She left her daughters without food, electricity, or running water. Thank God, for nosy neighbors. They paid for the electricity and water, no questions asked, out of pity.

The babysitting services her older sister provided neighbors in exchange for food would only last so long. Otherwise, they would starve. Kathy also kept her out of sight so not-so-understanding neighbors wouldn't realize she hadn't been to school in months and call the authorities.

Kathy depended on adages like out-of-sight, *out-of-mind* to keep questions to a minimum. Selfless to a fault, she cared for her little sister better than any mother. They were a team. Kathy's mature appearance aided in keeping suspicions low. Her body had matured light years ahead of her twelve years. She possessed a gentle, almost fragile soul. An iron will and fierce loyalty assured she did the necessary without complaint. Even though their mother let them down in so many ways, misguided belief ensured she never betrayed their mother's secrets. Kathy had a near child-like naivety. For her, the same couldn't be said.

While only five, she'd been born an adult. Possessed an arcane knowledge of people and the world. Being a child wasn't a luxury she could afford. Her older sister loved their mother and gave her the benefit of the doubt. She didn't.

The junky reached down, picked something off the floor. "Mama's gon' go make this money right quick. Sell this"—holding up a dark blue carrying case—"blow dryer. I'll be back."

She and Kathy traded sidelong, skeptical looks. "Mama, they're gonna evict us," Kathy pleaded.

"I know, baby. That's why I need to see bout this money now. I'ma be back," their mother crooned, pulling the front door open. She disappeared before either child could protest.

Ten minutes later, Kathy sat on the couch reading one of the two books they owned. Fortunately, books weren't an accepted form of currency for crack, or they'd have no source of entertainment.

The five-year-old made her way toward the front door.

"Uh... excuse me," Kathy said, turning to watch her sister, "where you goin'?"

All-too-knowing, brown eyes collided with questioning onyx ones. "The porch." A small brown hand yanked the door open before Kathy asked anything else.

She knew the answer, but something inside her needed undeniable proof. Maybe a tiny part of her wanted to believe it wasn't true. Perhaps she wasn't as jaded as she thought. Whatever it was, she had to know.

Relentless Arizona sun smacked her. Her skin flushed as she stepped onto the porch. To her immediate left, the storage closet. With unnecessary caution, she approached the closed door. She sucked in a deep breath through her mouth, then opened the door. Froze. There was the blue bag their mother went to "sell" on the cement floor.

Chapter One

"**H**ow's the bulge?" Christopher Clark sauntered into his roommate and best friend's bedroom.

Green eyes full of murderous intent shot toward where he stood in the doorway. "Are you fuckin' serious? I'm not checking out your dick print, bro."

Chris examined his childhood friend, Andrew "Drew" Sutton, through narrow eyes. Creased gray slacks, black long-sleeved dress shirt, black silk tie, and black dress shoes—what the...? He wasn't into guys or anything, but his six-foot-three, brown-haired, green-eyed friend never looked this good. "Where the hell are you going?"

Sliding his mirrored closet door closed, Drew turned toward him. "It's called a date. You know, one of those things a man takes a woman on. Man picks said woman up, takes her some-where nice, they eat, get to know each other, then man pays and escorts woman back home. They don't have sex on the table or in the car."

Frowning, Chris rolled his eyes. He knew what dates were. Just didn't believe in them. Pot. Kettle. Who was Drew to criti-cize...?

They'd been friends their whole twenty-seven years on Earth. They'd been born within days of each other, and their parents were best friends. He knew Drew. And knew when he was being lied to. Until a couple of months ago, the asshole had the same philosophy on women as he did: if there's grass in the field... play ball! Now, some mystery woman had Romeo's punk-ass sprung. Just the thought of being whooped over some chick gave Chris the shakes. Unless...

Not going there. He didn't want or need a subscription to her issues. He liked his bachelor status. There were too many women in the world. God did not bless him with his rock-hard body, six-five height, blond hair, blue eyes, and nine-and-a-half-inch dick to give it to one woman for the rest of his life. Especially not a woman who made being sodomized by Satan with a spiked club sound fun.

Chris stood next to Drew and checked himself out in the mirror. Fixing his hair and straightening his clothes, he didn't miss the incredulous side-eye coming from Andrew—nor did he care.

"Oh, I'm sorry, *Your Highness*, was I in your way in my room, standing in front of my mirror? Asshole."

"You know, you're gonna go gray from all the whining you do. Unclench. Let the stick fall out."

"Stress—*jackass*—stress makes you go gray. If you, being annoying, turned me gray... I would've been completely gray in second grade. Anyway, this is my room. I'm allowed to not want you in it. And there's a mirror in your room. Several, to be exact." His best friend pointed out.

"We were in the same kindergarten class. You were there when we learned to share. Plus, the mirror in my room is portrait size," he informed Drew. "I need a good look at the package since some people—who shall remain nameless—are no help."

Damn, I'm fine!

Chris continued fixing his wavy hair. He wagged his eyebrows at his reflection. Cupped himself. "I know what women want."

Chapter Two

R evulsion curled Andrew's upper lip. He glared at the image his friend presented in the mirror.

Dick.

The guy was a grade "A" jackass. He loved him like a brother, but like a brother, Chris pissed him off to no end. So far past conceited—dude couldn't see conceited if it head-butted him. The fact Chris hadn't forgone women altogether in favor of asexuality shocked him. The narcissist attached mirrors to his bedroom ceiling, not because he was a visual man. No, he did it to evaluate himself during sex. Make sure he didn't sweat too much or make any unattractive expressions.

Had Chris been anybody else, Drew would've beaten his ass and disowned the self-proclaimed "cookie crook" long ago. God, if his little sister ever met a guy like Chris, he'd kill him. Given his profession, he knew how and where to hide the body. Buuut, Chris had good qualities... deep, deep, deep down.

Somewhere trapped inside him was a fiercely loyal, chubby, acne-riddled kid. He'd give the shirt off his back to anyone in need. Of course, there were other reasons for their continued friendship. Chris's invaluable, no-bullshit honesty—no matter how blunt—was one. Chris was Chris; take him or leave him. No guesswork required. He was a straight shooter. Told it like it was, and Andrew appreciated that.

Andrew's ire cooled a bit. Yes, if he were being honest and risking sounding a little gay, he'd admit his friend was attractive. He looked better than most male models, even dressed in simple blue jeans and a black T-shirt with his multi-hued blond hair artfully mussed. Not only did he get mistaken for a young Matthew McConaughey, but the guy possessed the deep, slight, southern drawl to boot. No cap. It was how he spoke, which shocked the shit out of Andrew since they were both born and raised here in Arizona.

Finished with his covert appraisal of Chris, something on his king-sized bed caught his attention. Shit! He forgot. The usually unobservant Chris noticed, too.

Fuck!

"Movin' out?" Chris asked, gaze fixed on the large, black duffel bag atop Andrew's royal blue comforter.

Damn, damn, dammit! He'd hoped to get away without Chris knowing. Typically, Andrew told Chris everything. Borderline, TMI-style, everything. However, he didn't prefer to share this one of two things. The first, he kept from Chris and everyone. It wasn't only his secret, and he wasn't ready to go public. The second—this—he kept from Chris for his sanity.

"If I say yes, will you pretend you didn't see that?"

"What the fuck, man?" Chris snapped. "Why all the secrecy? We're supposed to be boys. Now I'm public enemy number one—you keep shit from me? I'm the bad guy—fuck you, too, dude."

Damn! Leave it to Chris to go all little girl sensitive. "If I tell you, promise not to ask to come."

"Go wherever you want. I'm a grown man, not a lost puppy. I don't need to follow you around. I've got people to see and women to screw. And, in the immortal words of Reverend Lil' Wayne, I'm the pussy monster. Ladies need me around here. I can't take a day off." Chris boasted, planting himself on the corner of his mahogany desk. Arms crossed, he watched Andrew.

Andrew released a loud, long-suffering breath. If only it were that simple. But for reasons unknown to him, he knew the second he told his best friend, he'd want to come with him. Chris liked to live dangerously. After a deep sigh, he conceded. "You know my parents' anniversary is in a couple of days, right?"

Chris arched a thick, golden brow. Nodded.

"They're going to Hawaii on some sort of second honeymoon type deal the day after tomorrow. I'm house-sitting until they get back."

Chris sat, eyes narrowed. Pensive. "Why would you need to house sit? Isn't—when do we leave?" he asked, interrupting himself as realization struck. He hopped to his feet.

Andrew raked a hand through his brown locks. Sighed. "Chris, that's why I didn't say anything. What happened to you being a grown man? Thought you had pussy to attend to?"

An indecipherable expression flashed in Chris's deep blue eyes but disappeared before Andrew could decipher its meaning. "I am a grown man and as such… I choose to go with you. Ain't shit to do here."

"You have work to do," Andrew pointed out, knowing he'd already lost this battle. Chris would reschedule all his training sessions at the gym, where he worked as a personal trainer and nutritionist. Funny, he'd never pegged Chris as a masochist.

"What? You don't think I'm up for a little sparring match?" Chris smirked, lifting his fists and mimicking a couple of boxing jabs. "Afraid I won't be able to take a few punches from little Sugar Ray Leonard?"

Drew rolled his eyes. No, he in no way, shape, or form wanted to spend his much-needed, eight-week-long vacation playing referee. "I always thought you liked your dick?" As soon as the words left his lips, he and Chris winced in unison at the memory they invoked.

"Poor… poor… Rand," Chris said in a mocking, sympathetic tone, shaking his head. "At least the one nutt still works."

Poor one-testicle Rand. He'd never seen it coming. When they were around fifteen, he, Chris, and their other two best friends, Alex and Rand, had been hanging out in the kitchen of his childhood home when his twelve-year-old sister came in. Rand said something to the effect of… she'd filled out. Andrew would've gladly readjusted his friend's nose for the comment, but the little ninja got to Rand first. One well-placed kick turned him into Mr. Uni-ball. Blood everywhere.

With that, his thoughts took an unpleasant turn. He'd hurt her, too. To refocus on the here and now, he shook his head. "You can't come. My parents didn't invite you."

Chris snorted. "Please! Since when do I need an invitation? I'm always welcome. Your casa es my casa."

"What about Samantha? She'll be pissed if you up and disappear for two months. Don't you guys have some other restaurant, amusement park, mall, church, or somewhere to defile?"

"First—motherfucker—I don't answer to her. She can throw a tantrum all she wants, but she knows the score. Second, there are these newfangled devices called cell phones I can use to tell her I'm gone if I choose. She'll wait. Who's better than me?" Chris grinned.

"I don't know. I mean, you're so humble. How could she ever tire of waiting for a catch like you—douchebag?" Andrew sat on his bed.

"You really don't want me to go, huh?" Chris asked, crossing his arms over his heavily, muscled chest.

"No. I don't. You know how it'll turn out. I don't want to play mediator, UFC referee, bodyguard, or judge," Andrew answered, hoping to appeal to some latent sense of decency within his friend.

Chris almost ran his fingers through his perfectly coiffed hair but stopped mid-action. His hand fell to his side. God forbid his hair should ever be out of place. He exhaled a clement breath. Shrugged. "Fine. If it matters that much, I won't go." And with that, his usual self-centered friend strutted out of his room.

Ho-ly, shit! Christopher Patrick Clark was doing something unselfish. Where was a camera when he needed one?

Chapter Three

"And how does that make you feel?" asked a smooth, soothing professional tone.

"I couldn't give a shit less," Renée Sutton answered. "It was nineteen years ago. I'm over it. I'm not the first kid it's happened to, and I won't be the last. It was a dream. I only told you because you give out the meds." Yeah, that voice was supposed to calm her, or whatever, but it pissed Renée off to no end.

Hazel eyes narrowed, condemned. Mrs. Anne Mendoza, M.D., seemed to have a hard time keeping her emotions in check, sitting behind her large oak desk. She struggled to pinch her too many times tucked face while twisting in her big, black, I'm-somebody-important leather chair. The degrees hanging on the wall gave her the authority to prescribe medicine and the right to think she knew everything.

Looks like someone's giving away their power, Renée thought. It took conscious effort to keep her mental sarcasm off her face.

She'd been told that same thing during one, or forty, of her sessions with Dr. Mendoza over the last three years. According to Dr. Mendoza, no one can make another feel anything without their permission. To let someone provoke you to anger gives away your power. Damn, therapist psychobabble! Renée didn't buy it, which was why she worked extra hard to poke the bear.

Renée was here for two reasons. Neither had anything to do with thinking this white blond haired, middle-aged lady in her gray pants suit knew anything. At least, not anything about her. This fulfilled one of her well-meaning parents' stipulations for her "moving" back home. The second reason: the excellent psychiatrist prescribed the only Western medicine Renée would take.

Usually, she stayed pretty healthy. She rarely drank. Didn't smoke. Didn't eat meat. Exercised her mind and body. She used natural remedies for any aches, pains, or illnesses. But, there was one condition nothing but good old-fashioned Xanax would cure: panic attacks. Her traitorous nervous system... Hangnails and being held at gunpoint elicited the same physical response.

"Renée? Renée, did you hear me?" Dr. Mendoza asked, breaking into her reverie.

"No. What'd you say?"

"How are you and your parents getting along? Your living situation?"

"Great, it's the best experience of my life. I love it. I recommend every twenty-four-year-old be forced under the threat of an involuntary psychiatric hold to move back home," she said, then tossed in a grin for good measure.

What did she mean—how were they getting along? They got along like too many queens in a castle. Barely.

"You know, sometimes sarcasm is used to hide deeper pain," the good doctor informed in the condescending tone that drove her crazy. "It's a way of deflecting."

"And sometimes sarcasm keeps annoying people from asking too many questions," Renée rebutted condescendingly.

"Renée, I'm here to help. Have you given any more thought to our discussion from a few weeks ago?"

God, give it up, lady! Less talk, more prescription writing. "Jeez, memories, dreams, they're all the same. Everybody dreams. Once I dreamed, I married a big, nine-foot-tall slug. Should I find a slug to keep that dream at bay? See if we have any chemistry? Or, wait, you know... I had a dream about being alive inside my coffin at my funeral. Should I go down to the local funeral home and lay in a pine box?" She shuddered. "No. Thank. You."

Dr. Mendoza ran a shaky hand through her chin-length hair. "Ms. Sutton, you could try the patience of a saint."

Gotcha, bitch! "I do what I can," she said in a breathy, dreamy voice.

"You can't keep running from your past—your feelings—forever. Waiting to examine things until later. The past will catch up with you. Confront those things that haunt your nightmares. For instance, you could try talking to me about them. Your parents pay for these sessions. The least you could do is use me. These degrees here,"—she pointed to the wall behind her—"aren't just for covering the holes I punch in the wall after our sessions, you know?"

Renée flashed a brief smile. Okay, that was funny. She didn't mean to be such an ass. But she didn't want to talk about it. For years, she'd been having nightmares about her past. But they weren't dreams. They were memories of the most harrowing experiences of her childhood and life. Memories she'd love to forget. But her subconscious didn't get the memo. And after "The Event" three years ago, the memory nightmares increased, which meant so did her anxiety attacks.

Dr. Mendoza believed the increased dreams and panic attacks were because of Post-Traumatic Stress Syndrome, PTSD. Renée agreed. After "The Event," she couldn't take another trauma or stressful situation in her life. The next big thing would more than likely kill her. Her fragile mental health couldn't endure another hit.

"This isn't my first rodeo. I've talked about this stuff with therapists before. It doesn't go away, no matter how many times I repeat the stories. Nobody understands what it was like for me, and I'm honestly over it. But, hey, good lookin' out." To further illustrate her point that the topic was closed for discussion, she gave Dr. Mendoza the wink and the gun.

"So, how are our relationships?" the doctor asked, changing the subject to one she thought safer. "Your friends? Your brother? Are we dating yet?"

The doctor didn't understand the universal sign for stop-talking-and-get-to-the-prescription-writing.

Hmm... she'd have to work on her sign-giving. "Er, I don't know about you, but I'd rather clear out my right and left eye with a rusty nail than date anybody. On a happier note, friends are good. The brother's doing well, I guess. We don't speak much."

With a smile and nod, the doctor reached into her desk drawer—a white prescription pad.

Thank God!

"Have you given any more thought to how you identify?" Dr. Mendoza asked, fancy pen tip to paper.

What the hell was she doing? Besides her resolve to never date or marry and her hate of mouth noises, everybody knew—very well—Renée had zero patience. And this bitch was toying with her. Yeah, patience wasn't a virtue she possessed. We all have our battles.

"My identity isn't wrapped up in skin color. Some people get left. Kids get left. There's no deeper meaning," she snapped, harsher than intended. The very idea she might not be as comfortable with herself as she believed didn't sit well with her. It had weighed on her mind since her psychiatrist brought it up a month ago. But she'd be damned if she admitted it. "I identify with me."

Thankfully, her response seemed to suffice because the pen glided across the paper. Sweet freedom was within her grasp. An hour had never seemed so long.

*A*rizona sun pummeled asphalt. Blurry, shimmering heat haze distorted a rundown beige and brown townhouse. Two white, four-door sedans were parked outside of it. Doors of *the idling vehicles hung open. A black, spear-top iron perimeter fence bordered an Astroturf-covered front porch.*

The home's front door flew open. Distraught screams and cries rent the air.

"No! Please..." screamed five-year-old Renée. A young, light brown-haired, professionally dressed Caucasian man struggled under her slight weight. "I don't want to go!" she yelled. "Kathy!" Tears streamed down a tiny, round chocolate face. Brown eyes were wild.

Kathy followed close behind, sedate. Her mouth turned down, a frown of resignation. A petite, red-haired woman with worried green eyes—dressed in a professional A-lined, gray skirt and sleeveless, cowl neck, black blouse—escorted her from the house.

"It's okay, it's not forever. We'll see each other again," came Kathy's hollow assurance. The woman led her to one car. The man led Renée to the other. "Renée, it's okay. Shh... I love you."

The attempt at comfort fell upon deaf ears. Renée knew better. She kicked, struggled harder against the man's hold. He forced her into the back seat. A jagged piece of metal from the doorframe sliced through her right wrist. Cut to the bone. Blood ran from her wrist to her elbow. She didn't feel it. Deeper, excruciating pain lanced her heart. Overshadowed the physical pain as she watched the other car pull away. The only person in the world who loved her sat rigid in the back seat, facing forward. Kathy never looked back.

Renée jolted awake. It was dark. Sweat ran from her forehead, down her hairline, off her chin. Her body shook. Tears flowed, unchecked, down her cheeks. Her heart compressed yet thundered in her chest. Breath ragged, she reached toward the nightstand beside her bed. Hand bumping into the lamp atop it. She tapped the metal shade. Muted light trickled out. She turned her alarm clock toward her—three-thirty-three in the morning.

Great!

Hands shaking, she opened her top drawer. Pulled out a prescription bottle, opened it, shook out two pills, and swallowed them dry. To give the Xanax time to do its thing, Renée focused on breathing. In through the nose. Out through the mouth. Waiting for her body to relax, she scanned her room. She attempted to re-familiarize herself with her surroundings.

Hoping to make her feel comfortable after her adoption fourteen years ago, her parents allowed her to paint the walls her favorite color: maroon. Her other favorite colors, black and royal blue, which were the colors of her bedsheets, always brought her peace. Right now, she needed all the peace she could get. She gazed across the room at her oak dresser with an attached mirror. In the mirror's frame, she'd tucked pictures of her friends. On the dresser were more framed photos.

As her medication calmed her system, flashes of her memory-dream replayed in her mind. She didn't allow her conscious mind to dwell in the past, but the chances of falling back asleep now were slim to none. So, she let her mind wander down the cracked memory lane. The day her sister had called Child Protective Services and reported that their mother abandoned them was as clear as if it happened yesterday.

She remembered most of her life experiences and events as if they'd happened yesterday. They'd diagnosed her at twelve years old with Hyperthymesia. People with the syndrome have superior autobiographical memory. Her memory was her most significant ally, and worst enemy. It reminded her of all the things she wanted, never wanted, and never wanted to happen again. It kept her grounded, maybe too grounded, which left the guard walls around her heart high with barbed wire and choked full of electricity. No one got in, or out, easily.

Of course, she knew her thinking wasn't healthy, and it limited her, but that didn't make it any less a part of her, nor did she know how, or even if, she wanted to fix it. Most people weren't worthy of her heart, anyway. Her guard wall allowed her to stay aloof. Able to detach from anyone. Barring two events in nineteen years, she never let her guard down. Let no one in that she couldn't kick out in a nanosecond. Those two exceptions only fortified her resolve, especially the last slip-up.

It pained her on a soul-deep level to have to maintain such a view of people. More than anything, she wanted to let someone in. Be close to someone. Have someone see her. Know her. But every time she tried, she learned the accurate measure of mankind the hard way. Humans' penchant for committing brutal, cruel, cold, and heartless acts against each other confounded her. She couldn't be that way. Yes, she treated people like they were disposable, but that covered her genuine care. It killed her inside.

Although she knew now that her five-year-old self's thought process wasn't fair... it didn't change the fact that Renée included Kathy in the long list of people who'd abandoned her. Who'd let her down. Now, of course, she realized Kathy hadn't known they'd be tossed knee-deep into the craptastic foster care system and separated. But some wounds run to the very fiber of a person's being. Age and wisdom scabbed them over, but they never truly heal.

Three weeks after their "mother" said she'd be right back, neighbors got wise to their situation. One neighbor Kathy babysat for threatened to call the police. Scared, Kathy did the only thing she could think of: She called the police herself.

Less than twenty-four hours later, two social workers came to investigate. One look at their barely furnished townhouse—barely furnished because their tweaker mom sold anything of value for drugs—empty refrigerator and cupboards. They seized emergency custody. They took her and her sister that same day, each with a tiny garbage bag of dirty clothes. Renée never saw Kathy again.

Kathy could have found her later in life; they were seven years apart. She'd reached adulthood far before Renée. Yet she never came back. Never looked for her.

Renée rubbed the crescent moon-shaped scar on her right wrist and yawned. She laid down. Her final conscious thought: *Does she ever think about me?*

"Isn't it a little early to set up camp in front of the TV, young lady?" a rumbling voice asked.

Turning from her position, curled up at the end of the stone-colored plush sectional, Renée dropped the television remote. She squinted. When filtered through off-white curtains, the sun bathed the contemporary-style living room in a harsh orange glow, making it hard to discern her father's image in the arched entryway.

Randall Sutton. Possibly the most handsome fifty-six-year-old man alive—at least in her opinion. At six-three, he was a big man, but not fat. He was in fantastic shape for his age. Cropped brown hair peppered with gray complimented sky-blue eyes. Lugging four large, black suitcases—one under each arm and one in each hand—he'd forgone his usual cowboy attire. In its place, he wore a tacky, multi-colored, floral print, button-down shirt with khaki shorts, and Timberland boots.

Not every outfit can be a winner, I guess.

"Don't you have work to get ready for? Or a mall excursion to plan?" Randall asked.

Renée gave a wide, ditzy smile and twirled a lock of long, mahogany hair around her finger. "Like, OMG, Dad. Like, the mall's not even open this early. Duh!" she said, affecting her best Valley Girl accent, which wasn't far from her usual speech pattern.

"Hilarious, Renée," he replied, eyes narrowed. "Is this your plan for the entire time your mother and I are gone? Watching soap operas?"

"Dad!" she exclaimed, offended. "Do you see how fast I'm flipping through the channels? I couldn't be watching anything if I tried. I'm surfing. And soap operas aren't really a thing anymore."

God, the way her dad made it sound, one would think she asked to live here. She wasn't some freeloader mooching off her parents. She managed a luxury apartment community close to their Paradise Valley home. On-call all the time, this was the first day of a much-needed vacation. Shit!

Randall put down the luggage. Sat in his favorite, ugly brown La-Z-Boy recliner. It contrasted starkly against the other furniture: the curved stone sectional where she sat, the plush stone couch, her mother's stone recliner, the glass-top oak coffee table with matching end tables, and a burnish-brown oak entertainment center. His La-Z-boy was also a source of contention between her parents.

A familiar, disapproving clucking echoed through the hall, grew louder by the second, and annoyed the shit out of Renée. Six seconds later, buxom, five foot five, Susan Sutton came into sight. Her outfit was almost identical to her husband's, except she wore flat white sandals and a black carry-on bag. Censure dimmed emerald eyes. Pink gloss-coated lips pressed into a firm line in a wrinkle-free, heart-shaped face. Her honey blond hair, up in a ponytail, made her look younger than her fifty-two years.

Eyes cut at her daughter and a hand propped on her hip, she shook her head. "Always sarcasm from you and your brother. A simple 'No, I'm not watching TV,' would suffice." She turned to her husband. "Honey, remember I told you Née has the next few weeks off?"

Randall arched a curious brow in Renée's direction.

Susan returned her attention to Renée. "You doing anything today, or just hanging around the house?"

Renée released a deep sigh. It's not like they'd be here. What did they care? This over-interest in her life shtick pissed her off. Too much. Her interrupted night's sleep was catching up with her. She glanced at each of her parents; warmth and love warred with annoyance. "Gosh, sorry, you act like you don't want me here. What? Afraid I'll throw a wild party? I will gladly move out if it helps alleviate your fears."

Susan entered the room and sat at the opposite end of the sectional. "Stop, Renée," she chided. "We were just curious—no ulterior motive or hidden agenda. And we said we didn't want you to move out before you were ready. You're not ready," she clarified.

Renée understood her mother's comment for what it was, a command. Oh, so now they were splitting hairs. Two could play that—

Ding. Dong!

Saved by the bell. Thank God! She would've given the *I have to potty* excuse to escape this escalating conversation in another minute. She hopped up on bare feet to answer the door. Renée pulled the door open and froze.

A smile lit Renée's face. "Hey, you!" she exclaimed. "Nice of you to grace us with your presence." No sooner than the words left her lips, she jumped up and threw her arms around Andrew's neck.

He looked good. Debonair in his gray T-shirt and jeans. She'd almost forgotten what he looked like in casual clothes. Since moving out, whenever he came by, it was after some meeting with a client, so he wore business attire. A successful private investigator, Andrew could not only find half a needle in a haystack but also determine who put it there, why they put it there, when they put it there, and get pictures of it happening in seconds.

He was one of only three men she tolerated. The serious workaholic never dated, which was sad because he was gorgeous with above-average height, green eyes, and chiseled features.

Bone-crushing strength returned her gentle embrace. He lifted her off her feet. She'd missed him but would bite her tongue off before voicing such a weakness. Renée glanced over Andrew's shoulder. Something—yeah, some-*thing*—caught her eye. Her smile morphed into a fierce scowl. She backed out of her brother's arms, grabbed the door, and pulled it close to her body. Wrapping her left arm around it, she blocked entry into the house.

Just when she thought the day couldn't get any worse. Now, all that was missing was an AK-47 and a rooftop.

Chapter Four

"Andrew," Renée said, glaring daggers over her brother's shoulder, "aren't you breaking some leash law for your dog?"

"Missed you, too, Renée," Chris greeted in his sinfully deep bass.

Tingles shot down her spine. A rush of liquid fire pooled between her thighs.

Damn him!

In black cargo shorts, flip-flops, black muscle shirt with a white short-sleeved shirt left unbuttoned over it, he looked hotter than sin. Thank God, dark black tinted Oakley's hid Windex blue eyes that could turn her into jelly. He looked… disgusting! No, she wouldn't think of anything, but how gross he looked with tanned, muscular calves, arms, and rock-hard pecs. The man bled charm and game. If looks could kill… he'd be a nuclear weapon. And that irked her to no end. Of course, stupid, shallow, self-centered, dumbass jerks got all the looks—*asshole!*

She didn't voice her ire, but she'd been working on her nonverbal communication skills since her session with Dr. Mendoza. She hoped her glacial stare conveyed the message.

It didn't, or the bastard was slow on the uptake. He broke into a straight, pearly white-toothed, panty-dropping smile. But not her panties, no sirree Bob—nuh-uh—she wouldn't have it. Nor would she acknowledge the pulsing ache and wetness between her thighs. No, not wetness; it was... dew. Yeah, dew. Her shorts were tight, and it was a hot day. Her panties were firmly in place.

As the thought crossed her mind, his smile grew wider. It was as if he could read her thoughts—*jackass!*

Yeah, read that!

If eyes were indeed windows to the soul, his spoke volumes. She didn't have to see him to know they were empty. Full of deception and shallow, like him.

Chris always stood sure of himself: tall and straight with his broad shoulders, large muscular arms crossed over a wide, lickable chest. No! Not lickable, disgusting. His large muscular arms crossed over a wide lick—disgusting chest. *Shit!*

Standing must make her light-headed. It had to be because Hell would freeze over, thaw, and then freeze over again before she licked his chest. Half the Arizona female population had licked that chest. She'd be damned if she got added to his roster.

Chris's smile widened, unbothered by her rage. He always acted so unflappable, but she'd be damned if she didn't rattle him constantly. Nobody could be that sure of themselves; it wasn't natural. He needed to be knocked down a few pegs.

"Been saving that one for a while?" Chris drawled, deepening his voice. Renée tried to hide her desire, but he saw the flames clear as day in those hypnotic, bourbon-colored eyes, and he knew exactly the effect his voice had on her. He also noticed how her tongue snaked out to glide across her bottom, then top, lip. The way her eyes perused his body. "I'm happy you think about me so much."

To his utter amazement, Renée's face lit up. She gifted him with a sexy yet adorable, dimpled smile that nearly knocked him to his knees in front of his best friend, God, and everyone outside. "Oh, Christopher," she said with a sigh. He tried not to cringe at the use of his government name. "I think about you all the time."

His heart stuttered.

"Late at night, when I'm sitting alone in my room, I think about you," Renée admitted. "And all the ways I could kill you without going to jail." She released an exaggerated breath.

It was his turn to glare. Though it seemed longer, their entire exchange lasted a brief minute, and he'd done well masking his desire with practiced aloofness. He couldn't hold his annoyance now. For years he'd known, should his genuine feelings for Renée become public knowledge, it would ruin his friendship with Drew. End it altogether.

Although they seemed to have drifted apart, Drew and Renée were super close. Given that there were only three years between them and most of their respective friends, they both had strict rules about dating each other's friends. Chris was one hundred percent certain those rules were more brutal on Drew's side with his friends dating his beloved, pain-in-the-ass sister. To date, no one had ever tried to do the unspoken and forbidden: date Renée. And he didn't plan on doing it either—kinda.

He'd tried to talk himself out of coming with Drew—he did! He wanted to be the good, selfless friend Drew needed, but in the end, he was Chris. And Chris wasn't known for his patience, but he'd given the ever-mercurial Renée five years to run from their mounting attraction, what they could have, and he could wait no more. He'd stayed with his grandparents in Flagstaff for over a year, so she didn't tempt him to cross the line before he thought she could handle the type of relationship he expected with her. Age was no longer a factor. Neither of them was seeing anyone. See, he didn't want to date her. He wanted her.

Completely.

Mind, body, and spirit.

Forever.

Something inside her called to him on a primal, life-altering, heart-capturing level. Chris was tired of living without her, tired of denying, not only himself but her, too, what belonged to the other. He was hers, and she was his. Now he needed to convince her of that.

"Seriously, Christopher," Renée said, breaking into his planning, "why do you come here? I don't think we have enough mirrors to feed your insatiable need for your own company."

Chris gritted his teeth. He hated being called Christopher, and she knew it. He allowed only his elders to get away with it.

Biting back his irritation, he responded, "Not an issue. I brought a couple portable ones and a compact. I'll be fine. But, thanks for your concern. And, please, call me Chris."

"I reserve nicknames for my friends, Christopher." She smirked.

"Chris," he corrected, narrowing his gaze.

"Chris-to-pher," she responded, enunciating each syllable.

She enjoyed getting on his nerves. If she wanted to play, he'd play. Though she wasn't ready for the game he wanted to play. He played dirty. For keeps. Chris trapped her with a hard, penetrating stare.

With the lesser part of his attention, he caught Drew's groans, but he wasn't about to back down. He had a feeling no man ever challenged Renée. "Chris."

"Christoph—"

"Renée Marie Sutton, stop!" a booming voice ordered from somewhere behind the door.

Since Renée still blocked their entrance, he couldn't see where the voice came from, but he recognized Mr. Sutton.

"Let them in already. I reckon it's mighty hard to house-sit from outside the house—no matter how appealing that idea is to you, young lady," Mr. Sutton continued.

With a last glare, Renée let her breath out in a huff, stepped back, and opened the door wide enough for him and Drew to enter.

"Explain to me again why you need Andrew to house-sit?" Renée asked through clenched teeth, shutting and locking the front door. She followed them the short distance to the living room, where Mr. and Mrs. Sutton sat. "Aren't I a better choice? I mean, I live here. He doesn't," she complained, sitting opposite her mother on the stone-colored sectional.

"C'mon, sis," Drew said, sitting on the arm of the sectional beside Renée. "You know as well as I do you can't be trusted home alone, no matter how old you are."

Chris settled in for the show on the comfortable couch near Mrs. Sutton. This was about to get good. Renée bitched and whined with the best of them. Don't get him wrong, he adored his little firecracker. Especially loved the way her five-two, petite, Coke-bottle frame poured into her tiny navy-blue shorts and white, lace-trimmed, V-neck camisole that showed a healthy portion of her full, milk chocolate breasts. But the girl carried a King Kong-sized chip on her shoulder.

She took everything the wrong way. In her mind, everything was a ploy to do her wrong. An angle to get over on her somehow. However, he supposed the situation would frustrate or insult him if he were her, too.

He didn't understand why her parents needed Drew to watch the house when she was here either. Nothing made sense about how the Suttons, including Andrew, were suddenly overprotective of Renée in the last few years. They walked on eggshells around her most times and tolerated her little temper tantrums like she was a toddler. They'd always been protective of her, but they'd never been as indulgent as they'd become in the last three years. He'd have to break her out of her bratty behavior.

Renée grimaced at her brother. "What will I do by myself? I'm twenty-four. I'm all growed up now," she said, mocking a child's voice.

This was one side of Renée Chris rarely saw. He loved her playful sarcasm. There were more, gentler, layers to her. He knew it. Couldn't wait to pull back that hard shell to find them all.

Randall Sutton stood, stretched, and then patted Renée on the head. "We're more worried about what you'll do to the house, sweetheart, not yourself. And... we might be concerned about our little girl's safety," he teased, going over to the mouth of the hall where several black suitcases sat.

"I've never been a little girl, Dad," Renée snapped. "And anyway, I'm more mature than Drew on my worst day."

Andrew snatched up a maroon throw pillow and bopped his sister in the head with it. "You say that now, but when you see a scorpion or hear a noise in the middle of the night, you'll be screaming, 'Drew, help! Drew, did you hear that? Drew, kill it!'" he said, impersonating her voice, then he finished in his regular baritone, "Like a little girl."

Renée turned a glare on her brother so fierce it should've eviscerated him on the spot. Then a quick, playful smile spread her lips.

God, he wanted to be the one she had fun with. He'd never admit it, but he was jealous of his friend. She'd never looked at him that way before. Not playfully, anyway.

Dismissing his surge of irrational jealousy, he tossed his arm around the back of the couch and patted Susan Sutton on the arm. "Hey, Mrs. Sutton, excited about your big trip? Gonna give the resort something to talk about?" He winked.

Andrew and Renée made gagging sounds in unison.

"Hay is for horses, Christopher," Susan reprimanded, getting to her feet. "And I'd appreciate you not using filthy talk around my poor, innocent babies," she crooned. A hint of humor laced the last part.

Innocent his ass! He couldn't say for sure, but he'd be willing to bet with her fiery temper and tight little body. Renée might not be too experienced, but she wasn't innocent. As for Andrew? *Puh-lease!*

Drew's world was full of pussy. Girls found out he was a P.I., which they equated with danger. Drew needed a catcher's mitt for all the pussy thrown his way. The guy got more ass than a toilet seat. Shit! He almost got more ass than him. At least, he did until a few months ago.

Susan picked up a black carry-on resting at her feet. "We better get going."

"Need a ride to the airport?" Drew asked.

"Thanks, sweetie, but no. We're stopping at one of your father's friend's houses. He and his wife are borrowing the truck. He'll drop us." She rushed over to Drew and Renée, gave them each a quick squeeze. After a slight hesitation, she turned and gave him a brief one-armed hug. Susan's strong perfume drowned him, filled his nostrils.

Randall grabbed the suitcases, one under each arm and one in each hand.

"Need help, Dad?" Drew offered, standing.

"Yeah, let us help with that," Chris chimed in, not wanting to seem like a total ass.

Randall scowled at both younger men. "I'm not that old yet, boys. I can carry my own bags. Besides, wouldn't want Christopher to break a nail." He chuckled, turned, and walked toward the front entrance.

"Hilarious!" Chris hollered after Randall Sutton, who might as well be an uncle, considering he'd known him all his life and ribbed him like one.

"I thought so. You kids be good," he called, heading down the short hall.

"One day, that man's going to hurt himself, thinking he's gotta compete with you boys," Susan groused, following her husband. "Goodbye, my sweethearts. Be careful. Don't destroy the house. No parties! We have our cell phones for emergencies, and please, look after each other like I would look after you. Understood?" She yelled from down the hall, opening the front door.

In unison, Andrew, Renée, and Chris shouted, "Understood!"

"Damn, twenty-seven years old, and she treats me like I'm fifteen," Drew complained.

"Andrew David Sutton!" Susan yelled, "I heard that! You're not too old to put across my knee."

"Sorry, Mom!" Drew shouted and then asked under his breath, "Exactly what age does hearing go?"

Chapter Five

"Hey, Née, isn't your brother staying with you?"

Soft-spoken Christina Lee, one of two of Renée's best friends, asked two weeks after her unwelcome house guests arrived. A sizable green umbrella shaded the three friends from the brutal afternoon sun while sitting at a table outside Starbucks.

Chris had tried to corner her a million different times, a million different ways, every day since he got there. Places to hide were scarce. Pretending to be in the bathroom or sleeping took a toll, especially when it meant going to bed at seven to avoid him. One time, he attempted to follow her into the bathroom, but Drew walked by, and he made some lame excuse and left. She didn't know what his game was, but she wasn't playing.

"Oh, yeah... Isn't he supposed to be babysitting you or something?" her other best friend, Ashley Moore, asked in her I'm-always-up-for-stirring-some-shit-up voice.

Renée regarded her friends through narrowed eyes. The two women couldn't be more different.

Twenty-three-year-old, five-foot-four Ashley, had an average frame—not too big, not too small, but just right—and a light smattering of freckles on the bridge of her nose. Her eyes were a beautiful hazel, strawberry blond hair hung in waves to the middle of her back, and she wore her trademark jeans and T-shirt ensemble. Guys referred to Ashley as adorable until she opened her mouth and spit fire. No one ever saw that coming. Ashley believed in living life out loud—literally. The mouthpiece of the group, she spoke her mind all the time and screw the person who didn't want her opinion. They got it no matter how they felt about it.

Christina was the total opposite. A pretty Asian and petite like her—maybe an inch taller—black-as-night hair hung stick straight to the top of her shoulders, but today, she wore it in a ponytail. Soft brown eyes complemented her gentle nature. Christina screamed girlie girl. On rare occasions, she wore jeans. Still, her usual go-to was what she rocked today: modest pumps, a cute frilly shirt, and a flowing skirt.

Two years ago, Renée and Ashley had encountered a distraught Christina sitting in the food court of Paradise Valley Mall. Ashley, being Ashley, helped herself to a seat at Christina's table and a nose into her business. They bonded over shitty boyfriends, annoying parents, Jacob Elordi's abs, and Oreo blizzards. They'd been inseparable ever since.

All their personalities were distinct. Renée was the mama bear of the group, or The Godmother, as some called her. She didn't let many into her circle, but once she cared about you and you were in—you were in. The only way out was death. Renée protected those she cared for with ferocity, the likes of which the world would never suspect someone of her size capable. She could also go girlie like Christina or casual like Ashley and be comfortable.

She loved her friends and would do anything for them, but she'd cut them off if they screwed her over.

Renée threw a glare at each friend. "I'm not being babysat at all—ass," she snapped at Ashley after a sip of her caramel macchiato. "He's staying there because my parents don't want me to be alone—which I don't understand. But, yes, he's there. Along with his annoying friend, meaning I won't be there as much as possible," she said, dousing each word in all the aggravation she felt.

Christina wiggled her eyebrows at Ashley, then Renée, from behind brown-tinted Gucci sunglasses. "You mean to tell me you have your brother and one of his many hot friends staying with you?" she asked, propping her elbow on the table to support her chin. "Life is so unfair."

"Annoying friend?" Ashley asked, brows furrowed behind oversized pink Dolce & Gabbana sunglasses. "Which annoying friend?"

Renée lifted her cheap brown Target sunglasses and rubbed the bridge of her nose before replacing them. With her uncanny ability to lose sunglasses, no way in Hell would she waste money on expensive ones. She could buy twelve of the cheap ones for forty dollars. "It's not a good thing, Chrissy. For one, it's my brother, so, ew, what do I care? And second, I could never be attracted to his friend. Plus, he can't attract anyone. He's too busy admiring himself. He makes me sick."

Ashley pushed her grande caramel Frappuccino away as if it disgusted her. "Ugh... Chris," she said, groaning. "Say no more. I hate those types of guys."

"Me, too." She sighed in agreement.

Chris was the type of guy a girl had to watch her make-up around—not that he wore make-up. She likened being with Chris to how Prince's wife must have felt. The guy was an extraordinary musician, a legend. But that poor lady probably had to hide her shoes every night just to keep him from stealing them. So vain!

She hated girlie men, or "metrosexuals," as they were now called. Being metrosexual wasn't a bad thing. It just wasn't her thing. Yes, she used to have a crush on Axel Rose, but that was different. He oozed raw sex appeal; '80s hairband rockers were manly. Kind of like Chri—shit! What the Hell was she thinking? Scratch that thought.

"Oh, really? You hate those types of guys, too?" Christina asked, pulling Renée out of her stupid ruminations. "Let's recap, shall we,"—she ticked off each point on her fingers—"white guys aren't your type. Black guys aren't your type. Asian guys aren't your type. No Germans, Russians, Serbians, Croatians, Italians, British, Scottish, Australians, Irish, Native Americans, and no Mexicans. Oh, and let's not forget, no tall, short, hot, or ugly guys." She arched a brow. "That rules out all guys. So, what exactly is your type of guy? Do you even have one? Or... are you playing for the home team now?"

Ashley laughed, then choked on her drink.

"See? That's what you get. No, Chrissy. I'm strictly dickly, thanks," she snidely responded. "There's a type, but I can't be in a relationship right now. My focus is elsewhere. I need to find myself."

Ashley slammed her hand against the table. Their drinks wobbled. "Find yourself? Née, don't start this shit again," she scolded. "How long have I known you? Since what, before the Suttons—fourth grade? Before all this shit." Waving her hand, she encompassed the general area. "If you don't know who you are—I do. You don't need some people you don't know, who just so happen to share some DNA with you, to tell you who you are. And, no offense, but it's not like they've been knocking down your door to get to know you. Remember, they left you."

She didn't want to have this conversation in front of Starbucks. Unlike Ashley, she knew a thing or two about privacy.

Christina looked as uncomfortable as Renée felt. Stupid her for confiding in her friends about her talk with the good doctor, Anne Mendoza. The whole, "Who do you identify with?" question had gotten to her more than she cared to admit. So much so, she'd shared her concern with Christina and the Queen of Little Tact. With an overabundance of memory dreams and the ever-exciting panic attacks, she'd been tossing around the idea of finding her birth family. She'd told them that, too.

Of course, she'd heard bits and pieces about her birth family from different caseworkers over the years. All they'd ever told her was that they were unfit and had some emotional issues. The state had to think that to justify taking kids into the system. But she didn't know how much truth there was to that assessment.

"How long has your puppet master—oh, excuse me, therapist—been suggesting you go find your loser family?" Ashley asked, bringing her back to the topic at hand.

"She hasn't been suggesting I find them. At least, she says that's not what she means. But how else does a person confront their past? Just talking about the past doesn't help."

"Maybe she's on to something," Christina mused. "Have you ever looked for any of them? Found anybody?"

Laughing without humor, Ashley rolled her eyes. "Or maybe, just maybe, that quack is full of shit."

Damn, Ashley had a way with words. However, her thoughts weren't far from Renée's own. Most counselors, therapists, and psychiatrists were full of shit. At least, she thought so. They based their entire modus operandi on knowledge from books. Not experience. People were complicated. Unique. Not meant to be forced into nice, neat, labeled boxes. What worked for one might not work for another. However, this nagging feeling in the pit of her stomach made her want to know. What if finding them filled in the gaps of her identity? Helped her move on in life? She was tired of surviving life. She wanted to live.

"Ash," she said with a sigh. She finished her drink before going on. "I know you don't think it matters, but it does. This crap with my past needs to stop. It impedes everything. This waiting for life to start? I don't want to end up some eighty-year-old woman with a million cats, still having panic attacks and bitchin' about what might have been. I gotta do something."

"So, is that a yes? You have found somebody from your family or a no you haven't?" Christina inquired, picking a piece of ice out of her tea and popping it into her mouth. She was always chewing ice, constantly hot, just like this conversation.

That girl was far too observant. Renée had told no one that she'd searched online for family members she had names, or parts of names, for.

"Yes and no." She hesitated, confirming her friend's assumption. "I found some names, but no addresses or anything of any actual use."

Crazy enough, for the wealth of information the Internet possessed, it couldn't deliver something as simple as an address without charging an arm and a leg for it. And none of her birth family had any social media. To be fair, her parents didn't either; they could barely email with an attachment.

"You know," Christina said around the ice in her mouth, "there is one person you could ask for help. He wouldn't be offended. He might even understand if you explain everything."

"How would this offend him?" Renée argued. "What I'm doing can't offend anyone. I'm not trying to take anything from my adoptive family or be disloyal. I'm trying to improve myself like they want me to."

"If you believed that, you would've told your parents. And you might've mentioned it to your brother, The King of Research. He could've gotten names, numbers, addresses, and social security numbers in five minutes," Christina pointed out.

"He's not my keeper," Renée spat, speaking more harshly than intended. It wasn't Christina's fault she and Andrew weren't as close as they once were. It also wasn't her fault she felt guilty. Searching for her birth family made her feel like she was betraying her adoptive family.

The next time she spoke, her words came calmer. "It's none of his business. I don't have to tell him everything."

"Renée," Ashley chimed in, "since when is Andrew someone you keep out of the loop? You guys used to be close—uncomfortably so. Best friends. Gag reflex-triggering, close. Tell him what's up and move on. Stop punishing him for something he had no control over."

Yep, no heartfelt conversation was complete without Ashley chucking her fifty cents at you. She wanted bygones to be bygones with Andrew. After all, it was her fault their relationship changed. Intellectually, she knew that, but when it came right down to it, she couldn't get past it.

"You guys ready to go?" Christina asked, fanning herself with her hand. "I'm hot. Hanging out at Starbucks shouldn't be a major life choice. We've been here for three hours."

Later that night, after another of her all-too-common, startling flashback dreams, Renée padded on bare feet to the kitchen. She searched the cabinets for her favorite comfort food: Cinnamon Toast Crunch. Her mom always stashed a box behind the fat-free oatmeal cookies, oat bran, and other crap Renée wouldn't eat with someone else's mouth. So, she didn't see her dreaded nemesis move through the kitchen and over to the pantry in stealthy silence. But she felt it. Her body tensed.

She got a bowl down, poured her cereal and milk, put them both away, grabbed a spoon, and sat at the oak table before being forced to look at him.

Damn! She glared at—and checked out—his broad, corded, naked tan back while he dug through the pantry. He looked like a freakin' Calvin Klein model in low-slung, plaid pajama pants.

She squirmed in her chair, focused extra hard on eating her cereal and not drooling over his tight gluts. The boy could crack walnuts with that ass. She'd never been an ass woman, but his was worthy of praise... or a smack.

Crap! *What am I thinking?* This was Chris. Chris, the town bicycle—every girl over eighteen got a ride. He made Narcissus seem modest.

He turned around. Noticed her sitting there. Renée rolled her eyes to mask the desire, need, and longing in them. Although, what she wanted was to go over and brush back the wet strands of blond hair falling over his eyes.

Chris's cocky grin took her breath away. "Hey there, short stack," he said, unwrapping one of two power bars he held. "You always eat cereal at one in the morning?"

"What's it matter to you? Do you always walk around someone else's house like you're expecting a camera crew to pop up?" she retorted. Renée shoved a spoonful of cereal into her mouth before she said anything else stupid.

Chris arched a brow at her compliment. And aggressive chewing. *Progress already, excellent.* "So, what you're saying is... you like the way I look?" he asked, taking a seat across from her at the table.

In all honesty, he shouldn't eat this late either. It went against his meal plan. But when he'd heard Renée's bedroom door open, he'd needed some excuse to be in the kitchen with her. He didn't think she'd appreciate him coming in and just staring.

For two weeks, she'd avoided him like the plague, and he'd had as much of that shit as he could take. She would talk to him tonight.

When he came into the kitchen, he'd nearly forgotten himself, ran over to her, bent her over the counter, and thrust into her with gusto. She looked scrumptious in a pair of black boxers—which he refused to believe belonged to another man—and a sports bra. Her hair was in a sloppy ponytail that he'd love to pull while he hit it from behind.

Good thing she'd been busy getting her cereal because, at that moment, his dick could've drilled through granite. He'd needed those few minutes in the pantry to regain composure. If she had looked at him with those honey-brown bedroom eyes of hers, it would've been all over.

An awful sound from Renée pulled him from his pleasant thoughts but did nothing to lower the tent his reverie raised in his pants. Thank goodness he sat down.

Renée inclined her head toward his snack. "Are we watching our weight? Having fat camp flashbacks, Chub-chub," she asked, using the nickname he'd love to leave in the past where it belonged.

He knew she needled him to distract herself from his effect on her. Chris wouldn't let her get to him. He saw the spark of desire she couldn't hide when he approached. She wanted him. He wanted her, too. Patience was needed here because when he claimed her, it would be irrevocable—no turning back for either of them. No more letting her treat him like crap. No more hiding their feelings.

"I don't need to watch my weight," he said in answer to her question, though he knew she didn't expect a reply. "You're watching it for me."

At that, warm brown eyes bored into his. Chris allowed everything he felt for her: hunger, lust, and need to seep through his intense stare. She saw it. Might never admit it, but she did. He knew it. He kept her trapped in his gaze for several moments before she broke away and took an extreme interest in her cereal.

"I wouldn't watch anything, or care to watch anything, about you," she said, maintaining her fascination with her cereal. "Your arrogance disgusts me. I can't stand you or this conversation for another second," she growled, looking him in the eye.

Glare trained on him, Renée pushed back from the table, got up, and then shoved the heavy oak chair back under the table. The chair slammed into the table, tipped on its hind legs, and crashed to the floor. On top of Renée's foot.

"Ow! Shit! Ow!" She hopped around, hit the table, and almost knocked over her cereal bowl full of milk.

Trying hard not to laugh, Chris rushed around the table and picked up the chair. "Smooth move, Ex-Lax." He chuckled, bending to look at her toe.

Renée glowered at him. Jerked her foot away. "Shut up! You think I meant to do that?"

He reached to pull her foot toward him.

"Keep your hands off me. I don't need your help!" Renée shouted, backing away so fast she nearly fell. She grabbed the table to steady herself.

Amusement upturned the corners of Chris's mouth. He tried smothering his smile, but Renée's attempts to avoid his touch were too cute. Like him, she probably knew one touch would change their relationship. Something he counted on.

He reached for her again.

She shrugged away. Teetered.

"Oh, yeah, sure, you don't need help. Do you have some sort of ability to walk on one foot I don't know about?" He laughed. "You can barely stand."

It was too late before either of them guessed the other's intentions. Renée reached to steady herself on the chair. At that exact moment, Chris went to pull it out for her. Their hands touched. Something he could only describe as an electrical shock hit him. Tingles shot up his arm. He didn't have to ask. The startled expression on Renée's face and sharp intake of breath confirmed she felt it.

He'd felt nothing like it before. It was like his every desire, need, and vulnerability burst from his body and into hers. Had she not already owned him, she did now. That one touch sealed them for all eternity. As corny as it might sound, the electricity between them seemed to fuse their souls, making them one. She would forever be a part of him, and he'd forever be a part of her.

Their eyes locked. Every emotion coursing through him shone in her brown eyes. Matched his intensity. Except for the flash of fear.

Chris tried to pull her into his arms and protect her from whatever frightened her. He made a silent promise to her. Let it flare in his eyes. As long as he drew breath, no harm would come to her again. He would care for her. Protect her with his life. It might be too soon, but he didn't care. He was kissing her—tonight. Right now.

Quick on the heels of that thought, she evanesced. Vanished, as if she'd never been.

Chapter Six

Pitch black. She couldn't even see a hand in front of her face.

But she heard footsteps. They were coming toward her. Her heart pounded so loud in her ears, it drowned out all other sounds, which scared her more because now she couldn't tell where the footsteps were or how fast they were coming.

Seconds that seemed like hours ticked by, and now, not only couldn't she hear or see, but she couldn't move. And...

Someone was close, very close. She felt it. Hot breath came from above. Right above her. And oddly enough, someone was behind her too. A shorter person, her height. Innocuous.

"I told you I would be back in fifteen minutes!" the deep male voice roared as loud as thunder.

Her heart stopped. Then it took off at beat-neck speed. Her stomach dropped. She knew that voice, recognized this moment.

Knowing what was to come, she squeezed her eyes shut. Her throat went dry. Tears stung her eyes. Her palms sweat.

"That was six hours ago! Where the Hell have you been?" her voice shouted from behind her.

"I told you not to talk to me that way. You're not my mother. I have a mother, and she wasn't a short, black, ugly bitch last time I checked! Watch your mouth when you talk to me. I'm the man in this relationship," the man hollered.

Renée made a loud sound at the back of her throat. "Making fun of women? Some man you turned out to be," her past self-retorted.

A loud bang reverberated through the emptiness. Only an observer in this black obis. Yet the blow felt like it'd been dealt to her again.

Finally, a dim spotlight lit the angry pale face of a tall, blond-haired, brown-eyed man.

Fear was a living, breathing entity. Her breath hitched. Not one word escaped her lips, or the lips of her past self, who lay crumpled against the floor in a whisper.

Not a word. One name. "Corey."

Renée and Ashley walked through the Hall of Fame, her parents' loving name for the long hall, separating family bedrooms and bathrooms from the rest of the house. Pictures of Renée's and Andrew's age progression through the years and members of their extended family as they grew over the years lined each wall. For whatever reason, whenever Ashley or Christina visited, they loved to scope out and make fun of the pictures. Since Susan Sutton religiously updated the walls, there was always something new.

The lady was a ninja photographer. Renée didn't even remember half the candid pictures being taken, but there they were. Documented proof of her awkwardness, which is why she called the hall: The Dreaded Hall of Blackmail.

While her friend giggled at a picture of Andrew picking his nose in his sleep—two years ago—Renée stopped. Stared at one of her dad from last Christmas. He wore a red T-shirt with green lettering that read: *Sit on Santa's lap. Let's talk about the first thing that pops up.* An arrow pointed to his lap. Yeah, her brother and father thought the shirt hilarious. She and her mother... not so much.

Thoughts wandering to the previous night, she stared through the photo. As much as she hated to admit it, her memory-dream, or rather nightmare, still had her on edge. Last night was the first time she'd ever had two nightmares: one before she ate her cereal and one after. Her nerves were all over the map. She'd taken her Xanax twice already, and it was only two in the afternoon.

That wasn't the only thing weighing on her mind, though. The moment in the kitchen with Chris hadn't escaped her notice. Had she stayed there, he would've kissed her. She knew it like she knew her name. Why he'd want to do that made no sense, but his intentions had been clear as day. Worst of all, for a split second, she wanted him to kiss her. She'd *wanted* his firm lips against her softer ones. Have his muscular arms embrace her—protect her. Something indefinable passed between them in their pseudo moment, and it scared her shitless. Hurt toe or no hurt toe, she'd run out of there so fast she left a vapor trail in her wake.

If it was such a non-moment, then why did it affect you so much?

She didn't know the answer and didn't want to examine it too closely, either. Something told her she wouldn't like what she discovered.

Renée looked askance at her best friend, clad in a violet satin, spaghetti strap tank top with lighter purple trim. Worn, skimpy blue jean shorts with strategic holes placed in the back and flip-flops. Her hair braided in low pigtails. For the first time in quite some time, Ashley dressed girlie. Renée might as well be wearing a moo-moo instead of red sweetheart boxers with hearts all over them and a scoop-neck black tank top.

Silly her, she'd invited her beloved, obnoxious friend over to help dull the weird feelings and terrible memories of a time she'd rather forget. However, she suspected that the whole Chris incident triggered the nightmare too. The last thing she needed was another nightmare trigger. She had plenty of those.

"So, Chris is still staying here, huh?" Ashley asked in a ho-hum voice, knowing full well he was. When she didn't answer but stared at the side of her friend's head, Ashley turned, wagged her eyebrows, and grinned.

She didn't appreciate the insinuation behind Ashley's grin. *I knew I shouldn't have told her about last night—shit!* "What?" she asked, pretending she didn't know what that stupid grin meant.

"Don't play dumb with me, bitch, you know what."

Renée narrowed her eyes at Ashley.

Ashley's grin turned into a full-fledged "Hey, Kool-Aid" smile.

"Shut up," she snapped. This was why she didn't tell Ashley about this stuff. Since Christina was at work, and she needed to talk, she'd buckled and called her. When would she ever learn? She knew what the strawberry blonde was getting at. "I was thirteen," she reminded her.

"Mm-hm..." Ashley nodded. "You could still be carrying a torch for him."

"Uh... No. There's a lot of stuff I liked then that I don't like now. Come to think of it. There's a person I liked a second ago. That I won't like too much longer if she doesn't stop talking about the thing she vowed never to speak of again in mixed company."

Ashley flinched, wrinkling her nose. "Mixed company? We're the only two people out here," she pointed out. "Who is there to hear me mention the enormous crush you had on Chris that made you cut his picture out of Drew's yearbook? And who could hear me say that when Drew asked what happened, you told him he did it in his sleep?"

Mouth pinched tight, Renée gave Ashley a wide-eyed, murderous glare.

"What?" Ashley asked. "Have I said too much? You worried Chris'll come out here, and what... spank you?"

Renée was about to tell Ashley where she could stick her bullshit opinion when she heard a voice she hadn't heard in eons, come from behind Drew's closed bedroom door. She stepped closer to listen.

"What are you—?" Ashley whispered, joining her.
"Shh..." she mouthed, putting a finger to her lips.

Chapter Seven

"Dude, when did you get back?" Drew asked, bouncing his miniature orange basketball, preparing to shoot it into the mini basketball hoop mounted on the back of his bedroom door.

His parents had months to do anything they wanted with his room. Most would've turned it into a den or a sewing room, but not his parents. They left it just as he had. The walls were still indigo. His cherry wood, executive-style desk remained in the corner, making his childhood room seem smaller. They hadn't so much as touched a paper clip since he'd moved out.

The only exceptions were his king-size bed sheets. When he'd left his *Ace Ventura*, sheets covered the bed. Now, a thick, black, goose-down feather comforter was in their place and matching black with white sheets. It stunned him that his mom would go through the trouble of changing the sheets—it wasn't like he was an actual guest. Of course, that wasn't the only surprise he'd gotten in the last two weeks of being back in his parents' home.

The second shock showed up unannounced, about an hour ago. A twenty-six-year-old, six-foot-tall, dark brown-haired, rich brown-eyed, light caramel-skinned, Latino man with a lean body that was muscled more than he remembered. It'd been a little over three years since he'd seen the man. It felt like some weird lucid dream when he saw him standing on his front porch.

Shooting the ball—and missing the basket he wasn't even a foot away from—he looked at his friend expectantly. Alejandro "Alex or Lex" Gutierrez lay kicked back on his bed dressed in gray and blue Ballin shorts, gray muscle shirt, and a backward black hat. Hands behind his head, he leaned against the wall and crossed his legs at the ankles. White sneakers hung over the edge like he owned the place. Or better yet, like he'd never left.

"Today," he answered, yawning. "The parents and I agreed it was time. Three years is long enough—don't you think?" He shrugged. "So, I jumped in the car, and six hours later... heeeeere's Alex!"

"Man, I think your sister's gonna try to kill me in my sleep." Chris, sitting at the desk, chimed in off-topic.

The off-topic part wasn't shocking. Self-centered Chris rarely paid much attention to conversations or anything not about him. While Alex had been updating them on his life in California, Chris had been where he loved to be, a world of his own. Here and there, he contributed an "oh, really," and "uh-huh," or a "no way," or nod to the conversation, but nothing else.

"Did you see how she looked at me earlier this morning? Shit, the last couple weeks I've been here...?" Chris continued.

Alex laughed and caught the ball. "Why wait 'till you're asleep?" he muttered.

Chris glared at Alex. Flipped him the bird. He picked something up off his desk and extended it to him.

Drew felt the blood rush out of his face as he saw what his friend held. Shit!

About the author

Advice writers receive: Write what you know.

I know darkness. I grew up in Scottsdale, Paradise Valley, and Glendale, Arizona. Knowing the uglier sides of life there weren't a lot of options available to me. At least, that's what the world would have me believe. I could've succumbed to the hopelessness and despair that come with having the kind of childhood and adolescence better suited for a Lifetime Channel movie or a cautionary tale. Become a statistic. Or I could allow my past to fuel my creativity.

I devoured anything I could read as an escape. Writing became my calm in the storm. My constant. I published my first book at ten years old. Through college where I studied Social Work, trying to effect change from within the system—I wrote. Modeled a bit. Sang. Became an on-air radio personality. Acted. And still, I wrote. Poetry. Screenplays. Novels. Even placed in the 2010 Beverly Hills Film Festival. All roads lead back to writing. Now, I write dark. Dark paranormal romance. Dark urban fantasy. Psychological and supernatural thrillers. And dark contemporary romance under the pseudonym Wilt Rhys. Because the one thing life's taught me, everything done in the dark comes to the light.

If you're interested in dark contemporary romance check out my other pseudonym Wilt Rhys.

<u>Connect Online</u>
Website: www.piperanderson.org
TikTok: @thepiedwriter
Instagram: @that_chick_piper_tv
Facebook: Author Piper Anderson